"I had to go."

"I got that."

She felt close to tears. "I appreciate what you did for me, but please, why won't you just leave me alone?"

"Because I can't," he said simply. "Not until I know you'll be okay."

She covered her face to keep from crying—or laughing. "It's because I'm a woman, isn't it? No matter what I've done, you refuse to see me as a threat."

"Hardly," he rumbled, bending near. "Women are terrifying. You, I'm sure, spit venom and eat men alive. But I'm offering you help right now, and you can take it or leave it."

"I left it," she told him, peering up into his eyes. "But you followed. For all you know I might be a murderer."

"Are you?" he asked.

"I don't know . . ."

By Marjorie M. Liu

Marjorie M. Liu

The Wild Road

A DIRK & STEELE NOVEL

AVON

An Imprint of HarperCollinsPublishers

This is a work of fiction. Names, characters, places, and incidents are products of the author's imagination or are used fictitiously and are not to be construed as real. Any resemblance to actual events, locales, organizations, or persons, living or dead, is entirely coincidental.

AVON BOOKS
An Imprint of HarperCollins*Publishers*
10 East 53rd Street
New York, New York 10022-5299

Copyright © 2008 by Marjorie M. Liu
ISBN 978-0-06-202018-5
www.avonromance.com

First Avon Books mass market printing: July 2011

Avon Trademark Reg. U.S. Pat. Off. and in Other Countries, Marca Registrada, Hecho en U.S.A.
HarperCollins® is a registered trademark of HarperCollins Publishers.

Printed in the U.S.A.

10 9 8 7 6 5 4 3 2

To those who must begin their lives again,
may you find your way amongst
the shadows and thorns:
strong of heart, full of faith, sunlit with dreams.

ACKNOWLEDGMENTS

This book would not have been possible without the patience, goodwill, and kindness of my editor, Chris Keeslar, and Director of Art and Production, Tracy Heydweiller. Many thanks to all the wonderful people at Dorchester Publishing, as well as my agent, Lucienne Diver.

One need not be a chamber to be haunted;
One need not be a house;
The brain has corridors surpassing
Material place.

EMILY DICKINSON, "Time and Eternity"

CHAPTER ONE

T HE woman smelled smoke in her dreams.
        She smelled it still, when she opened her eyes. A
bad way to wake. She lay motionless, stunned and dis-
oriented, lost in a dark room, stretched on a bed. Shouts
filled her ears, footsteps pounding. Sirens wailed. The
woman flexed her hands and gripped rumpled covers.
She wiggled her toes. Her feet were bare, though she
wore other clothing.

Her head hurt. So did her heart, like she had been
crying. Or maybe that was her lungs. Smoke was in the
air, faintly illuminated by some ambient light far on her
left. Her eyes stung. Her mind tried to catch up with
what she was breathing and seeing.

"Shit," she muttered hoarsely, and the sound of her
voice—rough, awful, hardly discernable beneath the
cascading sirens—felt like a baseball bat against her
back. One good swing. Move it or lose it. Live or die.

The woman scrambled off the bed, landing hard on
the floor, keeping below the thickening smoke. The carpet felt odd. Wet and sticky. She could not immediately

see why, but when she moved a fraction to the left, her hand hit something solid and warm. She ignored it and started crawling until she bumped into another, similar obstacle. Only this time, something inside her screamed, choking on more than smoke. She reached out blindly, jaw clenched.

Her hand landed on a face. Rough with stubble, a sticky nose, broad forehead. The woman froze, horrified—then shoved the man, hard.

"Hello," she whispered.

He did not move. She fumbled for his neck, searching for a pulse. Instead of finding a heartbeat, her fingers dipped into a wet ragged hole.

The woman gasped, scrabbling backward. Terrified. She tried to remember what had happened. She tried to remember how she had gotten here.

Nothing. She had no idea where she was. Not one clue. No memory of where she had been before this room.

No time, whispered a small voice inside her head. *Go. Get out of here.*

But she did not. Coughing, eyes burning, she spun around on her knees, fumbling her way back up the length of the bed. She found a nightstand and grappled for a light. Switched it on. Wished immediately she had not.

At first it was like being blind. Blinded by tears and light, startling splashes of color. Bodies. Three men in dark clothing, sprawled dead. The carpet beneath them—beneath her—saturated dark with blood. Her mind could not adjust, could only soak up in numb horror a sight that could not be real.

The woman slapped a hand over her mouth, trying not to scream. A sharp metallic scent instantly invaded her nose. Her fingers were wet. She remembered touching the man and recoiled from herself, choking, staring down at her hands. Her palms were covered in blood.

The knees of her jeans were soaked with it, too, the denim hot and wet against her skin. Something was pinned to her blood-spattered jacket. A piece of paper. The woman touched it, hand shaking, leaving red fingerprints. She stared at the word written in big black letters.

RUN, she read.

The woman felt faint, and she shut her eyes, breathing deep—which made her choke immediately. Smoke curled along the entire ceiling now, wafting down, thick and heavy. She looked once again at the bodies, those faces: three men in their thirties, big and strong, dark hair cut short against their scalps. One of them, she saw, held a gun in his hand.

The light by her head flickered out for a brief moment. The woman looked around, quick. She was in a hotel room. The door was behind her. The light flickered again and she hoisted herself onto the bed, scrabbling over it toward the exit. She saw nothing worth taking—no purse, no personal items of any kind. No shoes.

The lights went out just as the woman reached the door. She heard screams outside in the hall and pressed the back of her hand against the wood and the metal knob. Both were cool. She opened the door and crawled out of the room. It was pitch dark in the hall, but she heard and felt people running, saw a flashlight beam bouncing far on her right and took off after it. She kept low, pulling the collar of her T-shirt over her nose and mouth. She smelled blood. Tried not to think of the dead men in the room behind her. Or why she could not remember how she had gotten there.

Keep it simple, she thought, heart pounding. *Get out, then freak.*

The woman got jostled, slammed by running bodies, her ears ringing with sirens and screams and hacking coughs, but she kept going, fast, nearly blind, keeping one hand on the wall to guide her. No emergency lights, nothing to see by. The flashlight was gone. Glass shattered inside a room she passed. Ahead, the timbre of voices changed, became echoey, hollow and bouncy. Cool air brushed against her face. The exit.

She fumbled ahead, found a door swinging shut and forced her way into a metal and concrete stairwell that was relatively smoke free and blissfully cold. She almost fell down the stairs—her knees ready to buckle out from under her—but she saw more flashlights winking up through the darkness, accompanied by shouts. She felt her way down, bumped and pushed by other people trying to evacuate the building. Her hand kept grazing her jacket where the note was pinned. She ripped the thing off and stuffed it into her pocket.

The woman did not think she would ever forget the expression of the first firefighter who shone a beam into her face. He was a young kid, hauling gear up the stairs, oxygen mask hanging around his neck and a brilliant light blazing from his helmet. His eyes widened. He reached for her and she evaded him by moving deeper into the throng of other evacuees, afraid on a gut level of the questions he would ask, moving by instinct.

Run.

A small army of uniformed men and women waited for the evacuees at the bottom of the stairwell. Cold air rushed over her face, and an oxygen mask was held up. She used it. Hands touched her shoulders, guiding her away from the building. She looked back once, and saw that it was a fancy piece of architecture, tall and made of steel and glass and stone. Fire and smoke poured from one of the upper floors. Her floor, she suspected. She started to rub her eyes, and remembered her bloody hands, drying now, but still sticky. The woman wanted to vomit.

"Sit down," said a low male voice. She tried to resist, but the guiding hand tightened around her arm, and she did not want to make a scene. She pretended obedience, sat at the back of an ambulance, her coughs easing as she breathed deep from the oxygen mask. So many lights and people. Hard to look at all of them. All she wanted to do was run.

An older man in a blue jacket and pants peered down at her face, then at the rest of her body. "Ma'am, you're covered in blood. Are you injured?"

The woman said nothing and stared past his shoulder, affecting a glassy stare. A small part of her wanted to break loose, start screaming—about the men, the blood—but again, her instincts prevailed.

Subterfuge, whispered a voice. *Illusion*.

And, *Get away. Run like hell*.

The man frowned, but behind him a shout went up and he turned briefly, walking only a few steps away. The woman did not hesitate, hardly felt as though she owned her body. She slipped off the back of the ambulance and strode quickly around the vehicle.

It was easy to get lost in the crowd. So many emergency vehicles and workers, curious onlookers. The woman was almost stopped by a concerned police officer, but she croaked, "Water," and when he turned to look for some, she slid behind a fire truck and found herself beside a dim long stretch of alley.

The woman was barefoot, the concrete wet and slick. She got lucky. Nothing cut her feet as she ran through the shadows, away from the chaos of lights and uniforms, all of which felt as threatening as the fire and the terrible room she had left behind, the contents of which still covered her body. More or less.

She did not go far. The base of her skull began to throb again. Her side hurt. She stepped deeper into shadows, coughing, fighting for breath. Knees weak. She bent over, trying to control the aching fear in her chest, struggling not to be sick. She could still see those men. There was no escaping the scent of blood. Not when the front of her jeans was still damp and her hands sticky. She felt something heavy against her back and tentatively reached under her jacket . . . touching leather, then cold hard steel.

A gun.

The woman slowly drew the weapon. The weight felt good in her hand. She forced herself to look down, taking in the long, sleek form.

Semiautomatic rimfire pistol with suppressor, rattled the voice in her mind. *Ruger, .22 caliber.*

Before she could stop herself, she checked the clip. Found it empty, no more ammunition. Her hands moved without pause, without thought.

She almost dropped the gun, but her fingers tightened and she slid the weapon back into the waist of her jeans. Shaken. Dazed. Three armed men, shot to death . . . and she, at the scene, covered in blood. Carrying a gun.

A gun she did not remember. A gun her hands knew how to use, even if her conscious mind did not.

No, thought the woman, even as she realized something else in that moment, something far more horrifying. She did not remember anything of her life before opening her eyes in the hotel room. The thought cascaded into other realizations, equally terrifying:

The woman did not know her name.

She did not remember herself.

She had no memories.

It took a moment to digest this, a long moment. She did not want to believe. Here she was, walking around, alert, proactive. Not entirely insane. She had to remember something. Anything. She patted down her pockets for ID, a card, some hint. She found nothing.

The woman closed her eyes, battling herself—but it was like being caught on the other side of a dark wall.

There, but not. She could almost taste some shadow of knowledge just out of reach, maddeningly beyond her, and she pressed grimy knuckles to her forehead, digging in until her brow hurt. Sirens filled the background, the hiss of tires on the road, the distant groans of some drunk.

She did not even know what she looked like. Just that she was covered in blood. A gun with a silencer was tucked into the back of her jeans. She was barefoot, nothing in her pockets except a crumpled note that said to run.

Bad clues. No clues.

I might be a killer, she thought, frightened; and then, *I need to get the hell out of here.*

And the woman, discovering that she was an efficient individual, set about doing just that.

CHAPTER TWO

NOTHING less than the death of Frederick Brimley's three-hundred-year-old family Bible could have convinced Lannes Hannelore to leave the island in Maine, and when he got the call from his old friend that it was only a matter of time before the delicate binding fell to pieces, he packed a small bag, rode a boat to the public marina to retrieve his car and drove twelve hundred miles to Chicago to play artist and surgeon upon the priceless eighteenth-century tome.

"You are a genius," Frederick said three weeks later, surrounded by a haze of cigarette smoke that clung to his tattered gray cashmere sweater. He was in his eighties but was still strong and straight as an iron post, his long silver hair pulled back in a loose tail. Only his hands revealed the ravages of age, trembling uncontrollably to the point that he was forced to clutch them in his lap, holding tight until the tremors passed.

He was doing so now. Lannes pretended not to notice. He had other problems, including the brunette staring at him from across the small dark jazz club that he

and Frederick had come to—a night for them to cele-
brate, to enjoy music, to reminisce over a seventy-year
friendship that both of them knew would not last forever. Time was running out for Frederick in ways that
would not touch Lannes, not for more than another
century yet. Though he could restore the Brimley family
Bible, there was little that Lannes could do to reverse
the effects of time.

"Thank your father," Lannes replied, perched uncomfortably on the edge of his chair. He clutched his
cup of tea, a drink order that had generated some dis-
dainful looks, and tried not to yawn. "He taught us
both."

"But you were always the better student. Bookbinding and restoration were never my first loves."

"You just liked writing in the pages. What are you
working on now? Your thirtieth novel?"

"Haven't started." Frederick glanced down at his
clasped hands, the tendons in his wrists straining. "One
must be in the right mood. Though, since you asked, I
was thinking of telling a children's story this time. Old
age, you know, makes one wish for golden days."

"And?"

"And," said the elderly man, drawing out the word
with a smile, "I thought it would be about a young boy
who lives in an ancient wood, friend to all the magic
beasts, including one, their guardian. A lonely gargoyle.
A creature of books and tea."

"Such an imagination you have," Lannes replied.
"Magic beasts. Ancient woods."

Frederick's smile widened. "Gargoyles?"

"I was never lonely," he muttered.

The old man laughed and unclenched his hands, stretching his fingers. No more tremors. He took a sip of Guinness and glanced up at the stage. Lannes forced himself not to look at the brunette and followed his friend's gaze.

The Underground Wonder Bar had live music three hundred sixty-five days of the year, and tonight, a young black man sat in the spotlight against a painted backdrop of van Gogh's *Starry Night*. His name was Donny Shill, and according to Frederick he was new to the scene—even if he played like he had fifty years of hard living under his belt. He knocked the strings of his battered double cutaway Kay like there were wings on his long fingers, his shoulders hunched and his head bowed close to the microphone standing near his mouth. He had a voice like a slow-rolling train with tracks made of velvet, and except for a brilliant cover of B. B. King's "Every Day I Have the Blues," his music was original, straight from the heart. Lannes could have listened to him all night.

Except for the brunette still staring at him.

Except for the walls and the clinging shadows that suddenly reminded him too much of the bad days, the old days, the frozen-stone days waiting for the witch to carve on his brother.

Frederick took another sip of his beer. "You're all wound up. Is it the crowd? If you're worried about your appearance—"

"No," Lannes interrupted quietly, knowing his voice was almost lost beneath the music. "I know the illusion is working. But the crowd *is* part of it. Been a while since I left the island."

The old man's eyes were far too keen. "You've been shy of the world ever since you and your brothers came home from that . . . extended trip. You never did tell me what that was about."

Death, Lannes thought, ducking his head to drink some tea. *Imprisonment. Insanity.*

He was afraid his memories would show on his face; the human illusion he wore was too good at mirroring his heart. Pretending to examine the contents of his cup, he said, "Another time, Freddy."

"Keep that up, and I'll be in my grave before you tell the story."

Lannes finally looked at him. "No."

Frederick sighed. "You always seem more frightened than I by the prospect of my demise."

"You're not dead yet," Lannes grumbled. "You still have another ten or twenty years in you. Maybe thirty."

"You should try bottling that optimism," Frederick shot back. "I'm healthy but not immortal. I'm only human. And even if I weren't, everyone dies."

Or else you sell your soul for the privilege of staying alive, Lannes thought, but that was another memory he did not want to invoke—not now.

"I don't have many friends," he said instead. "You can't blame me for wanting them to stick around."

Frederick made no reply. His gaze flicked sideways, and Lannes turned just in time to see a delicate hand reach for his shoulder. He flinched, jolting away, and almost fell out of his chair.

It was the brunette. Quiet as a cat. A bombshell, a buxom woman whose assets overflowed like Niagara bound in black leather, and a gaze that, perhaps inappropriately, reminded Lannes of hot oozing oil: likely to burn, hard to clean off. Her small round face was framed by hair that curled loose around her bare shoulders. She wore a gold necklace with a charm shaped like a heart that dipped deep into her cleavage. Her eyeliner was heavy, her lips full and pink, and she had a sultry smile that should have warmed Lannes to the bone—but instead unnerved the hell out of him. He had not affected this human appearance quite long enough to appreciate a strange woman's admiring focus.

It made him nervous. Because even if Lannes *looked* human, he most certainly was not. And no illusion, no matter how fine, could hide the physical fact that beneath a guise of tanned skin and pleasant features, his real body was rather different from other—human—men.

Wings. Skin the color of dark silver. Long black hair. A face made of craggy lines and ears that tapered to a sharp point. The only similarities between reality and illusion were his eyes and the breadth and strength of his body: broad shoulders, powerful limbs, hard muscle made for war and a height that skimmed seven feet. Lannes felt like a giant tiptoeing around fine china. Especially here, with so many people. He had been forced to bind his wings, strapping them to his body with a wide leather belt that cinched around his back and chest. Highly uncomfortable, but better than accidentally brushing against someone observant enough to notice that Lannes did not feel the same way he looked. His wings resembled those of a bat—pliant, flexible, and highly articulated, consisting of numerous small joints covered by a thin, highly sensitive membrane that draped around him like a cape.

A gargoyle. The last of a dying race. No one could be allowed to discover his kind. He took enough risks as it was, relying on magic to walk the world.

"Jumpy," said the woman, her voice husky and nearly lost in the music pouring from the stage.

"You startled me," Lannes replied, struggling to sound polite, calm, even though his heart hammered and it was suddenly hard to breathe. He should have felt her near him, should have known she was close enough to touch, but the bar was crowded and he was not exactly at the top of his game.

He sidled out of his chair and stood, towering over the woman. He rubbed his arm where she had touched him, feeling flesh beneath the illusion of clothing. Only his jeans were real. The rest? Nothing but a psychic trick, a mental barrier. He had rooted the illusion in his spirit, like armor in the shape of human skin.

Up on stage, Donny Shill slid into a fast hard wail of notes, cascading against Lannes like the open sky, the long road. Freedom soared in that music. The woman smiled, flipping back her hair with one hand while the other reached again for him, ostensibly to slide those manicured fingers up his arm. Friendly, flirtatious, meant to soothe the strange man with the nerves.

He stepped just beyond her reach. "No, thank you."

She looked at him with a hint of amusement. "The polite rejection?"

"You're lovely, truly. But I'm not interested."

"Girl at home?"

"Something like that," he lied, wishing desperately it were the truth.

The woman sighed, mouth curling into a wry smile. "Handsome and loyal. You make me want you even more."

Lannes said nothing, and she sighed again, backing up a step. "Message received. But you, gorgeous, better stay out of places like this if you want to lay low. Face like yours, there's no such thing as being left alone." She flashed him a brilliant sultry smile and swayed away, each stiletto step timed to the music. Such great legs. Lannes watched her go, mouth dry. Kicking himself for things he could not change.

Frederick pushed back his chair and tossed some money on the table. "You're pathetic."

Lannes gave him a dirty look. "Let's go."

It was a crisp September night outside, past midnight. There was no moon, but plenty of city—canyons of men and their roaring machines that filled the air with the bitter acrid scent of exhaust. Chicago smelled worn-out, bowed and surly beneath the weight of its sprawl. Lake Michigan hardly seemed to exist. Lannes missed Maine, the cold ocean winds strong enough to bear the weight of a man.

"I don't know why you like this city," he muttered to Frederick, wings aching almost as badly as his heart.

"It's home," his friend said simply, and struggled to swing on his suede coat. His hands shook too much. Lannes wordlessly took the garment and helped him stick his arms in. "You should stay longer. No need to rush off in the morning."

Lannes hesitated. "I have commissions."

"Commissions," Frederick scoffed, gaze sharp. "You don't need the money, I know that."

"I like the work."

Frederick started walking down the sidewalk toward the tree-lined neighborhood of fine brownstones less than two blocks away. Part of the Gold Coast neighborhood, near Lake Shore. "Maybe. But I know you, Lannes, and I know your kind. You'll let decades pass with your head buried in your tools and books and 'commissions,' all to avoid the world, this sweet desperate world. And you'll be alone. You'll be alone, my friend. And I cannot stand the idea."

Lannes stumbled, staring. "I have my brothers."

"Brotherhood is hardly what I am talking about."

Lannes' face warmed. "Leave it alone, Freddy."

"Leave it alone, as *you* want to be left alone?" The old man shook his head. "I have watched heads turn all night simply to take you in. For a man who wants solitude, you did a poor job of choosing your appearance. You should have woven a different mask. Become a potbellied, washed-up, breast-heavy bald man of middling years."

"I was in a hurry," Lannes said stiffly. "I had to use my own face as the template."

"Now you're bragging on yourself."

Lannes stared, incredulous. "Absolutely *not*."

Frederick made a dismissive gesture. "That was a beautiful woman back there. And she *wanted* you."

"That beautiful woman would have stuck a pitchfork in my face if she knew what I really looked like."

"You underestimate the ability of some people to handle the truth."

Lannes grunted, a familiar ache creeping into his chest. "That was not a woman who could have handled the truth. I don't think such a woman exists."

"Charlie found one," Frederick replied, rather cagily. "Or so I hear."

Lannes shot him a sharp look. "You've been talking to my brother?"

"Here and there."

"Charlie never said a word."

"Really?"

"Really," Lannes said, sensing a conspiracy. "But since you mentioned it, yes, he did find someone. A lovely woman. But the circumstances were . . . unique."

Unique. Impossible. Stuff of fairy tales. Brothers, turned to stone, captured by a witch who wanted their souls. Until a human woman had broken the spell, a brave woman who killed the witch, beating her at her own game.

Lannes remembered. He remembered the weight of stillness. He remembered being helpless. Caged. Unable to move or scream. He remembered pain as though underneath the stone had moved needles and fire, embracing his skin, invading muscle, becoming bone.

He remembered being alone.

"Her name is Agatha Durand," Lannes said quietly, struggling with his memories. "I suppose Charlie told you that. They adopted a little girl. Emma."

"Remarkable," said Frederick. "And the child . . . I assume she knows what her new father is?"

"She knows. Doesn't care."

The old man hummed a low note and shoved his hands deeper into his pockets. "And will they have children of their own? Is such a thing possible?"

Lannes felt like a football was pushing up his throat. "Must we talk about this?"

Frederick hesitated. "No. I suppose not."

Lannes said nothing, just kept walking, careful to measure his steps so that his friend did not tire. He made no sound. His feet were bare, though he wore the illusion of shoes, brown oxfords. His soles were tough as rawhide, calluses hard as stone. He could have found shoes that fit, but he preferred the sensation of concrete. It grounded him. As did watching the world. A breeze ruffled his hair beneath the illusion, caressing his bound wings. He sank into the sensation and held on dearly, using the comfort of the wind as a line of power to enrich his senses. A quiet magic.

I could stay another day, thought Lannes as the din of the city dimmed beneath the old trees lining the street of elegant brownstones. Golden windows surrounded him, pouring out light and voices, the clink of dishes, a dash of jazz. *I can hide here as well as anywhere*.

Little comfort, hiding. Feeling like a fox in a hole.

Frederick resided in a narrow three-story building, a

single residence, one of the few that had not been converted into condos and apartments. Made of brick and
stained glass, the structure was covered in thick vines
of creeping ivy. An art-deco iron fence surrounded the
tiny yard, and beyond, an American flag hung by the
arched double doors. The air was heady with the scent
of late-blooming roses. Frederick unlocked the fence,
then the front door. Lannes watched but did not follow
him inside.

A look of uncertainty passed over the old man's
face. "You're not leaving now, are you?"

"No," Lannes said gently, realizing in that moment
just what a fool he had been. Frederick had no one, either. His wife was long dead, as were his parents and
siblings. At least Lannes had his brothers. "I thought I
would just . . . stretch . . . a bit."

"Ah." Frederick smiled, his relief painful to witness. "Well, then."

Lannes backed away. "Don't wait up."

"How delightfully rapscallion," replied the old man,
and shut the door.

Lannes, thinking hard, locked the gate behind him.
Ten, twenty years? Even thirty. Time went so quickly.
He could rearrange some things in his life. Find a
home in Chicago. Be here for Frederick. Make certain
the old man did not spend his last decades without . . .
family. No matter how odd that family might be.

Freddy would hate you for your pity, whispered a
small voice in his head. Lannes shook it off. There
wasn't a hateful bone in Frederick Brimley's body. His
father had been the same. This made it easy to trust

them, even with secrets as big as gargoyles—nonhuman, a sentient, magical species hiding in plain sight, rubbing shoulders with the rest of society. It boggled the mind sometimes, even for Lannes.

He found himself thinking about the woman from the bar. Wondering how she would react to the truth. What it would be like to just let go and be with someone. Without fear. Without question.

It was late, the sidewalk dark and empty. He started walking and unbuckled the belt cinched around his chest, sighing with relief as his wings stretched free. They were still invisible, which was an odd thing for him when he glanced over his shoulder and saw nothing but the street. His wings were phantoms, ghosts that were attached to his back. Only the belt winked into view, but Lannes quickly wrapped the long strap of leather around his forearm and it faded again out of sight. The illusion he had cast in Maine hid anything that rested flat against his skin.

He spread his wings against the night breeze, savoring the rush of blood through them, the stretch of the thin skin filling like sails. Not much good for anything but gliding. There was a reason birds had small bodies and hollow bones.

But even with a high point to jump from, the city was a bad place for flight. Too many eyes. Not like on the island, or in the skies above the long rocky Maine coast. Chasing beams of moonlight while his hands skimmed the cold froth of the Atlantic. Being himself, truly himself. He missed that so much. The leaves would be turning by now. Storms moving in. Home, sweet home.

Lannes turned at the corner and saw his car parked along the street. The Impala. It was a muscle machine, long and hard and black as pitch—a relic from the late sixties, a masterpiece of design that combined all the best of beauty and power. Classic, wild.

Someone was trying to break into it.

Lannes had excellent night vision. The thief was a woman. She held a dark object in her hands—a hammer, perhaps—and looked ready to smash in his window. He started running. Made no secret of his approach. The woman heard him coming. Their eyes locked—

And his vision blurred. Just for a moment. All Lannes could see was a halo of blond hair. Stunning. Unnerving. Nothing like the woman from the bar. She looked like she was in the first stage of a panic attack, all heart and fear and claustrophobia. Powerful, overwhelming. She was a woman cornered, dangerous.

And then her hand moved, and he realized she held a gun, not a hammer, a slender black weapon that seemed as natural to her hand as a fine glove. Lannes stopped in his tracks. Power simmered beneath his skin. Heat gathered in his chest. He was less afraid of a gun than walls, less fearful of death than capture. His heart did not thunder, but held steady, true.

"Back off," ordered the woman. "Do it."

Lannes did not move. Blood drew his eye—rusty stains on the knees of her jeans, on the front of the white T-shirt half-hidden beneath her denim jacket. Blood, crusty and smeared, covered the woman's chin and lower cheek. Her fingers were dark with it. As were her feet. No shoes. A metallic stench wafted from her body. She looked like she had escaped a war zone. Run through hell.

"You're hurt," he said quietly. "Someone hurt you."

"No," she said, unsteadily. "Please. Turn around. Walk away."

Please. A soft, desperate word. Lannes took a step, and the woman backed up. He felt her tension, her fear, and it radiated into his body like a hot wind off a fire. Wave after wave. She was terrified of him. If not of him then of something else. Which, he supposed, was obvious.

The top of her head was level with his throat, which placed her height at six feet, more or less. Her hair was tangled, her eyes clear and green. Fine bones, strong body. She looked like a natural athlete, a good runner. Or a chaser.

"I won't hurt you," he said. "Put down the gun."

"Don't," she replied. "I'll shoot."

Small thing. Being shot would not be the worst he had ever endured. Lannes very slowly reached into his jeans and pulled out his car keys. The woman's gaze flickered between his hand and the Impala.

Lannes took another step. "I'll take you to the hospital."

Her gaze fractured with distrust, pain. He thought she might shoot him or cry, and he did not know which would be worse. He was not afraid—for the first time since arriving in this city, he was not even a bit afraid—and it was suddenly incredibly easy to remember who he was: torn, disparate, made of whole and half spirits, a creature who would rather face a woman with a gun than a woman with lust in her eyes.

In the distance, a siren wailed. The woman flinched. Shame passed through her face, and she lowered the gun. Backed up. He followed, just one step, unable to look away from her. He had never seen such a gaze, filled with a sudden horror and humiliation that reminded Lannes too much of himself. Two years free, he was still unable to shake the sense that he was trapped in stone. Unable to see himself in a mirror without feeling like a parody of who he had been long ago.

"I'm sorry," murmured the woman, still backing away. "Forget this happened."

If only. Lannes followed. "You need help."

The woman said nothing. She tucked the gun into the back of her jeans, turned and hobbled away. She left a trail of blood. Lannes did not go after her. Frozen in place, immobile in his skin. All the good strong comfort he had taken in being outside seemed to fade in direct proportion to the rise of a sudden squeezing sensation around his heart—but his heart was also straining outward, toward the woman. Inexplicable. Mystifying.

Terrifying. He did not want to take responsibility for a mystery he could not name—this human woman, walking away from him. *A criminal*, he thought. Trouble. Certainly no damsel in distress. Nor was he some iron-clad knight from human storybooks, the likes of whom had once killed his kind. No, no. No matter what his instincts were telling him, this was a bad idea.

She needs you, whispered a small voice in his mind. *You must.*

And then, *Catch her.*

Catch her. The two words burned through his heart. More than words. Instinct. Hard, violent, instinct—the kind that had saved his life more than once. The same instinct he had ignored long ago, leading to tragic results.

Lannes flipped his wings close against his body and moved silently across the street. Blood ran hot in his veins, his heart pounding—like during flight, like the moon in his eyes. Each step swallowed him deeper into another life, somewhere on the other side of the fork in the road. He could feel it, like magic: moments bound together to form a tapestry. A crossroads of fate bringing him here to this moment, with this woman and her gun.

She whipped around before he got close. Her hand touched the weapon at the small of her back. Eyes narrowed, mouth set in a grim line. Fierce. But there were shadows, hollows in her face, and the harsh light from a nearby streetlamp made her look exhausted, even ghastly.

"Keep away," she warned.

"Let me help you," he said, helpless to do otherwise. "Please."

She shook her head and started limping backward, one hand on the gun. Lannes did not move. He felt like he was walking on broken glass, some hulking beast towering over a lost maiden in the woods. Fairy tales, magic. He did not know what he was doing.

Not that it mattered. The woman, still moving backward, faltered. Swaying. Blinking hard. She touched her brow, sucking in her breath with a hiss . . . and quite suddenly collapsed. Dropped like a stone onto the road. Lannes was too surprised, too far away to catch her, but the woman was conscious when she hit the concrete—enough to brace herself—and was still awake, barely, when Lannes crouched at her side. Her eyes refused to focus on his face, and her breathing was shallow. Sweat glistened on her brow. Blood dotted her chin and the corner of her mouth. Her terror made him sick to his stomach.

They were in the middle of the street. No cars, no one on the sidewalk. A sleeping city, secrets in the shadows. Lannes had a cell phone. He considered calling the police, washing his hands of the whole mess. It was what anyone else would do. What he *should* do. The alternative made no sense. He had secrets to keep and no way of knowing what kind of threat this woman posed.

But after very little thought and with a great deal of instinct, Lannes scooped the woman up into his arms. He held his breath, afraid of his own strength, of hurting her. He had never held a human woman. She was tall but slender. Hardly a burden. And she was finally, thankfully, unconscious.

Lannes—feeling more than a little helpless and very much as though he were about to throw himself upon the mercy of some hoary, horrific beast of fate—turned and carried her away.

CHAPTER THREE

THE first thing the woman noticed, before opening her eyes, was that she was in bed again. A soft bed, heavy with downy comforters that smelled fresh and clean. Music played in the background. A flute. Mozart. She knew it, could taste the name on her tongue.

But not her own name. Not that.

A bad dream, she told herself, willing it to be true. Just a dream. She knew her name. She must; it was there, waiting. The woman fought to remember, to push past the dark wall inside her mind. It felt like a battle, a war. But she had no weapons, no clue. Nothing.

Hands touched her feet. Her eyes flew open. A dazzle of light momentarily blinded her. All she could see was color—gold and brown and red—rich as some treasure of rubies and doubloons, sparkling softly. She blinked hard, her vision clearing, and found herself in a room full of shadows, rich with wood paneling and creamy walls hidden behind antiques carved and heavy with dark twining bodies lost in flowers and vines. A silk comforter covered her, threads coarse and red, embroidered with glints of gold. A single lamp burned.

And at the bottom of the bed, still as stone, sat a man.

She remembered him from the street, and she rode a hot flash of fear—rode upon it like a bird, soaring low—allowing adrenaline to run its course while she lay quiet and unmoving, staring into his face without making a sound. Her heart thundered. She was glad to be lying down.

The man was handsome. The woman had no frame of reference with which to judge attractiveness, but she had a feeling he might be the best-looking individual she had ever encountered. He was like some throwback to an earlier age—effortlessly masculine, his face tanned and craggy as though he had spent a life on the remote frontier, on a mountain braving sun and wind. Wild. Elegant. Dark hair curled loosely around his face. His blue eyes were piercing, sharp with intelligence. Eyes that missed nothing. Eyes she could not look away from.

It was a disconcerting effect. She was here, in a bed—in *his* bed, maybe—and while she might not have her memories, she had an excellent grasp of all the awful things that could happen to a person in her position.

"Hello," said the man quietly, his voice deep, slightly hoarse.

The woman did not move. "Where am I?"

"The home of a friend. Near where I found you." He glanced down, and she saw her feet sticking out from under the covers. A tube of antibacterial ointment lay on top of the bed, along with a plastic bowl filled with bloodstained rags. "You had glass in your feet. I'm almost done, if you don't mind keeping still a while longer."

Her soles throbbed, the pain radiating up her ankles and into her calves. The woman remembered her misstep—crossing over a park, of all places. She had pulled out the largest pieces and tried to ignore the rest. Which had been agony. "Did you call the police?"

"No." He searched her eyes. "Are you going to give me a reason to?"

"Besides trying to steal your car? Pulling a gun on you?" She tensed and shoved her hand beneath her back, searching. The weapon was gone. At least she had her clothes on.

The man still studied her. "You can't be surprised I took it from you."

She forced herself to breathe. "No. And I don't suppose you'll give it back."

"I doubt it matters. You have no bullets."

She wondered briefly whether she could kick him in the face hard enough to get away. "What are you going to do with me?"

"Do?"

"Why am I here?"

He blinked. "You passed out."

"And you didn't call an ambulance?"

"I had the sense you'd be unenthused about the idea."

"I pulled a gun on you."

"Yes . . . we've established that."

"You're an idiot," she said. "Or a pervert."

"Oh, well. You've found me out," he said dryly. "I've brought you here for nefarious purposes. Nothing better than a mysterious woman with glass in her feet, trailing blood all over the floors."

She stared. His gaze faltered, and for a moment she saw profound uncertainty in his eyes, which was more comforting than his kindness. He glanced down—at his hands or the floor, she could not tell—but his jaw flexed and his massive shoulders slumped, and it was as though a great weight bore down on him that was so palpable, so real, she could almost see it.

"Despite . . . what you did," he said quietly, "you looked like you needed help. That's all. Allow a man one stupid moment in his life."

One stupid moment. She wondered if it could be that simple, and thought about the dead men in the hotel room. Had that been a stupid moment? Someone had killed them. Maybe her. Maybe? Probably. If she could do it once, she could do it again, no matter how abhorrent the idea currently seemed.

You're not safe to be around. You need to run.

Run. Or turn herself in. But when she began to tell the man to call the police, her dry throat caught up with her and she started coughing.

The man stood. He was big, larger than life, broad and muscular beneath his long-sleeved navy crew and jeans. His hands were the size of baseball mitts, but he did not lumber when he moved. He was graceful, careful, as though he was aware of his size and strength, the damage he could do.

He moved up the bed and she turned her head, saw a bottle of water on the nightstand. She struggled to sit up, and he held out his hand. He kept his distance, but she felt the strength of that gesture and froze.

"Keep your feet still," he said, looking almost embarrassed. "Let me."

He handed her the water bottle, which was new and sealed. The woman would not have taken it otherwise. She unscrewed the lid, leaned back against the pillows and drank. Her throat was dry, painful. The water tasted so good she wanted to cry. She drained it. The man had another waiting for her when she finished, and she took it from him gingerly.

He did not try to touch her. He seemed to go out of his way not to, holding the bottle at the very top with just two of his fingers.

She drank a little, then stopped as the man moved back down to the end of the bed. He sat, staring at her feet, a furrow forming between his eyebrows. Behind him, at the door, there was a shuffling sound.

The door opened. An old man peered into the room. He had a clear blue gaze and trim features. A dark red robe covered his slender frame, and a knit cap of the same color perched upon his head. Dapper, elegant. His eyes traveled from the man at the foot of the bed and found her face. He looked worried, but he gave her a small smile and the woman relaxed a little, in spite of herself.

"You're awake," he said.

"For the last few minutes," added the first man, not meeting her gaze. "I think I woke her."

"Where am I?" she asked, again.

"Astor Street," replied the old man promptly. "Gold Coast district . . ."

"Chicago," she finished, realizing just in that moment how selective amnesia could be. Bits and tendrils of information streamed into her mind. Chicago. Gold Coast. The second richest neighborhood in the United States.

The woman would rather have remembered her name.

"I am Frederick," said the old man formally, his hands beginning to tremble. "The gentleman working on your feet is Lannes."

Lannes did not look at her. He held tweezers, and in one swift move put them against the bottom of her right toe. She felt a sharp pain, flinched, and he leaned back, a small piece of glass held glistening and red. He dropped it and the tweezers into the bowl. Reached back to rub his neck.

"That's it," he said with a sigh. "I got it all."

"Thank you," she told him, still afraid but unsure what to do about it.

The man—Lannes—made no reply. He reached down, out of sight, and came back with a pair of thick white socks that were so massive she felt certain they could only belong to him. He began to put one on her, hesitated just short of wrapping his hand around her foot, and glanced back at Frederick.

The old man blinked, and the woman saw surprise, then understanding pass over his face. Tremors still wracked his hands, but he took the sock from Lannes.

The woman sat up, pushing away the covers. The sudden movement made her dizzy, but she fought past the sensation. "Let me do it."

"You're hurt," said Frederick.

"Just my feet," she replied. "I can dress myself."

A faint blush rode up the old man's cheeks, and he passed the bit of clothing to Lannes, who in turn reached across the bed to place both socks in her hand. She met his eyes briefly and felt a hot thrill race through her: fear, uncertainty, confusion. Everything. She could hardly judge what rested in his own gaze, but it felt like a mirror, as though he was just as unsettled by her presence.

The woman pushed aside the covers even more so that she could reach her feet. She stopped, though, when she saw the knees of her jeans. Bloodstains covered them. Brown, thick, crusty. Nausea crawled up her throat, and she swallowed hard. Unable to look away.

"Frederick," Lannes said quietly.

"Yes, of course," replied the old man, and left the room. The woman sucked in a deep breath—once, twice, until she felt heady with oxygen—and then slowly, carefully, leaned over the stains in her jeans and reached for her throbbing feet. Her hands shook slightly. She felt the man staring.

"What happened to you?" he whispered.

The woman almost told him. Part of her begged to say the words. He would call her crazy, a liar, and maybe she was. Hard to tell. Hard to know anything true about who she was—except that she lived, breathed, and had nothing to claim but blood, a gun and memories of the dead.

But Frederick came back, pushed open the door with his arms full of clothing, and Lannes stood to help him. He towered over the old man, and she watched his care, his gentleness. She judged it, just as she judged everything else about him . . . and did not find it wanting.

"My wife," Frederick said breathlessly, "was not a tall woman, but she liked her things comfortable. There should be something in here that you can use."

His wife. It was not his use of the past tense that told the tale of her death, but rather his voice, the look in his eyes, as though he still suffered from the old burn, so deep in his heart that it was part of his blood, his dreams. The woman stared, helpless. She did not deserve to use his wife's belongings. She had not earned the right, nor was she worthy of such kindness, she was sure of it.

She was also quite certain she would not be around long enough to repay him. And while stealing a car seemed a forgivable offense, walking off with the clothes of this man's dead wife felt like a crime without hope of absolution.

"I can't," she protested. "They're special to you."

"My wife was special," he said firmly. "Not her clothes."

The woman squeezed the socks, unable to respond. Lannes spread the clothes on the bed beside her, then stood back, touching Frederick's elbow. He guided the old man toward the bedroom door and glanced over his shoulder, his eyes meeting hers. "Call if you need anything."

She nodded, but it was a lie. The less said, the less they interacted, the better. She had to get away. She had to take what kindness had been offered, then run like hell. It did not matter where. Just that she move. Better that than put these two men at risk—from her, from someone else.

Lannes held her gaze a moment longer than was comfortable, almost as if he could read her thoughts. She did not look away from him.

He ducked out into the hall and shut the door behind him. The woman listened to his footsteps recede, and let out her breath. This was hell.

She examined her feet before she rolled on the socks. Cuts covered her soles, but the bleeding had stopped, and Band-Aids hid the worst injuries. The man had washed her feet and slathered them in antibacterial ointment. His kindness was disconcerting. There was no good reason for it. She did not trust compassion.

The socks felt lush and warm on her feet, which she dangled over the side of the bed as she rummaged through the clothes. She tugged free long silk skirts that flowed and shimmered in lovely shades of dark green. They tangled gracefully with oversized cashmere sweaters that were as creamy as dark vanilla and sported wide shawl collars draped against long bell sleeves. The woman felt like a trespasser handling these clothes, but she forced herself to change. When she stood, her feet hurt. They ached so badly she was hardly certain she would be able to walk out of the place.

She looked for a mirror but found nothing. She still did not know what her face looked like. The skin around her knees was stained with blood, but she had no place, no time, to wash herself. The skirt came down to her calves. The woman touched her chin and felt smooth clean skin. The blood was gone. She hoped.

The woman found a garbage bin by the bed. Empty, except for a plastic bag. She stuffed her old clothes inside and tied the loops tight, swung it between her fingers and hobbled to the door. The hall outside was quiet, empty, elegantly decorated in neutral tones and antiques. She held her breath and started walking, each step pure agony. The floor did not creak. At the top of the stairs, she heard faint voices, dishes rattling.

"Well, I can see you're not a lost cause," said Frederick, sounding exasperated. "You go to such trouble to avoid others, and in the same night, you bring home a strange woman?"

"She needed help," replied Lannes, his voice low, practically a growl. "Did you expect me to leave her in the road?"

"Of course not. But—oh, damn my hands. Give me that towel, will you?"

"I'll clean it up. Here, just . . . just sit. Rest. I'm sorry I got you up."

"I would have been furious if you hadn't."

"I didn't know what to do. She collapsed."

"It could have been a ruse."

"You don't believe that, not after meeting her."

"No," said the old man quietly. "But *some* crime has been committed. The blood on her clothing, the gun . . ."

"Unloaded. And even if it hadn't been, she couldn't have hurt me."

"You're too sure of yourself."

"Better than the alternative," said Lannes grimly, and for a moment the woman wanted to go to him. She wanted to find those two men and ask for their help. Maybe they would turn her in, maybe they would hurt her, but the risk seemed small compared to the possibility of getting what she needed.

What did she need? A kind word. Some sense, even for a short time, that she was safe. Not alone. Protected from a solitude so gaping, so terrible, she could hardly stand it. Her entire history, all her memories, fit within the last three hours. She did not know who she was.

But you know what you feel. Count on that if nothing else. Rely on nothing else.

Her only other option was to give up. Not to the police, but on life. Find a nice bridge somewhere and jump. But the idea filled her with such skin-crawling revulsion—such anger at herself—that she abandoned it in less than a heartbeat.

She was not going to take the easy way out. She refused. An awful thing had happened—*she* might have done an awful thing—and it was up to her to find out what and why. Somehow. Even if she had no idea where to begin.

You won't find out who you are here. Alone is bet-
ter. No one else will get hurt.

Maybe. The woman sidled down the stairs, feet
throbbing. It was incredibly difficult to walk. Directly
ahead was the front door. Dishes still rattled—behind
her, down another hall—and she held her breath, moving as fast as she could. The socks were so large on
her feet the toes flopped, but at least they were silent.
She kept expecting to hear footsteps behind her, a
shout, but nothing happened. Not even when she un-
bolted the door and turned the knob.

Cold air rushed over her face. She stepped over the
threshold. Behind her, she heard, "Wait."

The woman did not wait. She slipped into the night,
slamming the door behind her, and took off, hobbling
as fast as she could past the gate to the sidewalk. Her
heart pounded in her ears and her breathing rasped.
Her feet felt like they were on fire. She heard nothing behind her, not a single sound of pursuit . . .
but before she had gone half a block, heat washed
down her back and she glanced over her shoulder in
time to see Lannes bearing down on her, massive
and silent.

She stumbled. He caught her. Just for a moment,
the briefest of touches. And then his hands disappeared and he stepped back, leaving the glow of the
streetlight for the shadows of a tree. He looked menacing, dangerous—and that was only his silhouette.

The woman steadied herself, mouth dry. "I had
to go."

"I got that," he rumbled. "Do you have a place? Somewhere you're headed?"

She hesitated. "I can't stay here."

"You didn't answer the question."

The woman turned and started walking, but the pain was worse and she hobbled as though tiptoeing over hot coals, feeling ridiculous and miserable. She glanced over her shoulder. Lannes followed, close enough to touch.

"Stop," she said, "please."

"*You* stop. You can't walk like this."

"I believe I'm doing so."

"How far? Where are you going?" Lannes stepped in front of her, effectively blocking the sidewalk. He was too large to go around, with cars on one side and an iron fence on the other. "If you have a place in mind, I'll drive you. I'll get you there safely. I promise."

She felt close to tears, something she was uncertain her pride could handle. "I appreciate what you did for me, but please, why won't you just leave me alone?"

"Because I can't," he said simply. "Not until I know you'll be okay."

"I *threatened* you."

"I remember."

"I could be crazed."

"Possibly."

"Jesus," she muttered. "Grow a brain."

"Too late," he replied, a grim smile touching his mouth. "Jiminy Cricket ate it."

She covered her face to keep from crying—or

laughing. "It's because I'm a woman, isn't it? No matter what I've done, you refuse to see me as a threat."

"Hardly," he rumbled, bending near. "Women are terrifying. You, I'm sure, spit venom and eat men alive. But I'm offering you help right now, and you can take it or leave it."

"I left it," she told him, peering up into his eyes. "But you followed."

"Well." Lannes hesitated, frowning. "I won't again. If you mean it."

She wanted his help. She wanted it desperately. But it terrified her that she could be misjudging his intentions—or that she might be overestimating her own sanity.

"For all you know," she said softly, "I might be a murderer."

"And are you?" he asked, just as quiet, with such startling directness, she swayed as though hit. She remembered the scent of blood. Felt sick.

"I don't know," she whispered, trying not to vomit. "I don't know what happened."

Lannes studied her in silence, his gaze unflinching. Then slowly, he took a step back, and she thought, *That did it, he's done with me*, which was less of a relief than it should have been. But he stopped after that one step, paused and said, "Are you coming?"

Her breath left in a rush. "You're insane. I could be dangerous."

"You've certainly worked hard enough to convince me of that."

She shook her head. "If you want to help, give me your car. I'll leave it someplace safe. The police will find it. You'll have it back in days."

He ignored that. "Is someone chasing you?"

She felt ill. "I don't know."

"You don't know a lot of things." Lannes took another step, his gaze never leaving her face. "I won't hurt you."

"You expect me to trust that?"

"As much as I'm trusting you. Just for the night. To rest your feet."

One night. A night almost gone by now. She swayed toward him, feeling everything inside her settle quiet as death. "I'd like my gun back."

"Okay." His mouth tilted into another grim smile. "When you're ready to leave."

The woman wanted to say no. She wanted to turn and walk away into the shadows. She wanted to do it and know she would be okay. No matter what. Strong enough, resourceful enough.

And you are. You're all of those things. She felt it in her gut.

But there was also nothing wrong with taking a risk on kindness. No matter how terrifying it might be. No matter how much the awful little voice in her head disagreed.

Run, it kept whispering. *Run far.*

"If you try anything . . . ," she began, and stopped, feeling ridiculous.

"If I try anything . . . ," he said gently—then he also

hesitated, finally sighing. "Never mind. I need some tea. Are you coming?"

The woman said nothing, but hobbled toward him. He was a big man, no doubt strong, but he did not touch or help her, just kept his pace slow. She appreciated that. Even if he still scared her.

She was just too desperate to care.

CHAPTER FOUR

WHILE Lannes could not in good conscience disagree with the woman's assessment that he was indeed an idiot, he knew several things about himself that she did not. First and foremost, he was a Mage—a fairly accomplished one, at that, and therefore capable of knowing certain things about other people that might not or could not be readily divulged.

He had learned some things about the woman while she lay unconscious.

She sat before him now in Frederick's kitchen, perched on a stool at the butcher-block counter. Her blond hair was a fine mess around her face, and the skin around her eyes looked pinched with exhaustion. He had cleaned blood from her chin earlier, after carrying her into the house. Wiped it away with a hot rag. She had looked pained even while asleep.

Now was little better. A small furrow cut between her eyebrows—a permanent fixture since she had awakened—and her mouth held a worried frown.

She had said almost nothing since following him home. Just a nod here, a shake of the head there. Not a word when asked her name, though the anxiety that rolled from her made him never want to inquire again.

So, they sat. In silence. Regarding each other. The woman clutched a white steaming mug of some aromatic green tea that always gave Lannes a terrible stomachache. He preferred dark brews, breakfast blends steeped in fine Irish Belleek porcelain. Bits of lemon thrown in. No sugar, which for him obscured the taste of a good tea.

He had his own cup in front of him, half-drained. Fredrick was back in bed, though not likely asleep. Listening to an audiobook, perhaps, or keeping his ear pressed to the door.

"This is a nice home," said the woman suddenly, as though the silence was finally too much to bear. She glanced from him to the rest of the kitchen: cream-colored cabinets, sandstone floors and pale accents. Frederick had a woman come every day to cook for him and do the dishes. It had been that way since Clarissa died.

"It has a lot of heart," Lannes agreed, and added, "You can eat, you know. Sandwich, leftovers."

"Maybe later," she said, but he knew she intended on bolting as soon as she was able. He had known she would try to escape when he left her alone in that room to dress, though he'd had little choice but to let her try. To do otherwise would have terrified her even more, made her feel like she was in a cage, captured. His own nightmare.

His puzzle, too. He could still hear a single word, one small word, reverberating from her mind to his.

Run.

Lannes pushed back his chair and took his cup to the sink. Felt the woman watching him. Her intensity was unnerving, her eyes so piercing that he half-expected her to see through the illusion to his real face and start screaming. What he was doing, the risk he was taking . . .

Frederick was right to question your actions, he thought, dragging a loaf of bread from the cabinet. *This is not you.*

Not him. Not entirely. Before the witch had stolen and tortured him and his brothers, he had gone out into the world. He had . . . mingled, used magic to hide in plain view and had seen . . . wonders. He had glided through the Himalayas searching for Shangri-la. Perched atop Notre Dame under a full moon and composed lines of bad maudlin poetry. Trekked with amateurish delight through Rome and Spain, apprenticing himself when he could to the old dying masters of the art of bookbinding. Touched the earth and skies of more places than he could count. And everywhere he had found awe and marvel and beauty—in nature, in people, in the things that people could create.

He loved humans. That he feared and was sometimes disgusted by them as well did not lessen his appreciation. His brothers felt the same, as did their parents, though he knew quite well that many of the remaining clans, scattered in remote reaches of the world, would have preferred a little less humanity, less war and other human folly.

"Are you a vegetarian?" Lannes asked, opening the refrigerator. He had bound his wings again, and the ache threatened to turn his mood even sourer.

The woman said nothing. He glanced at her. She was staring at the open refrigerator with such confusion— even despair—that he felt instantly sorry he had asked.

"No," she finally said, slowly. "I don't think I am."

It was the perfect opening—and Lannes almost took that moment to pin her down with his questions. He stopped himself, though. Remembered what it had felt like up in that room while she lay unconscious, as he touched her face—with his hands, with a washrag— enveloping her in his magic to make her sleep. Trying, as he did, to see into her mind.

Not easy to do. The process never had been, for him. It required prolonged touching, skin-to-skin contact. He could cast an illusion, influence a body's ability to heal—as he had done with the woman's feet, so that she could walk. Little things here and there. But to reach into a mind was a different business, unsavory at best. This woman was his first attempt in years, and he would not have tried at all had he not been so concerned about her presence in Frederick's home.

But what he had seen—what he had *not* seen— troubled him more than it reassured.

Run, he remembered, pulling leftover chicken and slices of cheddar from the refrigerator, along with bits of cucumber and onion. He got down a plate, careful of his strength, and made the woman a rough, sloppy sandwich that he hoped tasted better than it looked.

He handed her the plate. She stared at it, then him.

"Not poisoned," he said.

"Thanks," she replied dryly, and then in a softer tone, "Really, thank you."

He shrugged, keenly aware that anything he might say—*You're welcome, not a problem, anytime*—would sound trite, patronizing. Silence was safer. Lannes stepped back, pretending to busy himself with refilling the electric kettle. But he watched out of the corner of his eye as she gingerly picked up the sandwich and took a bite.

Hunger flashed across her face. Her next bite was larger, faster.

Lannes turned his back on her, his wings hot. His heart hot. He needed more tea. Anything to settle his nerves. He marveled that the woman could maintain such calm when he knew—he *knew*—what lay inside her.

Confusion. Terror. Loss. Bigger than her body, bigger than the sky.

He could still feel his hands upon her face, the softness of her skin. Her emotions, overwhelming him even though subconscious. And beyond her fear, something else. Blood. Smoke. Horror. Escaping down a black road, filled with a small voice whispering, *Run, run, run.*

Then, nothing else. A hole. A void. So dark, so empty, it had frightened him into withdrawing. The woman was missing part of her mind.

Stolen, not lost. Lannes could feel it. He knew the difference, had some experience with amnesia. On his travels, long ago, an old Tuscan man had suffered a minor blow to the head, lost a month of his life, an important month—a wedding, a dinner with a dying friend. Lannes had pretended to know something about medicine. Talked big, made claims about Asian reflexology that to this day still made him blush in shame. He had touched the old man, held his breath the entire time, hoping Alberto Guarnieri would not notice the difference between reality and illusion. Worth the risk, though. Alberto's memories had still been there. Intact. Just . . . lost behind a wall. Sheltered. All it had taken was a minor trick to free his thoughts. Nothing but patience. Ten minutes of his time.

This woman had none of that. No walls. No trace. This was not some dissociative fugue. It was as though her life had been erased entirely. No accident could have hurt her so badly. No blow to the head, or stroke.

No, someone had ripped away her memories, excised them with breathtaking precision. And not just one or two memories, but a great many. Perhaps all, though he had no way to be certain. She might know her name, though he doubted it now. He was also quite certain those lost memories were gone for good. Not a trace of them remained. Not even an echo.

The kettle began to whistle. Lannes shut it off. "More tea?"

"No thanks," she said, carefully standing and carrying her plate to the sink. Limping heavily. He wanted to tell the woman to stay off her feet, but she looked stubborn, and he stepped sideways in a subtle dance, trying to keep his distance. Frederick's kitchen was large, but not big enough for a gargoyle attempting to keep a woman from brushing up against his wings.

She gave him a curious look and turned on the faucet, dashed some liquid soap over the plate and began washing it. Lannes poured himself tea.

"I'm sorry," she suddenly said, glancing at him, the kitchen lights catching the gold in her hair like a halo. She was a beautiful woman, if a bit haggard. Lannes found himself leaning back against the counter merely to drink her in, and felt the base of the electric kettle burn his wing. He tried not to flinch.

"Sorry?" he echoed, weakly. "For what?"

She looked at him with a hint of dry humor. "Think about it for a minute."

Lannes shrugged. "You were desperate."

"I committed a crime. You don't take someone into your home for that."

"Maybe I'm a Boy Scout. Delusions of Superman." His favorite comic book character. Lannes had first begun reading the comic in the forties, along with everything else he could get his hands on. As a child, he had been dazzled with the idea of a man being able to fly—or at the very least, jump far. He had been swept in by the idea of a secret identity—glasses and a tie—transforming one of the most powerful men in the world into just another Joe Average. Hiding in plain sight.

"I didn't think Superman ever let anyone but Lois

into his Fortress of Solitude," mused the woman—then she stopped, frowning, and looked down at the sink.

Lannes asked, "What is it?"

She shook her head, fingers grazing her brow as though she hurt. "Nothing. Just . . . strange things pop into my head."

Strange things. Lannes wanted to touch her again. He needed to, if he was going to examine the cut inside her mind. That she could function, recite random facts . . .

He turned away, busying himself with his tea. He was afraid to look at her. He had never been good at hiding his emotions, and what he felt—what had driven him out into the night to bring her back here—was more than he could name. But it felt like anger. Profound, terrible anger. Because he knew this. He knew what it was like to have his life stolen. To be trapped in a cage, just as this woman was trapped. Not by stone, but by circumstance. No money, no friends, no one to turn to. Violated, in ways that Lannes could not even begin to fathom.

And the blood? The gun?

He glanced over his shoulder and found the woman hobbling back to her stool. He moved past her, careful to keep his distance, and snagged the seat with one long arm. He placed it beside her so that she would not have to walk so far, and she gave him a tense, guarded nod of thanks.

"There's a bathroom upstairs," he said. "Towels."

Her jaw tightened. "A lock on the door?"

He was not offended. "Yes."

"Okay," she said, her tension so raw he could taste it. Which was exactly his problem.

He could *feel* the woman. Ever since he had entered her mind. Like a walnut lodged in the back of his brain, hard and unyielding. A strong presence. As though part of her had taken refuge with him when he pulled away from his examination of her memories. And no matter how hard he tried, he could not rid himself of her. Mentally, physically—it was all the same. Lannes was stuck with her. And she was stuck with him, whether she realized it or not.

He had to find the person who had harmed her, and the only way to do that was to keep her around. Use her. Learn from her mind, if he could. He could not allow such a violation to stand unpunished or leave open the possibility of it happening again.

And the woman . . . she needed help. He might not be able to explain the blood or the weapon, but he had seen enough. Felt enough. Until this was done, he would take care of her. One way or another. Even if it was just as a shadow at her back. He could track her now. That presence in his mind might as well have been a chain between them. He could follow her anywhere.

"You're staring at me," she said, breaking him from his reverie.

"Ditto," he replied, trying to sound cool, unaffected. Feeling like an idiot. "I'll see if I can find you some comfortable shoes. Slippers, maybe."

Her gaze remained steady. "I'm leaving in the morning."

Then we both are, he thought. "I'd appreciate you saying good-bye first."

A very faint smile touched her mouth. "You'll try to talk me out of going, Boy Scout."

"Maybe," he admitted, and backed away as she slid off the stool. "Think I might succeed?"

"I hope not," she said, and he told her where to find the bathroom.

HE WENT TO FREDERICK'S WORKSHOP WHEN HE HEARD the water start. His friend had converted a bedroom and its adjoined study into an office that doubled as a place to indulge the craft Frederick's father had taught him. Alex Brimley, master bookbinder: a man whose patrons had included royalty and the finest libraries and museums in the world, a clientele that had gone to Lannes after Alex's death. Not to Frederick, who preferred scholarship, the written word, no matter the disappointment this had caused his father.

But that was neither here nor there. Alex Brimley's workshop still existed. Lovingly recreated from memory.

Memories make us, Lannes thought, settling onto the large, steel-enforced stool that Frederick had bought specially for him. *Memories are the bricks of our souls.*

And if you lost those bricks? The woman was no shell. She had thoughts, feelings. She knew things. But her predicament was, to Lannes, the same as being born again. Forced to start anew. A babe in the woods.

Tools lay scattered on the long table in front of him. Some resembled screwdrivers, but the shapes of their

long tips ranged from needle thin to scalloped and flat
as a duck's beak. He smelled leather, paper, glue. A
small refrigerator full of eggs hummed near his feet.
He had been using egg whites earlier, mixed with
natural chemicals, to apply gold leaf to the etchings of a
special journal he was making for Frederick. The old
man had written twenty novels within Lannes' cre-
ations before sending them on to a secretary to be tran-
scribed onto a computer. He called the journals his
lucky charms.

Lannes wondered if Frederick's hands would let
him write in this one. Likely enough, his next book would
have to be of the spoken variety, recorded on tape or
computer.

He heard the old man's footsteps and sat back, pre-
paring himself. Frederick did not disappoint.

"I can die happy," said his friend upon entering the
room, "now that I finally know what it feels like to
harbor a criminal." He slouched into a wooden arm-
chair near the workbench in the study and stared at a
picture of his father, a black-and-white still of a young
man in a dark suit, fair hair slicked back, standing
stiffly in front of a painted floral tapestry. The photo
had been taken in the late 1920s in Maine. Lannes'
father had a copy in his own study.

"She's not a criminal," Lannes replied, balancing
the base of a screwdriver on his palm. "At least, I don't
think she is. What she said is true, I guarantee you that.
Her memories *are* gone."

Frederick shook his head, looking away from his

father's picture. His fingers danced and trembled. "This is strange business, Lannes. Dare I say, even unnatural."

"That's what you get for being friends with a gargoyle."

"Oh, the pain." Frederick stood, and stretched. "All right, then. I will make my evening call to Sal, and then off to bed."

Sal. Lannes had not heard that name in some time. For some reason, it was always a minor shock for him to remember that Frederick had other friends. Human friends. Men and women Frederick had known almost as long as Lannes. He wondered, suddenly, how Frederick had coped all these years, living a double life between magic and the mundane.

"How is Sal?" Lannes asked. "Still in the nursing home?"

"Coma," Frederick said, simply. "He had another stroke."

Lannes sat back, staring. "I'm sorry. I know you're close."

"More than seventy years we've known each other. We might not be as close as you and I, but we are still like brothers." Frederick suddenly seemed very small and frail, every bit his age. "I call, and the nurse supposedly holds the phone up to his ear. It's the best I can do, at the moment."

"Would you like to visit him?" Lannes asked. "I'll take you, wherever he is."

"Maybe. Or perhaps it is better to remember him as he was. Which was never that good, anyway." The old man studied his slippers. "And the woman? I'm concerned with her state of mind, her circumstances notwithstanding. I'm also worried about you."

Lannes turned his thoughts inward, focusing on the hard sensation of the woman's presence burning at the back of his mind. She felt like a small flame—brighter now, growing in strength. He did not know what that meant, but it was not a concern. Yet. His brothers might not feel the same way. Any kind of mental link, accidental or not, always posed a risk.

But he knew where she was, just by thinking about it, and he found that to be an odd comfort.

"Don't," Lannes said. "I can take care of myself."

"And I suppose you were . . . taking care of yourself . . . during that extended vacation?" Frederick's jaw flexed, his eyes hard. "I found your parents, Lannes. I suppose they didn't tell you that, did they? I found them after they had stopped searching for you and your brothers. We thought you were all dead."

Lannes closed his eyes and gripped the screwdriver between his hands. The plastic handle cracked. "You didn't say anything."

"I thought *you* would. Eventually. But this . . . this woman . . . changes everything."

He felt sick. "I don't see how."

"Your father said it was a trap."

Lannes tried not to think of it, but images flashed through his mind. His wings ached. "Wasn't anything like this. If it was, do you think I would be helping her?"

"I think helping others is in your nature. I doubt you can resist."

"Don't say it like that."

"I worry," said Frederick quietly. "I can't see into her mind the way you can, but I still can't help but wonder at the coincidence of her meeting *you*, of all the people in this city. You, Lannes. What are the odds?"

Lannes opened his eyes and very carefully set down the mangled remains of the screwdriver. He could not look at his old friend. "Good night, Frederick."

"Lannes."

But Lannes said nothing. He did not want to remember. And though it was childish, he kept his head down until the old man shuffled from the room. Yet, when he was finally alone, shame crept over him. Frederick deserved better. Lannes was in no position to take for granted the concern of a friend.

He sighed and reached for the phone. Dialed a number. His brother Charlie answered on the third ring.

"Hey," Lannes said, "it's me."

"Better be good," Charlie muttered hoarsely. "Three in the morning here, man."

A two-hour difference between Chicago and San Francisco. It was going to be dawn soon. "I have a problem."

Charlie said nothing for a long moment, but when he spoke, his voice sounded clearer. Like he was fully awake. Sitting up. "What happened?"

Lannes told him. About the woman and the gun. The blood. The hole in her mind. He did not mention the link between them. There was no good reason for the omission, except that it felt personal, somehow. Intimate.

"So?" Lannes asked, when he was done. "Verdict?"

"I got nothing," said Charlie. "You're screwed."

"Thanks, genius."

"Good way to get a date."

"Not funny."

"Sorry." His brother went silent. "I need to talk to Aggie about this."

Which was the reason Lannes had called Charlie instead of his other brothers. Agatha knew people. People with resources who would not look twice at a gargoyle or dismiss claims of psychic mutilation out of hand.

Lannes had to marvel at his brother sometimes. His luck. His life. Charlie, through nothing more than an act of sheer desperation and compassion, had opened up a new world to them all—and found himself married, with a child, working now for an agency that operated out of San Francisco: a group of men and women, human and inhuman, shape-shifters, human psychics, all of whom masqueraded as little more than highly trained private detectives, mercenaries and bodyguards, simply in order to use their abilities, psychic and magical, to help others.

Dirk & Steele. An agency that operated in public merely to maintain a guise of human normalcy. Fooling the world with the greatest trick of all—hiding in plain sight. Much like Lannes and the rest of his kind. He could never have imagined such an organization existed before Agatha had come into their lives. It was an extraordinary twist of fate. Destiny. Magic. Mysteries beyond reckoning.

"Agatha isn't at home?" asked Lannes.

"Not for a bit. She was sent to Argentina. Investigating that gnome scare."

Lannes hesitated, trying to decide if he had heard right. "Gnomes?"

"You know, little dudes with pointy hats? Big white beards and blue coats?"

"That's a *commercial*, Charlie."

"Whatever. A kid took some creepy footage down in Salta. Little guy wearing a pointed hat, moving with a weird sideways walk. People got freaked."

"It's probably just a prank."

"Sure. But Roland wanted it checked out. Just in case."

Lannes frowned, unbinding his wings with one hand. "*Gnomes*? Seriously?"

"Gargoyles? Shape-shifters? My wife who can tell the future?"

Lannes grunted, stretching his wings. "Fine. But that doesn't help *me*."

"I'll make some calls. In the meantime, *be careful*. You can't be certain this isn't just a ruse. Another way to . . . get at us. Again."

Lannes almost asked if he and Frederick had been talking. The possibility of a trap was impossible to forget. Pressure, those lines of fate knotting tighter: coincidence and chance, quirk and happenstance. To have been chased out of a bar by a woman just at the moment when he would witness his car stolen—a theft intended by another woman. An armed, bloody woman. A lifetime of tenuous moments bringing him here and now.

The idea of being tricked scared him. But so did the idea of being wrong in another way. Because if the woman was innocent in all this—and he thought she was, he truly did—then abandoning her would be the same as a slow murder. He could not do that. Not without losing a part of himself that would be impossible to regain.

Determination was stronger than fear. He had to get this done. He had to be strong enough.

The witch did not break me. She did not.

Upstairs, he heard the water stop. Charlie said, "Are you there?"

"Thinking," Lannes muttered. "Ask around. I'll call if anything changes."

He hung up on his brother's good-bye and sat still, wracking his brain. Coming up with nothing. He was going to have to ride this through. Play the situation by ear.

Lannes heard footsteps on the stairs. Quiet. Careful. He half-expected the woman to make a run for the front door again, but after a long minute of silence, he heard her walking down the hall toward the study.

He said, "I'm in here."

The woman peered around the door. She still wore Clarissa's old clothes, and her hair was wet. Her face was scrubbed clean and pink. She looked tired and tense, but there was a strength in her gaze that was sharper, clearer. Like she had gotten her second wind. He liked that. She was not a whiner. Not a quitter. And she had every reason to quit, based on what little he had gleaned.

"Feel better?" he asked, still seated.

She nodded, peering at the workshop, the glow of the antique lamps warm on her face. She carried the scent of lavender with her, and her feet, wrapped again in his big socks, flopped charmingly. The small garbage bag crammed with her old clothes swung from her hand.

She limped near, gazed down at the table covered in tools and paper. She seemed especially fascinated with the partial cover he had been working on, which was still laid out in loose form.

"Ulrich Schreier," she murmured. "Your work is similar. And it looks as though you're using the cuir-ciselé process."

Lannes stared, heart thudding faster. "That's a very obscure name. And a little known technique."

She blinked, ripping her gaze from the table to stare at him. "Is it?"

He forced himself to breathe and folded his wings tighter around his body. He was wishing suddenly that he had not been so quick to free them. "Schreier was a fifteenth-century Austrian artisan. Famous in his time. But usually only bookbinders are familiar with his work."

Her cheeks flushed. "Is that what you are?"

"It's one of the things. I restore books. I make them, too."

"Useful."

"Not many would say so."

"Then they're not readers," she said simply and frowned again, briefly shutting her eyes. Lannes leaned back, trying not to react. Her memories might be gone, but her spirit remained. Personality, likes and dislikes. A storehouse of random information.

"You should rest," he said. "You can take the room you woke up in."

"The sun will be up soon."

"Does it matter?"

"I should say good-bye."

"Sleep first, then good-bye."

"What makes you think I don't have somewhere to get to?"

"Because you would have gotten there by now." Lannes wanted to stand, but his wings were pressing against the worktable, and that was probably the safest place for them. "The bedroom door has a lock, too, if you're worried."

The woman faltered, staring. "Why are you doing this?"

He smiled, sadly. "The way you ask . . . You think I'm going to hurt you."

"I think you'll want something, eventually."

"You're jaded."

"I'm realistic."

"Fair enough." Lannes tried to think of anything that would reassure her, but nothing came to mind. She had a right to be scared. He was a big man with a suspicious absence of motives.

Lannes heard something outside the room. A click. Not from the stairs, not on the second floor, but closer. He froze, then stood so swiftly the woman backpedaled away from him. He did not try to reassure her, just walked into the hall. He tasted night on his tongue and moved faster, almost at a run, until he found himself in the foyer.

The front door was open. Not just a crack, but thrown wide. Heat washed over his back, and he moved aside as the woman drew up beside him. She stared at the door and went very still.

"I didn't do that," she whispered.

"I know," he breathed. "Go upstairs, second door on your right. If Freddy is there, stay with him."

"What about you?"

"Go," he muttered. "Just go."

She went, hobbling as fast as she could. Lannes glided toward the front door, listening hard. Hearing nothing but the wind. He stretched out his senses, feeling for the passage of another, the passage of a stranger.

All he found on the front steps was a piece of paper weighed down with a rock. He did not need to pick it up to read its message. The letters were large, bold, and in black.

FIND ORWELL PRICE, he read.

And at the bottom, *RUN*.

CHAPTER FIVE

THE lights were off in Frederick's room when the woman knocked and entered. She heard a man's voice reciting from a book. Fredrick, stretched on the bed and illuminated by light from the hall, immediately sat up and turned on a bedside lamp. He clapped his hands and the audio shut off.

"What do you want?" he asked, with such tension that the woman realized with utter certainty that he did not trust her—that he might even be afraid of her. This was such a bizarre relief, such a pure gasp of *normal*, she had to lean against the door to catch her breath. Maybe no one here wanted to hurt her, after all. Maybe, just maybe, she had found herself a real, honest Good Samaritan.

"Lannes told me to come up here," she whispered. "Someone might have broken in."

The old man threw back his covers and rolled out of bed. He moved with enviable grace. "He's down there now?"

"He said to wait here."

Frederick gave her a sharp look and swept past. "Do you listen to everything strangers tell you?"

"Apparently not," she muttered, and followed him. Not far, though. Lannes was already running up the stairs. His mouth was set in a grim line, and his eyes held a look that made the woman feel as though she were seeing dead bodies all over again. Something terrible, awful. Horrific.

"Pack a bag," Lannes said to Frederick. "I'm taking you to a hotel."

The old man froze. "Excuse me?"

"A bag. Anything you need. Five minutes." He pushed Frederick toward his room and flipped on the overhead light, glancing back at the woman. "You and I need to talk."

Her feet throbbed. So did her heart. "What happened?"

Lannes pulled a crumpled note from his pocket and showed it to her. Her knees buckled. Lannes caught her arm. She began to lean against him and he pushed her firmly toward the wall.

"I don't know what that means," she murmured, pain threading through her skull.

"I think the meaning is self-explanatory," he replied tersely. "Do you know this name?"

"No." She pushed herself toward the stairs, desperate. "I should go. I'm sorry. I'm so sorry."

He moved fast for a man his size, and blocked her path. His eyes were intense, searching. She wanted to hit him, to scream in his face, but her throat felt too full for words, and her hands, curled into fists, dug against her stomach. She was trying to hold in her fear.

"This message was *not* just for you," he said quietly.

"You're wrong," she told him, hoarse. "You don't understand. I was left a similar note. Earlier."

"Run," he breathed, as though the word meant something to him beyond the note in his hand.

"Run," she agreed. "But just me. Not you. I don't know anything about finding a man."

He leaned in. "Who would do this? Do you have any idea?"

"I don't know. I don't remember."

"*What* don't you remember?"

"Everything," she whispered, horrified at herself. "Just that I woke up in a hotel room, and there was smoke, and bodies—"

Her voice crumpled. So did her face, tears breaking free. She tried to speak again, but all that came out was a hoarse cracking sound, and she sagged against the wall, bent over her stomach, hands pressed against her mouth. Fighting herself. Fighting grief. Ashamed for not being stronger.

Lannes crouched, keeping his distance. The woman could not meet his eyes. She was too afraid of what she would see. Disbelief. Suspicion. She expected him to call her a liar. Or worse.

But all he whispered was, "It'll be all right. I believe you."

She shook her head, squeezing shut her eyes. Wishing she were alone. Grateful she was not. "I don't know who I am. I don't know anything."

"You know Ulrich Schreier," he murmured, leaning closer. "You know Superman, and you know Chicago. You like books. And you are very stubborn. That's something. That's a great deal."

The woman finally forced herself to look at him. "It's not enough."

Lannes' shoulders slumped. Frederick appeared in the bedroom doorway dressed in loose slacks and cashmere, with a small canvas rucksack hanging from his shoulder. He looked ready for a stroll along the Seine, though his hands shook slightly and his eyes were fraught with concern. Especially when he looked at the woman.

"What," he asked slowly, "has happened now?"

Lannes hesitated, but the woman felt as though truth serum had been poured down her throat. "I don't know who I am," she confessed wearily. "I may have put you in danger."

Frederick stared a moment then looked at Lannes, who tilted his head in a half shrug, his expression unreadable. The old man tucked his chin against his chest, still staring, and tossed his bag on the floor. His hands shook. He jammed them into his pockets.

"Lannes," he said, rather fiercely. "The bedroom, if you will."

"No time to talk," replied the big man, bending down to pick up the bag. "We have to go."

The woman wiped her nose with the back of her hand. "You should call the police. Report this. Turn me in." She hesitated when they remained silent. "Unless you have something to hide."

"You are an extremely suspicious woman," Lannes replied, but there was no malice in his tone. Just kindness and a very quiet exasperation.

She found that unnerving. His motives were mystifying. As were his eyes, the way he moved. His stillness. The longer she was around him, the more she felt like those were the only parts of him that were real, and that the rest was a mask polished to craggy perfection.

"Boy Scout," she muttered. "Why do you care?"

Lannes said nothing. Frederick gave her a stern look. "Because he is kind, madam. Do not take that for granted."

Frederick's words rang inside her head. She thought he might be right. And she did not take it for granted.

Which was why she said, "I may have killed three men. Shot them."

Frederick's gaze faltered, and he glanced quickly at Lannes. But the big man remained silent, studying her face with those eyes that seemed to see right through her.

She leaned against the wall, palms sweaty. "Did you hear me?" she asked, nauseated.

"Do you remember pulling the trigger?" he asked.

She thought about lying, shrieking *Yes!*, but could not bring herself to say that one small word. She shook her head, numb, and Lannes made a small sound, glancing at Frederick. "Innocent until proven guilty."

"That's dumb," she said. "I had a gun in my possession."

"You're suffering from amnesia," Lannes replied.

"I could be lying about that."

"But I happen to know you aren't."

"How could you possibly know that?" she asked.

"Boy Scout magic." A grim smile flickered across his mouth.

"Oh, for God's sake," Frederick snapped, pointing to his bedroom. "Lannes, I insist. One minute will not harm any of us."

Lannes sighed, and glanced at the woman. "Stay here."

Like hell, she thought, and watched him disappear into Frederick's bedroom and shut the door softly behind him. The woman immediately struggled toward the stairs. Her feet hurt too badly for speed, though her stomach twisted with urgency. Near the bottom, she looked at the closed front door and felt chills, pure sickening dread. She imagined she heard breathing. In the night. Waiting for her.

Find Orwell Price. Run.

A name. A real name. Answers, maybe. Or danger. Someone had followed her here. The same person who had left that note pinned to her jacket. The handwriting was the same. But the message, the name . . .

None of this made any sense.

The woman hobbled to the kitchen. The blinds were down, which was some relief. She had a fear of mirrors now, after seeing herself in one. Not because she looked bad—that much had been a pleasant if useless surprise—but because her eyes frightened her. Looking into her own gaze had felt like enduring the stare of Medusa, like being cast in stone. Becoming withered and cold and hollow. Lost girl. Trapped.

The phone was red and hung on the wall. The woman perched on a stool to rest her feet and picked up the receiver. Her finger hovered over the number nine, but she did not touch it. She wanted to. She wanted to turn herself in. She had to. Let the police sort it out. But the dread that crawled into her body nearly choked her.

The woman pressed her forehead against the cool wall, thinking hard. Looking deep inside herself. She was not afraid of arrest, was too exhausted to care. No, she was afraid of being found.

The woman closed her eyes, searching her memories, fighting for something, anything. All she recalled, though, was the hotel room—and that was enough. She hung up the phone.

Then she picked it up again. Chicago, she told herself. She was in Chicago. And just like that, area codes and phone numbers slipped into her mind. Like magic.

The woman dialed directory assistance. When the operator answered, asking for city and state, she said, "Chicago. Illinois."

"Listing?"

"Orwell Price."

"Hold on."

And the woman held on, leaning against the wall. Until, moments later, she heard a click—and a computerized voice rattled off a phone number. The woman listened, stunned, then got over her surprise just in time to hear the digits repeated. She memorized them. And when the computer asked if she wanted to make the call, she affirmed it with another push of a button. Waiting. Breathless.

She heard ringing. She also heard footsteps on the stairs: a quick heavy tread, followed by a lighter slower one. Both men, Lannes and Frederick, were coming to find her. She hardly cared. The phone was still ringing.

Until, suddenly, a voice answered after a great deal of fumbling and mumbled, "'Lo?"

The woman hung up fast. Lannes and Frederick walked into the kitchen. The men stopped when they saw her—froze in their tracks—but not, she thought, because they were surprised to see her. She felt her stunned amazement reflected back in the way they looked at her, and her voice clawed up her throat like a wild thing.

"I think I found Orwell Price," she whispered.

LANNES DROVE. FREDERICK SAT UP FRONT.

The Impala's interior was flawless. The woman reclined on black leather that had never known a scratch and wondered how she had gone from waking up in a burning hotel to this—driving in the dark near dawn with two strangers. It was dumb. Incredibly dumb.

"Drop me off somewhere," she said. "I'll take it from there."

"Young lady," replied Frederick, "you must be crazy."

"Well, yes," she said. "Deliriously so."

Frederick turned in his seat to look at her. The suspicion was gone from his eyes, replaced instead with a thoughtfulness that was cautious but kind. As kind as

he had been earlier, when he had brought her his
wife's clothing. She wondered what, exactly, Lannes
had said to him up in that bedroom.

"Perhaps you suffer from the onset of a fugue," said
the old man, so calm one might have thought he was
discussing a wine list or the weather.

"A fugue," she said, assailed by facts. "A disor-
dered state of mind in which somebody wanders from
home and experiences loss of memory."

"Men and women *have* been known to spontane-
ously forget themselves. Afterwards, they are often pos-
sessed with a desire to . . . flee."

Sounded familiar. She found Lannes watching her
in the rearview mirror. A hot flush stole through her,
a sensation with which she was becoming familiar
in his presence. He seemed to fill the entire front
seat, and it was not her imagination that the car
dipped slightly on his side. Frederick sat pressed
against the passenger door, his hands shaking against
his thighs.

At a stoplight, Lannes pulled out a battered cell
phone and dialed a number. "Charlie," he said quietly, "something happened. I need you to send someone to the Peninsula in Chicago to look after Freddy.
As soon as possible. I don't care who. Just make sure
they're good. And look someone up for me. Orwell
Price."

He recited the phone number she had given him back
at the house, then hung up. The woman leaned forward.
"Who was that?"

"My brother," Lannes said awkwardly, leaning away from her. "My brother, who happens to work for a . . . detective agency."

Her stomach dropped. "You told him? How much?"

"Everything." He looked at her in the rearview mirror. "You can trust him."

She leaned back and closed her eyes against the city lights. Frederick muttered, "Really, Lannes. Bald statements like that would hardly comfort *me*."

Lannes muttered a tense reply, which was lost beneath the roar of the engine. The woman almost smiled. Almost. It was either that or cry again, and she was determined not to let *that* happen.

It was almost six in the morning, and the sky was beginning to lighten. Not enough to dismiss the night. They reached Superior Street, downtown, and pulled up in front of an immense art-deco monolith with an entrance composed of glittering golden glass and marble, doors framed by pillars, and stone lions that were distinctly Asian in design. The Peninsula Hotel.

A doorman approached. Lannes turned off the car engine, twisted in his seat and said, "You can come or stay, lady. But if you stay, I want your word that you won't run or hot-wire my car."

Frederick stared at the big man. "You're not both staying with me?"

It was of some interest to the woman that Lannes squirmed. "Charlie will probably call back soon. No time, Freddy. I'll make sure you're safe in the room before I go."

"That's not the point. I would like to go, too. And help."

"Freddy."

"Don't let these useless hands fool you."

Lannes rested his own hand on the old man's shoulder, and the compassion on his face, the sadness, was enough to take the woman's breath away. She forgot herself for a moment as he very quietly said, "Never would I be fooled by anything so shallow."

"Ah," breathed Frederick, sagging against the seat. "But I've become old, haven't I? What happened to those years, Lannes?"

"They're still here," he said firmly. "But I won't put you in danger."

Danger I caused, added the woman silently, feeling very insignificant and helpless. Frederick glanced at her almost as though he had heard her thoughts, but she saw no accusation on his face. Just concern.

Behind him, the doorman waited, one gloved hand resting on the car. Frederick took a deep breath, tore his gaze from the woman and fumbled for the door himself. It was immediately opened from the outside.

But Frederick paused, looking back again at the woman. "You, young lady," he said quietly, "I hope you find yourself. But if you do not, remember that there are worse things than . . . choosing the course of a new life."

Then he was gone, rising out of the Impala with as much dignity as a king. Lannes shot the woman a brief look, then followed Frederick, keeping close, one hand under the old man's elbow. He loomed over everyone else, and as she watched him, Frederick's words rang inside her head. She thought he might be right: there *were* worse things than starting a life afresh.

Here she was, too, sitting in the backseat of a car just ripe for stealing. No keys, but there was a something twitching at the back of her mind that might have been a skill for stripping wires. So very tempting.

She got out of the car, ignoring the incredulous look the doorman gave her as he stared at her floppy socks and ill-fitting clothes, and climbed into the passenger seat. She leaned back and studied the steering wheel.

I am a practical woman, she told herself, willing it to be true. And Lannes was a resource, an opportunity. She needed him. Or someone like him. And while she could bemoan the safety of that, or its ethics—or beat her chest in some mocking, woe-is-me roar—the facts were dead simple: she did not know who she was, she had no money or friends, and she had only a name, only one clue to what might have happened to her. Giving that up was no longer an option.

So she waited. And locked the doors. Watched the street and the lightening sky.

The woman sat for almost twenty minutes before Lannes returned—a remarkable length of time that eventually felt like playing chicken with a freight train, a train rumbling toward her filled with the ominous specters of police and blood and murder. But finally, *finally*, she saw the big man exit the hotel.

He did not look entirely surprised to see her waiting for him, which the woman found a bit insulting, but he did give her a small grateful smile that felt almost unbearably sweet to her raw ticking nerves. She unlocked his door. He slid in, carrying with him the scent of earth and something delicate, like orchids.

"Is he all right?" she found herself saying, genuinely concerned.

Lannes shrugged, frowning. "No one likes being left behind. But . . . thank you for asking."

"I like him," she said simply. "And I'm sorry for the trouble I've caused. It's not too late to ditch me, you know."

"Maybe later," he said. "I'm curious now."

The woman could not help herself. "No matter what happens? How do you know I'm not lying to you? Or that I didn't plant that note at your front door? I could be anyone in the world."

"I haven't forgotten that," he said, pinning her with a look that made her feel very small. "This isn't an easy thing for me. But I believe you. I see a person who needs help. And if *I* don't help you, I'm afraid no one will."

The woman stared at him in silence. Lannes sighed, put the Impala in gear and drove away from the curb. The sun was rising. A hint of golden light twinkled between the skyscrapers, reflected by glass and steel. It was going to be a pretty day.

"My brother called," Lannes said. "He found Price."

"Okay," the woman whispered, hardly hearing him. She was thinking instead that she should have thrown survival to the wind and done the right thing after all, embraced a little self-sacrifice and saved this man from his moral compass. She should have stolen his car while she had the chance.

CHAPTER SIX

O RWELL Price lived in a gritty little neighborhood
on the far west side of Chicago. Not much in the
way of personality. All the houses were small and made
of brick, with wide porches and scrappy yards.

The Impala purred. Lannes parked behind a white
pickup. He and the woman got out of the car. The air
was cool.

The neighborhood was quiet, but that was merely a
lull—he heard doors banging and car engines roaring, saw tiny children crying and screaming, throwing
down their book bags on the concrete sidewalks while
their mothers ignored them and leaned on chain link
fences, cigarettes dangling from their fingers.

Folks going to work, school. It was only Thursday.

Lannes stood for a moment, watching the woman
posed frozen on the sidewalk, her gaze sharp, thoughtful. She was still wearing only socks. He needed to get
her some good shoes if they were going to keep on
like this. A first-aid kit for her feet, maybe.

They walked down the sidewalk to a small brick

house surrounded by a chain-link fence decorated
with plastic windmills shaped like birds. Yellow grass
and bushy weeds filled the small lawn, which was covered in stone birdbaths and bird feeders that hung
from iron poles jammed into the earth, leaning at an
angle. The feeders were empty, and there was no water
in the baths.

The fence gate stood ajar. Lannes and the woman
hesitated, staring over the threshold at dirty windows
covered in curtains yellowed with age.

"Think the boogeyman lives in there?" asked the
woman. "Or Mister Rogers?"

Lannes grunted, extending his senses into the home.
Listening with his mind. Someone was in there . . . but
that was all he could determine.

"Stay behind me," he said, ignoring the amused surprise that flashed through her eyes—an amusement that
faded just as soon as he started walking up the path to
the front door, deliberately taking long strides so that he
would reach the house before her. The woman hobbled
behind him, her presence at the back of his mind spark-
ing with irritation. It made him think of Charlie.

Wait, his brother had said. *I'm sending help. Don't
go alone.*

Well. He was not alone. And he could not wait.
Those instincts in his heart had been pushing and pulling from the moment he had found that note—earlier
even, if he considered the woman—and it was now or
never. He knew it. Even if he did not understand why.

*Fate. Moments passing in time. Moments that will
never come again.*

And knowing just when to catch them was another kind of magic all of its own.

Lannes knocked on the front door, stepping sideways as the woman neared. His bound wings ached. So did his nerves. He had spent too much time alone to be well equipped for playing hero. Up until now, his only purposes in life had been simple: Mind his own business. Cause no harm. Never be discovered.

He heard a shuffling sound. The door opened. An old man stood on the other side of the screen, wearing a ratty blue bathrobe that gaped at the front revealing a scarred pale torso and a pair of striped pajama bottoms that hung low over wide hips. His face sagged. His nose was red. He had no hair on his head, but plenty on his chest. White and bristly.

Find Orwell Price, the note had said.

"Who the hell are you?" growled the man.

"Mr. Price?" Lannes inquired. "We were hoping to speak with you."

"I'm not buying, I'm not converting, and everyone under the age of thirty-five deserves to be shot," the man snapped. "Get off my porch."

"Hey," said the woman, stepping close to the screen door. "This is important."

"I've got jock itch more important than you, lady," he replied, then looked at her. Lannes was certain Orwell had already seen the woman, but perhaps his eyesight was bad. He blinked, reaching up to rub his left eye . . . and went very still.

The woman's breath caught. "Do you know me?"

"No," Orwell whispered, sagging backward. "No. Who did . . . who did you say you were again?"

"We didn't," Lannes said. "But we were told to find you."

Orwell was still looking at the woman, who shifted uncomfortably, leaning in toward Lannes. She said, "Please, we need to talk."

"Talk," echoed the old man, his eyes narrowing. At first Lannes thought he meant for them to continue standing on the porch, but then, haltingly, he unlocked the screen door. He did not open it. He backed away, deeper into the shadows of the house. Lannes and the woman shared a quick look, but it was done, they were here. No turning back.

Lannes entered first. Very reluctantly. It was dark inside. Piles of laundry, dirty or otherwise, were on the floor, along with stacks of magazines that had fallen over and some bags of rank-smelling garbage that needed to be taken out. A television buzzed in the background. Some news program. Talk of a major hotel fire in Chicago. Investigation ongoing.

It was a small house with a lot of walls. Lannes' chest tightened. It was hard to breathe. He swallowed hard, trying to focus on the woman, the old man and nothing else. No time for claustrophobia. No time.

"Ignore the mess," Orwell said gruffly. "I don't get company."

"Why did you let us in?" Lannes asked. "Do you know this woman?"

The old man ignored his questions. "You said you were told to find me? Who did that?"

"It was on a note," replied the woman carefully. "Some . . . odd things have been happening to me. We hoped you could explain them."

"Explain odd things?" Orwell laughed, but it was tinged with nervousness. "That's rich. Did Simon send you? Mr. Simon Says?"

Lannes frowned. "As she explained, your name was on a note left on my doorstep. Who's Simon?"

"A nobody. Just like me." The old man shot the woman a thoughtful look. "He wouldn't have sent a girl. He doesn't like girls."

"You recognized me," she pressed.

"You look like someone," Price admitted. "But she's dead."

The woman tensed, but Orwell turned and shuffled deeper into his living room. He kicked aside some clothes and stooped with a groan to pick up a can of beer on the floor by the sagging couch. Taking a long drink, he gave Lannes and the woman a hard look.

"So," he said. "Mind if I see the note?"

Lannes very carefully unfolded it from his pocket, but he did not move. This felt wrong. Not just the mess or the tight space, but the air when breathed seemed to enter his heart instead of his lungs, and it was as though he could taste the miasma of darkness that had settled over this house like an illness, or death.

Bad vibes.

The woman also did not move. Her stillness felt the same as that of a fox sniffing out a trap—sharp, smart, hunted. Good instincts. Lannes held up the note like a sign, uncertain the old man's vision would let him see it but unwilling to go any deeper into the house.

The old man took another drink of beer and squinted at the note. Then he took a step closer, and another. Until he stopped, staring. Calm enough, on the surface. Perfectly calm. So calm he looked like a mannequin, plastic and frozen.

"Where did you get that?" he asked, and Lannes realized something in that moment that made him want to take a slow careful step out of Orwell Price's house: he could not sense the old man's mind. Not a hint nor trace of it. It was like standing in the presence of the dead, of something empty and hollow.

Impossible. Lannes was a poor mind reader, but at least he could *feel* minds. He could sense the weight of thoughts. Orwell Price had none. This confused Lannes at first. And then it frightened him. Normal people did not put walls in their minds. Normal people would never consider it necessary. Normal people would not have the mental strength to do such a thing.

Which meant that the old man was . . . something else.

I should have listened to Charlie.

Lannes took a risk on the woman. He touched her arm, wrapped his fingers lightly around it, grateful for her thick sweater, and tugged slightly. She glanced at him but did not protest as he made her move toward the door.

"Don't go yet," said Orwell, quietly. "I still haven't

heard about that note. Interesting handwriting, don't you think?"

"It's just writing," said the woman, as Lannes stuffed the paper back into his pocket. "Unless you recognize it?"

"I recognize a lot of things," Price whispered, knuckles white as he crumpled the beer can in his fist. "I recognize the morning, and the shit taste in my mouth when I open my eyes after a bad night's sleep. I recognize the pain in my gut when I've eaten something I know is bad for me, and I recognize, too, that I have no self-control. But sometimes a man needs to eat some shit. No matter what it costs."

Lannes stepped in front of the woman, his wings straining against the belt. Power gathered in his chest and his skin tingled. Every instinct was pulsing. The walls were closing in. He put one hand behind him and pushed the woman back toward the door.

"The note," Orwell whispered. "Goddamn that note."

He threw aside the beer can. It hit the television. In the same swing, he swooped down with surprising speed and jammed his hand past the cushions of the couch. He came back up with a gun. Behind Lannes, the woman made a sound.

Orwell shot him. No hesitation, not even a blink as he pulled the trigger. The bullet slammed into Lannes' chest just below his heart, shattering ribs. Lannes staggered, almost blind with pain, but his adrenaline kicked in and his vision cleared in moments. He was certain there must be a hole in his torso the size of his fist, but when he glanced down, he saw no wound.

Just the illusion of clothing. He looked up and found Orwell staring in disbelief.

Lannes charged. Orwell managed to get off another shot that hit him in the shoulder, smashing bone and spraying blood—which spattered through the illusion and hit the wall. He staggered but had just enough momentum to slam seven feet of hard muscle into an old man who was soft and weak limbed. Both of them went down. Lannes heard ominous crunching sounds beneath him. Orwell howled.

Lannes wanted to scream, too, but he kept his mouth shut. This was not going to kill him. No gunshot had ever taken out a gargoyle; it took a grenade to do that. Blow him to bits and he'd never regenerate. Cut off his head, burn him to ash—these things would kill him for good. His wounds would be fine in hours.

The problem was the woman. Orwell Price. Witnesses. They had seen him shot point-blank. He hoped neither noticed the fine mist of blood on the wall.

The woman fell on her knees beside them. Her concern rolled through Lannes' mind like a warm bath, until it was all he could do to focus on disarming the man beneath him. He had never felt anything like her heart. Her compassion could have been a drug. He would have been happy enough to lie still and savor the heat of her mind, like a monstrous Rip van Winkle, lost for years in a dream. Her presence, for one brief moment, drowned the pain.

And then that pain hit him again, and he swallowed a groan. Orwell Price did no such thing. He squealed like a stuck pig, screaming obscenities. Lannes had his gun hand pinned. The old man loosed another round, which hit the wall, and then the woman leaned backward, scrabbling toward the television, and returned with a ten-pound dumbbell that she raised above her head. Orwell's eyes widened. He tried to move. The woman brought the weight down hard on his wrist.

Another crunch, another scream. The old man released the gun. The woman grabbed it.

And then something odd happened. Lannes felt her mind change.

Her emotions were so deeply embedded inside him that he sensed the shift immediately. As though something . . . suddenly joined her. A completely different vibration. She was not alone in her mind. It felt the same as two brains stuffed in a jar, but only one of them was in control.

Lannes grabbed her wrist, trying to see deeper. All he found was another wall. A wall like the one keeping him out of Orwell's thoughts. And a presence that was cold and old and alien. An intruder.

He had no time for horror. The psychic intruder twisted the woman's mouth into a hideous forced grimace, which might have been a smile but looked more like she was about to sink her teeth into the old man's throat. Her eyes darkened. Her skin drained of color and her lips turned white.

"Murderer," she whispered to Orwell, and the fear that rolled off the old man was so thick, so repulsive, Lannes wanted to gag.

"It *is* you," Orwell breathed.

"Yes," the woman murmured, and raised the dumbbell above his head one-handed, aiming like she was going to punch his face into pulp. Lannes let go of the old man and grabbed both her wrists, dragging her close. He tried to force himself into her mind, clawing at the psychic wall.

For one moment, across their link, he felt the woman—the woman he knew—doing the same on the other side. She was fighting desperately. Trying to regain control over herself. Like dragging her nails down the inside of a coffin. No yield, no freedom. Just death.

He tried to close the gap between them, but the wall pressed forward, shutting him out of her mind. Pain flashed through his eyes. He heard a voice inside his head, soft and sibilant, but the words made no sense. He tried to hold onto both her mind and body, but the woman—the intruder *inside* the woman—was too strong.

You cannot stop me, whispered the voice. *You, monster.*

An immense force slammed into his chest. A wave of hard air. He lost his grip on the woman's wrists and tumbled backward, landing painfully on his bound wings. Invisible fingers tore at the wounds in his chest hard enough to make him scream. Orwell also cried out. The old man began scuttling across the carpet toward the kitchen. The woman leapt over his fat body and pinned his wrinkled neck with her knee.

All the fight went out of him. He lay as still and dull as a rag doll, but his gaze rolled sideways, searching out Lannes, and the terror the gargoyle saw in that brief glance was rich and real and desperate. Orwell flung out his hand, and for one brief moment, the walls surrounding his mind tumbled down.

Lannes caught flashes: a forest, a wild garden filled with dried cracked fountains and a shining red dome. An old graveyard and crows staring with death in their eyes. He saw children sitting in a circle, holding hands. He felt power.

The woman raised the dumbbell above Orwell's head. Lannes, still caught in memories not his own, could not move fast enough to stop her.

She crushed the old man's skull.

CHAPTER SEVEN

*T*HIS *is the way he goes*, whispered a voice. *And it is a good way.*

Good way, bad way—it was part of a nightmare the woman could not free herself from. Memories lost, and now her free will. Everything had gone insane.

She felt the impact of slamming a heavy weight into Orwell Price's head. She heard the crunch of bone and saw with sick horror the dent she had made in his face. But she could not stop herself, not for all her strength. And when she screamed, nothing came out of her mouth but a sigh of satisfaction—and when she kept screaming, her voice split against the inside of her skull like a bird tearing its wings against a wall of knives.

Hush, said that satisfied voice. *This will be over soon.*

Stop, replied the woman, desperate and grieving. *Please, stop.*

Not until I am free, whispered the voice, and the woman felt a presence like fire lick at her mind, burning her down to the soul.

Then, nothing. The ghost in her heart disappeared, and its sudden absence made the woman feel so light she thought she might float away. Her mind felt raw, as though her thoughts had scratch marks, or as though open sores pocked the inside of her skull. Pain pulsed between her eyes, but only for a moment, replaced by overwhelming languor. Her eyelids drooped. She wanted to sleep.

Instead, she told herself to flex her fingers and curled them into a fist. Her legs tingled and her feet ached. Her lungs felt as though she had been breathing flames.

She had her body back. Her mind. And a murder on her hands.

The woman yanked herself from Orwell's warm corpse and felt hands touch her waist. She shrieked . . . then remembered Lannes and spun around on her knees, desperate to see his face; something, anything familiar.

For a moment, he was nothing but a blur inside her vision: darker, larger, his face craggier and his hair longer—and then everything coalesced with crystalline clarity, and he was as she remembered.

Except, there was a hollowness in his eyes, a bleakness in the way he looked at her, which made the woman want to throw her hands over her face and run.

She almost did. He grabbed her wrists. His skin was warm, his grip strong.

"Are you okay?" he asked, his voice strained. She could not answer him. Too dumbstruck. Still horrified by what she had watched herself do. He stared a moment longer; then, almost reluctantly pulled her close. She did not resist. She did not touch him back. She could not. He kept her arms pinned to her sides and his voice filled her ear, a low murmuring rumble. She started shaking. He held her tighter, against a chest that was broad and smooth and felt suspiciously like warm skin. She thought she felt blood, but when she looked there was nothing. Her hands, though, glistened red and sticky.

Déjà vu.

Lannes pulled away just enough to stare into her eyes. Again, for a moment his body blurred, and something just behind his shoulders wavered like a ghost—but then she blinked and nothing odd was there. He was just a man.

Looking into his eyes was like getting hit in the face with cold water. She shuddered, trying to free herself, and glanced down. Got another shock. The front of her sweater was smeared in blood—bright red blood, where there had been none only moments before. Black spots filled her vision. Lannes caught her, and she was too numb to shake him off.

"You've been hurt," she mumbled, hardly able to speak.

"I'm fine," he whispered.

"We need to call an ambulance."

"No."

"Look, blood." But the only blood was on her hands, and not his body. He had no visible wounds. She *was* losing it. She'd already lost her mind.

Her gaze fell again on the old man. The dumbbell was embedded in his face. Blood pooled around his head. He was so very still. Maybe she had missed a step. Perhaps the blood on her hands and sweater was from him. It made sense.

The woman tried to go back to the old man, but Lannes held her still. "Don't. It's too late."

"No," she said, and he let her go, though she felt his palm trail warm and heavy down her spine as she scrambled away from him toward Orwell. She only got halfway. She had to swing back, palm pressed to her mouth, fighting not to vomit.

"I killed him," she rasped. "Oh, God, I *killed* him."

"You're wrong," Lannes said, his voice strained. He started to stand, but moved stiffly. The woman did not think. She tried to help him, reaching for his back.

He flinched. "Don't touch me."

The woman backed off. Red-hot shame poured through her. Lannes, staring, said, "No, don't . . . that's not what I meant."

But she understood. It made sense. She had just killed a man.

No, she told herself in the next breath. It had *not* been her. Not *just* her, at any rate. Someone else had been in her mind. Not that anyone would believe that.

Tears filled her eyes. She stumbled sideways, looking for a phone, and found one beside some withered and yellowing issues of *Playboy* magazine.

"What are you doing?" Lannes asked sharply.

"I need to report this to the police," she shot back. "I can't just leave him."

"You have to," he growled. "We made too much noise. We need to get out of here."

The woman hesitated, torn. It was not right. Not right at all. But after a moment staring at the phone, she nodded. No arrest. No confessions. She did not want Lannes to get in trouble. And she needed her freedom if she was going to learn the reasons for what had just happened.

She did not, however, return to Lannes. She saw a door in front of her. Ignoring his hisses to stop, she hobbled into a bedroom, standing for a moment in its dark shadows and smelling the overwhelming scents of moldy old carpet and dirty body. Rumpled covers filled the bed, and stacked boxes lined the cracked wall. More clothes were on the floor. No pictures. Nothing personal. Nothing that rang a bell.

She heard Lannes in the hall, breathing hard. He took up the entire space, was almost too large for the house. She smelled blood and at first thought he was bleeding, but his chest appeared miraculously unscathed by the bullets Orwell had fired, and the dark brown carpet—if there was blood on it—hid stains well.

"Find anything?" asked Lannes, and when she shook her head, he said, "Come on, then. We have other options."

She could not imagine what those were, but she was already having trouble thinking. Her mind felt numb. Death on one side, life on the other. She washed the blood off her hands in the bathroom, and closed her eyes rather than look at her reflection in the mirror above the sink.

But when she passed Orwell's body, her stomach rebelled—as did her heart. She remembered again his terror, and the impact of the dumbbell as it crushed his skull. She could still hear the echo of that presence speaking through her. Using her to kill.

A sob crawled up her throat. Lannes grabbed her arm, practically lifting her off her feet in his haste to get her to the door. He glanced back at the dead man. "I'm sorry I brought you here."

"You couldn't know," she whispered, feeling awful. Like a monster.

Lannes gave her a hard look. "I'm not sorry he died. I'm sorry you're suffering because of him."

She stared. He opened the front door and shoved her into the sunlight.

THEY DID NOT DRIVE BACK TO DOWNTOWN OR RETURN TO Frederick's home. Lannes got on I-294 and headed south, out of Chicago. After twenty minutes spent in utter silence, the woman said, "Where are we going?"

"I don't know," said Lannes. "South feels right."

Nothing felt right. She had awakened in a nightmare that was only growing larger, stranger. She could not imagine where it would end.

The woman rubbed her hands together, felt they were sticky, and stared at the odd dark puddle collecting against the Impala's leather seats beneath Lannes. It took her a moment to figure out what it was.

"Oh, God," she whispered. "You *are* bleeding."

"It's fine," he rumbled. "*I'm* fine."

She saw no wounds, nothing that could be the source of all that blood. "Lannes—"

He cut her off. "Orwell recognized you."

His abruptness, and his words, took her off guard. "I don't know how. You have to believe me."

"Belief isn't the issue. I want to know why. Why that note changed everything when he saw it."

"I'm being played," she said instinctively, still staring at the blood leaking onto the seat. It was very strange, the way it looked, almost as though it were coming not from his body but out of thin air.

"Look at me," Lannes said sharply, glancing at her before returning his gaze to the road. "We're going to figure this out."

"You just saw me kill."

"It wasn't you."

"There's no way you can know that."

"*You* know it." He shot her a grim look. "Tell me I'm wrong."

She leaned back against the passenger door, feeling as though she were seeing Lannes for the first time. "How could you know that?"

"Maybe I have an instinct," he muttered, looking uncomfortable. "Or maybe I just believe in strange things."

"No," she whispered. "You watched me kill an old man. A normal person . . . a normal person would call it as they see it. They'd believe they know what I am. Murderer. Psychopath. Not . . . not something else. Not innocent."

Lannes said nothing. She could not bear to ask. Saying the words, speaking of what had happened in Orwell Price's home, would feel like reliving it again.

Which she was already doing—tasting every nuance, trying to understand how and why. Had someone truly been controlling her? How was such a thing possible? It was easier to believe she was crazy.

She looked down again at the blood on his seat. Just blood and no wounds. As though the air was bleeding. She closed her eyes, dragging in a deep breath, and heard several metallic clinks that made the hairs on the back of her neck rise. She looked again, searching for the source of that sound, and saw steel glinting on the car floor behind his heels.

Bullets. Slick and red.

The woman began to reach down, but Lannes knocked the slugs away from her.

"Don't," he said.

"Don't look? Don't touch?" she asked him, beginning to tremble. "What is this?"

He shot her a fierce look. "Nothing."

"Bullshit."

"Let it go," he growled. "Please."

Please. She had used that word on him, with the same pleading anger. It hurt to hear almost as much as it had hurt to say. The woman leaned back against the passenger door, the seatbelt cutting into her neck, and stared at Lannes' profile. He was too big for the Impala. He drove with his shoulders hunched, slouched in the seat. He crowded her with his broad shoulders.

Words filled her. She swallowed them, turned away to stare out the windshield like some head on a stick, all feeling gone from her body, nothing but eyes and ears. Her heart was dead. She could not feel it.

Lannes drove south out of Chicago. The woman did not care. She sat very still and kept her hands curled in her lap. Hands that still felt filthy.

Two hours later, after driving just below the speed limit through a countryside of wide-open spaces, Lannes pulled off the highway, bought gas and drove into the parking lot of a one-story brick motel lined with blue doors.

Lannes pushed open his door and uncurled himself from the driver's seat. The woman also stumbled from the Impala, trying not to hiss as her feet throbbed. The air was cold. Her eyes felt dry and were burning. Lannes hesitated, glancing at her over the roof of the car, but she did not walk around the hood to join him.

"We need to rest," he said. "A place to think."

"Okay," she said.

He hesitated. "I don't think it's safe to get two rooms."

The woman thought it might be a great deal safer to have two rooms—safer for him, anyway—but she said nothing, and after they stared at each other for a long moment, he went inside the front office to rent a room. She watched him go. Wondered distantly whether if it would be one bed or two. It did not matter. She was more afraid of herself than of him now.

In the end, it was two beds—in a small white room with orange curtains, brown carpet, and a television that was bolted to a plastic dresser that had been carved with hearts and arrows. The woman hobbled straight into the bathroom, socks flopping. She fumbled with the soap, digging her nails under its paper wrapper, tearing it free. Ran the faucet until the water steamed. She washed her hands. She scrubbed her skin until it was red and burning, and did not stop.

She made the mistake of looking into the mirror and found nothing but a stranger, a woman with haunted hollow eyes and pale cheeks lost behind tangled hair. A woman who might forget herself at any moment.

A large hand reached in and closed around her wrist. Lannes rumbled, "Stop. You're hurting yourself."

His hand was warm and strong. Her wrist looked very tiny in his grip, and his skin felt strange. She went still, remembering how he had told her not to touch him. Remembering the blood on her hands when she had. Blood on her sweater, in the car. Bullets on the floor.

Lannes let go long enough to turn off the water and pull down a towel. He made her drop the soap in the sink and began drying her hands. She did not resist.

"He let us in," she whispered suddenly, and Lannes stopped, looking at her. "He let us in because he knew me. Someone like me. A woman . . . who was supposed to be dead."

"That's not your fault," Lannes murmured, and pulled her back into the bedroom, making her sit on the edge of a dark mauve floral comforter that felt more like plastic than cloth. He walked around her and tugged down the covers. Then he knelt, studying her feet, which were still snug in the floppy socks he had given her. The fabric was grimy now, more gray than white.

He began tugging off her socks—awkwardly, like he was afraid of hurting her. The woman stopped him and kicked them off herself. Her feet throbbed. When she stretched them, the cuts in her arches felt as though they were splitting apart.

She crawled backward, under the covers. The sheets were cold. She curled into a ball.

"Sleep," Lannes whispered, standing beside the bed. "Don't be afraid."

She *was* afraid, more afraid than she could imagine anyone ever being. But the softness of the pillow felt good, and the room was dark, like a cocoon. She tried to say something to Lannes, but her throat would not work.

I'm sorry, she thought, exhausted.

Then she fell asleep.

CHAPTER EIGHT

T EN minutes after the woman's breathing slowed, Lannes left the room. He tried to be quiet. She did not seem to wake as he shut the door behind him. The cold afternoon air felt good on his face and wings, as did the freedom of the open sky. Those walls, that dark space—it all had been too close for comfort.

The Impala was parked just outside the room. He got in, sat in the blood-stiff leather, and took a deep breath as he unbuckled his aching wings. Driving a car meant sitting on them like the ends of a cape, but that was hard on the skin—first abrasive, then numbing. When he was driving alone, he could take frequent breaks, could stretch out his wings as he was doing now.

His chest hurt, but the bleeding had stopped soon after driving out of Chicago, and the holes had nearly closed. Regenerative abilities aside, the difficulties of being wounded while wearing the illusion were not something he had anticipated. The damage, close to his body, could not be seen. The blood was another matter once it left the confines of his illusion. As were the bullets that had been rejected from his body.

You should never have hugged her, Lannes chastised himself. He still could not believe how easy it had been to pull her close—but then he remembered her stricken face, her despair as it had rolled through his mind, and he could forgive himself, just a little. Her pain might as well have been his. He could not divorce himself from the link between their minds.

Nothing to be done, he told himself, more concerned by the grief he had caused the woman by telling her not to touch his back. Her eyes, the way she had looked at him—like he thought she was a monster . . .

Slightly sickened, he turned on his cell phone and dialed. Charlie answered on the third ring. Lannes heard a little girl singing in the background, accompanied by the clinking sounds of dishes being washed. Despite the circumstances, Lannes smiled. His brother, gargoyle and domestic warrior.

"Emma trying out for *American Idol*?" he asked.

Charlie grunted. "She watched *The Lion King* this morning. You know, it has music."

Lannes did *not* know, not about children's movies or lion kings, but Emma was still singing, and she had a good voice.

"Your phone has been off," Charlie said, a hard note entering his voice. "I got a bad feeling a couple hours ago. So did Magnus and Arthur."

"Did you now?" Lannes tried to sound calmer than he felt, especially at the mention of his other brothers. "And what do you think happened?"

"I think someone died," said his brother. "Two of our guys caught a morning flight out of New York and got to Frederick. As soon as they made sure he was all right, they went to Orwell Price's home."

"Ah," Lannes said, feeling rather ill. "Had the police come?"

Charlie was quiet. "No. And they won't."

"Sounds like you work for the Mafia instead of a detective agency."

"I wonder myself sometimes. But I need answers. Like now."

Lannes needed answers, too. He thought of the woman sleeping less than thirty feet away—a woman he had held in his arms longer than he had ever held anyone—and told the story. Charlie did not interrupt once. It hardly seemed he was on the line.

Lannes tapped his fingers against the steering wheel. "Hello?"

"I'm thinking," said his brother.

"Think faster. Orwell was not a normal human man. And whatever was inside this woman's brain . . ." He stopped, unable to put words to what he had felt. The coldness of it.

Charlie said, "Are you sure it wasn't her? Putting on a good act?"

Lannes hesitated, searching his heart. He remembered her eyes afterwards, his sense of her emotions embedded in his mind, how they fluttered as though her heart were beating itself to death in horror.

"I'm sure," he said.

"Then we need to find out what connects her to the victim. And what happened in that hotel room. You mentioned smoke, right? I'll look for mentions of fire in the news and see if we can pin down the location." Charlie hesitated. "How are you handling this? You know, such close quarters?"

"Fine," Lannes replied.

"Because you haven't been around anyone but us and Frederick in a year."

"I'm fine," Lannes said again.

Charlie hesitated. "Is she cute?"

Lannes almost hung up. "She's fine."

" 'Fine,' " said his brother. "That could mean a lot of things."

A lot. A great deal more than Lannes wished to talk about. But he stayed silent too long—too long for someone as perceptive as Charlie—and his brother very softly said, "Ah."

"Stop it," Lannes told him. "Mind your own business."

"Fine." He sounded far too mild. "Just . . . be careful."

"There's nothing to be careful about. I don't know the woman. And she certainly doesn't know me."

"That can be less of a barrier than you think."

Lannes gritted his teeth. "Just say it. You think I'll be played as a fool."

"If you fall, we all fall," Charlie said.

Not something he could stand to hear. "I'm going now. Call when you know something."

His brother very reluctantly said he would. Told him to lie low. Hide the car. And that was that.

Lannes did not, however, return to the motel room—nor did he move the car to a less visible location. He sat, staring out the windshield at the battered door, the closed curtains, and thought about the woman sleeping inside.

He had touched her. He had held her. He had fought for her. And he had not been afraid. No thought of witches and stone, no feeling of the walls closing in. His only thought had been for the woman. Even now he was thinking of her, knowing she was close. He could sense her presence, however small, inside his mind.

That scared him. It also thrilled him in ways he could not explain. She made him feel strong. Gave him no choice but to be strong. Lannes might have been sleepwalking until now, the feeling was so raw, as though something was waking in his blood: genetic, primal, an imperative too long suppressed. It was simple, that desire. Easy as breathing. He wanted to protect the woman. He *needed* to protect her. A desire that went beyond his earlier, more intellectual excuses for involving himself in her welfare.

It was in a gargoyle's nature to protect, even if their kind had been forced to adapt to different lifestyles. It was safer now to ignore suffering and turn a blind eye, to exist in hiding away from others, relying on magic, subterfuge. The instinct to protect had become a liability, sternly repressed. Lannes had not realized quite how sternly, until now, and he felt as though he was committing some crime, as though his desire was somehow against his species. To protect this woman, to give her what she needed, meant putting himself at risk—his body, his secrets. This was something that had been at the back of his mind from the beginning, but it suddenly hit him hard, with terrifying clarity. He was jeopardizing the secrets of an entire species.

Charlie did it. He challenged tradition.

To save a little girl's life. A little girl who was now his daughter in every way but blood. A child unafraid of Charlie's real face, who loved him as he was. Father. Rescuer. Protector.

Lannes stared down at his hands. Human. They looked normal, were illusions he could never dream to match. He wondered how the woman inside the motel would react if she knew the truth. What would she do?

Stop. Enough. You have bigger problems. So does she.

Something had been in her head. He could still feel the tangle of its presence: cold, old, furious. Powerful. Perhaps it was the force that had stolen her memories. It frightened Lannes. Taking over minds was tricky business. To control a person over a long distance was even trickier. It took a connection, permission. Like what the witch who'd captured them had wanted Lannes and his brothers to give.

A simple yes would do. A mere acquiescence, however innocent. A person had to be ever vigilant with the mind. To do less was to lose everything. Or to be vulnerable to everything.

Lannes started the Impala's engine and drove around to the back of the motel. He parked out of sight of the freeway and walked back around the building. Clouds had begun to move across the sun, but only a scattering of them. He wondered if the woman's jacket would be warm enough.

A name, he thought, binding his wings again. *She needs a name.*

Lannes was trying to think of one when he felt a spark of heartache pulse along their link. He turned the corner and found the woman standing in the doorway of their room, gazing out at where the Impala had been with such a look of disappointment and hollow resignation that he almost ran to her.

She saw him coming. Her hair hung in a soft tangle around her face. Her cheeks were flushed, her eyes green as sun-bathed grass. She blinked several times, almost as though she was surprised to see him.

"Out for a walk?" she asked mildly.

"Moved the car so it couldn't be seen from the road. Police might be looking for us."

She nodded, still with a pinch of stress around her eyes, and gazed out at the barren parking lot. A strip of earth and a chain-link fence separated them from the highway. Cars roared past.

"You need to rest," he said.

"I did. A little. I heard the car start." Her mouth quirked into a sad smile. "It's a distinct sound."

"I'm sorry." Lannes leaned against the door frame

feeling awkward, exposed. His wings curled tight around his back. He suspected the illusion made his shoulders appear hunched. "You thought I was abandoning you."

"Crossed my mind," she admitted. "I wouldn't blame you."

Lannes held her gaze, willing her to understand. "We need to get something straight. I'm not leaving you."

"Right. Because you're just that nice."

"Nice has nothing to do with it. You need help. Do you understand? I'm here because you need someone."

"That's being nice *and* dumb. I might hurt you."

"I can take care of myself."

"Can you? What's happening . . . it's not normal. It's not . . . human."

Chills raced up his spine. "Is that what you think?"

"I know it." She pressed her fist to her chest. "Here. Call me crazy, and maybe I am—"

"No, you're not crazy."

"But something took me over." She hesitated, cheeks flushed, studying his face with an unnerving intensity that made him want to search out a mirror and check his illusion for cracks. "You really don't think I'm nuts? A psychopath?"

He smiled gently. "Go. Rest. I'll warn you the next time I decide to go out."

The woman backed up, her gaze pale and hollow. "*You* should rest. You haven't slept since we met."

Lannes said nothing and gestured for her to precede

him into the room. He locked the door behind them. The room felt darker than he remembered. More oppressive. His skin crawled.

The woman slid back under the covers of her bed. He lay down on the other mattress, his healing ribs aching, his wings smashed like a soft, articulated blanket. The mattress groaned beneath him. He thought it would be impossible for him to relax, but after a tense minute, his muscles began to sag and his breathing slowed.

Think of the woman. You need to hold it together. Walls are nothing. Walls are not stone on your skin or the bars of a cage. The witch is dead. The wicked witch at last is dead. Let the joyous news be spread, Lannes told himself, reciting from *The Wizard of Oz.* All he needed now was a heart and a brain, and some courage. Anything, to help the woman near him find her way home.

The woman said, "This isn't over. I'm afraid I'm going to hurt someone else."

Her certainty was as disquieting as her self-loathing. Lannes rolled onto his side. "What do you want to do?"

"I want to stop it," she said immediately. "Find who's doing this. Learn why."

"First thing you have to stop is blaming yourself."

Her jaw tightened. "It was my hands that did the deed. That puts Orwell Price's death inside me."

You take too much responsibility, Lannes wanted to tell her, but he knew what it was like to second-guess things that could not be changed. So he said, "I called my brother. Explained the situation to him. He's going to look for more information on Price."

She paled. "Did you tell him what happened at the house?"

"I had to."

"And?"

"And, nothing. I told you, he's going to help. Find the connections."

"She called Orwell a murderer. She, me, whatever."

"If someone was murdered, there should be a way to link Price to it, no matter how distant in the past."

The woman shuddered. But that was all. No hysterics, no tears. Just calm, grim determination. "That doesn't explain how anyone managed to reach into my mind. I must be crazy, to believe it—that minds can be hijacked, stolen. But I felt it. And as for you . . ."

She did not finish. Lannes was afraid to ask. The woman pulled the covers higher over her shoulder.

Sometime later, when he thought she was asleep—when *he* was almost asleep—she said, "I want to trust you."

"So trust me," he said, and closed his eyes again. He heard her near-silent sigh. Listened to her toss and turn. He did not move or look at her. He tried not to think about how he was alone with a woman in a motel room. There was a joke in there somewhere.

His wings ached. So did his heart. He kept his eyes shut, and eventually he fell asleep.

IT WAS A BAD, HARD SLEEP. HE DREAMED. THE MOON WAS in the sky, filled with blood, and beneath him was no sea, no trees, no earth to fall upon. Merely stone, a living breathing stone, reaching up to grab him. He could not fly fast enough from it. He could not, no matter how hard he tried. Body heavy, wings weary, all his strength ebbing into sorrow. Magic, entirely out of reach. Helpless. Feeble. Stone touched him. He screamed—

And opened his eyes at the exact moment his fist connected with a soft body. A body that made a small sound of pain and rolled off the bed. Lannes stared, shocked and horrified. He scrambled forward, his claws digging into the covers, ripping them. The bed frame shook.

The woman lay on the floor, propped up on her elbow. One hand was holding her shoulder. She looked dazed.

Lannes fell beside her. He moved devoid of his usual caution—everything shook with his weight—but he did not touch her, and she hardly seemed to notice the minor earthquake his landing caused. He was so much larger than she. So much stronger. And her trust . . . her trust was already so tenuous. If he had hurt her . . .

"I'm sorry," he said, breathless. "I'm so sorry."

She shook her head. "You were dreaming."

"I hurt you." Lannes began to reach for her and stopped, afraid. But she shook her head again, and leaned toward him, just slightly, as she tried to push herself up.

He held his breath and placed one hand ever so carefully against her back. Her hair draped over his skin. Fine, feathery, soft as silk.

"Did I hit your shoulder?" His voice was so rough, so painful, he felt as though he had swallowed glass.

"I think so," she said, and winced. "Yes, definitely."

He briefly closed his eyes. "You should see a doctor."

"No."

"Please."

"No. It's not that bad."

"I hit you hard."

"Yes," she said, her voice far more gentle than he deserved. "But you were in a bad place."

A bad place. No worse than the place she was in.

Lannes swallowed hard. "If you won't see a doctor, then at least . . . at least let me see your shoulder. Or if you aren't comfortable with that, then go to the bathroom and use the mirror. Just . . . please. Being punched by me is not a good thing."

Her mouth tilted into a sad smile. "Given how dirty my own hands are, I don't think I have a right to complain."

"Don't think like that."

"I *killed* a man," she said, and lay back down on the floor, wincing. Her eyes stared up at the ceiling. She blinked once, twice. Tears glistened. Her voice dropped to a hoarse whisper. "I killed him."

Lannes hung his head, miserable. His wings ached. He leaned back against the edge of the bed, a good foot between himself and the woman . . . and all he wanted was to close the distance. Even just to take her hand.

"Please," he rumbled. "Please, listen to me."

"I already know what you're going to say."

Lannes braced his hand on the ground and leaned close, almost hovering over her. It was the kind of posture that might have been construed as threatening, but he needed to look into her eyes. He was ready to pull away if she seemed uncomfortable.

But she did not flinch, her gaze did not waver, and all he saw in her eyes was a pain that went so deep, was so wild, he felt hit with it, punished, as though it were *his* body lost to the will of another—as if his life, his mind, his heart, were all subject to whims not his own.

He knew this. He understood. Better than anyone could. He wished he could tell her. But that would have required opening up an entire world, more secrets than simply his own. Not his right. It just wasn't.

Just as she was not his.

"You were used," he said. "You believe that, don't you? You've said as much."

"Yes," she whispered, "I know it."

"So don't waste time being angry at yourself. Don't blame yourself for things you can't change." Lannes hesitated, considering his words—feeling as though he were talking to himself. "The past is done. You have to keep fighting. You have to find the person doing this to you and stop them."

She closed her eyes. "I don't know how."

"You don't have to," he promised her. "You're not alone."

Her face crumpled, and she rolled away from him. Sat up slowly. He did not touch her but watched as she stood, swaying. Her hand gripped her shoulder. She limped to the bathroom and shut the door.

Lannes sat, staring. His mind was numb, empty. He heard water run. Then, suddenly, the door opened a crack. The woman said, "I think I need help."

He was on his feet in an instant, at the bathroom in a heartbeat. She stepped back as he pushed open the door, and the space immediately felt too small for them both. She was a tall woman, and he felt huge compared to her. Awkward, lumbering, ill at ease. A fumbling, violent fool.

He hung back. The woman, her face flushed, tugged at the collar of her blood-matted sweater, trying to pull it past her shoulder. "I don't trust myself. Injuries are one thing I don't remember how to judge."

"I don't want to frighten you."

Her tearstained gaze remained steady. "What you did was an accident. I shouldn't have been so close."

He leaned against the doorframe, needing to steady himself. "Why were you?"

"You were suffering. I was going to wake you up."

"My brothers know to stay away from me when I have a nightmare. Or else they poke me with a baseball bat."

"You have bad dreams often?"

"Used to. Not for a while, though."

She smiled, briefly. "Must be the company."

"No. Could be the walls, though."

"Walls?"

He regretted opening his mouth. "I'm . . . mildly claustrophobic."

"Really." She glanced around the bathroom, frowning. "This must be awful for you."

"Let me look at your shoulder," he said gruffly. "If you still want me to."

The woman wordlessly tugged aside her collar. His

gaze traveled down her neck and throat—pale, fine, and strong—which put the rest of her into perspective when he saw the bright red, swelling curve of her upper-left shoulder. His breath hissed. He still felt the impact of his fist meeting her flesh. He was afraid to touch her again.

But he did. Carefully. Holding his breath, he used his knuckles to gently prod her shoulder. Her jaw tightened. She stared resolutely at the wall. He settled deeper into his mind, and used the opportunity to send a wave of healing energy into her body: into her shoulder, to soothe broken veins and muscle; into her feet, to encourage the healing of her cuts. The effort left him lightheaded.

"I'm no doctor," he murmured, keenly aware of how near they stood—how dangerous that was, how much he wished he could stand even closer. "But nothing seems broken. Can you roll your shoulder for me?"

She did, wincing slightly. Lannes softly directed, "Raise your arm."

She followed his instructions, still wincing. But only a little.

"You need ice," he said. "And my apologies, again."

"Unnecessary," she replied, "but accepted."

Lannes made the mistake of looking into her eyes. Her gaze was steady, straightforward, but with an undercurrent of that old loss and sorrow that made everything in his heart sing toward her. Every instinct demanded nothing less than that he wrap this woman in his arms and wings.

He forced himself to stop touching her. "I'll get you some ice. I think . . . I think there's a machine by the office."

"I'll go with you," she said, cheeks faintly flushed. "I could use some air."

Lannes almost tripped over himself moving away from her. She was close behind him. He was well into the middle of the room when someone knocked on the door. He froze. So did the woman.

He listened hard, heard nothing but faint breathing outside the room. Lannes glanced back at the woman. She was pulling her socks on, eyes narrowed, ready to run. He pointed to the wall behind the front door, and without a word she moved there. Light feet, silent. Lannes grasped the knob, braced his rear foot against the floor and opened the door just an inch.

It was almost dark outside. He and the woman had slept a long time.

The man knocking was from the front office of the motel. The manager. He was tall, skinny, and had a receding hairline that crawled well past the top of his head. His lower cheeks were soft and round, but the skin around his brow and eyes was so tight he could have been a Botox addict. He seemed faintly surprised when Lannes opened the door. He had a key in his hand.

"Oh," he said, "I thought you had gone."

"Oh," Lannes echoed. "And you thought you would invite yourself in?"

The motel manager took a quick step back, his palm

rubbing against his thigh. Nervous. He smelled acrid, bitter. "You seemed like the fly-by-the-hour type. I saw the woman earlier, and then your car was gone. . . ."

"Wham, bam, thank you, ma'am?" Lannes smiled coldly, wishing the man could see his real face. "No, I don't think so. And you should go. Now."

The motel manager turned without a word and strode quickly away down the sidewalk to the front office. Reaching for his cell phone.

Lannes closed the door and turned to the woman. "We have to go."

"I figured," she said. "What do you think he really wanted?"

"No idea. But I don't like it." Lannes went to the window and checked the parking lot, which was totally empty. He guessed they were the only ones left and would have found the isolation comforting only a moment before, but now it seemed vaguely threatening. Like something was coming. And no one would be around to bear witness when it did.

Again, you are hunted, his instincts whispered. *And you must fight or die.*

"I'll get you some ice at a gas station," he told her. "Some new clothes, too."

He and the woman exited the room, leaving the key on the nightstand, and walked as quickly as her feet would allow on a path around the motel to the rear parking lot. This was a poorly lit area, but the Impala waited, its gleaming black surface reflecting slivers of the thin moon and the tall security light on the other side of the lot.

Lannes unlocked the woman's door first, and as she was sliding in, he felt a breath of warning against the back of his neck, some instinct rising from his blood.

He turned but saw nothing. Tossing his thoughts wide, he searched for the unseen and caught a hint, a shadow, a taste that was old and dusty, with a scent like dirty socks and mothballs, a body left too long un-washed. He felt that presence tap against his mind just once and hurled it away with a snarl that started in his chest and rolled out of his mouth—deep, violent, bro-ken. Instinct filled him. He crouched, fingers slamming into the concrete, tearing trenches. Furious. Shaken.

The presence disappeared. Lannes searched for it but found no trace. Nothing.

He dragged in a deep breath. A hand touched his back. The woman. Only, instead of falling upon his shoulder, she laid her palm against a wing.

Lannes flinched, spinning from her, still on one knee. His heart thundered. He could hardly think straight. His focus narrowed to the woman sitting half in and half out of the Impala. Her hand hovered in the air, fingers curled, eyes huge, mouth open. He felt ashamed, terrified.

"What happened?" she whispered.

But Lannes had no time to tell her. Tires squealed. A tan sedan peeled around the corner of the motel, headlights blazing. A man in a black suit leaned out of the open driver-side window. He was alone in the car, and his lips were moving against the cell phone pressed to his ear. Probably talking to the motel manager,

Lannes reasoned. Bastard had been checking to see if they were still there. Setting them up as targets.

The world slowed down—the speeding car, Lannes' own heartbeat, the movement of the driver as the cell phone disappeared and was replaced by a handgun. The man aimed his weapon . . . not at Lannes, but at the woman.

"Shit," she rasped. Lannes threw himself in front of her as the first shot was fired.

Different gun, different bullets. Orwell's firepower had felt like bee stings compared to this. Each round tore through him like a small grenade, and Lannes, struggling to reach the sedan, went down on one knee. He had no magic to fight a gun. And even if he had, the pain was too much.

But it was not as bad as what the witch had done to him. Lannes managed to stand and staggered toward the shooter before getting punched just above the knee with a bullet. Blood sprayed from his body, but no wound showed.

The man pushed open his door with a frown, clearly not understanding what he was seeing. He began reloading. Lannes hoped the woman was running, but when he touched her heart—her heart, floating in his mind—he found her right on top of him.

"Go!" He screamed at her, but she stepped up to his side and he felt something from her, something entirely different than before, in Price's home. No one was controlling her this time. She was alone in her mind. Making her own choice to stay. To move forward.

He grabbed her ankle, trying to pull her back.

Fighting to stand. His vision blurred. Blood poured through the illusion, soaking the concrete around his knees. He looked down, and as he expected, his body still appeared unwounded. What a joke.

The gunman aimed at the woman. Lannes tried to pull her behind him. She resisted, lifting her hand—

—and the man flew backwards as if propelled by a rocket, so hard his head and most of his shoulders crashed through the side window of his car. His gun clattered to the ground. He did not move again.

Lannes stared. The woman made a small hiccupping sound, halfway between a sob and a gasp, and that was enough to snap him out of his shock. He tried to stand, then fell again, hard on his knees. The woman squatted beside him. Blood soaked her socks. Her face was so pale he was afraid she might pass out. He was afraid *he* would pass out.

He grabbed her hand, squeezing. Hardly able to think. "I dropped my keys. Get them. Get the car."

She nodded and disappeared. Moments later the Impala roared to life. She pulled up alongside him. He was already hauling himself inside by the time she shoved the gearshift into neutral.

The woman got out. She hobbled to the gunman and rifled through his pockets, found a wallet but did not take his gun. Lannes was glad she left it. In the distance he heard sirens. Small fortune, it was dark and the motel had no customers.

The woman shut his door, limped around the hood and slid behind the wheel. Her mouth was set, her eyes narrowed in determination.

"Where are we going?" she asked him.

"Just get out of here," Lannes said, eyes swimming shut.

She did. Fast.

CHAPTER NINE

THE woman drove for a long time. She headed south because it was the first entrance to the highway that she saw. No other thought was in her head. Her heart was pounding so hard she thought it might burst. She wanted to vomit. Dizziness made her lean against the wheel, gripping it so tightly her knuckles felt fit to burst. Chills shook her.

Lannes was unconscious. The big man was slumped against the passenger door, still breathing. Not one sign of an injury marred his body. Despite the fact that he was bleeding. Despite her having seen him hit.

And also despite the fact that she had touched his torso, trying to find those wounds, and discovered that Lannes really did feel a great deal different than he looked. She could not handle that. She could hardly handle the car.

She drove, looking for a good place to pull over. The highway itself was too risky. Exits seemed to lead to wide-open country lanes with no shoulder. Gas stations and fast-food restaurants had too much light in their parking lots.

In Lafayette, however, she saw a small sign advertising a Meijer's grocery store, and she envisioned an expanse of pavement that stretched like the bad yawn of a concrete monster. Lots of space. A anonymous parking lot. It would be exposed, but she had to stop. She had to check Lannes.

She took the highway exit and turned left, following her instincts more than the signs. She could not remember if she had ever been here, but her gut seemed familiar with the area, and when she passed Cracker Barrel on her left, she knew it. Meijer's would be on her right, ahead.

And it was. She pulled off the road, bouncing slightly over the curb, and started coasting for an out-of-the-way parking spot. She found one on the east side. No other cars around. No tall lights. Just darkness and solitude. For now.

The woman shut off the engine. Her hands shook the moment she took them off the wheel. She held them close to her stomach, rubbing her knuckles. Thinking about the man and his gun. What she had done to him.

Lannes, she told herself fiercely. *Worry about Lannes.*

She turned to him. Darkness was safer, but it limited what she could see. Which wasn't much. He looked fine. Healthy. But he lay still, and the scent and heat of his blood filled the Impala's interior, burning her heart.

The woman touched his shoulder, just to remind

herself. She did not feel a shirt. Just skin. Hot sticky skin. And past his shoulder, around his back, something even softer, like supple leather. Something bigger than his body. What she touched terrified her, but not nearly as much as the fact that she thought he was dying.

But she could not take him to a hospital. That much was clear.

Cell phone, she told herself. *He said he was talking to his brother.*

Her breath caught. She began patting his pockets, grateful that his jeans seemed to be real. She was losing her mind, losing her mind. Oh, God.

His jeans were soaked in blood, but she found the phone and wiggled it free. The case was also sticky, but she wiped it on her skirt and tried to make her hands stop shaking long enough to use the damn thing. Lannes stirred slightly, groaning. She whispered his name but he did not respond, not even with a flutter of an eyelid.

She managed to punch into the menu on his phone and found the last number dialed. It was labeled with a name, *Charlie*. She hoped that was the right person to call. She also hoped the battery lasted. The dial was red, and she heard a loud warning beep.

A man answered on the first ring. His voice sounded like Lannes'. The woman heard a cartoon blaring in the background, and had to take a breath.

Again, the man said, "Hello?"

"Hello," she whispered. "Are you Lannes' brother?"

There came no reply, but a moment later she heard a

click like a door closing, and the cartoon music faded. He said, "What happened? Where is he?"

She looked at Lannes, then twisted to peer out the car windows, checking to make sure they were still alone. The battery warning beeped. "Here with me. Someone came after us. He's been hurt. Shot. I don't know how to help him. I can't see the wounds, but I can feel them, and there's so much blood—"

Charlie interrupted. "Where are you?"

"Lafayette, Indiana. Meijer's parking lot, just off the highway."

"Stay there, if you can. If you have to move, call me. I'm sending help."

The phone beeped again. "*Wait.* What can I do?"

"Protect him," Charlie said grimly. "I'll call you when my friends are close."

And he hung up. The woman stared at the phone for a moment and slid it onto the dashboard. She looked out the windows again, taking in the mundane process of cars pulling in and out of the grocery store parking lot and the distant signs of restaurants and hotels. Normal lives, normal people.

Lannes made another small sound. She remembered what had happened the last time she got close while he was unconscious, but even though her shoulder was a painful reminder, she scooted as near as she could and rested her hand against his face. His skin was hot, even feverish. She cast about for something, anything she could use to help him, and found nothing in her immediate vicinity. She opened up the glove compartment, hoping at least for a cell-phone car charger.

She found nothing of the kind, though a block of wood fell out, an unevenly shaped chunk that looked as though it had been hacked from the heart of a tree. She picked it up off the car floor, turned it over in her hands. Six inches long and almost as wide. Part of it had been carved into what seemed to be the vague outline of a man with wings. Not much detail, but exquisite nonetheless. Every stroke was filled with character.

She focused again on the carved wooden wings and remembered the motel. She would never forget. Never. Even if her memories were stolen again, she knew something—something of *him*—would remain.

Lannes, stepping into the path of those bullets. Taking them. Protecting her. Falling to his knees. Getting back up again.

The woman looked over and saw a human man. A big, strong, handsome man. A man who looked healthy but who was dying, maybe. The closest thing she had to a friend in all the world.

"Don't go," she whispered. *Don't leave me. Don't leave me alone.*

He stirred. She touched his face—a careful, tentative brush of her fingers against his feverish cheek. His bone structure was strong, pronounced. Still craggy. Her heart rate began to slow. Her hands stopped shaking. She remembered touching him in the parking lot just before the gunman had arrived. She remembered the sensation of what she had felt. His horror when he had turned on her.

You're more mystery than I am, she thought, then

heard something behind her on the driver's side. A car engine idling.

Black Humvee. Huge car. She could hardly imagine how it had pulled up without her noticing, but its lights were off. The woman suddenly wished she had taken the gun with her. Or that she knew how to . . . to do that thing again. Whatever it was that had stopped the gunman. It had been a force in her mind that was hers and hers alone, not the work of an outside influence. Which was frightening, but not nearly as much as being unable to protect Lannes.

It was a woman who got out of the Humvee. An old woman, tall and slender, with short silver hair and a narrow face that sagged around her chin. She wore all black, except for a string of heavy pearls. She was elegant and feminine, but her gaze was as cold and sharp as knives.

The woman could not see if anyone else was inside the Humvee. She started the Impala's engine, shoved down the clutch and shifted into first gear. She did not go, though. She thought about Charlie. He had said he would call.

The old lady tapped on the car window with one slightly gnarled finger. "You. Open up."

Like hell. The woman glared, trying not to let on how frightened she was. "Who are you?"

"My name is Etta Bredow," said the old lady, speaking loudly. "I work with your friends."

"What friends?"

Etta's withered lips pulled into a hard smile. "Charlie. Fredrick."

The woman hesitated, then reached for the cell phone. Its battery light was shining red. She remembered Charlie's number and dialed quickly, trying not to take her eyes off the old lady, who stood back, arms folded over her sunken chest.

"I'm here," Charlie answered, his voice strained.

"I've got company," she said immediately. "A woman who says she knows—"

The battery finally went dead. She squeezed the phone until her knuckles ached and searched Etta's gaze. Wondering if *she* had a cell phone. All it would take was one call.

But Lannes suddenly coughed, and though it was dark, she felt something wet hit her face and she knew instantly it was blood. The woman stared, torn. Trying to listen to instincts that might as well have been stripped away with her memories.

Protect him.

She reached over to squeeze Lannes' hand and unlocked the car door. She pushed it open slowly and got out, keeping the door between herself and the old lady.

"You act like I'm a monster," said Etta. "You should relax."

"Of course I should," replied the woman dryly. "Are you alone?"

"Would you prefer an army of thugs at my back?" Etta smiled again, rather unpleasantly, and the woman had the distinct feeling she knew this person. Somehow. It was that smile that felt like proof. All teeth.

Etta peered into the Impala. "He's too big to move. Follow me in your car."

"Where are we going?"

"My home. It's close." Etta snapped her fingers to suggest they hurry. "Follow me."

The woman did not like her tone or the risk, but she saw little choice but to do as she was told. Lannes had to survive. He needed help that she could not give him. Not here, not in this car. She could not even rent them a hotel room, not looking as she did.

They drove. The woman lost track of all the twisting roads, though she saw signs for Purdue University and all the trappings of a major college town: restaurants and shops, small neighborhoods cluttered with trees and old homes perfect for students and professors. It was night, but the town glittered like a strip mall cut into chunks.

Etta led the woman to a dead end, a dark quiet neighborhood that looked like a burglar's paradise. Fat oaks, thick bushes, few lights. The driveway was shaped like a half-moon, and rather than follow Etta into the massive garage that opened before her, she pulled up parallel to the main entrance. The Impala would be easy enough to sabotage; she was not going to drive it into a cage.

She held the keys tight in her fist and opened up the passenger door. Etta appeared from the garage and stood for a moment, arms still folded over her chest, watching carefully.

"You sure you're here alone?" the woman asked.

"Still afraid?" replied Etta.

"No," she lied. "Show me where to take him."

Etta frowned. "You're going to move him by yourself?"

"Yes," she said firmly, unwilling to let the old lady touch Lannes. Charlie, if that was his brother, no doubt knew and understood the discrepancy between sight and touch when it came to him, but she had no faith in anyone else. And while the mystery of it both frightened and boggled her, Lannes had saved her life—in more ways than one—and she was willing to suspend her notions of reality to keep him safe.

But it was going to be a hell of a job.

Etta stood back, studying her. The woman thought about hopping in the car and driving away. She stopped herself, though. Blood dripped from the Impala's leather seats to the floor. When she leaned in, it smelled like a charnel house compared to the crisp night air.

"Lannes," she whispered in his ear. "Lannes, wake up."

He did not twitch or make a sound. Gritting her teeth, her feet throbbing, she raised his arm and slung it over her aching shoulder. She reached around his back, her hand gliding over soft skin that reminded her of thin leather. Appendages. Her fingers glided over the joints in his shoulders.

She had to take a moment, dizzy. And she found something else—a wide belt strapped around his chest and back. Holding down those . . . things.

Wings, said her mind. *Lannes has wings.*

She forced herself not to think about it. But she grabbed the belt and used that to tug on him. He would not budge. Too big, too heavy. Face flaming hot, more than a little desperate, the woman dug in her aching heels and pulled with all her strength.

Move, she thought. *Goddamnit, move.*

And just like that, something clicked inside her brain. It was the same sensation, the same instinct, from the motel parking lot, as though her brain had an extra arm.

She had felt hints of it ever since her encounter with Orwell Price. The thing that had invaded her mind had flung Lannes across the room—without laying a hand on him.

Right then, like wires crossing inside her brain, something had connected. As it had again.

Come on, she begged silently, wrapping her thoughts around Lannes. Needing him to move. Needing it with all her will. She yanked on the invisible belt strapped around his waist, groaning with the effort.

He moved. He was still unconscious, a dead weight, but she felt her thoughts squeeze around him as though he were inside her mind, like a hard silver marble. And like a marble, she was able to lift and pull until he slid free. It was a tremendous effort, though, more so than merely striking the gunman had been, and she held his arm across her shoulder so that he was bent over, his feet dragging. It was hard to breathe.

"Open the damn door," she muttered, sweating. But Etta was already there, holding it open, and the woman hauled Lannes into the house, step by painful step. Fighting not to lose her concentration.

She hardly noticed her surroundings. She could have been walking into a pair of iron jaws and she

would not have paid attention. Just one foot in front of
the other. Just one more. And another. Her hands and
clothes became soaked and slick with Lannes' blood.
She ignored that. Followed Etta to the kitchen. Blan-
kets had been spread on the floor.

"Put him down," Etta ordered. "I'll get towels."

The woman settled him with a stifled groan, her
back and arms screaming in protest as she straightened. Her mind still tingled. Every object around her
seemed vibrant, small, light as air. For one moment,
she could feel the entire kitchen inside her mind, and
it was a delirious sensation, wild and heady.

No. Stop. Focus on Lannes.

She crouched beside him as Etta appeared again.
The old lady carried towels and another blanket, as
well as scissors. She dropped them on the floor.

The woman said, "I need a phone."

"I already called Charlie," said Etta. "He's on the
way here. I let him know where we are."

"Really," said the woman. She glanced around the
kitchen but saw no phone. Just white countertop and
wallpaper covered in red roosters. The kitchen looked
as though it had not been used in some time. There
was dust on the stove.

"This your house?" she asked.

"It belongs to my family," replied Etta. "You're
safe here."

The woman gave her a sharp look. "What do you
know about it?"

"I know you are hunted," she said simply. "And I
know that neither of you are what you seem."

Etta backed up a step. Graceful, light-footed in black ballet flats. The woman felt like an exploding train wreck in comparison. She watched the old lady leave the kitchen and wanted to follow her with questions.

Instead she dug into the cabinets and found mixing bowls. A kettle was on the stove. She filled it with water and set it to boil. Then got down and began removing Lannes' clothes. Starting with the belt around his chest.

She could not see it, and feeling one thing while seeing another was too disconcerting. Especially when she noticed that the very tips of her fingers disappeared out of sight when they touched his skin.

She shut her eyes. Her fingers found the belt loop and she undid it, blind. But she was nervous. She was afraid he had it there for a good reason, and so left it on, but loose.

Lannes made a small sound. She whispered his name but got no response.

Her hands fluttered over his chest, searching for wounds. Every time she found one, she laid a towel over the spot, but some of the injuries were too massive. His chest was a mess. Her eyes burned with unshed tears.

You should be dead, she thought, and then, *Don't. Don't die. Don't leave me.*

Her mantra. Her prayer over him as she worked. *Don't leave me. Don't. Please. You're all I know. My biggest memory. My only friend. Don't leave me. Don't die. Don't.*

She found a hole in his upper thigh. She had to

cut away his jeans. Used a towel to make him decent once she had him fully disrobed. She had no idea what he really looked like—which was an odd thought in itself—but she supposed whatever his appearance, it must be radical. Truly wild.

The kettle whistled. The woman poured the steaming water into one of the mixing bowls, then set more to boil. She dumped two small towels into the hot water and, when it cooled, began washing Lannes' body. Most of the bleeding appeared to have stopped on its own, if the blanket he lay on was any indication. Stains, yes. But not the soaking that had occurred in the Impala. Incredible, miraculous.

Not human.

Maybe you're *not human*, she told herself. Maybe her entire definition of humanity was nothing but a joke. Perhaps her mind was so messed up she had forgotten the existence of men with wings or folks who had the power to control minds and turn normal women like herself into assassins. Maybe the world was strange, had always been strange, and amnesia had turned her into such a square peg she had forgotten it all.

Maybe all of this is one big hallucination.

Maybe you should be afraid of him.

Maybe be afraid of yourself.

All kinds of maybes. She hated every single one.

She listened for Etta as she worked but heard nothing in the rest of the house. It was like she and Lannes were alone. She wondered if the Impala's tires had already been slashed. She wondered if men with guns were coming.

The woman could not be certain how well she was washing the blood from him, but four bowls of hot water later, she called it quits. All she could ask for was a heartbeat and working lungs, and Lannes was giving her both. She cleared away the dirty towels and his ruined jeans and leaned up hard against the kitchen cabinet near his head. She smelled like blood. She had a feeling she had more of it on her than he had on him.

The woman drank some water. Poured a little down his throat. Somewhere, a clock ticked. It matched time to her heart and to the words in her head.

Don't. Don't. Don't.

The woman sank closer to Lannes and curled into a tight ball. She reached out just slightly and let her pinky rest on the invisible edge of something soft that was not a blanket, and not her imagination.

A wing, she told herself, chilled to the bone.

But she did not stop touching him. She lay very still and waited for Lannes to wake.

CHAPTER TEN

WAKING was the hard part. Dreaming, unfortunately, was not.

Lannes lost himself in dreams. Part of him knew he was hurt, but it was a small thing, insignificant, compared to the visions inside his head.

He saw the witch who'd captured him and his brothers. He saw her for the first time, small and red-headed, a sultry smile that seemed to cut right through him. She wanted him to restore a book, a seventeenth-century grimoire that she claimed to have purchased at auction.

He knew it was a lie. But it was a rare book, a decaying relic of some human's attempt at magic, successful or not. He could not help himself.

And so, he lost himself.

"Magic is a tricky thing," he heard his father whisper, as he drifted in darkness. "We have never cultivated it for attack or for the harm of others. Not for thousands of years. And so we have lost the seeds

*of such abilities. But there are others, Lanny. There
are others who have no such compunctions. And the
seeds of their darkness are strong, as well.*

"My boy. My poor son."

And then, another voice in the dark, soft and broken:

"Don't. Don't leave me."

*The woman. Lannes struggled toward her. He had
to find her. She needed to be protected. . . .*

"Please, Lannes—"

He had left her, she had no one.

"No one—"

You have me, he wanted to tell her.

"My friend—"

I'm coming, he thought. Stay alive, stay safe, I'm—

"Here," he mumbled, and just like that, he felt the
heat of her presence flood through his mind like a warm
soft light, and it was amazing to him, amazing how
good it felt, and how familiar.

His lips were cracked. His mouth was as dry as
sandpaper. He tried to open his eyes, and they felt glued
shut; only it was not glue, but a cold rag. He tried to
move his arm to take it off his eyes, and everything—
from the top of his head to the tips of his toes—felt
like it was on fire. Regeneration was an awful thing
when you took near lethal damage. Charlie had suffered it countless times simply to save his daughter.
This was a first for Lannes. He had new admiration for
his brother.

He reached along the mental chain binding him to
the woman. He felt her right beside him. Her mind si-

lent. He pulled off the rag, blinked hard and painfully, and glanced sideways.

She was asleep, curled on her side, snug against him. Touching his skin. Covered in blood.

Alarm filled him, until he realized she was unharmed. His unease, however, did not fade. Lannes was well and truly naked beneath his blanket. Even the belt was undone, though it still lay close enough to his skin to remain invisible.

The woman, he realized, must have had her hands all over him. And while some deep part of him found that rather titillating, the sensible portion of his brain was quite tempted to pull up its proverbial stakes and start running for the hills.

Calm down. She's still here. Asleep. Obviously not terrorized by anything she might have discovered about you. You'd feel that, if it were the case. Idiot.

Lannes exhaled slowly, his ribs protesting. The woman stirred slightly but did not wake. She looked exhausted and pale, her hair tangled, dirty. Dried blood smudged her cheek.

But she was lovely. So very lovely. Quite likely the dearest, most beautiful face he had ever seen. He was scared of himself for finding her so attractive—had been scared from the beginning—but he had as much choice in the matter as he had breathing. And breathing—being alive—was in his estimate a most delightful blessing.

He looked around, slightly puzzled that he was on the floor of a kitchen. The woman stirred again. He gritted his teeth against the pain and reached out to touch her hair. He was not certain how many chances he would have to do so. Might as well store up the memories like secret jewels.

Her hair was soft and fine, golden against the illusion of his human fingers. He tried to imagine how her hair would look spread across his real skin, and the quiet fantasy shot such longing through his heart that it was suddenly hard to breathe. He wanted to see it. He wanted to know what it would feel like to have her arms wrapped around his body, even in something as simple as a hug, and not be afraid of what she might discover. He wanted her to smile at him, the real him, and not this mask.

He wanted to kiss her.

Lannes closed his eyes and pressed his lips against the tip of his finger. Then, very carefully, he brushed that finger against the corner of her mouth. A ghost kiss. A phantom heart.

She opened her eyes. He had forgotten how green they were: a deep, vibrant color like malachite hewn and polished to a glowing shine.

"You're awake," she breathed, and began to sit up. Lannes, unthinking, touched her arm and lightly held her still. When he remembered himself, he drew away quickly. If she noticed, she showed nothing. Her gaze remained locked on his, and he felt and saw her uncertainty—and the dizzying strength of her relief.

"I thought you were going to die," she whispered.

"I'm hard to kill," he said hoarsely. "Where are we?"

"Near Purdue University, I think. Some woman

brought me here. She said she knows your brother and Frederick, but I don't trust her. I couldn't find a phone to confirm with him, either, and I was too scared to leave you."

"My brother," Lannes said. "You talked to him?"

"You said you had been speaking to him about my situation. I called the most recent number on your cell phone." A weak smile flitted across her mouth and she pointed at her head. "Don't have all my brain, but I've got some."

Lannes grinned, though it quickly faded. "What about the woman? What's her name?"

"She calls herself Etta Bredow."

"Anyone else with her?"

"Don't think so, but it's impossible to know."

"How did you get me in here?"

The woman glanced away from him. "I, um, carried you."

"Carried me," he said. "I'm . . . huge."

I also have wings you must have felt, he thought, alarmed. But the woman flushed a faint red and said, "I'm . . . not quite what I think I am."

Lannes coughed, and she sat up, reaching for a glass of water. He drained it—hardly enough to quench his thirst—in seconds, but he kept her from getting him more. He wanted to hear this.

"Tell me," he said, remembering the gunman hurled backward into his car.

Her gaze became haunted. "You first."

That was *not* what Lannes wanted to hear. He tried to sit up, clutching the blanket around his hips. But he forgot the belt, which had somehow loosened. It slipped totally free, clattering on the floor behind him, fully visible. He felt the size of an elephant and like he was juggling apples and standing on one leg.

He looked at the belt. So did the woman.

"Well," she said dryly, "that's interesting."

"I could use some more water," Lannes said.

"You seem to be feeling better," she remarked. "Although I wouldn't know for sure, seeing as how *I can't see your wounds*."

He pointed at the glass. "My throat. Burning."

The woman sighed. He tried to read her emotions, but there were so many of them, so tangled, that he could not make sense of even one. But he did not expect her to suddenly press her hands against his face. And he did not expect that she would sit up on her knees and lean in close enough to kiss. He sat, frozen. Breathless. Afraid to move. Desperate to close the distance between them. Her hands felt too good.

"Your eyes," she whispered. "Lannes. At least tell me your eyes are real."

He swallowed hard, quite certain he was plunging off a cliff. "Real as yours."

She hesitated, searching his gaze. "And the rest?"

Lannes' heart thudded like a freight train. He reached up and covered her hand with his own. Pulled it down to rest against his chest.

"What matters is real," he murmured.

She stared at their linked hands and closed her eyes. Lannes, aching, driven by everything that was wrong and foolish with his heart, also closed his eyes and brought her hand to his mouth. He kissed her palm. Poured himself into that one act, as though it would be his last. And it was, he was certain of it.

The woman made a low sound, deep in her throat. He forced himself to look at her. Found her staring at him. In his mind, her heart thundered. Or maybe that was him. A storm in his veins.

Until, quite suddenly, he sensed they were not alone.

He looked up and saw no one at all, but the woman stiffened, retreating from him. She stood on wobbly legs. Lannes also tried to stand but had to stop when bits and pieces of him pulled and tore in ways that were distinctly painful. He forced himself to breathe.

A pair of pale slender hands appeared around his arm. Lannes flinched but forced himself not to pull away. The woman tugged. He finally stood, swaying. The blanket was wrapped around his waist. His wings trailed behind him. His jeans were in tatters on the floor.

Lannes cleared his throat, distinctly uncomfortable. Even with the witch, he had never felt so vulnerable. This was either a nightmare or the best moment of his life. Maybe both. "Could you, ah, hand me that belt?"

The woman wordlessly gave it to him. Lannes knew he would never be able to bind his wings—not now—so he wrapped the belt around his forearm, his face hot, keenly aware of the woman watching. Pressed against his skin, the leather faded into the illusion of his shirt.

He could not look at her. "Did this . . . Etta . . ."

"No," she said quietly. "I made her leave. And I carried you in here myself."

His relief was overwhelming. "Thank you."

"You saved me," she said simply. "You saved me, no questions asked."

"Well," he said, smiling shakily, "maybe next time we can manage something less dramatic."

"Maybe next time," she replied slowly, "I can see what your smile really looks like."

Lannes stared. She patted his arm—so natural, so casual, as if there was nothing to it—and pointed toward the hall. "If you feel up to it."

He was forced to nod. No voice left. She led the way, limping and covered in his blood, and he followed close behind, wings loose. Everything aching. Except his heart. His heart felt good.

Afraid, but good.

THEY FOUND ETTA BREDOW IN THE LIVING ROOM, WHICH flowed outward, spacious, with a wall made entirely of windows that reflected back an area full of golden lamps and soft long sofas. Bookcases lined one of the walls. Golden shag carpet covered the floor. A gas flame flickered in the fireplace.

Etta was a spare woman, so skinny her shoulders seemed more in common with a clothes hanger than flesh and bone. Everything about her was hollow, except for her eyes: cold and piercing, brilliant with intelligence. She held a novel in her lap. *The Hunchback of Notre Dame*. Lannes wondered if there was a message in her choice of reading material.

"So," he said. "You know my brother."

"No," said Etta, closing the book, "I lied."

"Well," replied the other woman sarcastically. "At least you're honest."

Lannes focused his energies, opening himself to the rest of the house, searching for other signs of life. No one else was present. He tried to do the same to Etta and ran up against a wall. Like with Orwell. A barricade in her mind. He wondered if this was going to turn into another fight.

He wondered, too, at the nature of coincidence: of all the individuals in Chicago, he had been the one drawn into circumstances that no one else could possibly be suited to handle. Not that he was doing such a great job. Still, it made him uneasy, as though he was being manipulated. Something he could not blame on the woman at his side. If anything, they were both pawns.

He stared at Etta. "How do you know my brother's name?"

She set aside her book. "Same way I know yours, Mr. Hannelore. Mutual acquaintance. One who shall remain unnamed, in case you're thinking of asking. Suffice it to say, he asked me to intercede on your behalf."

"Sure," Lannes replied, struggling to control his fear. "That's acceptably vague."

"As if you should talk," she replied, raking him with a glance. "Lannes Hannelore, master of bookbinding. And other things. Nice mask, by the way." She tapped the corner of her eye. "You take too much for granted."

Dread filled him. "Why *are* we here?"

Etta gave her female guest a hard look. "To pay an old debt."

Lannes' companion pushed back her tangle of hair and limped deeper into the living room, posture stiff, as though she were being drawn forward against her will. Lannes felt a moment of alarm, but there was nothing wrong with the presence in her mind: no duality, no shadow of another.

"Do you know who I am?" she asked Etta.

"You ask that like you think you're somebody," replied the old lady. "But you're not. Just a slip of a thing, being used."

Lannes moved closer. "What do you know about it?"

"Not enough. More than I want." A look of disgust passed over her face. "I can't tell you about the man who wants you dead. I won't. All I can do is give you sanctuary. But he'll come for you again. And next time he won't use hired guns. He'll do it himself. He'll follow your example and borrow another mind."

The young woman's hand flew up to her throat. "That's peculiar wording."

"Is it?" asked Etta heavily. "History, my dear, tends to repeat itself."

"What was, what is, and what will be," Lannes murmured. "That's no answer. And I can't believe you lured us here for riddles."

"I did what was asked of me," Etta replied disdainfully. "I'm tired of looking over my shoulder."

Lannes suddenly wished his brothers were here—Arthur, maybe, who was a far stronger telepath, and who could slide through mental shields like a deadly ghost. "You want to play games with your life, fine. But not ours. Talk straight."

"And ruin the game?" Etta smiled bitterly. "No. In seventy years, all I've been able to maintain is an illusion of pride, a semblance of dignity. Smoke and mirrors, my good monster. And I won't throw that away on you. Not even to save my life."

"Then what's the point of luring us here?" asked the young woman, her voice filled with anger, her mind with despair. "If you know something—"

"Simon," interrupted Etta. "I know Simon. The man who is trying to kill you."

"Orwell mentioned that name," Lannes replied, losing patience. "Simon Says."

"'Simon says *jump*, and you jump,'" whispered the old lady, with a weariness that seemed to add another ten years to her face. "Ah, Simon. He started this, and he'll finish it. As long as you keep coming for us. His old, dear, friends."

Blond hair fell over the young woman's face, hiding her eyes. "I can't control that. Something . . . comes over me."

"Not something," said Etta softly. "*Someone.*"

Lannes' wings flared slightly. "And who would that be?"

Etta did not answer. She stood and walked toward the windows. Lannes saw his own reflection: a big man, dark hair, blurry features. He had managed to avoid most mirrors while wearing his illusion. He disliked seeing a stranger when he looked at himself—which was too close to the truth for comfort.

Etta turned, folding her arms over her hollow chest. Feet slightly apart, braced like she was facing a storm.

"Orwell Price," she murmured. "He's dead, now. You killed him."

"No," Lannes began, but the woman beside him shook her head.

"I killed him," she admitted. "More or less."

"More or less," agreed Etta, and placed a wrinkled hand over her heart. "I felt it, when he died. Right here."

The woman flinched. "I'm sorry."

Etta did not seem sorry, nor full of any particular regret. Her voice was strong when she said, "We should have seen it coming."

"We," Lannes said. "Who's *we*? Simon, Orwell?"

"All of us," said Etta slowly, "who are obliged to die."

"Everyone dies. What makes all of you so special?"

She smiled. "The quality of the sin, Mr. Hannelore."

"Murder," said the blond woman softly. "You and Orwell murdered someone."

Etta's mental shield wavered, enough so that despite her calm face, he knew she was raging underneath, raging with sorrow or anger or guilt, raging with something almost too big for her body to contain. A chill filled him, matched only by the one in the old woman's eyes, which were pitiless and hard as stone. Powerful eyes. Frightening.

Etta turned those eyes on Lannes' companion, who did not blink or look away but met the gaze with a power that seemed to rise, warm and steady, against the old lady. Lannes could feel it in his head, and it made him want to take a step back. He moved forward instead, close against his companion's back.

"I'm going to make this easy on you," Etta said. "It's not the reason I was asked to bring you here, but I know the score. I know what's coming. And I might as well do one good deed before I die. Something to ease the way to the other side."

"You're not going to die," said the woman.

Etta swayed, arms still folded across her chest. "You won't have a choice."

The blond woman paled. Lannes grabbed her arm. Etta smiled at him, though it seemed sickly, like she was nauseated. "You were right about my reading material, Mr. Hannelore. I did choose it for a reason."

Anger clawed into the woman beside him. He felt it, was surprised by the intensity of it, and squeezed her arm, gently. "If you know who's controlling her or where this Simon is—"

"There is nothing I could tell you that would help," she interrupted, rubbing her brow. "Knowledge can make things worse, Mr. Hannelore. Take my word for it."

"No," said the woman beside him, trembling. "I don't accept that."

"You should," Etta whispered, a faint sheen of sweat breaking out on her brow. "You, of all people."

The woman stiffened. So did Lannes, but before he could say a word, Etta's eyes unfocused and her knees buckled. She managed to stay on her feet, barely, but that lasted only a moment. Her left leg collapsed, and she started to go down, hard.

Lannes caught her. He lowered her hollow body to the carpet, nothing but bone and sinew beneath his hands. She reached past him for his companion and caught her wrist.

"I know you can hear me," Etta whispered, blinking hard, struggling to focus. "Bitch."

The young woman frowned, clearly confused—and then, quite suddenly, hissed in pain. Her eyes squeezed shut, mouth twisting in an awful grimace.

Lannes felt a tremor along their link, a rupture— and a shadow emerged. A second heart, pressed atop the woman's mind. The intruder.

All it took was a moment. Lannes could do nothing to stop it. He stared into her eyes and found a stranger. The woman he knew, locked behind a wall. Her skin paled to a ghostly white, as did her lips. All the color in her body leached away.

No windows were open in the room, but her blond hair stirred as though she stood in a storm, and her green eyes glowed briefly, as though emerald fireflies hid there. Lannes stared, stricken. Realizing suddenly that the woman might be several more degrees past human than he had imagined. He tried to make contact through the link between their minds, but slammed against a barrier. He imagined a scream from the other side.

"How could you?" whispered the intruder to Etta, her voice several octaves lower and shaking with fury. "You owed me. You were *mine*."

"Maybe," rasped Etta weakly. "But the girl you're using owes you nothing. You put blood on her hands that doesn't belong there. And that is *not* your right."

"I have every right," snarled the intruder, grabbing Etta's throat.

Lannes snatched her wrist and closed his eyes, once again throwing himself down the mental link, hurling into the barrier with all his strength. He felt the woman—his woman—on the other side, and he hit the wall again and again, even after he lost his grip on the woman's wrist and felt his physical body flung aside. His ribs hit the sharp edge of a table, and the pain almost made him black out.

Etta started laughing. Her voice, the satisfaction in it, sent a tremor through the intruder that Lannes felt in his mind and in the air itself, as though the world around him shivered.

"Go," rasped Etta, smiling coldly. "Finish me off if you like, but you'll always know I beat you."

The intruder went very still, gazing down at Etta with such hate, the room seemed to crawl with shadows. Lights flickered. Windows rattled.

"You do not deserve mercy," whispered the intruder, blond hair blowing around her pale, stolen face. "Not for what you did to her. Not for what you made me watch. God damn you, Etta Bredow."

And without another word, the intruder vanished from the woman's brain. Like the shadow of an eclipse lifted off the sun. The mental barrier disintegrated.

Lannes, still fighting against it, fell through into his companion's mind with such force he momentarily became tangled in her thoughts. He caught flashes— witnessed her hands washing the blood off his body, her care as she looked for his wounds. Her fingers grazing his invisible wings.

He felt her fear. He felt her heart, thundering as though it were his own.

Lannes fled to his own mind and lay on the floor, breathing hard, eyes burning with unshed tears. He rolled on his side, and found his companion crouched on her hands and knees, shuddering. He crawled to her and, without a word and only a brief hesitation, wrapped his arms around her waist and tugged her into the curve of his body, laying them both down on the carpet. Holding her tight as she shook uncontrollably, teeth chattering. His arm beneath her cheek felt wet with tears.

Etta whispered, "It worked. Oh, God. I didn't think it would."

"You poisoned yourself," murmured the young woman unsteadily, her breath warm on Lannes' arm. "I felt it in her thoughts. She knew it. You've killed yourself."

The old lady remained sprawled on the carpet, sweating profusely. "My hand or hers, through you. I thought I would spare you the death, little girl. And stick it in her craw while I was at it."

The young woman trembled. "Who is she?"

Etta's eyes drifted shut. "A mistake. Too many secrets in that mistake for me to tell the story. But you have to stop her, girl. You have to get rid of her. You'll never be free if you don't. How, I cannot imagine. Must be blood. Your face . . . Oh, damn."

Lannes rumbled. "Why did you bring us here if

you knew how it would end? And why didn't she kill you as soon as we met?"

"Takes energy. Takes time to be strong enough. She would have dragged you to me if I hadn't found you first. Saved you the trip." Etta smiled weakly, eyes closed. "I'm tired of running from my memories."

The young woman struggled to crawl from Lannes' arms. "You *can't* die."

"Go to hell," muttered Etta. "Better yet, go south. Find the dome. Find the farm. Someone will be waiting for you there. Son of a bitch."

Lannes said, "We can still get you to a hospital."

"Too late," Etta mumbled, eyes briefly drifting open to look at them. "This is what I get for being a punk."

The young woman knelt beside her. Lannes reached out and held Etta's hand. She stopped breathing soon after.

CHAPTER ELEVEN

THOUGH the woman remembered nothing of her life before waking in that Chicago hotel room, she was quite certain—hopeful, if nothing else—that her existence had been mundane and riddle-free, full of lazy evenings and warm apple pie, and nothing more upsetting than the spiteful remark of an irate neighbor or co-worker. That was the fantasy. No murder, no blood, no voices in her mind. No old women committing suicide and dying in her arms.

No men with wings.

"Up," Lannes murmured, dragging her to her feet, away from Etta. "Come on."

"We let her die," she rasped, fighting the urge to puke. "Jesus. What did I do?"

"Nothing," he snapped, holding her chin, forcing her to look at him. Close up, she thought it was a miracle she had ever mistaken him for human—it was in his eyes, shot dark with blue but glowing with electric veins of light that pulsed and flickered like tiny gasps of lightning.

"You did nothing," he said again, softer, though he did not release her. If anything, he pulled her closer, and though she did not mean to, her hands pressed against his chest, sinking through the illusion of a shirt to hot smooth skin and muscle hard as stone. She was too close to miss the sharp intake of his breath, and after a moment of pure stillness he pulled away. She let him, quivering with cold.

"Terrible disguise," she rasped. "You can't let anyone get close."

His gaze was haunted. "Never."

Lannes bent and scooped Etta into his arms. He carried her the short distance to the couch and set her down very gently. The old lady looked like a stick figure against him, nothing left but skin and bone.

She tried not to cry, the woman, not when she looked at Etta's pale hollow face, not when Lannes unfolded a blanket that had been resting on the back of the couch and draped it over Etta's head and body. The woman did not know if they should say a prayer or some words of passage. Instead she stayed quiet, holding down terrible emotions, and made her heart cold and numb.

There was another blanket on the couch. Lannes shook it loose and draped it around the woman's shoulders. She felt very small beside him.

Suck it up, she told herself, and Lannes said, "I need to find a phone and call my brother. You rest."

The woman glanced down at Etta and shuddered. "Nice try."

Lannes' jaw tightened. "Come on."

He held her hand. His palm was large and warm, and felt no different from any other hand, though she could not remember anything, or anyone, with whom to compare him. Lannes led her down a long hall off the living room, and they found a bathroom and three bedrooms. There was no one else.

But the house still felt creepy. Lannes squeezed her hand, gently. "Clean up if you can. I'll be close by."

I don't want to be left alone, she almost told him, but that would have been pathetic, so all she did was nod.

Lannes gave her a knowing look. "I won't let anything happen to you."

Never, she imagined him saying in her mind, with such clarity she wondered if it was more than her imagination.

Lannes released her hand and stepped away, but the distance meant nothing. He still held her gaze, and the power of that, the intimacy of his intensity, felt the same as a touch. The woman wished, more than anything, that she had memories to draw from—experience—but she felt like a blank slate when it came to human contact. And Lannes, no matter what he looked like, was so much more than that. She did not know how to react.

And does he? *What makes you think his experience is any greater than yours?*

You can't let anyone get close.

Never.

She battled a perverse desire to touch him again, just because . . . just because she needed to feel his warmth and she was cold, so cold she might have been standing chest-deep in a glacier, but she felt his tension roll over her—tension and even, she imagined, fear—and she stayed rooted in one spot. Sick and swaying.

Lannes looked little better. He bowed his head and backed away, leaving her alone in the doorway of the bedroom.

She watched him disappear at the end of the hall, and sucked in a deep breath. Her spine felt like it was made of ice cubes, and she clutched the blanket tighter, forcing herself to go deeper into the bedroom. It was a large and simple space. Closet doors were already open, which was some relief. She felt like a little kid terrorized by shadows.

It was an eerie thing, rifling through a dead lady's closet, but the woman had little choice in the matter. She needed clothes.

Wherever Etta was from, she had not lived in this house—if at all—in a long time. As with the kitchen, a fine layer of dust covered everything, and the few clothes in the closet, while in good condition, smelled musty. Some belonged to men. Some dresses were clearly from the fifties and had more in common with flowered curtains than high fashion.

The woman pulled down some clothes and clutched them in her arms. She crossed the hall and found bedrooms that had belonged to children. One of them was decorated in pink bunnies; the other had wallpaper covered in an old-fashioned montage of cowboys and Indians. In that bedroom, the woman discovered a shoe box, contents already poured on the hard narrow bed—as though Etta had been in here going through some

things. At least, she hoped it was Etta; the idea of someone else being here made the woman uneasy.

Still clutching the blanket and clothes with one hand,
she pushed aside the shoe box and sat down on the
bed. There were black-and-white photographs in front
of her, a feather, a piece of folded pink stationery and
several yellowed postcards, one of which showed a
man with red clothes and skin, horns on his head and
a tail that ended in a dagger point. A sword was buckled to his side, and his hand was raised in an oddly
delicate gesture.

PLUTO WATER, read the postcard. FRENCH LICK
SPRINGS HOTEL.

The image was both disturbing and compelling.
Pluto. Hades. God of the underworld. She looked on
the back of the card and saw a short message written in
neat, childish script.

Dear Etta,

*I am sorry you are sick. Mama says you will be
coming soon to the Springs, and I cannot wait.
Simon is here. So are the others. It is hot.*

Yours,
Marcel

The photographs were creased and old. One of
them showed a group of children standing in front of
a graveyard. It was a faintly ominous picture, filled
with two little girls who could not have been older

than ten, and four boys who seemed to range in age from three to eighteen. The girls were sitting in the grass, round faces framed in curls and ribbons. They looked happy.

Only two of the boys were smiling—they could have been ten or twelve and were lounging against the fence bordering the graveyard. Dressed in slacks and suit jackets, hair slicked back. They looked like trouble, the kind that might throw rocks at dogs or yank the skirts of girls.

The other two boys were different. The older was tall and strong looking, with an honest face and a clear gaze. The woman liked him immediately. She also liked the little boy he held, who seemed shy of the camera and had his face partially hidden by his hand and a shadow. There was something familiar about the curve of his cheek. It nagged at her.

The back of the photo had an inscription:
From Will. Late '30s. Indiana. Summer.

The woman stared at the photograph a moment longer then tucked it away in the shoe box along with all the other little knickknacks. She gathered up the box and took it with her to the bathroom, placing it on top of the clean clothes she had found in the closet.

The woman locked the door and kept her back to the mirror. She took a shower. There was only a dried-up sliver of soap in the stall, and some old shampoo that looked like it had not been used in ten years.

It was hard to scrub off the blood. She had to use her fingernails and left welts in her skin. But the hot water felt so good she never wanted to turn it off, and

she bowed her head, pummeled by the near-scalding
stream, inhaling steam, knuckling her burning eyes.
Her feet stung and her shoulder ached. She had almost
managed to forget both. She supposed that meant she
was healing. Or maybe she had been running on nothing but adrenaline.

Beyond the shower curtain, she heard knocking at
the bathroom door. It made her jump, but she heard
Lannes' muffled rumbling voice and forced herself to
breathe.

"Yes?" she said shakily.

"You've been in there awhile," came his gruff reply. "I wanted to make sure you're all right."

"Fine," she said, and shut off the water. Cold air
seemed to blast her, and she fumbled for a towel, which
smelled musty and old. Her hair was a snarled mess,
dripping down her back. When she stepped from the
stall, she caught her reflection in the mirror.

Pale face, hollow eyes. Bruises all over, especially
her shoulder. She still did not recognize herself. She
could have been in a chicken suit, and she would have
felt the same numb disconnect.

It was not a bad body. But it was just a body.

She heard nothing on the other side of the door, but
she sensed him there, like a tickle on the edge of her
mind. More than instinct. She began to dress and said,
"Did you call your brother?"

"He's sending help. He . . . asked after you."

The woman nodded to herself, but said nothing.
She dressed in loose black slacks and a black sweater,
as well as a soft pair of black leather shoes she had

found in the closet. She found them a little snug, but it didn't matter. Wearing shoes was almost enough to make her feel like a new woman. Even her feet did not hurt as much. Her shoulder was slightly stiff, but not nearly as mangled and sore as it should have been, considering the blow she'd taken. Maybe it wasn't just adrenaline.

Lannes, she thought. *He had something to do with it, this healing.*

Taking care of her. Saving her life. All of which was enough to cut through any mystery, no matter how bizarre. She could not think of him without a twist in her heart.

Her hair was a snarled mess, but she opened the door and found Lannes leaning against the wall, across the hall from the bathroom. His eyes were the only part of him she looked at. The only part that mattered.

The only true piece of you I can see.

She searched his gaze for the same look he had given her earlier, when she had opened her eyes and found him watching her. As though she was the most beautiful thing he had ever seen. She had felt beautiful in that moment. Haunted, as well. And the way he had kissed her hand . . .

Her heart lurched. She stopped herself from thinking of it. Wrong time, wrong place.

His jeans looked different. "Real or illusion?" she asked, pointing.

Lannes seemed embarrassed by her question. "Real. I had some clothes in the back of the car."

"Ah," she said, smiling briefly. "I'm glad you're wearing pants."

He grunted. "How do you feel?"

"I'm still standing."

"Your shoulder?"

"You did something to help it heal," she suggested. No matter how impossible that seemed—even now, with everything she had seen.

"Maybe," he replied. "But you didn't answer my question."

"Still hurts a little," she admitted.

Lannes pushed away from the wall and filled up the bathroom doorway. "I can look at it again."

The woman's heart beat a little faster, and she slowly, carefully, tugged aside the soft collar of the sweater. Lannes edged into the bathroom, huge and solid, and very gently grazed his knuckles against her shoulder.

She shivered, but not from cold—and quickly averted her eyes, afraid of what he might see in her face. She folded her arms over her breasts, too. She had no bra, and her reaction to him was obvious in other ways. Embarrassing. Totally inexplicable. Utterly improper, given the circumstances.

But she was hungry for his touch. Aching for it. And when his knuckles finally rested heavily on her sore shoulder, every part of her stilled in utter focus on that one small connection. His nearness made it difficult to breathe—but then it stopped being about him, and instead she noted an odd tingling heat that spread through her skin. The pain eased. Her feet stopped throbbing, though the lessening discomfort was preceded by a pronounced burning sensation in her soles.

She finally braved a look at Lannes' face, and found his eyes slightly unfocused; he was lost in concentration.

Healing me, she told herself, filled with wonder; followed by: *What are you?*

And then: *What am I?*

Lannes' hand shifted, sliding slightly down her arm, against her sweater. His eyes focused on her face with an intensity that made her blush, though she felt more grim than shy.

"You're not scared," he said quietly. "Not of me."

"I should be. You're a walking lie. But I suppose I'm not much better."

"I lie by choice," he replied. "You have none."

She smiled bitterly. "I might have forgotten a lot of things, but not, I hope, my common sense. You have . . . limbs . . . attached to your body that I don't think you could show this world, any more than I can remember my name. Tell me I'm wrong."

"You're not," he said, and she felt his tension roll over her, hard and hot. "Which is why you're such a puzzle. In more ways than one."

"Ah," she replied. "You expect screaming."

"Pitchforks, at the very least."

"Boiling oil? Flame-tipped arrows?"

"Aimed for my heart." A faint, grim smile touched his mouth. "Try to match *some* of my expectations, why don't you?"

"Sorry," she said. "What you see is what you get."

Lannes hesitated. "Yes. I suppose it is."

The woman could not help herself. She touched him again, pressing her palm flat against his chest, watching her skin shimmer and disappear into his body, as though his shirt was made of nothing but shadows. She felt no wounds, though his skin seemed slightly sticky. She had not cleaned off all the blood, after all.

Her hand slid down slightly, and encountered the hard leather ridge of the belt. He covered her hand.

"We should go."

"I know," she said, staring at their hands. "But I'm tired of running."

Lannes' other hand, very carefully, slid against her neck into her tangled hair. His palm seemed to engulf the entire left side of her head. She fought the urge to lean into his touch, but the effort was overwhelming, and she finally gave in, swaying forward, digging her fingers into the invisible belt strapped again around his massive body. Lannes did not move as she pressed her forehead against him, though she felt the rise and fall of his chest, and his scent, though unidentifiable, was musky and warm. He felt so good. Like a wall against the world.

She fought the urge to press even closer, trying to ignore the parts of her body that wanted to touch him in ways that were totally inappropriate. Jesus, but she was in trouble.

And it wasn't just her, she realized. Lannes' breathing seemed to be just a little faster, and she felt something—an energy from him that seemed to run deep as her mind, and that sank bolts of liquid heat through her limbs. His hand tightened in her hair and she sagged against him, just a little more, her breasts finally rubbing against his torso. She had to bite her bottom lip to keep silent, and was instantly ashamed of herself. There was a dead woman in the other room, four dead men in her past. She had no memories, and there were things in her mind that could not be explained.

Lannes could not be explained. And here she was, every part of her humming, wanting nothing more than to reach beneath that illusion and . . . fuck the hell out of him?

He sucked in a deep ragged breath and began to pull away, but not before she closed the distance between them one last time and felt against her hip the long hard line of his cock pushing against his jeans. She was all instinct in that moment, part of her primitive as some animal lost in heat, and she rubbed against him, briefly, savoring the shock of pure lust that slammed heavy and wet between her legs.

"Lannes," she breathed.

"You don't know what you're asking," he muttered hoarsely. "You have no idea."

The woman swallowed hard, trying to control herself. "I know. I'm sorry. I won't . . . I won't touch you again."

A short bitter gasp of laughter escaped him. "Trying to kill me, aren't you?"

She almost forgot. For a moment, she was so lost

inside him, being near him, those words nearly passed over her. But then they hit her like a brick, and all the cold and pain returned with such force that it was all she could do not to sit down on the floor.

"No," Lannes said, dismayed, but she tore herself away from him, grabbed the shoe box of Etta's possessions and staggered from the bathroom.

He caught up with her in one step, his fingers grazing her arm. She wrenched away, running past Etta's corpse in the living room—trying not to vomit when she saw it—and headed for the front door.

Lannes stepped in front of her, blocking the way out. Big as a mountain, all muscle and sinew beneath that illusion of his shirt. Her hands remembered what it felt like to touch him. His power was no fantasy. Not a play of smoke and mirrors. He was as strong as he looked. Probably stronger.

But it was his eyes she could not look away from. Those damn beautiful eyes. Filled now with a peculiar grief and desperation that made her heart ache.

"That's not what I meant," he said quietly, "and you know it."

"Yes," she told him, clutching the shoe box to her chest. "But there was truth to it. I might hurt you. I already have."

"If that's easier for you to believe." Lannes took a step toward her, and it was hard not to back away. "You're not what I wanted in my life. Not what I needed. Not in a million years. But there you were, and here we are, and I don't care about a little pain. So I won't leave you. I won't let you walk away. And I won't—" He stopped abruptly, looking down at his hands, which curled into massive fists.

I won't stop wanting to touch you, she imagined him saying, hearing it so clearly she might have thought he had spoken out loud if her gaze had not been solely on his mouth. Instead his words rang through her head, and she was hard pressed not to respond. With what, she had no idea.

Lannes finally met her gaze again, and his expression was haunted. No words, though. He stepped aside and opened the front door. The woman hesitated, glancing over her shoulder into the living room. She could not see Etta's body, but knowing it was there made the pain just as acute.

"I know," Lannes said quietly, as if in response to her hesitation. "I hate the idea of leaving her, too. My brother is sending someone to take care of her body, but it still doesn't seem right."

Nothing seemed right, least of all Etta's death. "We could wait."

He hesitated. "Feels like a trap to sit still."

"Do you think she was telling the truth?"

"I don't know. Did you feel anything? When that . . . thing . . . was inside you?"

"Just anger. I was shut off from everything else."

"In a bubble," he said quietly, gaze distant. "Walls around you."

A chill raced through her. "How did you know?"

"Lucky guess," he said, but she did not believe him. She would have said so, but her stomach growled. Lannes' mouth softened with faint amusement.

"We need to eat," he said.

"Seems wrong to admit I'm hungry. I shouldn't have an appetite."

"You have a good survival instinct. Nothing wrong with that."

They left the front light off and went outside, in the dark, to the Impala. There was a small pile of garbage bags by the back wheel. Lannes popped the trunk, threw them inside, and then pulled out a flannel blanket.

The woman did not ask why it was in there. She took it from him, and spread a blanket over the grisly front seat. The blood had dried, but the interior still smelled. They both rolled down the front windows and sat there for a moment, staring at the house.

"I can't take much more of this," the woman said.

"You'll have to," Lannes replied, and started the engine.

She watched him drive, wondering what to believe. Not so long ago, he had been the one slumped in the passenger seat leaking buckets of blood. Now he looked the same as he ever had, sitting straight and tall behind the wheel of his car.

But everything was different now. Everything.

It was three in the morning. Lannes found a Denny's. The young woman felt like a fugitive walking in. There weren't many people in there: some college students with their books out, a few grizzled men hunched over empty plates and cups of coffee. Not much talking was going on. Frank Sinatra crooned.

The waitress gave Lannes and his companion a booth in the corner, away from the windows, where they sat facing the front door. There was a good view of everyone coming and going. It was hard for the woman to relax. She was afraid someone would come in shooting. She still held the shoe box and put it on the chair beside her.

Lannes seemed uncomfortable, too. He looked so much larger than the seat and table, as though he might break both with one wrong move. She wondered about his claustrophobia. His nightmares.

His wings.

"We can go someplace else if you want," she said. "Or wait until morning when the drive-up windows open."

Lannes hesitated, surprise flickering through his eyes. "No. But . . . thank you. I appreciate the thought."

The woman shrugged, flipping open the menu, afraid to look at him again.

She ordered a burger and fries with a strawberry milkshake. Lannes got two club sandwiches, a side order of onion rings, and as an afterthought, a Philly melt and lemonade. The waitress took it all in stride, all smiles for him. She winked at them both, actually.

After the waitress left, Lannes and the woman sat in awkward silence. He started playing with his fork. She tore her napkin into bits.

"Remind me," she finally said, slowly, "is the rest of the world as strange as we are, or are we just . . . unique?"

Lannes looked amused. "I guess that depends on what your definition of strange is. Because I see some things on television that make me feel positively normal."

She bit back a smile. "I'm serious."

"I know," he said, his own smile fading. "But I don't like the answer."

She nodded slowly. "Six billion humans in this world. How many of you?"

He seemed taken aback by her question, but after a tense moment, relaxed. "A handful in comparison. Hardly a wink of the eye."

"And you survive by . . . hiding your appearance?"

Again, tension. But this time she seemed to feel his anxiety in her mind as if there were a link between them. It was not intrusive, but it was distinct, as though her brain contained a separate room, a place where odd notions and power lived. And the door was creaking open.

She took a long drink of water, trying to hide her unease. But Lannes was looking at her with a curious consideration that made her feel like he could see right through her.

"Some of us mask our appearances," he said slowly, still searching her face. "Others just . . . hide. Big world. There are still places where people don't go."

She closed her eyes. "I didn't expect this. The hotel room and amnesia were enough."

"I would never have told you," he said quietly. "I would never have taken the risk."

She understood. She did not know what he was, but she understood his fear on a gut level. "Then why did you help me?"

He looked down at his hands. "I still don't understand why you're so calm about all this."

"Why, Lannes? Why did you do it?"

He hesitated, still not looking at her. "I wish you wouldn't ask."

She did not give him the easy way out. Lannes rolled his shoulders and took a drink of water. "I helped you because I was hurt once. Not like you, but similar. My life was . . . stolen from me." He stopped, finally meeting her gaze, and the weight of it was like being punched.

"I understood you," he said. "That's all. I understood."

Her fingers dug into the seat. The waitress approached with their plates and set them down. When she walked away, Lannes said, "You need a name."

"Do I?" she said weakly. "I don't know if I feel comfortable giving myself a name not my own."

"I have to call you *something*."

She grabbed some French fries, then dropped them to pick up the ketchup. Squirting some on the rim of her plate, she offered him the bottle. He shook his head. "Thanks."

And then, "A name."

She grumbled under her breath, rolling some fries in ketchup and cramming them into her mouth. She sat back, chewing, then repeated the process—efficient, no-nonsense, all business.

"Jane," she said. "See Jane run."

"No," he replied. "Let's not."

Her mouth twitched. "Becky."

"Only if you plan on wearing pigtails."

"Ashley."

"I'll leave you at the side of the road, Valley girl."

"Aretha."

"Blasphemy."

"I thought this was supposed to be my name, and not yours."

He half grinned. "I'll be the one saying it."

She made a face and went after her hamburger, using her palm to flatten it against the plate until it was little more than a bread-and-meat pancake. Amnesiac, maybe, but she had some definite habits.

"Who named you?" she asked abruptly.

Lannes swallowed. "My mother. She brought the name with her from Europe. France, maybe."

"Jean Lannes," she said. "One of Napoleon's generals."

"Ah. Well, I don't think I'm named for—" He stopped. "I'm amazed at the things you seem to remember."

She shrugged and ate more of her burger. "It's random. What was your mother's name?"

"Chloe," he said, after a moment. "She and my father live in northern Canada, up around Hudson Bay."

"You?"

"Maine. With my brothers."

"How many?"

Again, he hesitated. "Four. I'm the second oldest."

"No sisters?" When he shook his head, she added, "You'll be missed, won't you? You can't keep gallivanting around with me."

"You already know I work from home." Lannes hunched lower into the seat. "This was supposed to be a vacation."

"I'm sorry. I guess that means you don't have a family. Kids and a wife."

It was hard to say those words, surprisingly so. Nor did it help that Lannes took a long time to answer. He bit into his sandwich, as though mulling over his words.

"No," he finally said, avoiding her gaze. "No one."

And then, "Isn't there *any* name that resonates with you?"

She shook her head, stabbing some more fries into the ketchup—also keeping her gaze down, afraid he might see relief in her eyes. "You might as well call me after this restaurant. Nothing strikes a bell."

"Denny," he said. "You want to answer to that?"

She rolled it around in her mouth. "Not really. But I will if I have to."

"Denny," he tried again, looking into her eyes. "No. That's not right. Maybe something symbolic. Like . . . Lethe."

"Lethe," she echoed. "That's a loaded name."

"Means forgetfulness in Greek."

"It's also a river in Hades. Those who drink from it forget everything."

"But only so they can be reincarnated without the burden of past lives." Lannes smiled. "Appropriate, I think."

"I would rather remember my past, bad or good."

"And if you don't?"

Something in his voice made her heart hurt. "You don't think I'm going to get my memories back."

Lannes poked his sandwich. "I think it would be . . . prudent to prepare for the possibility."

"Prudent," she echoed, going cold. "You know something, don't you?"

"No," he said, but it was too late. Words and moments fell into place, little pieces adding up into the larger puzzle, and she had an insight that filled her with dread, even while it seemed impossible. Impossible, relatively speaking.

"You can read my mind," she said. "Oh, God."

"It's not like that," he told her.

"Bullshit. You can hear my thoughts."

"No," Lannes muttered sharply. "Not all the time anyway."

The woman threw up her hands. "Thanks a lot."

Exasperation filled his face, and he tore apart his sandwich, tossing it in pieces on his plate. "The big stuff happens only when we're touching. Strengthens the link. And I had no choice the first time. I had to make certain you weren't a threat to Frederick."

"The *first* time. First of many, I assume."

"You have a loud mind," he growled.

"Fantastic." She looked away from him, suffering an odd panic and humiliation. Lannes had been in her mind, what little was left of it. She'd had some rather embarrassing thoughts. Not to mention she had enough people in her mind. Mucking around, screwing up her life.

Enough. No time for this. Suck it up.

Just like everything else. The woman forced herself to breathe, and rested her elbows on the table. "Fine. You read minds, you heal yourself and others, you only *look* human, and you have some goddamn wings. Am I forgetting anything?"

"I'm handy with leather," he replied dryly.

"Boy Scout," she muttered. "You're not telling me everything."

"Should I?" He leaned in—a giant, powerful. "I'm trying to protect you."

"And if you're not around?" she asked. He started to protest and she held up her hand, stopping him. "Please. Please, Lannes. The truth."

"Truth," he said softly. "The truth is in your mind. Your mind, which has been . . . tampered with. Your memories were ripped out. I could feel it when we first met."

She no longer felt hungry, and shoved away her plate. "I can get them back."

Lannes shook his head. "Doesn't work that way."

"I guess you're the expert."

"Expert enough. But not like some."

"Then don't . . . ," she began, and stopped, swallowing hard. "Don't tell me things like that."

"I'm sorry," he whispered. "But you could have a family. Children. A husband."

She closed her eyes. "Don't say that."

"You have to consider it."

"I have," she said sharply. "I can't take it. I can't handle the idea that there might be people out there who know and love me, when I can't remember their faces."

It frightened her, to be honest—almost as much as

172   Marjorie M. Liu

the idea that she might not be capable of loving such people again, even if she found them. This very thought had been plaguing her.

Face it. No matter how much you want to have a past, it would be easier if you didn't. Easier if you were never found.

Horrible. But she felt an odd relief at the possibility. A lifting of tension she had not known she carried. No past. Nothing to hold her back. Nothing to be afraid of.

Do not let yourself be found, whispered a small voice in her heart. *Stay small, stay hidden. Start fresh. You are Lethe. Forget. Then find yourself again.*

"Hey," Lannes murmured. "Are you okay?"

The woman shook herself. "Yes, I'm . . . fine."

He frowned, and she found herself wondering how much of that frown was him, or whether everything was part of a mask. She could not imagine such a thing, not when he looked so real. So human.

His cell phone buzzed. A car charger had been on the floor in the back of the Impala. She had kicked herself when he pulled it free and plugged it into the cigarette lighter. His phone's battery was nowhere close to being fully recharged, but it was good enough for calls. At least until they were back in the car. "Charlie," Lannes said into the phone. "Yes, we're fine. Nearby at Denny's."

And then he listened for a long time, jaw tight, staring at his half-eaten sandwich with a distant intensity that made his companion lean forward, watching the tick of his heartbeat in his throat. So real. So damn real.

"I understand," he said, glancing up. "I need to talk to her first, but I'll let you know."

He hung up and was silent. As was she. Letting him gather his thoughts. Until, finally, he said, "My brother found the hotel you were at. It was in the news because of the fire. According to him, the hotel matched up the evacuees to the names on their files. As of tonight, only three people hadn't checked in with the authorities, and all of them were women. One of the ladies has a Chinese last name, while the other two women are above the age of sixty-five. Same booking, senior rate. You weren't registered at the hotel."

"Those dead men in the room with me?" It occurred to her that she had not given Lannes many details of their discovery, but he kept talking as though she had—and if he *could* look into her mind, then chances were good he already knew everything she needed to tell him.

Creepy. So creepy.

"Police found their bodies. Burned to a crisp, though there were bullets inside them, visible to the naked eye. It was obvious they had been shot."

She leaned back, remembering the feeling of that gun in her hands, how familiar she had been with its use. Lannes said, "One more thing. Orwell Price didn't give us his real name. He was born Marcellus Bredow."

Chills rolled down her spine. She thought of the postcard in the box. "Bredow?"

"She was his twin."

A sucker punch would have been kinder. "No way."

"Charlie found the paper trail. Orwell—Marcellus—changed his name in his late teens. Don't know why."

She placed her hand on the shoe box. "Any word on a man named Simon?"

"No. And Charlie didn't know how Etta found us. He asked around, and there's no . . . mutual acquaintance that he's aware of."

"The gunman? The men in the hotel room where I woke up? Is there any connection there?"

"Not yet. And the manager at that motel where the last attack occurred confessed only to being promised cash if he would find out whether or not we were still in our room."

The woman forced herself to breathe, wondering briefly if she would have to run to the bathroom to puke up her guts. But the nausea passed, and she slid the shoe box across the table. "There's a picture in there and a note to Etta from her brother. Marcel, he called himself. Everything seems to be from Indiana. Down south."

"That's where she said to go," Lannes murmured, poking through the box and pulling out the picture. It looked very small in his hand. He frowned, his gaze roving over the faces of the children. He checked the back. "No names, except for 'Will.' Whoever he is."

"Wanna bet one of those boys is named Simon?"

Lannes kept frowning, eyes narrowed. "Marcellus and Etta must be among these children, too. But that leaves three others." His expression turned even darker.

The woman said, "What is it?"

"Nothing," he muttered, his finger pressed alongside the half-hidden face of the little boy in the young man's arms. "Just . . . a tickle in my brain."

"I don't know what that means, coming from you."

He flashed her a quick smile. "Nothing bizarre. Just instinct."

"And?"

"And I don't know. Something about these two." He tapped the young man and the little boy. "They don't belong with the others."

"They look . . . nicer."

Lannes flipped over the card. "Will . . . . Which one do you think he is? The older kid or the baby?"

"Doesn't matter. He might not even be in the picture. But if he is, consider him another possible target."

Lannes made a small sound of agreement and placed the photo back in the box. He rummaged through the rest, glancing at the postcard with amusement and a shake of his head.

"So," said the woman. "South?"

"Etta said to find a dome."

"Unless she was messing with us. We're relying on the word of a person no one knows."

"Sounds familiar." He flashed her a smile. "Getting anything from that extraordinary brain of yours?"

"I wish."

Lannes sighed, and glanced around until he saw the waitress. He waved at her, and she swayed over with a little hop in her step. His companion guessed that being waved at by someone who looked like Lannes was not such a bad thing. Even if it was just an illusion—the

idea of which made her head hurt. She could not begin
to imagine how it was possible.

Magic, whispered her mind. *Magic. Something you
know.*

She rubbed her eyes. The waitress said, "Ready for
dessert?"

"Actually," Lannes said, "we're touring the state and
heard something about a dome. We're not sure where
or what, but—"

"I know what you're talking about," interrupted the
waitress cheerfully. "You want to head down to West
Baden. Just drive through Indianapolis on I-270, then
follow 37 all the way south through Paoli. You'll see
signs. Got a new casino down there and everything."

"And the dome?"

"I'll let you be surprised," she said, smiling mysteri-
ously. "Wasn't called the 'Eighth Wonder of the World'
for nothing."

Then she asked if they wanted dessert, which they
did not, and she left the check.

"Well," said the woman, "I guess we have a desti-
nation. What little help that is."

"The question is, do we go?" Lannes dropped several twenties on the table to cover the bill. "My brother
offered you a safe place to stay until we understand
what's happening."

"A hidey-hole, you mean."

"Something like that."

"Wouldn't do any good, would it? That . . . thing . . .
that comes into my mind can find me anywhere. It
might even be listening to us now."

Lannes frowned, rubbing lines through the condensation on his glass. "I could try to check. Get a sense of just how . . . compromised you are."

He made her sound like a nuclear weapon. "You can do that?"

"I can," he said quietly. "I'll have to touch you."

She felt the weight of his conflict as well as her own. "I don't know if I'm comfortable with that. Doesn't it bother you?"

"It's complicated."

"I don't know what that means."

"It means . . ." Lannes stopped, sighing. "It doesn't matter what it means. It needs to be done."

Yes, she thought, and then leaned back, marveling at the fact that she felt nothing but acceptance for what should have been considered a truly odd conversation.

"What?" Lannes asked suspiciously.

She shook her head, grasping for words. "I can't believe I'm listening to this as though it's normal. I keep telling myself I'm crazy, but I'm not, am I? The world is just . . ."

"Strange," Lannes finished. "Infinitely strange."

"Yes," she replied. "I don't even know what *you* are."

He hesitated, apprehension rocking through his eyes. She took pity on him and said, "Tell your brother thank you, but no. I won't run. I won't hide."

"Okay," he said, so easily, with such acceptance, she was unsure whether to laugh or cry.

"You don't have to come with me," she said. "It's not your fight. No reason for you to risk your life."

"It's my life," he told her, leaning in. "And you need me. You need a friend. Don't pretend otherwise."

"How could I?" she muttered. "Jesus. Who am I?"

"It doesn't matter," he said quietly. "No matter what you call yourself, no matter who you were, you are brave and strong. And you'll always be that woman to me."

She stared. Lannes looked like he wanted to say more, but he glanced away and carefully pulled out his keys. He pushed the shoe box back to her. "Come on," he said gently, with what she imagined was pain his eyes. "Time to run."

Run, whispered her heart. *Run*.

She managed to hold it together long enough for them to get outside. It was cold, but the crisp air felt good in her lungs and calmed her stomach. She had no coat, so she stood close to Lannes while he unlocked her door. Though she breathed deep of the night air, she was grateful for his warmth.

Just as he was about to turn from her to walk around the car, she grabbed his arm. Her hand sank through the illusion of cloth and touched warm skin. He went very still even when she moved close, craving with all her heart for some small comfort to ease the loneliness crawling through her soul.

She pressed her cheek against his arm. Less than a hug, more than a caress. It felt so good, touching him that way. It was like medicine for her aching heart.

"Lannes," she whispered.

"Yes," he breathed, big and solid as a mountain.

"You're right that I need a name," she said. "Call me Lethe."

"Lethe." Her name sounded like an echo from a fairy tale when he said it, and when she closed her eyes, she could imagine them in a dark wood instead of a parking lot, and beyond them, the wind and the stars, and the wolves closing in.

And in the heart of the wood, a mysterious creature, a man or monster, protector and fighter.

And lonely. So lonely, she thought, instinctively. Living a life of masks, never able to be yourself. Always afraid of discovery. This was something she was beginning to understand.

His hand closed around her arm, and for a moment she felt as though his mind—his heart—was open to her, and it felt like a gaping wound, torn and perilous and anguished. But he did not say a word, and a moment later pulled away. She kept her head down, the loss of his heat a painful thing, and slipped into the car. As he walked around to the other side, she glanced out the window.

She saw a crow watching them. It was perched on the roof of a truck parked beside the Impala. She imagined a flash of gold in its eyes, and then the bird flapped its wings and flew away into the shadows.

It felt like an omen. Of what, she did not know.

Lannes got in and started the Impala's engine. "Ready?"

"Run," she murmured, and closed her eyes.

CHAPTER TWELVE

It was 1950, and Lannes was twenty years old the first time he left the island in Maine. It had been under cover of darkness, in the back of an old car, rattling down a dirt road on a moonless night with Frederick at the wheel. His friend hardly knew how to drive, and he certainly was not supposed to be using his father's car for joyriding through the wild back roads of Maine, but Lannes had been stir-crazy and wanted to see things.

What he had found was a small town filled with golden lights, and men and women walking down narrow streets, together and apart. He had heard laughter and listened to jingles on the radios playing through open windows, and after Frederick ran into an ice cream shop for cones, the two of them sat together eating chocolate and vanilla, dreaming of the places they would go when they were older.

Only, Frederick had gotten older faster than Lannes, and had gone away to college. Lannes had remained behind, learning from books special-ordered and delivered to the island, devouring pictures and words, dreaming big. Working hard to cast his illusions so that he could hide and pretend to be one of the many.

Which he did, eventually. But by then things had changed again. Frederick had a life—a new girlfriend, a career as a writer, human friends he enjoyed spending time with. A hard realization for Lannes, but not a bitter one. Wistful, maybe.

And though he knew his brothers would go with him, Lannes had decided to travel alone. On the island he had never been alone, except with his kind. He had wanted something different.

Something different. That seemed so innocent now. Seventy years of his life, always dreaming big, and the witch had stolen that desire to do more, be more. Had bent it, almost broken it. Had made him afraid to venture beyond rock and ocean and old trees.

Only Frederick had been able to pull him away.

And now this woman.

He could hardly believe himself. Throwing his heart, his life, to the wolves—lost in a journey not his own. Nor could he be certain of his own motives, though he knew one thing for certain: even if the woman had no clue what he was, even if she had not shown one iota of care for him, he would still be helping her.

That she *did* have some inkling and had not run— indeed, she had suggested the almost inconceivable possibility that she liked him as something more than a resource—was more than he dared contemplate.

Lannes thought, perhaps, he would rather face the witch again than the risk that he might be wrong.

You are a pathetic bastard. But he glanced sideways

at the woman and felt her resting in his mind, a warm presence, and he considered that there were worse things than being desperately and distractedly wretched.

He drove for more than two hours. The urge to keep moving was overwhelming, as was his need to go south. He had felt that way since leaving Orwell Price's home—as though there were lines hooked into his spirit, drawing him in. His kind was sensitive to energy in all its forms. But the ability to sense it was not usually accompanied by compulsion.

The fact that this was a compulsion complemented by the words of a dying old woman was of great concern to him.

More than twenty minutes south of Indianapolis, in a town called Martinsville, he found a Wal-Mart. The parking lot was huge, and he pulled into a distant corner, tucked away from the bright lights. It was very dark out. His companion was asleep, but as soon as the radio turned off—Eric Clapton was interrupted in the middle of a slow riff—she opened her eyes and sucked in a long breath that was mostly a yawn. She squinted at him, rubbing her eyes, and looked so young and fragile that it was hard for him to believe the danger she posed, both to herself and others.

Lethe, he thought.

"Why are we stopped?" she asked blearily.

Lannes swallowed hard, his hands still tight on the wheel. "I thought this would be a good place to . . . do what we discussed. Checking your mind."

"Oh," she said. "Of course."

"I don't think we should wait," he said. "Just in case."

"I know." Her mouth tightened into a faint frown. "I don't like this. I don't have much left that's private."

"And the mind is the last sanctuary," Lannes murmured, thinking of his father's stern lessons in ethics and propriety. "I'm so sorry you've had to endure such violations."

She frowned. "You're not including yourself as one of the perpetrators, are you?"

"Is that how you feel about me?"

"No," she said. "I just don't like you reading my mind."

I can't help what I hear, he wanted to tell her. *But even if I could, I wouldn't change a thing.*

Not now. Not after what he had felt from her in that bathroom: her hunger for him, her desire. It was staggering, arousing, and the most shocking reaction to *him* that he had *never* imagined. Only a lifetime of ingrained habits—his own damned fear—had kept him from doing more, filling his palms with her curves, tasting her mouth and her hot, wet, scent.

Remembering was nothing but misery. Lannes was still hard. He had no idea what it was like for human men—that was one topic he and Frederick had managed to avoid—but once aroused, it was incredibly difficult for a gargoyle to defuse the situation. Touching himself was an option, but he hadn't exactly been swimming in time or opportunities to be alone. Not to mention, there was a chemical imbalance that would ensue.

"I'm sorry," he said again, lamely. "If it makes you

feel better, I can't sit here and listen to your thoughts. Only touch allows me to go deeper."

"So all those other times you touched me—"

"No," Lannes cut her off. "I didn't touch you because of that."

I touched you because I care about you. Because I want to protect you. Because I want to rip off your clothes and see you naked.

He was suddenly grateful for the illusion. Heat suffused his face, partially due to shame. Feeling awkward, he said, "I wasn't listening to you all that time. I promise you that much."

"Okay," she said softly, her gaze far too perceptive. "What do I do?"

He let out a breath he did not know he had been holding. "Just relax. Take my hands."

She started to, then stopped and scooted closer across the seat. Her scent was clean, faint with soap, and with her hair pushed back, it was easier to see more of her face. His heart started thudding faster. He could not believe he was doing this. She had already seen too much of him.

And what would I do? Strip those memories from her?

He held out his hands, and she placed her palms against his. His hands resembled baseball mitts in comparison—huge, brown and leathery. And that was just the illusion. Everything about her was incredibly delicate. Her wrists felt as fragile as silk. He was afraid of hurting her.

"Just relax," he whispered.

She smiled. "You first."

His wings twitched. Lannes tossed himself down the link.

It was different this time, now that she was aware of what he was doing. Her focus surrounded him, bearing down with startling awareness, as though he had the mental equivalent of an eyeball skimming every part of his presence inside her brain. The intensity of her perception surprised him.

You are naïve to assume anything about this woman, he thought to himself, and imagined a ripple as though she had heard him. Was that possible?

"Humor me," Lannes murmured. "Have you been manifesting any odd abilities, besides the . . . telekinesis?"

Her thoughts became tinged with incredulity. "Telekinesis?"

Yes, he spoke into her mind, testing her. She flinched, physically and mentally, and began to pull away from him. He tightened his hold on her hands, just slightly.

"I'm sorry," he said, opening his eyes. "I wanted to see if you could hear me."

Lethe said nothing, nor did she look at him. Her eyes were squeezed shut, lips compressed into a hard line.

I can hear you, she suddenly said, inside his mind. Faint, delicate, less than a whisper.

Lannes exhaled slowly. *Good. Now relax.*

She did not relax, but she did not fight him, either, as he slid deeper into her mind, skirting the edge of the chasm where her memories had lived. The edges of the injury were not as raw as they had been, but the cut was clean and final. There was nothing left.

"Oh," she whispered, and then, *I had no idea that was what it looked like.*

You were hurt deliberately, he told her grimly. *I need to go in. Stay here.*

"Lannes," she said out loud, but he did not listen. He jumped into the chasm.

It was more like floating in free fall than flying, a slow descent that reminded him of an old *Alice in Wonderland* cartoon, drifting down the rabbit hole past bits and pieces of an odd material world; except in the darkness, he found scraps of thought instead of alarm clocks and teacups. Recent memories. Of himself. Frederick. Etta and Orwell. As though coating the walls with ivy, new roots that would grow and flower. But they faded the deeper he fell, until the shadows swallowed him in a cocoon that was endless, suffocating.

It was too much like living in stone, frozen and dying in place. He and his brothers had been imprisoned, trapped as statues in the home of the witch, while Charlie—who had come to rescue them—had suffered in another cage, a sandy circle just within sight. Lannes would never forget. The witch had forced them to watch as she tortured his brother, cut him up for her stews. She killed him slowly, again and again, knowing he would resurrect.

It was something Charlie had encouraged, after a time—because it allowed his spirit to escape. He was the only one of them granted freedom, of a kind.

Lannes had been almost crazed with envy. Occasionally, he still was. His memories were almost as bad as the reality had been. So much that Lannes sometimes thought he would never have true freedom.

He felt a moment of envy that this woman—Lethe—had no memory. *He* wanted to forget. Not everything, but enough. Enough.

He went deeper. He sank into the abyss. His fear faded. And Lannes felt instead the woman's emotions. Her own terror was buried deep: a primal, sickening horror that coiled around him like a leech, latching onto his mind. And for one reason only. She was afraid of being found. He could feel it—a profound terror at the possibility of being discovered. By whom, he had no idea.

I don't know why, he heard her whisper, surprising him. He had not felt her follow him into the abyss.

Feels like the boogeyman, she added. *Whatever it is . . . it's something terrible.*

Something you were running from when you lost your memories? Lannes inquired gently. *Is it possible you did this to yourself, that you cut your own recollections away?*

It was a horrible thing to ask, and he would never have considered it before now, but the potential ability was there. Telepaths could inflict wounds on themselves, though it was rare and extremely difficult. Minds, human or otherwise, were embedded in layers of protection. Attacking them was like peeling back the skin of an onion. Which was why this hole, drilled straight through her memories, was so remarkable. And so grue-some.

Lethe denied nothing outright. Until finally, she said, *I don't know. But if I did, then I don't want to remember.*

He did not blame her. It was difficult untangling himself from the grasping roots of terror flooding her deep unconscious, but he sensed the presence of the woman bound close to his side like a warm shadow, and it helped center him. Together, as minds alone, they were not so different; he could almost forget the disparity of the flesh.

No more masks, whispered the woman. *Not after this.*

You don't understand, he told her.

I know you're afraid. We both are. Just of different things.

She was calmer than he. Lannes could not under-stand that.

Neither can I, she replied. *But I must have known what I was before I lost my memories. And down here, wherever "here" is, I feel closer to myself.*

Lethe, he said, tasting her new name. *Do you re-member anything?*

No, she murmured, *but I feel something strange.*

A moment later, so did Lannes. Just out of reach. Hard, like a small pearl. Another mind.

No, he realized, a moment later. It was a *doorway* to another mind. An anchor.

Fear spiked through the woman, but she stayed with him as they drifted through the spiritual abyss, hover-ing close to the anchor glistening tiny and round in the shadows. Lannes touched it, tentative, but nothing stirred, and though he sensed a slight hum of energy, it was not anything immediately dangerous.

Feels dormant, he said quietly, surrounding the anchor, searching out its roots. *But she can enter you at any time. It's a hook. All barbs beneath.*

Can you get rid of it?

No. Not without the other side letting go. Or dying.

Lethe drifted from him. *Let's go, then. Before she wakes.*

But Lannes hesitated, still listening to the pulse of the anchor, feeling its energy fill him. Tasting it. Catching the hum against his mind where he sank into its mental footprint. He wanted to know whom, or what, they were dealing with.

But all he felt of the spirit behind the anchor was something wilder than the heart of a raging river, chaotic, unstoppable—and in the next moment as still and flimsy as a rag doll. There were two sides to the creature, so very opposite that they hardly seemed to belong to the same individual.

Lannes wanted to stay longer, but Lethe drifted farther away, floating up the walls of the abyss, the chasm of her lost memories. He watched her, and she was a mote of light, like a fairy surrounded by moonglow and wisps of stars. He followed, aware of every shifting nuance in her heart, hungry for her luminosity.

He started up, passed the memories residing close to the mouth of the abyss until he and Lethe were free, perched at the top of her mind. Then, not even that. Lannes returned to his own body, and the divorce between his mind and hers hit him so hard that he doubled over fighting for breath. He felt hands slide against his healing chest, small and warm, and he struggled to sit up. Instead, a slender sweet-smelling body followed those hands, the woman slumping against him, also shuddering.

Lannes could not help himself; he touched her waist, loneliness roaring through him with such force that his heart felt as though it would stop dead. He closed his eyes, afraid to move, breathless when her hands slid over his shoulders, grazed his wings. Heat pulsed through him.

Desire. Such longing, such desperate need—he was suddenly afraid of himself.

Her breath stirred warm against his neck, and his jaw tightened so painfully that his teeth ached. Among other things.

"You were in my mind," she whispered, incredulous. "I can still feel you. Like an echo."

He fought for his voice. "I'm sorry if it was intrusive."

Lethe leaned back to peer into his eyes, solemn and unafraid. "It was illuminating," she said, but before he could worry himself sick over what *that* meant, she added, "How . . . how would something like that anchor . . . get into a person's brain?"

"It takes permission," Lannes said, thinking of the witch. "The mind has to accept things. It has to say yes."

"You have to give in, you mean. Even just a little?"

Lannes hesitated, and the woman bowed her head.

He touched the back of her neck, holding his breath as he drew her closer. She did not resist, burying her face against his chest.

"So," she said quietly, "I did this to myself."

He held the woman tighter, keenly aware of his strength, his size—feeling like a giant, a monster in comparison. "She could have caught you at a bad moment. Or . . . forced you. Tortured your mind and body. If that happened, losing yourself might have sounded like the more pleasant alternative."

She went very still. "Is that what happened to you?"

His skin crawled, and though being in the car had never bothered him before, he suddenly needed air. Lannes fumbled for the door. Lethe caught his arm, her hands small against him. He froze, her body pressed close.

"I'm sorry," she said.

"Don't be," he told her roughly. "It's been years."

Her tension did not ease. "The claustrophobia. It's because of what you went through."

"I couldn't move," he whispered, trapped by her eyes, unable to share anything but the truth. His heart was aching with such furious pain, he had trouble breathing.

Lannes sucked in a deep breath and shoved open the door, tumbling outside onto the pavement. He sat on the concrete for a moment, feeling pathetic but too glad to be out of the car to care. Cold night air swept over him, soothed his flushed skin. His healing wounds protested, but he ignored the pain.

Behind him, Lethe crawled from the passenger to the driver's seat and out the door beside him. She also sat on the concrete, cross-legged, staring at her hands. He had good night vision, and with the faint light cast by one of the towering security lights, he could see every line of her face and feel every nuance of her heart inside his mind.

Her breath puffed out white, and she slumped in front of him, looking very small and alone. But strong. He felt her strength radiating like sunlight, warm and true. It made him feel stronger. He had to be strong—for her.

"It was my fault," he said quietly, hearing cars on the highway, listening to the first morning warble of birdsong. The sky was growing lighter in the east, just a blush. "I was careless."

She did not ask for details. Lannes sighed, unbuckling his wings—forcing himself to do so in front of the woman no matter how much a part of him resisted. He let the belt rest in his lap, his wings stretching painfully, invisible as the air. She bit her bottom lip, then held out her hand. It took him a moment to understand what she wanted.

He gave her the belt. She hefted it in her hands then looked at him and at the area just behind his shoulder.

"Does it hurt?" she asked, which was not the question he expected.

"To bind them? Yes. But it's better than accidentally bumping into someone who wouldn't understand the discrepancy between sight and touch. Who wouldn't *appreciate* that discrepancy."

Lethe sat back for a moment, staring, then turned to scan the parking lot behind them. It was mostly empty, and they were far from the store. She started to stand, and he said, "Are you cold?"—but a moment later she was on her knees in front of him, and he lost his voice as she raised her hand, ever so tentatively.

"May I?" she asked, holding his gaze. He nodded, unable to speak, and she reached very carefully behind his shoulder. Her fingers grazed bone and skin, the hard thumb of his wing. He knew her intentions were innocent, born only of curiosity, but heat flowed through his body in slow aching waves, and the pleasure was so good, it was all he could do not to make a sound. He rested his head against the Impala door, trying desperately to control himself, when all he wanted— all he needed—was to take her in his arms, if only for a moment. Just one.

So he did just that.

Lannes ignored her gasp as he wrapped his arms around her waist, his hands sliding up her lean back, drawing her in. He held her as tightly as he dared, her body pressed against his own, and though he was mindful of his strength, he did not hold back. He was not shy. His blood was too hot for that, his need too great. And her body felt too good. Just holding her—as little a thing as that—was better than anything he could have imagined.

Then rational thought crept in, as did heartache. Lannes closed his eyes, bowing over her body, pressing his cheek against hers. He savored the stir of her breath, the sound of her heartbeat. Until, though he felt as though it would break him, he let her go.

Or rather, he tried to. Lethe did not move. She sat

very still in his lap, her emotions fluttering through their link like the wings of some desperate hungry butterfly.

"I lied to you," she whispered. "Back at the motel, when I asked for your help with my shoulder. I didn't need your opinion. I knew nothing was broken. I just . . . didn't want to be alone." She shut her eyes, trembling in his arms. "That's horrible, right? A person should be strong enough to be alone, but it terrifies me. My head is empty. I'm afraid it'll happen again. But when you're around I can pretend I'm safe, like I have an anchor. So that if I lose my mind . . ."

She did not finish. She did not need to. Lannes smoothed back her tangled hair and murmured, "So that even if you lose your mind, you'll still have a friend. You'll have someone who remembers you as you were. For a brief time, anyway."

Despair twisted down their link, across her face. "I shouldn't put that burden on you. I shouldn't even trust you with it. I shouldn't trust anyone."

Lannes held her away from him, forcing her to look into his eyes. "You think I feel differently? Do you know what would happen to my kind if I made a mistake—with you, with any other? Can you *imagine*?"

I don't want to, she whispered in his mind; deliberately or not, he couldn't tell—nor did it matter. He suddenly felt as though he had spent his entire life looking through windows, envying the closeness others seemed to have, and now, suddenly, he was his own window, with a life that someone else, gazing in, could envy.

But he hardly trusted it. No matter how much he

wanted. Not even though her body was snug in his lap, her curves soft under his hands, her mouth right in front of him, soft and open—and those eyes, her eyes, which were a mirror of her mind . . .

Stick with your own kind, he remembered his father saying. *Your fascination with humans is unhealthy. You can love them, but you cannot be with them.*

"Because it's dangerous?" asked the woman suddenly, and then blushed a bright red. "I'm sorry. I didn't mean to hear your thoughts."

"Touché," he said unsteadily, fighting the urge to push her away from him—which made him an insufferable hypocrite. "And yes, because it's unsafe. I suppose, too, because there are so few of us left. Survival of the species."

She was still flushed red, and refused to look him in the eye. But he felt her mind again, the hum of their link, and remembered how little flesh had seemed to matter when it was only their thoughts binding them. Floating in the abyss, together.

And with that thought came another, unbidden, an image in his mind of them entwined, naked, his body buried inside hers, thrusting hard.

It was an overpowering thought, visceral and hungry, and when the woman—Lethe—let out a muffled gasp, he realized with shame and horror that he had dragged her several inches closer, and that she was sitting snug and tight against the erection straining beneath his jeans.

But when he let go of her, she did not move. When

he tried to push her away, her arms flew around his neck and she held on.

And moved, slightly.

The pleasure was so intense he almost lost his mind. She did it again, and he realized with shock that it was on purpose.

I'm an idiot, she whispered, on the outskirts of his mind. *This is so dumb.*

Incredibly dumb, he told her, hardly able to think straight. *But don't stop.*

She burst out laughing, which was a delight, and not just because it made her jiggle against his aching groin. Lannes had never heard her laugh. He supposed she'd had no reason to, but it was beautiful. And short-lived. Her smile died into something small and sober, but though a trace of pain entered her gaze, he found warmth, too. Unaccountable, unfamiliar.

As though she liked him. *Him.* And not just because of the illusion. This woman had seen more of him than any other, protected him when he was vulnerable, taken care of him when she had no reason to. Accepted him without fear. For now.

Lethe held his gaze and moved again, grinding her hips against him. Her own pleasure rocked down their link, melding with his—and, feeling like a fool or some stripling hardly out of his first wing-growth, he cupped her breast in his hand.

They were sitting in the dark parking lot of Wal-Mart, totally exposed for the world to see, if anyone should glance in their direction, and he did not care. Neither did she, if her reaction was any indication.

She closed her eyes, breathing raggedly. Her nipple was hard through the sweater. No bra, which he found unbearably sexy.

He felt like he should warn her. Give her another chance to push him away.

"I'm not human," he said, which was the first thing that came to mind, and felt about as awkward and dumb as his overwhelming desire to unzip his pants.

"Whatever," she breathed dismissively, and then gasped as his thumb flecked her nipple, hard. "Oh . . . oh, do that again."

Make me forget, she said inside his mind. Which seemed to him the last thing she should want, though he understood.

Forget just a little, for a brief time. Forget the pain, the blood, the fear. Be here. Now.

Make a new memory. Something to fill the abyss.

But he never got the chance. An engine rumbled, ominous and loud. Lannes and the woman stiffened, and a moment later she began scrabbling off his lap. But in midmovement she leaned in close and her lips brushed his cheek.

At first he thought it was an accident—he could hardly believe otherwise, despite the intimacy of the last few moments—but he caught her gaze for one split second, and there was something in her eyes that shot through him like those bullets that had been flying so freely. She really did like him. Holy crap.

He stood beside her, placing his hand under her elbow as she swayed on her feet. A truck faced them, parked more than fifty feet away: a Toyota Tundra, huge with muscle. As soon as they looked at it, high beams switched on.

Fear spiked down their mental link. Lannes muttered, "How fast can you get in the car?"

"Faster than you," she said, under her breath.

Lannes' cell phone rang. Both he and Lethe flinched. He did not want to answer, but the ring tone belonged to his brother. And those headlights continued to burn, blinding him.

"Get in the car," he said. "Slowly."

Lethe did, sliding in on the driver's side and crawling into the passenger seat. Lannes got in after her, his gaze never leaving the truck. He gave his cell phone to Lethe and started the engine.

A new roar filled the air outside the Impala. The truck was revving its engine—and suddenly it accelerated toward them.

Lannes swore, slamming the car into reverse. He hit the accelerator, and the Impala lurched backward, tires squealing. His door was still open, but when he spun the Impala around, it slammed shut, right on the tip of his wing. He snarled. Beside him, Lethe was speaking frantically into the phone, fighting to get her seat belt on.

The truck scraped the rear bumper, but Lannes switched gears and slammed again on the accelerator. Lethe, one arm hooked through her seat belt, flew forward against the dash. Lannes flung his arm in front of her at the last moment and stopped her momentum.

The Impala roared across the parking lot, the truck close behind. He and Lethe should have had a substantial lead, but the other vehicle was surprisingly fast, and Lannes cut across a grassy zone, rocketing onto the four-lane highway that doubled as a city street for the town. Headlights flashed, brakes squealed, but no one got hit, and Lannes wrestled the Impala into the appropriate lane, gunning the engine.

The truck was still behind him, high beams reflected in the rearview mirror. He glanced sideways. "You okay?"

"Fine," Lethe snapped, one foot braced on the dash. "Your brother said help is close."

"Sure," Lannes muttered, seeing a red light ahead. "Hang on."

Lethe suddenly strained backward into her seat as Lannes punched down on the accelerator, hammering on his horn. Cars were turning at the intersection, but Lannes swerved around them by a hairbreadth. The truck had to slow—but not enough to put a sizeable distance between them.

Up ahead, there was more traffic on the road. Lannes swung onto the shoulder, still leaning on his horn, his left tires churning up grass as he accelerated past a long line of cars making steady progress in the lane beside him. Cars honked, swerving to get out of his way. Lethe ducked down, so low in her seat he could hardly see her. The truck gained. There was no way to see the driver, but Lannes assumed he or she was armed. If nothing else, the truck itself was a weapon. And at these speeds, one good blow on his bumper or side might spin him out of control. His *own* driving might do that.

The road emptied out just enough for him to swing off the shoulder and into the left lane. Beside him, Lethe said, "This can't go on forever. Someone's going to get hurt."

Lannes gritted his teeth, searching for a place to turn off the highway. He saw nothing. The truck roared up, rode his bumper, then swerved into the next lane, trying to creep up against their side. Engines snarled. The speedometer ticked close to one hundred miles per hour, and up ahead appeared taillights. More traffic.

"Lannes," hissed Lethe, glancing over her shoulder. He pushed the car a little more, outpacing the truck . . . but then it slammed into the corner of his bumper, nearly sending them out of control. Only brute force kept the Impala on the road. Lannes reached out, searching for the mind of the truck driver, trying to get a sense of who was chasing them. All he got was a barrier. A wall.

"He's going to try again," Lethe called out, her voice sharp with fear.

Lannes accelerated and wrenched the wheel to the left, cutting the truck off. He saw, in his rearview mirror, another car bearing down on them. A large dark mass. A Humvee.

The truck pulled behind him again, blocking out the sight. Ahead, more traffic. Lannes got ready to escape onto the shoulder again.

Until quite suddenly, he heard the screech of metal, and the truck lurched hard, swerving. Lannes glimpsed the Humvee, and braked just as the truck spun past him onto the heavily forested median, skimming so close it

ripped off the Impala's side mirror. The Humvee, show-
ing far more control, roared after the out-of-control
truck. As it passed, Lannes looked through the window
and saw a man staring down at him, face chiseled and
hard. Golden eyes flashed.

The truck crashed sideways against some trees.
Lannes was long past, but he braked hard, yanking left
on the wheel. Lethe let out a small yelp as the Impala's
tires squealed, and then suddenly they were spinning
off onto the median, making a tight circle. They stopped
on the median, facing the opposite direction of traffic.
In front of them was the Humvee. The truck lay on its
side against the trees. Other cars on the freeway were
slowing. People were pulling over. There was no time.

Lannes drove across the bumpy grass and watched
as two men leapt out of the Humvee. One of them, the
man who had matched his gaze, wore scrappy jeans
and an unbuttoned denim shirt that revealed a great
tangle of tattoos across his chest. He had a lean, tanned
face. Wild black hair. Golden eyes.

Golden, inhuman eyes.

The other man was also not human, but in some
indefinable way that made Lannes' skin crawl. *Danger*, he thought, looking at him. Impossibly dangerous. The man wore all black, and his skin was a light
brown color. Sharp green eyes glanced over at Lethe
as she exited the Impala. Lannes, instantly protective,
followed her. Two long steps around the hood of the
car, and he was at her side.

"Koni," the green-eyed man snapped, never taking
his gaze off Lethe. "Keep those gawkers back."

"Bossy," muttered the other man, but he ran gracefully across the median, shouting warnings at the gathered gawkers. His arms were like wings, Lannes thought, looking at him. Graceful, lean and strong. *Shape-shifter.*

Lannes ran to the truck, Lethe behind him. The green-eyed man was already there, face twisted with disgust. He climbed gracefully from the bumper onto the side of the vehicle, and Lannes joined him with one good leap—wings flaring slightly to keep him from landing hard on what could not possibly be solid footing.

The green-eyed man tried the driver's door, but it was locked. Lannes reached down, his fingers punching holes into the metal. Stealing energy from his surroundings, his chest hot, he yanked up with all his strength. Metal groaned. So did Lannes, but the door finally ripped off its hinges. He did not dare to look around to see if anyone had noticed. His only consolation was that it was still somewhat dark, though that was changing.

A middle-aged woman lay inside the car, slumped sideways against her seat belt. She had curly hair, and wore a loose flannel shirt. Glasses hung askew off her ear. Lannes saw no weapons. She was conscious, barely. Fury warred with caution, but he jammed his hand into the truck and grabbed her arm. He tried to punch into her mind—and slammed up against the old hateful wall.

The injured driver smiled, blood flecking her lips. "Well, I'll be damned. A real monster."

Her voice was rough, stilted, as though she was un-

used to talking. Lannes tightened his grip, listening
against the barrier in her mind. It reminded him of the
one that surrounded Lethe's thoughts when the intruder
awakened—only this was cruder. Given enough time,
he could exploit the chinks in this wall.

"Simon, I presume," said Lannes, remembering what
Etta had said.

"Not quite in the flesh," the woman—or at least her
controller—wheezed. "Where's the girl?"

"Down here," called Lethe dryly from outside the
truck, and held up her hands. Lannes grabbed them
with just one of his, and pulled her up beside him.
The green-eyed man, still perched on the other side
of the open driver's door, gave Lethe a long, thoughtful look.

The injured driver peered up at Lethe. "Hard girl to
kill. Those men in Chicago were supposed to be good.
I paid cash for their trigger fingers."

"Then you wasted your money," Lethe said. Lannes
felt a thread of horror winding down their link and
instinctively reached for her, mind to mind, bolstering
her strength with his. She glanced at him, startled, but
regained her composure in a heartbeat.

"Why are you trying to kill me?" she asked.

"It's not personal," said the woman, spitting blood.
"You're just a tool. But I won't die that way. I won't
go, crying into my bedpan."

Lannes heard sirens. The green-eyed man said,
"We gotta go now."

"Little girl," whispered the injured driver. "If you

kill the old hag first, I'll let you live. Find her. Strike her from your mind. We'll call it even."

"You'll do that anyway," Lannes rasped, but the injured woman laughed, an ugly sound that lasted only a moment before the barrier fell and Simon's presence fled. The driver in the truck lapsed into unconsciousness, though her heartbeat was strong.

The Humvee engine roared. The man named Koni stuck his head out its window, waving frantically. Lannes wanted to stay longer, examine the unconscious woman's mind for more traces of Simon, but there was no time. He jumped off the upended truck, reached up to grab Lethe around the waist and lift her down. The green-eyed man leapt gracefully from the truck and ran for the Humvee. Lannes did not watch him. He and Lethe raced up the median to the Impala.

By the time the police arrived, they were all long gone.

CHAPTER THIRTEEN

THERE are over five million miles of paved road in the United States, a black tangle weaving from east to west and all the directions of the wind in between, and Lethe was quite certain she was doomed to travel every inch of them. She was like some female Odysseus, condemned to wander—blood behind her, uncertainty in front, monsters lurking at every turn.

It was midmorning by the time they drove into West Baden. Dried cornfields lined the curving lane, filled with crows dancing on their wing tips. Golden light crested the tops of the trees. Lethe's eyes were gritty with exhaustion, but she was awake enough to appreciate the quiet beauty of the land.

She glanced at Lannes, who held himself rigid. His window was rolled all the way down to combat the smell of the dried blood soaked into the leather seats. Also, she thought, so that he could stay awake.

"You need to sleep," she said, examining the curve of

his shoulders, seeking out any indication of his wings. She saw nothing except a faint depression in the seat behind him, as well as a good inch of space between the leather and Lannes' back. She hesitated, then gently poked the air behind him. Her finger hit something solid. Lannes flinched.

"Sorry," she said, embarrassed. "Couldn't help my-self."

He grunted. "I suppose you should be curious."

"I suppose," she said dryly. "I have a lot of questions. What you are, exactly, is at the top of them."

"Gargoyle," he rumbled. "That's what my kind are called. Or Thunderbird. Mothman. Jersey Devil. Any legends involving humanoid types with wings are probably referring to my people."

"Huh." She leaned against the door, watching his human profile, which was craggy, weathered, and effort-lessly masculine. Same as his touch, which still made her shiver. Jesus. She could not imagine what he looked like beneath the mask, and wondered if she would feel the same way if he ended up having horns sticking out of his head, scaly skin, or teeth like a piranha.

"Has any of your kind ever been caught?" she asked him.

Lannes gave her a sidelong look that was distinctly uncomfortable. "Occasionally. In the late eighteen hun-dreds, some cowboys in Arizona managed to kill one of us. Staked him to the side of a barn and took pic-tures, for money. He had family, though. Some human friends. They managed to get his body away, and the photographs."

"I'm sorry," she said. "Have your . . . people been around for a long time?"

"A long time," he replied. "We were warriors once, and there was a battle between the creatures of this world. It resulted in a great cataclysm, and afterward we scattered and never fought again."

"But you hide. All of you."

"Some. Others have jobs, and families. We pay taxes. Most of our work can be done from home. Book-binding, writing, artisan-type skills." Lannes waved his very human-looking hand at her. "We hide in plain sight. And for those of us who can't wear a mask, human deformity can explain the rest. It's the twenty-first century. As long as you can pass, most people won't say a word. And if they do, it won't be to call you monster. Just ugly as hell."

She hesitated. "Is it lonely?"

"Sometimes," he admitted, and smiled. "Not now."

Lethe bit her bottom lip, trying not to return his smile, but it was impossible. Something about the warmth in his eyes, the kindness, made him irresistible.

Or maybe she was just desperately lonely. So lonely that anything—anyone—looked good.

That's a disservice to Lannes, she told herself. *He's better than that. So are you.*

Maybe. Or maybe it was better not to think too much about these things. She had a lifetime of memories to make. No doubt some of them—quite a few, at this rate—were going to be unpleasant.

Take the good while you can. Even if it turns out to be a mistake.

She was going to have a lot of those in her life, mistakes. Chances were good she had lost her mind over one.

"You travel much?" she asked Lannes, trying to make conversation—a distraction from her thoughts.

He shrugged. "Not anymore. But Frederick needed me for something."

She thought of the old man, so elegant and proper, and felt an odd affection that took her off guard. "How did you meet?"

"Our fathers knew each other. How *they* met . . ." Lannes hesitated. "It happened during the first World War. My father was in Germany helping to relocate some of our kind who had become trapped near the fighting. He came upon a child who seemed to have been abandoned. My father took care of him. Found a family in Scotland who was willing to take the boy. Alex Brimley. Frederick's father."

"Was Alex aware of your father's . . . differences?"

"He was when I knew him," Lannes replied. "No one ever explained how that happened. My brothers and I always took it for granted that we never had to hide from Alex or Frederick. Their wives were another matter."

He stifled a yawn, and Lethe said, "You really *do* need to rest."

"We're almost there," he replied grimly. "I'll rest then."

"If you get a chance."

He shot her a look that was so very human, she

wanted to reach out and touch his face to see if his mouth moved the same way beneath the illusion.

Lannes said, "I'm more worried about you."

I'll be fine, she almost said, but that would have been slightly ridiculous. She was not fine. But she was still standing. Still ready to fight. That was something.

She glanced over her shoulder at the Humvee. It was trailing them. Neither vehicle had stopped in the two hours since leaving the accident outside Martinsville. And thankfully, no cops had seen fit to haul either aside for questioning. She figured someone would, eventually. These were distinctive cars, and there had been a lot of witnesses.

It's not personal. You're just a tool.

Lethe closed her eyes, remembering those words, tasting them. Anger stirred. She felt Lannes glance at her—felt it even though she was not looking at him—and his concern flooded through her unbidden, warm and enveloping. Safe. Protected. Being around him felt the same as standing on a cliff edge but knowing she could fly.

He *can fly*, she guessed, trying to imagine such a thing. Not easy to do. There was still so much about him that he had hidden.

Except his heart. His conflicted, lonely heart. Mirror twin to her own.

At the intersection just before town, they passed a small used-car dealer. It was little more than a white square with some vehicles parked out front. Lannes turned left onto a road that curved past a lush tree line now burning with autumn. On the other side, to the right of the road, the land unexpectedly opened, revealing an immense green meadow covered with yet more trees. And just beyond that, surrounded by evergreens . . .

"Wow," said Lethe, staring. "I was totally not expecting that."

"That" being an immense dome. It was rather astonishing in size, with a red top that almost glowed in the morning light and four white turrets arranged in a half-moon design around the structure. Yellow walls and brick formed the base, which was mostly obscured by trees. It could have been a castle rising from the hills: an improbable sight, which should have been gaudy or bizarre, but instead was oddly enchanting.

"There's the entrance," she said, pointing to an arched gate on the right. Lannes pulled past, driving down a long cobblestone road. Workers were already out gardening, and some of them waved as Lannes drove past. The Humvee hugged the Impala's bumper.

Up close, the hotel was even more astonishing. Giant white columns framed an immense curving promenade lined in rocking chairs and the hanging boughs of old evergreens. The butter yellow of the bricks and walls glowed in the half shadows and sunlight of morning. On the left of the cobblestone drive was a wild garden filled with fountains and pavilions and paths that meandered into the trees, while in front of them, in the circle of the drive, was another stone fountain surrounded by flowers. Copper posts capped with the carved heads of horses lined a narrow walkway.

They parked on the far side of the hotel. The Humvee pulled in beside them. It was Etta's car, Lethe was certain of it. She sat still, suffering a moment's trepidation at having to face new strangers.

"I know how you feel," Lannes said.

She stared at him, startled. "Did you hear my thoughts that time?"

"No." He looked uncomfortable. "Just your emotions."

Knuckles rapped against her window and she flinched. A man stood on the other side of the door, dressed in a tight black shirt and black cargo pants. His skin was smooth and brown, and his green eyes were sharp with intelligence, much like the rest of his face, which resembled stone more than flesh.

A dangerous man, she thought, and opened her door, forcing him to step back—which he did, grudgingly. No shoes on his feet. She had noticed that last night, as well.

Behind him, leaning against the Humvee, was the tattooed man. Golden eyes glimmered, the sight of which stirred something deep inside her.

Koni, she remembered him being called. He stared at her with unnerving intensity, his mouth turned down in a frown.

"What?" she asked sharply. Her feet hurt, but her shoulder was better.

His golden eyes narrowed. "Nothing."

Lannes walked around the Impala to stand beside her. His craggy face looked grim, as did his eyes, and his invisible wings brushed against her arm like the whisper of a breeze. The belt he had bound them with was probably still in the parking lot of the Wal-Mart in Martinsville.

"Nice illusion," said the man in black, who then settled his gaze on Lethe. "You have a talent for making people dead."

"It's been a busy couple days," she replied coldly.

Lannes leaned forward, looming over the other man. "Are you here to help, or are we going to have a problem?"

"Rictor always has problems," said Koni, still leaning against the Humvee. "And I'm not much better. You're stuck with the assholes of the group, I'm afraid."

Lannes appeared less than pleased. "I suppose my brother filled you in?"

"Second-hand knowledge is shit," said the green-eyed man. *Rictor*, Lethe reminded herself. She found him familiar, and could not put her finger on why, which was maddening.

Rictor added, "We need to talk. Just us."

Just us. Lethe was obviously not included, a certainty that intensified when she glanced at Koni and found him staring at her dead on. Golden eyes. Suspicious eyes.

Trust, she thought. It always came down to trust. She had not trusted Lannes when she first met him, and now it was her turn to be on the receiving end of someone's suspicion.

Lannes brushed up against her arm, creating a link between them. *They have secrets to keep*, he whispered inside her mind. *All of us do.*

And I can rely on them? Lethe replied, falling easily into their mental connection. It had not surprised her as much as it should have; it was as though this was something she knew, like those random aberrant facts crowded in her brain. *Do* you *trust them?*

He never answered. Above their heads, a murder of crows swooped down from the trees, cawing raucously. Koni gave them a sharp look, and his eyes seemed to glow for the barest instant. Or maybe that was the sun, his irises catching that light. It sent shivers down her back, either way.

Lethe limped around the men and started strolling across the parking lot to the hotel entrance. A moment later, she heard three sets of footsteps behind her.

"Never mind following me," she called back, "since you obviously have things to discuss."

"Don't be ridiculous," Lannes muttered, easily catching up with her. She turned, hobbling backward to study Rictor and Koni openly.

"So," she said slowly, "you're . . . detectives."

"I suppose," Koni replied. "Though you could try not to say it like you're vomiting in your mouth."

"Why not?" Rictor muttered, glancing at the tree line with disgust. "This is humiliating."

Lannes and Lethe stopped walking. Koni gave the green-eyed man a dirty look, but the crows flying overhead began screaming again, and a similar expression of resigned dread passed over his tanned face. Lethe thought that the two men were very weird.

"Have you heard anything from Charlie about Etta

Bredow and her brother?" Lannes asked them. "How about this Simon?"

"Nothing," Rictor said, still staring at the trees.

Lethe frowned. "Are you an investigator or not?"

"Rictor is what he is," Koni replied, giving his companion another hard look. "I suppose that's true of all of us."

There was something in his tone, something in the way he suddenly looked at her, that made Lethe narrow her eyes. "Why do I get the sense that you know me?"

"I don't know," Koni said. "That would be impossible, wouldn't it?"

"I don't know," she replied, "seeing as how I can't remember a goddamn thing."

"Enough," Lannes rumbled, his gaze roving between the two men his brother had sent. "We're here to check things out. Let's stick with that plan."

Stick with a plan. Easier said than done. Especially as Lethe had no idea what she was looking for. She forced herself to take a deep breath, and the air smelled good and green, the cold wind on her face so sweet she wanted to close her eyes. It was good to be alive.

She noted Koni buttoning his denim shirt as they walked inside the hotel. All of them, except Lannes, appeared slightly rough and bedraggled. She certainly felt like something that had been dragged under a car, which was closer to the truth than she was entirely comfortable with.

Inside was another mystery of architecture: a passage from shadows and dark wood into a room that felt like it was made of air and light, a vast expanse echoing with every footstep and whisper. Above them, the dome. It was freestanding, floating, with nothing but arched and delicate steel girders holding everything in place. Immense glass panels allowed a cool radiance into the room that seemed to make everything, from people to furniture, appear impossibly delicate.

The walls rose six stories high and curved around the interior in a perfect circle lined by Grecian pillars. Dark windows filled the spaces in between, gazing inward like hundreds of dark eyes. A beautiful space—perhaps pretentious, certainly grand. Wild beyond any human purpose except, Lethe supposed, to prove that such a thing was possible.

She walked several steps away and swiped a brochure left on one of the chairs. She thumbed through it and shook her head. "Larger than the Pantheon and Saint Peter's Basilica in Rome. Built in 1902. Biggest freestanding dome in the world until 1965."

"So, why are we here?" Lannes murmured. Rictor and Koni stood behind him, scanning the small groups of people ranged across the massive atrium. Cameras flashed and some children laughed, chasing each other.

Children. Laughing.

Dizziness cut through Lethe, and for a moment her vision blurred, windows and people running together like pieces of a black web. At first she thought her eyes were dry, or that perhaps she was just tired, but she glanced at Lannes and he was clear as crystal—as were Rictor and Koni, though their skin seemed to shimmer.

Her neck ached. Her head felt heavy, tired.

This is where it began, whispered a voice inside her mind, and everything around her shifted as if a camera were panning sideways, fast. Lethe staggered . . . and the world changed. Like a snap.

She found herself alone beneath the heart of the dome, standing in the center of the cavernous room. Everyone was gone. Even Lannes. The air was dark. It must have been night. She turned, searching for anything familiar, but all she saw was empty floor and hundreds of black windows, which made her skin crawl. As though behind all that glass were eyes, staring.

Lethe heard uneasy laughter. Children. She tried to turn, but her feet refused to budge. Terror clawed up her throat. She felt a presence bearing down on her body, fat as a slug, and again the children squealed with delight.

They thought it was a game, whispered the voice. *They told my daughter it was a game, but it wasn't.*

The laughter of the children grew stronger, closer, and those dark windows shimmered as though made of water. She heard the slow shuffle of something immense directly behind her shoulder. Hot breath puffed against her neck, followed by the scent of blood, loose bowels.

The children began chanting—

—and Lethe woke up. She was stretched on a cold hard floor. It was day instead of night. Lannes crouched over her, holding her face between his hands. His eyes were impossibly grave. Nausea crawled up her throat, her nostrils still burning with that awful scent. Her ears rang. Lannes did not say a word.

"What happened?" she croaked, wiping the back of her hand across her mouth. Her throat hurt, her nose ran. Everything felt raw.

Lannes trailed his knuckle across her cheek. "You fell unconscious."

Lethe dragged in a deep breath. "How long?"

"Less than a minute."

Voices clamored, and she realized there was a crowd. The giant bulk of Lannes' body blocked much of it, and Rictor and Koni stood on her other side, imposing figures, keeping people back.

"Don't mind everyone," Lannes murmured, his hand smoothing back her hair, his touch so gentle that she hardly felt it. "You're okay now. You're fine."

She heard children laughing, but couldn't tell if it was real or an echo from the darkness. It was chilling either way. She tried to sit up, but Lannes scooped her into his arms. Faces passed in a blur, and then she was set down again, on a long couch.

"Incoming," Rictor murmured, somewhere on her right. She looked up and saw a very young woman in a dark suit running toward them. She carried a walkie-talkie, and her brown hair, pulled back into a sensible ponytail, bounced furiously.

"I'm fine," Lethe said before the woman reached her, and then louder, "I'm fine, really. Blood sugar. Happens sometimes."

The walkie-talkie crackled, and the woman frowned

with a concern that seemed genuine and very sweet. "Are you certain? We've already called an ambulance—"

"Cancel it," Lethe said firmly, lying so easily, with such conviction, she felt as though another part of her was suddenly a stranger, yet again. "Really. I should have snacked earlier."

The young woman hesitated. "Are you certain? This happened last time, ma'am."

Cold rushed down Lethe's spine. "Last time? I was here before?"

The woman frowned, confusion—or unease—filling her eyes. "A week ago, I think. You weren't a guest here. Just . . . passing through. I remember your face, because of what happened. You collapsed."

"Did she leave a name?" Lannes asked.

"No," replied the woman, glancing from him to Rictor and Koni. A faint flush rose in her cheeks. "You woke up and walked out before anyone could get a good look at you."

Koni flashed the hotel employee a surprisingly roguish grin. "Don't worry," he said with a conspiratorial shrug of his shoulder, "she's fine. Practically has to keep a candy bar in her mouth all the time, but hey. Not enough to call an ambulance on."

The woman smiled hesitantly, though she was polite enough to sober up when she looked again at Lethe. "If you're really fine . . ."

"I am," Lethe said.

The hotel employee nodded, concern still in her

eyes. "If you need anything, let us know. And . . . um . . . thank you for coming back to visit."

Lethe forced herself to smile. Koni slid in front of her and guided the slender young woman away, walking with her across the atrium. She never looked back. He had her entire attention.

"Well," Lannes said. Rictor grunted. Lethe wanted to put her head between her knees and practice breathing.

"I was here," she told the two men. "Oh, my God."

This is where it began, she heard inside her head, but it was only an echo. She grabbed Lannes' hand. "Did you feel her inside me? Is she still awake?"

Lannes' expression turned profoundly solemn. "I felt her. But she's quiet now."

Quiet now. No way to know how long that would last. Lethe felt as though she were living on borrowed time. Or that everything she was—what little had been left to her—would be swallowed by the creature living in the cave of her mind; like a dragon, jaws straining over her heart.

"She showed me something," Lethe told the two men. "It was night. I heard children laughing, and there was this . . . thing . . . behind me. Breathing down my neck. It was terrifying."

Rictor folded his arms over his chest. "Do you trust what you saw? Could it have been manipulated?"

"It felt real. But I'm no expert."

"Expert enough," he said, with a dark humor in his voice that again made her uneasy. Lannes gave the green-eyed man a hard frown, and for a moment Lethe's vision blurred again and his body wavered. She thought she saw wings folded against his back, hanging from him like a cloak.

Then, nothing. She rubbed her eyes and looked at him again. His features seemed craggier than before. Less perfect, but no less handsome.

Rictor said, "Are we staying here?"

"At least one night," Lannes said, and the other man walked away without a word, following Koni, who had only just reached the other side of the atrium, the hotel employee still at his side.

"This is where it began," Lethe whispered, terrified. "That's what she said."

"You weren't a guest," Lannes said thoughtfully. "I wonder why you were here?"

"Because I'm crazy," muttered Lethe, needing to hear those words, though saying them felt more like a force of habit than actual belief. She wondered if part of her would be more content as an insane person. At least that would be a reason for what was going on. A real reason. More real than mind control or men with wings. More real than murder and visions that terrified the heck out of her.

Lannes gave her a long steady look. "You're not crazy. You've been hurt. In impossible ways." He began to lean in, then stopped, jaw tight, something terrible moving through his eyes. "You scared me. I was afraid you weren't going to wake up."

She stopped breathing for a moment then centered herself, holding his gaze—allowing herself to sink deep into the roar of her aching heart. So deep, so hungry.

Her heart was hungry. And there were so many reasons not to trust that, no matter how much she wanted
to. Words slipped from her mouth; they were nonsensi-
cal, humiliating.

"I don't trust myself," she whispered, and knew
instantly he understood what she meant, because she
could see it in his eyes, which grew haunted and tense
and echoed the loneliness driving a knife through her.

"We're both vulnerable," he said quietly. "And here
we are, forced together. I don't trust myself, either."

Lethe reached for his large sinewy hand, which felt
strong and hard but curled ever so carefully around her
own. "I like this," she told him, staring at their joined
hands. "I don't know what you are underneath your
mask, but I like this. And I like you. That, I trust."

"You might not," he murmured. "You might change
your mind if you saw me as I am."

She shoved at his shoulder gently, but only because
she wanted to touch the warm skin she knew existed
beneath the illusion of his shirt. She remembered the
hard silk of his body against her hands, the shocking
desire she had felt when he dragged her into his lap.
Sitting on the ground in a Wal-Mart parking lot, and
there had been things she wanted to do in that moment that still taunted her.

"If you don't let me see," she told him, "neither of
us will ever know."

He pulled away. "It's not that easy."

No, she thought, considering her own situation. *I
suppose it isn't*.

They walked across the atrium. Her feet still hurt,

and she limped. Lannes took her hand, squeezing gently. Her soles tingled. She shouldn't have been startled, but she was, and had to stop walking as the skin of her feet began crawling, the muscles twitching. The pain eased, though, as did the other sensations of discomfort.

Lannes let out a slow breath, swaying slightly. Lethe touched his chest, but only briefly, afraid someone would notice how her fingertips faded into the illusion.

"You okay?" she asked.

"Fine," he said, but inside her mind she felt a pulse, slow and heavy, and she knew it was him.

"You're exhausted," she whispered, and even though he shook his head in disagreement, there was no hiding the shadows in his eyes. She had no idea how to help him, though. Other than a bed and quiet. Both of which had been in short supply since she had met him.

To her left, Lethe saw a crowd gathered. A tour group. An old man was giving them a lecture. They stood in front of a massive fireplace that must have been at least twenty feet wide and was certainly tall enough to stand in.

She stopped walking, staring at it. Lannes said, "What?"

"I don't know." But after a brief hesitation, she began a slow approach, studying the fireplace—studying herself as well, trying to understand why it bothered her so.

Because you were here before, she told herself. *Even if you don't remember.*

The fireplace was rather odd looking compared to the rest of the building interior, decorated in stone with a colorful mural that was almost clumsy, even tacky, compared to the rest of the atrium. It was disturbing, too, in ways that Lethe could not explain.

The mural's design should have been innocent: a depiction of a river and a tree heavy with wisteria or grapes, a green meadow just behind its branches. But in the far-right corner, perched on a rock, a little man had been painted. He was dressed entirely in red, with a long beard and small pointed cap. The tips of his ears were sharp, and he had a crazed look in his eyes.

"That's . . . weird," Lannes said.

"Yeah," Lethe agreed, grateful for a distraction. "Jesus."

A strange look passed over his face. "Looks like a . . . a . . ."

"Damn gnome," said a rough voice behind them. Rictor. Koni stood at his side, head tilted as he stared at the fireplace.

"A gnome," Lannes said heavily. "As in, from Argentina?"

"Argentina, my ass," Rictor replied. "They'll live anywhere you find bat caves. Dirty little bastards."

Lethe stared. "Um. Dare I ask?"

"No," Lannes and Koni said in unison, voices firm. They gave each other suspicious looks.

Which, of course, only piqued her curiosity more. But she did not ask. She happened to glance right—and found an old man staring at her.

He stood less than twenty feet away and was the

seeming leader of the tour group. He wore a badge, thick black glasses and a yellow polo shirt tucked into khakis. His white hair was thin and had been combed over. He was all skin and bone.

His querulous lecture had been part of the background, but he was silent now, and the people in the tour were glancing at each other and Lethe. One of them, much to her embarrassment, waved a hand over the old man's face. He blinked, but instead of looking at the owner of that hand, he lurched through the tour group and headed straight toward her.

Fear hit Lethe. Lannes grabbed her arm. Rictor and Koni slid in front of them, silent, graceful. Dangerous.

The old man hesitated when he saw the men, but he did not break into shouts or pull a gun or knife from under his shirt. Instead he stood, swaying, peering between the men at Lethe. His pale bleary eyes searched her face, and his wrinkled mouth trembled.

"My God," he whispered. "Runa."

Runa. Run? She felt her gut twist, and not in a good way.

"Do you know me?" Lethe asked, moving closer.

Maybe it was her voice that broke the spell. The old man suddenly blinked, leaning back. Disappointment filled his face, so bitter it seemed to snake through the air.

"No, of course not. You couldn't be her. I'm so sorry. I . . ." He stopped, disappointment becoming red-faced shame, even sorrow. "I got old-age disease."

He started to pull away. Lethe pushed between Rictor and Koni. Hands caught at her, but not before she grabbed the old man's arm. "Wait. Why couldn't I be the person you think I am?"

"Oh," he said, his voice heavy with grief. "She's dead."

CHAPTER FOURTEEN

THE old man called himself Ed. He had to finish his tour, so they waited for him outside on the promenade, which was deep and elegant and felt like an island among the evergreens.

Lannes leaned against one of the wide pillars, his hip neatly balanced on the wide banister. His wings draped over the side, invisible but caught in a breeze. It felt good, as did the sun on his back.

The other two men ranged around him. Koni also perched on the banister, with a light-boned grace that was effortless and dangerous. *Shape-shifter*, Lannes thought again. He did not know what animal called to this man's blood, but it hardly mattered. His brother had told him that Dirk & Steele had the "golden eyes" among its agents, but seeing was different than believing. And it had been thirty years since he had crossed paths with a true shape-shifter.

Rictor stood behind Lethe, who was the only one sitting, her body curled up tight in a wicker chair covered in thick cushions decorated with embroidered flowers. The entire veranda was filled with an assortment of outdoor seating. Lethe's eyes were closed, her long pale throat exposed. Merely looking at her was enough to make him feel aroused, but fortunately, it was an easier reaction to control with some distance between them. Lannes wished he could have been more cerebral about the matter.

He found Rictor glancing at him, though the man's eyes—and mind—gave away nothing of what he thought. He was closed up tight. The only thing Lannes could sense was that he was not human. Just how far past human? That was another matter entirely.

There are mysteries I have not dreamed, Frederick had once written, and it was true. Mysteries walking a world that had no room or heart for them.

You are one of those mysteries, Lannes thought at Lethe, wishing he knew what she was thinking. All he felt from her presence in his mind was quiet determination.

"So," Koni said, "that was awkward."

"Just a bit," replied Lethe, opening her eyes to glance up and down the empty porch. "Obviously, I'm not dead."

"Obviously," Lannes said. "But even Orwell seemed to recognize your face. Which means you resemble *someone*."

"I must be a goddamn twin," she muttered, rubbing her arms. "Did you see the way that man looked at me? Like I was a ghost."

A ghost Ed missed very much, if his initial reaction and subsequent disappointment were any indication.

But the whole situation made Lannes uneasy, and he stretched his wings, gazing down at the garden beneath him.

"Run," he said quietly. "Runa."

Lethe's face paled. "Could it have been a play on her name? Not telling me to run, but a fragment, a clue to the identity of the thing inside my head?"

"Maybe all of this is a coincidence. Might have nothing to do with you," Koni postulated. "Maybe you only *look* like someone."

"Someone who could be used to scare men and women like Orwell and Etta," Lannes added thoughtfully. "Because they committed a crime."

Lethe stared at her hands. "Murder."

Rictor stirred, arms folded over his chest, staring at the back of Lethe's head. His gaze was thoughtful, almost disturbingly so, but Lannes did not call him on it. He was afraid of what the green-eyed man would say.

Footsteps echoed. It was Ed. He walked quickly, with a slight stoop to his shoulders. He was still red-faced, his lips compressed in a hard line.

"I'm so sorry," he said when he was close enough to speak without shouting. "Truly, I didn't mean to embarrass you like that. But I saw you, and I just . . ."

"It's okay." Lethe patted the chair beside her. "I don't suppose you happened to see me around last week, did you?"

Ed looked startled. "I was on vacation. But if I had seen you, I suppose my reaction would have been much the same." He gave the other men an uneasy once-over. "All of you friends?"

"Family," Koni said. "Adopted."

"Coerced," Rictor muttered.

Lannes smiled to himself. Lethe shook her head, the corner of her mouth hooking wryly. "Ignore them, Ed. Tell us about Runa."

"You look like her," he said immediately. "My God, but you're a spitting image."

"Maybe I'm related."

Ed hesitated. "Would be hard to believe it. She had a daughter, Milly, but the little girl passed away around the same time as her mother. If there was other family, none of us in town ever knew it."

"When did she die?" Lannes asked.

"Oh, back in the 1930s." Ed smiled at his reaction. "I know. You were expecting something more recent."

"Well," Lethe said, and the old man tapped his skull.

"Photographic memory. I don't forget a thing. Got almost eighty years of living crammed into this head. I could tell you what I had for breakfast when I was six years old."

"That's practically inhuman," Rictor said.

Ed grinned with self-satisfaction. "Some superpower, huh?"

Koni chuckled. Lannes glanced at Lethe, and her smile made his heart swell inside his chest like an incendiary balloon.

Pop, he thought. *There goes my heart.*

"So," Lethe said, "she was a friend of yours?"

Ed laughed. "A friend to us all. She was one of the adults. Used to come here in the summers with her daughter. Good people. She made the best fudge and sugar cookies in the county. Had a soft touch." He glanced sideways, his smile fading just slightly. *"Amazing* how much you look like her."

Lethe stirred uneasily. "Do you remember her last name?"

Ed shook his head. "Never asked, never mentioned. She was just Runa."

"How did she die?"

Ed faltered, hands curling in his lap. "She was found here, on these grounds, by one of the Jesuits. The dome had been turned into a seminary by then because of the Depression. And she was just . . . out there one morning. Not a mark on her. No signs of foul play."

"Sounds foul to me," Lannes said. "Did they find who killed her?"

"That's just it. The police never ruled it a murder."

"That doesn't make sense," Lethe told him. "I assume she was still young. How did they think she died?"

"She had friends, and they were rich. They told the police to drop it, or so I heard. The police did. Never sat well with us kids, but you know kids." Ed smiled again, though it was bitter. "Big imaginations."

Lethe fingered her throat. "I'm sorry you lost her."

Ed searched her face with a quiet sadness that made Lannes hurt for the old man. "I'm sorry, too. She was nice to me, and not many were. So I took it real hard when she died. Looked for clues and everything."

"Did you find any?"

Ed hesitated, rubbing his hands together, then staring at his palms like he was going to read from them. "Just . . . odd things. Maybe not odd. But secretive. Runa was friends with several families that would come down here every summer. Real clannish. The kids stuck together and never talked much to us locals. Not too strange, I guess. Always been like that since the hotels went up. We had Capone down here, Franklin Roosevelt, even the Marx Brothers. All kinds. But those families *really* stuck together. Real quiet about it, too."

"You think they knew something about Runa's death?"

"I thought so, since they were the ones who hushed it up. But see, she died near the end of summer, and they were all gone not long after. The next year, most didn't come back. So the trail," he said, with a sad smile, "went cold."

"What about her daughter?" Lannes asked. "You said she passed away, too."

"Milly," said Ed. "Oh, she was cute. She disappeared, that's all. Up and gone. There was a search, but no one ever found a body."

"Some coincidence," Koni said.

Something cold entered Ed's gaze. "Like I said, big imagination."

Lethe rubbed her arms. "Do you know where they used to live?"

"Down where the lake is now. Patoka Lake, that is. Part of a reservoir that was built in the seventies, but the state had to steal from farms to do it. My daddy's was one of them. We had to move to town, and he went to work making golf balls. It wasted him."

Lannes bowed his head, fingers digging into the banister. "Ed. Do you remember the names of those other children?"

Ed smiled again, but it did not reach his eyes. "Bredow, they called themselves. Marcellus and Etta."

"Anyone named Simon?"

The old man went very still. "How do you know that name?"

Lannes wanted to kick himself. Koni, glancing at him, said, "We came down here because a friend of ours died and left some paperwork behind. Bragged about this area. One of the names was Simon. I might have even seen a Bredow in there, but I can't really remember."

Not smooth enough, Lannes thought. Ed still looked suspicious, his heart closing up a little towards them. As though bringing up that name had created an undesirable association.

"Simon," murmured the old man, a hard look entering his eyes. "Simon Says. Yeah, he played with those children. Most of them—all of us, I guess—were the same age. I almost put a rock to his head once. He hit Milly in the face. I saw it."

The admission surprised Lannes, as did the rage still simmering in the old man. Rictor said, "Why didn't you?"

"I don't know," replied Ed simply. "Probably saved me that I didn't. I might have killed him. But at the time, it wouldn't have bothered me. He had no call to hurt Milly. She was . . . sweet. And just a little younger than us big boys."

His face crumpled. "Anyway. I had the rock in my hand, ready to throw. And Simon, he sees me, and I just stopped. Like my body didn't belong to me. I dropped the rock and turned around. Walked home like nothing happened, and all the while I didn't know why. Strangest goddamn thing ever. If I was a suspicious man . . ."

"You'd think he was controlling you," Lethe finished quietly.

Ed frowned. "Young lady. Why do I get the feeling you know more than what you're saying?"

Lethe hesitated, and looked into his eyes with a sadness that would have melted stone. "Would it matter? Would it bother you if I was looking for answers?"

Ed's breath caught. He leaned back sharply, staring. "What are you saying?"

"I don't know," she said. "But I was lucky to meet you, Ed."

The old man looked stricken, and he reached out slowly to touch Lethe's cheek with the back of his gnarled hand. "The honor was mine," he said.

ED HAD ANOTHER TOUR SCHEDULED. HE MADE THEM promise to say good-bye before they checked out of the hotel.

"It's obvious," Koni said to Lethe. "You were cloned."

"Gee," she replied. "Thanks."

They were upstairs on the fourth floor, in a suite: two adjoining rooms separated by a parlor. The decor was muted and cool, with pale silver walls and white trim. Shopping bags littered the floor, clothes from the high-end guest shops downstairs. Lethe had nothing, but Lannes had a credit card—a good match as far as he was concerned, though her anxiety at not being able to pay her own way had followed them from downstairs to upstairs, and had abated only slightly.

Trays of food covered the tables. Lannes stood by the window. He had tried to open it, but short of ripping it off the sill, that was not possible. No more cool breezes. Just a view of the garden and a sliver of late-afternoon sunlight. The room felt rather small to him.

Koni was sprawled on a couch. Rictor, who never seemed to sit, stood by the door. Lethe was curled up in the chair closest to Lannes.

"Okay," she said to them, sipping from a cup of green tea. "Let's assume, for the sake of argument, that a murder was committed. Let's also assume the victim was Runa, and quite possibly her daughter."

"That's a big assumption," Koni said.

"Not really," she replied, a wave of uneasiness washing through her link. "Call it instinct."

The shape-shifter shrugged. "Fine. And the perpetrators?"

"Simon and his friends."

"Who could be any number of people," Lannes spoke up, glancing at the two other men. "We found a group photo, but that might only be the tip of the iceberg."

"Show it to Ed," Lethe suggested. "He'll give us names."

"Consider that secondary," Rictor rumbled. "Your

main focus should be on finding Simon, and locating the source of the thing inside *her*."

"And how do you propose to find a ghost?" Lethe asked him sharply. Koni, cleaning his teeth with a toothpick, started humming the *Ghostbusters* theme.

Rictor gave his companion a hard look. "Find where the crime occurred, and you'll find the spirit."

"You're making the wrong assumption," Lannes said. "The thing hooked into her mind isn't the murder victim. It's alive. It has to be. No ghost, no *spirit*, could have that kind of control over a person."

"You're sure of that?" Rictor asked, a hint of disdain in his voice.

"I'm sure," Lannes told him. "At least, I'm sure about this. I felt the anchor. We're not dealing with a dead person."

Lethe set down her tea. "I can't live like this."

Koni frowned. "Are you sure you don't remember anything about your prior life?"

It was an unnecessary question, and something in the way the shape-shifter asked it made Lannes uneasy, a feeling he had harbored off and on, watching the two men from Dirk & Steele interact with Lethe. They were friendly enough sometimes, but he also sensed a tension he didn't think had anything to do with the fact that she was a stranger. Something else was going on.

Lethe sat up, stared at Koni. "Say what you mean. You think I might be faking the amnesia."

"I think you might be exaggerating it," he replied, with brutal honesty. "Because you need help."

"Stop," Lannes said.

"So you can ignore the coincidence of her stumbling on someone like you? With your history? Your . . . *background*?" Koni shook his head. "No, man. Don't be that dumb."

Lannes pushed away from the window. "I won't tell you again."

Koni narrowed his eyes. Rictor shrugged and said, "You can't blame him."

"Lethe," Lannes said, deadly quiet. "Now would be a good time to take that shower you were talking about."

"I never talked about a shower," she said. But she got up, sweeping shopping bags into her hand, and stared at Rictor and Koni. Spine straight, eyes hard. Anger and hurt were pulsing down the link with Lannes.

"I don't know who I was before," she said coldly, "but I'm no liar now. Don't *ever* accuse me of being one again. Especially when it comes to Lannes."

She left the parlor for the second bedroom. The door closed softly behind her. No one spoke. Not one word. Not for five long minutes, until Lannes heard the shower start.

Rictor stepped away from the wall and walked into the other bedroom. Koni followed. Lannes, after a moment, joined them. He shut the door, his wings folded tight, his heart settling into a dark, cold place.

Koni and Rictor stood before him, impassive, eyes glittering.

"My brother trusts the both of you," Lannes said.

"Otherwise, he wouldn't have sent you to help. So, that means something to me."

"But not enough to stop you from throwing me out a window, is that it?" Koni's eyes flashed, his mouth curling as a line of feathers erupted along the back of his hand. "Maybe you should try."

Rictor shook his head. "What do you know about the woman?"

I know her heart, Lannes wanted to say, but that would have been unforgivably sentimental. "I've been inside her mind. I've seen what was done . . . and it was nothing less than brutal. She can function, yes. But everything pertaining to her life was stolen."

"You're certain?" Rictor asked.

Lannes forced himself not to throw a chair at the green-eyed man's head. "If you know my brother, then you know what happened to me. If I had *any* doubts, I would not have risked my secrets with her. Not mine, not my brothers'."

"And her memories? Will they return?"

"The damage is irreversible. Everything she was is gone."

Rictor said nothing, impassive. Koni slumped in a chair, rubbing his face. Lannes dug his claws into his palms, drawing blood. "I understand you're trying to protect yourselves, but—"

"That's not what this is about," Rictor said. "Not for me. I have nothing left to protect."

Koni shook his head. "Bullshit."

Rictor looked away, out the window. "The woman isn't human."

Lannes hesitated. "I'm aware of her psychic powers."

"Nothing to do with that. This is about blood." Rictor's jaw tightened. "She is *not* human. Not entirely."

"None of us are. What's your point?"

Rictor's jaw tightened. "There are very few lineages left in the world that contain what's in her veins. And those with her particular bloodline are . . . especially troubled."

It took him a moment, but Lannes made the connection—and everything inside him stopped. Dread poured through him, a profound disappointment that rattled him to the core. With her amnesia, with her fears, Lethe had been his. Only his. Now she was going to belong to someone else.

"You know who she is," he said, stunned by the deception. "You've known all along."

Koni shifted uncomfortably. "Only when we saw her. But I know the woman differently than Rictor."

Lannes looked at Rictor and found an odd compassion in his eyes. Brief, gone in an instant, but unmistakable.

Lannes did not want that. Not at all. "Who is she?"

"Her real name is Alice," Koni said heavily, "and she's the grand-niece of the woman who tortured you and your brothers."

CHAPTER FIFTEEN

L ETHE was in the shower when she felt a tremor run down her link to Lannes. She had hardly been able to sense it until that moment, but the connection suddenly burned so bright in her head that she felt it as a thread made of liquid fire, shimmering hot and fine.

She almost went down on her knees, but instead she turned the water off and staggered from the stall, grasping blindly for a robe. The pain started to ease by the time she left the bathroom, but not enough to keep her from seeking Lannes out. No one was in the parlor. She heard voices in the other bedroom. She thought about grabbing a steak knife from the dinner tray, just in case, but kept her hands in the pockets of the robe.

Lethe opened the door. Lannes stood in front of it, his back to her. Just beyond him were Rictor and Koni. Both men had shadows in their eyes, but it was only Lannes who concerned her. She began to reach out, to touch him, but he stepped away from her at the last moment, turning to face her.

His gaze was terrible—so raw, so torn, staring at him felt the same as being punched in the face. She staggered back a step, feet aching, heart wrapped so tight in the link between them, she was afraid it might stop beating if she was cut off from him.

"What happened?" she whispered.

"Nothing," he rasped, and pushed past her. Moments later, a door slammed.

Lethe turned on the men. "What did you say to him?"

"Truth," Rictor replied. "Nothing but."

Koni would not look her in the eyes. "He'll be fine."

Then you're blind, she thought at him, still blistered by the look in Lannes' eyes.

Lethe limped quickly through the parlor, back into her room. She upended the bags of new clothes, pulling on soft black yoga pants, a tight hooded sweatshirt, a pair of thick socks and white tennis shoes. Her hair was wet, but she ran her fingers through it once. Grabbed a room key. And left.

She did not think, just followed her instincts. Breadcrumbs inside her heart. She ignored the elevator in favor of the stairs, hobbling down them as quickly as she could until she hit the first floor. From there she went outside, crossing the cobblestone drive for the garden.

Lethe found Lannes standing in the shadows of trees, near an old stone bridge. His back was turned against her. He cut a lonely figure, large and solid as an oak. It was easy to imagine wings.

She did not immediately approach him; she could not bring herself to. Lethe felt as though she was in the presence of something hurt and wild, and all she could offer was space and time and gentleness. So she sat on the grass, hugging her knees to her chest, wondering if this was what it felt like to be a little girl, lost and alone.

She waited a long time. She waited so long, she wondered if Lannes was aware of her presence, but then the link would pulse, and she knew he had a bead on her heart, just as she had a bead on his. Until finally, as the sun began falling into dusk, he stirred from under the trees and came to her.

Lethe did not stand as he approached. All she could do was watch him move—like a dancer, unspeakably graceful, with a lean coiled strength that was also, somehow, not nearly as attractive as his kindness.

She did not move, not even when he finally stood above her, big as the world. She wondered rather absurdly if invisible wings still cast shadows.

"Are you all right?" he whispered. "You've been sitting there a long time."

"I'm fine," she said. "You?"

Lannes glanced away from her, staring at the dome. "Better."

And then he reached down, grabbed her wrist and pulled her up hard against him. His arms snaked around her waist, and it felt so good to be held by him, she wanted to cry. A horrible weakness, but she could suffer it. Just as she could suffer the realization that losing him—in any form—was quite possibly the worst thing she could imagine happening to her.

"I was afraid," she confessed, craning her neck to peer into his eyes.

"I know. I felt it." Lannes hefted her higher in his arms, so that her feet dangled. "I had to figure something out."

"They gave you bad news."

"Depends." He searched her face, the edge of his mind pressing against her own. "Depends on a lot of things."

"And?"

"And nothing," he said roughly, and pressed his lips against her own.

She was not expecting to be kissed, but his mouth was hard, even desperate—and if he was gentle in some ways, his kiss was not. It stole her breath, every thought in her head, and it was good he was holding her because if she had been forced to stand, her legs might very well have betrayed her.

Lannes did not let go. He sank to his knees on the grass, taking her with him. They were kneeling together, tangled, her body draped in something heavy and warm that she could not see but that felt like leather or silk.

My wings, he murmured in her mind, and his kiss deepened to such an intensity that she lost herself, forgot everything. But only for a moment. Lannes pulled away, eyes shut, breathing hard. She was little better. Her heart was hammering, not an ounce of strength left in her body.

Afraid. Totally, desperately, afraid.

Don't let me remember my old life. Please, don't,

she prayed desperately. Not if it meant giving up this new existence, no matter how twisted and dangerous it had become. What she had now was better. It had to be.

It is, whispered her instincts. *Run from the rest. Run from them.*

Lannes opened his eyes. "Them."

Lethe wished he could not read her mind so easily. "The mysterious 'them.'"

Your family? Lannes thought, but the words were so fleeting, so rushed, she sensed he had not meant her to hear them. Nor had he expected her to see, like a flash of lightning, a rush of images: a woman with long brown hair shrouding her eyes, and a lush sultry pout; a knife, a flash of green light, blood soaking into white sand. Pain crept beneath her skin, as though her veins were kissing fire, and it was so sudden, so shocking, all she could do was suck in a hard fast breath.

Lannes grabbed her arms, steadying her. "No, don't look."

I can't help myself, she whispered, and his conflict was immediate, a tumbling force in his heart that made her mouth taste bitter and her body feel cold. She leaned back from him, rubbing her tingling face with her palm. Lannes' hands trailed away, as did the warmth of his invisible wings.

"They told you something about me," she said, full of dread. "Something bad."

"Nothing bad about you," he said quietly.

She shook her head, scooting backward on the grass. "I don't want to know."

Lannes said nothing, not with his voice, though his eyes were dark, his mouth set in a hard line. He stood and held out his hand.

"You're not alone," he rumbled. "No matter what happens."

Lethe closed her eyes. Strong fingers curled around her wrist, drawing her slowly up on her aching feet. She was afraid of seeing more from his mind, but her thoughts remained blissfully quiet.

"Look at me," he said.

Lethe did not. She turned and started limping back to the hotel. Her life felt perilous, built on air and matchsticks. There were no memories to fall back on, only whatever she had on hand: grit, stubbornness, a blind determination to stick one foot in front of the other. Nothing that could be stolen.

But tainted, maybe. Cut.

I won't cut you, said Lannes, and it surprised her that she could hear him without them touching. *I won't hurt you.*

Not now.

But later. Later was the problem.

She did not trust herself.

LETHE DID NOT SEE RICTOR OR KONI WHEN SHE RETURNED to the room, and all the doors stood open. There was no place to hide. She walked into her bedroom and shut herself in. Evening had fallen, full and heavy; there was no light outside except for some lamps in the garden below her window. She crawled under the covers and curled into a tight ball. She heard Lannes enter the suite's parlor, but he did not knock on her door or try to come in. He left her alone. Much as she had done for him.

Something bad, she thought. *Something in my past.*

Something inside her head, someone else trying to kill her.

Your family, she remembered him thinking, but pushed away the memory of the images that had fallen from his mind. Too disturbing. Filling her with dread. She did not want to think about the brunette or the bloody sand even for a moment.

Lethe sighed, punching her pillow, and tried to sleep. But every time she closed her eyes she saw other terrible visions. The dead men from the hotel in Chicago. Or Orwell Price's head crushed by a dumbbell. She saw Etta dying in her arms and a man with a gun flung through the window of a car. She saw, once again, her hands covered in blood.

Her eyes snapped open and she stared at the ceiling, then the wall. These were solid, firm objects. But the darkness crept in on her, and turning on a lamp almost made it worse. Too many shadows. So she switched off the light and huddled under the covers, battling memory, struggling against her need for the balm to that memory.

Lannes.

You should be stronger, she told herself. More stalwart than indulging some sniveling desire to have someone at her side—an anchor, a constant—as if to be near another would keep her from losing her mind all over again.

Yet, she could not help it. Solitude frightened her. Almost as much as the knowledge that at any moment she could turn into a robot made to kill. And there was the paradox: keeping anyone close was the same as putting them in danger.

Lannes, in danger. No matter who or what he might be.

She finally sat up. And after several minutes, she rolled out of bed and opened the door.

Lannes was in the parlor. The couch had been shoved back toward the wall, and he lay stretched on the floor with a blanket and pillow. There was no sign of Koni and Rictor, though the other bedroom door still stood open.

Lannes sat up. His shirt—that same blue shirt— looked perfectly clean and pressed. His hair fell around his craggy face. Lethe was tired of seeing the illusion. It seemed fake. Everything seemed fake but his eyes.

"I can't sleep," she said.

"It's the hotel," he said. "You're in a hotel again."

"No," she told him. "It's because I'm alone."

Lannes regarded her for a long moment, then carefully stood. He gathered up his blanket and pillow, and when Lethe backed into the bedroom, he followed and shut the door. Darkness swallowed her, but she kept moving until the backs of her knees hit the bed and she sat down.

Lannes was nothing but a dark mass. She heard him toss his blanket on the floor, but before he could settle down, her hand shot out and grabbed his wrist. She kept silent but tugged, falling into the heat of his skin and, past that, his mind. Touching him made everything feel more real.

I'm no anchor, he whispered in her thoughts. *I can hardly take care of myself.*

Bullshit, she replied, feeling that word drift like a dandelion seed, slow and wild. *I wouldn't be alive without you.*

You'd be alive, Lannes told her, and finally settled on the bed. He pulled back the covers. Lethe scooted under, and after a moment, he joined her. The mattress groaned, sinking under his weight, and she curled into a ball as he wrapped himself around her body. He was so much larger than her, his arms heavy and strong. His chest, rising and falling slowly against her back, felt hard as stone and hot as a furnace.

You'd be alive, he said again in her mind, almost like a prayer. *I know you would.*

He wanted to believe it—she could feel that much—but underneath his thoughts, she felt his doubt, and the lie. Lethe let him say the words, though. She needed to hear them.

His arms tightened, drawing her closer, and his lips brushed the back of her neck. "Wasn't a lie. I just happened to remember all those bullets."

"Right," she said. "I could have easily survived that."

Lannes sighed. Lethe tried to turn in his arms, but it took too much effort. "Do you still hurt?"

Be more specific, came the instant response, accompanied by a deep embarrassment that cut right into her heart. It forced her to take a moment, remembering again that this was a man—a creature and a man—who had lived a full life, and that unlike her, had the memories to go with it. And not all of them, she knew, were good.

"My wounds are almost gone," he said quietly, his warm breath ruffling her hair. "Like I told you, my kind heals fast."

"You don't feel much different from human. Except for your back."

"We're like you, for the most part. Humanoid. Bigger, stronger. Our . . . faces are alien, I suppose. We were mistaken for demons, long ago. Dragons, even. You can't imagine the numbers of virgins deposited near our flying grounds."

"Kinky," Lethe muttered, and finally forced herself to turn over. Lannes helped, sliding his strong hands around her waist and back. The room was dark, but she caught the glitter of his eyes, and laid her palm against his cheek. She felt bone beneath her hand, craggy and sharp, but nothing that frightened her. Her fingers trailed over an angular nose . . . and paused against his lips.

She remembered those lips. How they felt on her mouth. But the memory was tempered with the hard, bitter knowledge that he knew something about her. Something unpleasant. Something that had sent him from the hotel and made him stand alone until he could bear to be in her presence again.

"Don't," he whispered. "Don't think about it. Not yet."

Not yet, but soon. It made her sick.

His lips moved against her fingers, and she felt

heartache behind that gesture. "I told you not to think about it."

Heat pooled in her stomach. "Easier said than done."

"Try," he said, and one large hand slid down against her hip, tugging her closer. Lethe could not help herself. She reached under his arm and touched the base of his wing. He shuddered, closing his eyes, and between them she felt his sex thicken, a reaction that was so unexpectedly noticeable, her pulse began to pound. She hooked her leg over his hip, grinding against him, and the friction of his jeans through her thin pants tore a small soft sound from her throat.

His hand crept under her shirt. He had calluses she hadn't noticed, but they felt good on her skin, and she arched against him, unable to control the desire that raged through her as his knuckles grazed her aching breasts.

She stroked his wings again and he cried out, jerking against her in one hard thrust that made her see stars.

"Lethe," he gasped, his hand closing over her breast, squeezing. She muffled her own cry, baring her throat to him as his mouth closed against her neck, his teeth dragging along her skin in a savage kiss. She grabbed the waist of his jeans, scrabbling for the button, but it was too difficult to undo. She settled for sliding her hand down his stomach and her fingers brushed against something ridged, hot, and hard.

Lannes snarled breathlessly, covering her wrist with his hand. "*Don't.* Not unless . . ."

He stopped, but she could hear his words ringing in her head.

Not unless you want all of me.

She wanted him. She wanted him now. Inside her, on her, around her, any which way he would have her. She wanted to feel him thrust between her legs and steal the pain away.

But you're afraid, he whispered in her mind, going very still. *I can feel it.*

No, she told him, but even as that thought flitted across her mind, she felt the shiver in her heart. Not of him. But of herself.

Lannes dragged in a deep, ragged breath, and he very gently pulled her hand out of his jeans. He cradled it between them, twining her fingers through his.

"Afraid to be alone, but afraid to be with someone," he murmured. "How familiar."

"We're pathetic," she told him. "Me, more than you. I'm terrified to close my eyes."

"You're afraid you'll be someone else when you open them."

"It could happen," she said simply. "That . . . thing . . . still hasn't left my mind. I can feel the hook. I don't know why it—she—hasn't done anything yet."

Lannes sighed. "Maybe what it wants has less to do with power than fixing some old pain. Maybe all it wants is solace. I suppose that's what anyone ever wants who's been hurt."

"Like you," she whispered.

"Like *you*," he replied. "Though that doesn't . . . doesn't make it right to hurt others. To take out that fear and pain on innocents."

Then you're better than most, she thought at him,

and sidled closer, simply for comfort, needing to hear
his heart beat.

"Lannes," she said softly. "I want to see what you
look like."

He was silent for a very long time, and only the
pulse she felt within that odd little link told her that he
was awake.

Then, quietly: "Go to sleep, Lethe."

But when she did, she dreamed.

SHE WAS BACK IN THE DOME, AND IT WAS DARK AND SHE
*was not alone. Children laughed, squealing and shriek-
ing at echoes, and she heard the clicks and thunder-
ous claps of shoes racing on tile. They were slicing
through her, cutting like knives.*

*And . . . something was behind her, large and piti-
less and lost in stony slumber. Heaving great breaths
and tremulous sighs. A beast. A monster.*

*A line of poetry whispered in her ear, as though a
voice hovered in the air like a butterfly.*

*"The blood-dimmed tide is loosed," she heard, "and
everywhere the ceremony of innocence is drowned."*

*Drowned, dying, dead. She tried to turn, to see what
slept behind her, but it was no use. Her body refused
to move, and she endured, frozen and terrified, as the
laughter of the children neared and the thing behind
her began to stir like the slow grind of mountain rock.*

*It would eat her when it awakened. She knew that.
She was as much a sacrifice as a lamb is to a lion, and
she looked down suddenly and saw rope around her
wrists and feet. Terror clawed up her throat. She tried*

*to cry out, to scream, but could not make a sound.
Nothing but a squeak.*

*The children came closer, still laughing, but qui-
eter now. Hushed.*

*Until, suddenly, a shadow loomed, big as the dome,
and hands grabbed the rope around her wrists. A
woman's hands, a flash of blond hair, eyes that were
green and furious and frightened.*

*And then those eyes shifted to blue, and the face
became masculine and dark, and the hands melted
from woman's into man's, sinewy and large with muscle. Her vision blurred, shadows gathered around the
figure wrestling with her bindings, but she knew the
heart, and she knew those eyes.*

Lannes, *she thought.*

*"This is only a dream," he told her, but he sounded
afraid. The ropes would not loosen. When he tried to
pick her up, her feet would not budge from the tile floor.
They were glued there. Anchored.*

"Run," she told him. "Hurry."

*But he did not, merely stepped back, turning in place
to survey the cavernous room. And she saw something
that made her forget fear.*

*Lannes no longer appeared human. Immense wings
folded against his broad muscular back, wings made of
thin bones and pliable skin the color of silver and lavender. Between those wings was long dark hair, heavy
and shining, coarse as fish line. She glimpsed the edge
of his face: a craggy cheek, a jaw edged in a gently pro-
truding bone that swept up toward his pointed ear.*

He turned slightly to look at her, and she knew his

face, though it was alien and wild. His human mask had been less of an illusion than a simple softening of features—and it was some comfort that she could still recognize those craggy lines cut with shadows and sharp angles.

And his eyes . . . His eyes were exactly the same— dangerously intelligent, heartbreakingly compassion- ate. Otherworldly. A fairy tale.

Lannes looked past her, his eyes widening. She could not imagine what he saw, but air compressed around her body like a cocoon—not a hand or a body squeez- ing upon her, but instead a mind, a lumbering aware- ness finally shaking itself from sleep.

The children, somewhere, began chanting. It was different this time. Louder. Coarser.

Lannes pressed close, wrapping his wings around her. He tried to lift her, struggled to cut the ropes. Nothing worked. His desperation was horrific.

"It's just a dream," he hissed.

"No," she told him. "No."

Again, he looked over her shoulder. "Close your eyes."

"Lannes—"

"Do it now."

She closed her eyes, hardly able to breathe. Lannes wrapped himself around her body, pressing her face against his chest. Around them, the air closed like a fist and the voices of the children grew higher, shrill.

Until, quite suddenly, it all disappeared, swallowed by darkness.

Lannes was with her. Lethe could hear his heart

thudding in time to her own, their bodies pressed skin to skin, so close she could have been part of him.

"They sold my daughter," whispered a voice from the darkness, broken with grief. "Oh, Milly. Oh, God. They took her from me. They called it a game and they lured her, they enticed her, but it wasn't, it wasn't, and I couldn't save her, they wouldn't let me save her, and I would have died for her, I would have died—"

"Stop," Lethe breathed. "Stop, please."

"You see," said the voice. "You see why I stole you. Because you are of me, you are all I have, you are my blood. And you came here. You came here, and you were willing, and I will keep you until they are dead. All of them, dead. And when they are dead, you will be free."

"Don't make her kill," said Lannes. "Don't turn her into a monster."

"We are all monsters," whispered the voice.

Lethe struggled to protest, but everything inside her tightened like the stretching of a rubber band—the world heaving with shadows—and before she could ask who or how, she was flung back into her mind.

SHE OPENED HER EYES—THOUGHT SHE WAS TURNING somersaults, but that was just dizziness. She shut her eyes again, holding very still. Something moved beneath her: a warm chest, breathing in and out. A large hand that fell against the back of her neck.

She was on the floor. On top of Lannes. They had

fallen off the bed, both of them tangled in covers. His arms were wrapped around her. It was hard to breathe. Part of her was still wild with terror.

"Lethe," he mumbled, "Are you okay?"

She could not answer him. Her voice refused to work. Lannes sat up, groaning slightly as he carefully rolled her sideways so that she lay on her back on the hard floor. He leaned over her, massive as a mountain, his right hand moving lightly over her waist, up her ribs, following her arm to her wrist.

He checked her wrists. She tried to sit up, but he held her still.

"What?" she asked, and he held up her arm. Lethe squinted. "I can't see."

"Can you feel?" he asked, and the moment the question left his lips, she suddenly became aware of a burning sensation around her ankles and wrists. Fear spiked through her. She had to close her eyes.

"Oh, my God," she breathed. "It was real."

"Or it felt so real in our minds that our bodies reacted." Lannes ran his hand very lightly up her throat, his thumb brushing the edge of her collarbone with a gentleness that made her shudder.

"Something terrible happened here," she managed to whisper.

"Someone was sacrificed," Lannes replied, sounding ill. "That's what started this."

"Runa," Lethe said, then shook her head. "No. Her daughter. Milly. Those other kids hurt her."

"A game," Lannes growled, with such fury he almost

frightened her. "They used the little girl to summon something."

"You saw it."

He closed his eyes. "I felt it. There was nothing to see."

"Are you lying to me?"

"No," he said firmly.

Lethe wished she could see his eyes. "We almost died, didn't we?"

His silence was all the answer she needed, and she clamped her mouth tight, struggling for calm. Lannes leaned in even closer and pulled her into his arms with an ease that made her feel impossibly delicate.

"It's not safe for you here," he said. "We'll go as soon as possible."

"She'll just keep following me. She wants them dead. If what we saw was true, I don't blame her. Doesn't mean I want to do the deed, though."

"Etta and her brother. Simon. Who else? That name on the back of the postcard. Will . . . ?"

She hardly heard. Another memory tormented her. "What did she mean, Lannes, when she said . . . 'You are my blood'?"

"I don't . . ." He stopped. "I don't want to speculate."

"I might be related to Runa. That's what she meant, right? According to Ed, I look just like her." A horrifying thought slipped into her brain. "You don't think . . . I *am* Runa, do you?"

"Absolutely not," he said firmly. "*That* would be crazy."

She banged her head on the floor, frustrated. Lannes, swearing softly, slid his massive hand beneath her skull like a soft pillow. "Don't take this out on yourself. Not even in the smallest way."

"Lay off," she said.

"Trust me," he shot back. "Things are going to get worse. Take out your frustration on the enemy. Not yourself. Once you start that . . ." Lannes stopped, looking away. "Once you start, you'll lose part of yourself. More than your memories."

He began to pull away, and she grabbed his face, her thumbs caressing craggy lines and bone, and in her mind she saw again his true appearance. It was not nearly as shocking as she had believed it would be. And not in the slightest bit disgusting.

If he realized what she had seen in her vision, he gave no sign. She forced him to look at her. "Whoever hurt you . . . are they gone now?"

"Dead," he said, terrible tension raging through his body.

"Then stop. *You* let it go." Lethe curled her arm around his neck and pulled herself close, brushing her lips over his cheek. His arms squeezed.

She heard a distant thump and the low murmur of voices. Then came a knock at the bedroom door, which opened before either of them could say a word.

"Lady, you need to— Oh." Koni stopped, staring at them. His body was backlit by the lights in the parlor, preventing her from seeing his expression, but his silence was enough.

And then: "It's good you're both here. We need to go. Right now."

Lannes sat up, bringing Lethe with him. "What happened?"

"The police," Koni replied. "They're at the front desk. Looking for the woman."

CHAPTER SIXTEEN

T HEY took nothing with them except Lethe's new
    clothes. Just got up and walked out. Lannes flung
his thoughts ahead and behind, searching for any sur-
prises, but the hall was quiet and they found the stairs.
Five minutes later, they were in the parking lot, at the
cars. Rictor was already in the Humvee. Koni climbed
in. Lannes and Lethe slid into the Impala. They drove
away.

No one stopped them, though they passed an empty
police sedan parked by the front entrance. They drove
out of town, the Humvee in the lead, following a road
that traveled from West Baden into the deep country
night. Lannes did not know what time it was, but no
other cars were out, and when they left the small state
highway for an even smaller road, they passed old farm-
houses and small cottages framed by trees. At one point,
they were chased by a wickedly fast spotted dog that
leapt from behind a bush to snap at their wheels.

Lannes liked the near emptiness, the quiet. Reminded him of his youth, a world that no longer existed.

He was seventy years old, still young by gargoyle standards, but everything around him had deteriorated in the intervening years, turning from a land that was idealistic, full of hard-working pride, into a carnival of glitter and excess, where the superficial, the *artificial*, reigned supreme.

Not that Lannes was old-fashioned. Not exactly. But for someone who had watched the world turn for seventy years and would not hit a midlife crisis for seventy more, there was something to be said for the solid strength of a land not eaten by strip malls and parking lots.

Rictor and Koni led them to a state park, which was little more than a boat ramp at the edge of a lake. No one else was there, and the air was quiet except for the faint lapping of waves on the shore. It was cold out, and dark. Almost three in the morning. Lannes could see Lethe's breath, and he wished he had thought to buy her a coat.

Rictor walked a short distance away, down to the water's edge. Koni sat inside the Humvee, bracing his foot on the open door.

"We're being screwed with," Lethe suggested.

"It's an odd way to do it," Lannes replied. "If Simon is capable of taking over minds, then why not just jump into the police officer himself? He seems capable of tracking you, too. He wouldn't have needed to ask at the front desk."

She leaned against the car, rubbing her arms. "He must be old. If the thing inside me needs to rest after coming into my mind, what about him? Maybe he's getting too worn out, so he calls in a tip to the police, tells them about Orwell Price or the car chase. Maybe he makes something up."

That made a bit of sense but was of little comfort. Lannes had prided himself on a nice orderly life for decades, and this free spin had his nerves in a bind.

As did their recent shared vision.

As did Koni's revelation about the woman.

Alice. Lethe. Blood kin of the witch who had tried to enslave him and his brothers. Who had tortured him and nearly stolen both his soul and his mind. His brothers would shit themselves if they knew whom he was keeping company with. He wondered if Charlie had been made aware. There were no missed calls on his phone.

The devastation of the knowledge still rocked him. *So stupid*, he had thought. *So stupid.* He had thrown his heart to the world, and the world had burned it with venom. Even knowing what lay inside Lethe's mind— the wounds, the emptiness—had not been enough; everything, every memory of his captivity, had slammed him sideways. He could not stand to look at her.

I would have left her, he thought, staring at Lethe now, so slender and still beside him. *I would have given her to Koni and Rictor and run like hell.*

He would have. He definitely would have, if she had not come for him, her heart like a small bird in his mind, fluttering and strong. Filled with concern. Concern for him.

No deception, no lies. She had sat on that grass for hours only to make certain he was all right, and for all those hours he had listened to nothing but their link, searching it for even one trace of dislike or greed or selfishness. Just one stray emotion would have sent him fleeing.

He had found nothing but compassion. Nothing but distress at his obvious upset. Not an ounce of concern for herself. Lannes could not fight that. He had stood there trying to, and all he had done was burn a hole through his soul.

Her memories were gone. Who she had been, whom she had loved, the things she might have done—these things all meant nothing. He could not judge her. Not when he could see inside her heart.

And that kiss . . . and later, in the bedroom . . .

Lannes folded his arms over his chest, leaning on the Impala. "Koni. Something happened just before you came to get Lethe. The two of us . . . saw something. Another vision of what started this mess."

"We saw the murder," Lethe said. "We were . . . part of the murder."

"Not just a murder," Lannes corrected her grimly. "Ritual sacrifice. An attempt to summon something."

Rictor, down by the lake, turned around. His green eyes flashed. It was similar to the light Lannes had witnessed just once in Lethe's eyes. He started walking back toward them. Fast.

Koni frowned. "So, who's responsible for what, again?"

Lannes curled his hands into fists and ground them together. "It was evil. That's all I can tell you. Old and evil."

"They were just kids," Lethe remarked, rubbing the back of her neck. "Just kids, but . . ."

"Ed," Lannes replied. "We need to show him that photograph."

"And then what?" Koni asked, as Rictor joined them. "You find the kids who did the deed, and all you'll be doing is setting them up to die. Isn't that what this thing wants?"

"Maybe you can protect them from me," Lethe said, a note of desperation in her voice.

"Lady," Koni said, "no offense, but how long do you propose we do that?"

"He's right," Lannes told her. "We have to focus more on getting Runa out of your head. If she won't go willingly . . ."

"Doesn't seem right," muttered Lethe. "If this is Runa . . . Punishing a mother for wanting to hurt the people who killed her daughter and herself just feels wrong."

"And the alternative?"

She looked down at her hands, almost as though she were seeing blood. "I know. It's bad."

Rictor stared at the lake. "Did the sacrifice take place in the dome?"

"Seems that way."

"And you're sure the mother is the one responsible for using the woman?"

"I have a name," Lethe said. "I'm not 'the woman.'"

Rictor gave her a long look, then fixed his gaze back on Lannes. "Are you sure?"

For a moment, Lannes thought the man was still

talking to Lethe. She seemed to think so, too, given the hint of confusion pulsing from her mind.

Lannes finally said, "I'm sure."

"Then perhaps we *are* dealing with a ghost."

"If you're right, a ghost, a spirit, will make things more difficult."

"How difficult?" Lethe asked.

"Depends on the dead person," Rictor replied. "Yours will be . . . complicated."

"Oh," she said. "Lovely."

Koni leaned back into the Humvee, against the passenger seat, most of his face lost in shadow. "Lannes . . . maybe you should take a moment."

Lannes studied him. "A moment of what?"

But Koni made no reply, and the silence stretched into something uncomfortable.

Lethe tilted her head, gaze sharp. "A moment of your time," she answered for him, coldly. "With them."

Lannes reached for her, but she slid away and walked across the parking lot to the boat ramp. No backward glance, spine straight, tension rolling across their link. Her limp was almost gone.

Koni said, "Don't give me that look."

"Then tell me something," Lannes replied, fighting to control his temper. "What was her crime, when you knew her? You never told me."

The shape-shifter's golden eyes glittered. "There was no crime, as far as I know. She was kidnapped. I met her briefly, after she had been freed. It was her own family who hurt her. A great-aunt, I suppose. It happened more than a year ago in Vancouver. The old woman locked

Alice in a cage with a bunch of dead people, made her sit in her own shit for days, all because she needed a blood sacrifice. The old woman was trying to summon something. Maybe the same kind of thing you saw in your . . . vision."

Chills raced down Lannes' spine, chased by fury. Rictor grabbed him before he could do anything stupid. "Don't. Calm down."

"I'm calm," muttered Lannes. "But what you just told me isn't exactly an indictment of her character."

"Like hell," snapped Koni quietly. "And don't blame me for being cautious. Even if she doesn't remember who she is, you can bet her family hasn't forgotten. Most of them are normal. But there might be some who aren't, and they'll find her, eventually. And if she tells them what she's seen, what she knows about us—"

"How could they not know already?" Lannes shook off Rictor's arm and glanced over his shoulder. He saw Lethe's slender body standing at the end of the dock.

Feels like the boogeyman, she had said. *Something terrible.*

"She's afraid of being found," he told the other men, still watching her. "A deep fear, more instinct than anything else. She doesn't know why she feels that way, but I think she'd rather die than get caught."

"She'll get caught," Rictor said, with far too much certainty for comfort. "Family always catches up."

Lannes frowned at him. "And what do *you* do at the agency? Besides look menacing?"

Rictor gave him a cold, bitter smile. "Isn't that enough?"

Koni shook his head. "Never mind. There's something strange going on in this area. I wouldn't mention it, except for everything else that's happened. It might be connected."

"And?"

"And, it's the crows. They're . . . different."

"Different. What do you mean?"

"I mean, the crows in this area . . . have a different way of getting on. They're clannish. They don't talk. Not much, and not to me."

"You fly as a crow? That's your blood form?" Lannes asked, and when Koni shrugged, he added, "Not to diminish what you're telling me, but how are the talking habits of birds important?"

"I was out," Koni explained, pointing at the sky, "and when I tried to pass over one particular area, the local crows drove me away. That's never happened."

"What did you see?"

"Woods, water. Maybe a house. It was hard to say. Those birds are protecting at least three, four hundred acres."

"What do you think it means?"

"It means we should mind our own business," Rictor muttered.

Koni gave him a sharp look. "I don't get you."

"I don't give a fuck," Rictor said, and walked away. He disappeared in moments, lost in shadows.

"Asshole," Koni muttered.

"Who is he?" Lannes asked.

"Your guess is as good as mine. Rictor is as Rictor

does." The shape-shifter's golden eyes briefly glowed. "He's immortal."

"No such thing."

"Dude," Koni said, "you need to get out more."

Lannes let that slide. "You think it's possible to find out where Ed lives?"

"Hell of a lot easier than sitting in a car with *him* for eight hours." Koni slid out of the Humvee. Lannes looked back at Lethe and found her watching them. It was too dark to see much of her face, but he felt her curiosity in his mind.

"You came back to her," said Koni.

"You thought I wouldn't." Lannes folded his wings even tighter around his body. "Maybe you calculated it that way."

"No, but we knew it was a possibility. Better than lying to you." Koni craned his neck to peer at the night sky. "When are you going to tell her? Or are you?"

"She figured out on her own that you had bad news about her. You weren't subtle. Neither was I. She told me she doesn't want to know. When that changes . . . we'll see. I can't lie to her."

Koni remained silent. So did Lannes. Once upon a time, he would have marveled at standing beside a shape-shifter. Now, it felt like a burden.

But that was his fault. Until the witch, he had spent his life immersed in books, taking for granted the fact that the modern world was a soft world, without the dangers that had affected his kind before the age of steel and science. Superstition still existed, but it had been dampened with logic, with humanity's inexorable disbelief in strange things.

Yes, gargoyles might be few in number, but in some ways, it was easier now to live. You could be Godzilla in a tutu, but if you had e-mail and a telephone, no one would ever know.

No one. They had paid for safety with solitude. Inexperience. Innocence.

You wanted to be alone, whispered his mind, mockingly. He had wanted to be alone, and now he was very much *not*, but he was too far gone into the mystery, so far beyond the crossroads of that fateful meeting in Chicago, he could not conceive of his life before.

Never go back? He would not change a moment of his life even if he could, not if it meant losing Lethe.

"Can you find this tract of land at night?" Lannes asked Koni. "The tract protected by crows?"

"No," said the shape-shifter. "I need landmarks. I might even have to go into the air again. All I can tell you is that it's close."

"It'll be dawn in three hours. We should find Ed first. Show him that photo."

"If the police are looking for Alice—"

"Don't call her that," Lannes said sharply. "She goes by Lethe now."

Koni gave him a long steady look. "Is that for her benefit or yours?"

Lannes made himself breathe. "Find Ed."

Without waiting to see if Koni agreed, he started walking across the parking lot toward Lethe. Footsteps scuffed, and a strong hand grabbed his arm.

"Wait," Koni said, "there's something else. About her."

Rictor appeared from the shadows behind the car, utterly silent. "Don't."

"Don't what?" Lannes asked, his voice dangerously quiet.

"Don't," Rictor said again, staring at Koni. "You'll cause trouble."

Lannes grabbed the shape-shifter's arm and twisted it away. "Talk, or don't. But make up your mind."

Koni suddenly looked as though he wished he had kept his mouth shut. Lannes wished the same thing.

"Your lady friend," said Koni slowly. "Before she lost her memories, she knew a woman, one of us. Kit Bell. Kit can see when people are going to be murdered. She foresaw Alice's death."

Disbelief was the first thing Lannes felt, and then gut-wrenching horror. He stopped breathing. "How?"

"You don't—"

He slammed Koni against the car. *"Tell me."*

Rictor stepped close, gaze hooded, his mouth set in a hard line. But he did not intervene.

Koni's eyes flashed golden. "Stabbed. A knife in the eye."

Lannes let him go and spun away. He took several steps, stopped and could go no further. "When?"

"Don't know. Could be tomorrow, or fifty years from now." Koni's voice was soft, ragged. "But it'll happen. Far as we know, Kit is never wrong."

She will be wrong, Lannes thought desperately. *She will be wrong this time.*

He fought to pull himself together. He thought of Lethe—Lethe, feeling his emotions—and tried to put a wall between his heart and the bond they shared.

"I don't know you," Lannes growled at Koni. "I don't know this Kit. I sure as hell don't know why you told me this." He leaned in, holding the shape-shifter's gaze. "As far as I'm concerned, you're wrong. And I will *not* tell her. I will not frighten her. And neither will you."

Lannes held the shape-shifter's gaze for a moment longer, then started walking again toward Lethe. His wings stretched, catching the breeze, and his body tugged backward, aching to fly. Just one good leap was all it would take, but he kept his feet firmly on the ground.

She turned to face him. Alice. Lethe.

It will never last, he told himself. *After she finds out who she is, she will either go back to that life or start a new one. And just because she likes you now will mean nothing in the long term. She has no conception of what you are, and even if she had, even if she accepted you, hearts change. If you put too much weight on what you have with her, it will break.*

Talking himself out of things before they even happened? His brothers would call him an idiot. Frederick would, as well.

But he could not help himself. He had avoided, by accident and personal choice, most involvement with women, human or gargoyle. Humans, for all the obvious reasons. Gargoyle females, because there were so few, and most of them had used him, during brief courtships, as a means of getting to his brothers, Mag-

nus and Arthur—both of whom were far more powerful than Lannes or Charlie.

So, all these years and he had forced himself to be
cold. It was safer that way, easier. Problem was, Lannes
could not control his heart. Not with her. Not Lethe.
And he realized now that he did not know how to care
about someone in any other way except all the way. All
or nothing. He had too few friends to be cheap with his
heart.

And Lethe . . . was more than a friend.

*Even if her family can never be allowed to know
you exist.*

Lethe did not smile when he joined her at the water's edge. "You've escaped the male bonding. Any
scars to show for it?" she asked.

"I don't scar easily."

"Lucky," she whispered, and leaned against him,
hugging his arm. He felt her loneliness, her need for
him—her need *just* for him—and his heart fell apart
a little. And then it stitched itself together, encasing
bits and pieces of her mind inside his soul. Making
her part of him. Permanently. He could not help himself. If the link was lost, and he supposed it might be,
one day, he would still feel her. Always.

For good or ill.

"Lannes," she said, "I have a stupid question."

"Okay," he said.

She turned, facing him. "Was I a good person before?"

Lannes dug his claws into his palms. "I believe you
were."

"You don't seem too sure." She glanced across the parking lot. "Those two don't trust me."

"They're cautious with strangers."

A faint bitter smile tugged at her mouth. "They work for a detective agency, right? Same as your brother, who, I presume, is also a gargoyle?"

"True," he said, reluctantly.

"Which means that Rictor and Koni must know what he is."

Lannes said nothing, and she drummed her fingers against her leg. "Which means they don't care. Which also means they are very understanding . . . or they're just as different as you."

"I don't know much about my brother's work," Lannes finally said.

"You know enough. But really, a detective agency? It seems . . . odd."

"It's called Dirk & Steele."

"Or like a porn movie."

"They do good work. I think."

"And they're all . . . psychic?"

He shrugged. "I suppose the rest of the world thinks they're normal. But having the label of detective or bodyguard, even mercenary, allows them to use their gifts in ways that don't . . . draw attention."

"Like you, hiding in plain sight." She looked once again at the Humvee. Koni and Rictor were nowhere in sight. "I'm not a stranger to them, am I? And if they don't trust me . . . I suppose I can guess what that means."

"It's not like that. If you want to know—"

"Not yet." But she chewed her bottom lip, indecision flickering across her face. "Do I have children? A . . . husband?"

"I don't know," he said, feeling as though his heart were plunging onto a bed of knives. "But as for the rest, good or bad . . . all I can judge is the woman you are now. Nothing else matters."

She nodded tightly, but her unhappiness made him miserable. "And I suppose you don't hold hands with people you don't like."

"I would suppose you're right," he said gently, taking her hand in his.

"Well," she said, "then do something for me. Please."

"Lethe—"

"Stop me," she whispered. "If you get a hint that I'm . . . losing my mind to the thing inside me . . . do something. Knock me out. Tie me up. Don't wait, or second-guess. Just . . . stop me."

"I don't know if I can," Lannes said. "I haven't had much luck."

Lethe smiled bitterly. "I don't want to die. I don't want to be murdered by some old man with a grudge who's poking around people's brains. But I don't want to kill, Lannes. I don't want to kill, and that's more important to me than staying alive."

Lannes did not know how to reassure her. He was uncertain he could help, but the fear and dread that hummed around her presence was so acute that he could taste it as though it were his own sin to commit. Murder. Violation.

He pulled her close, wrapping his wings around her

body. She pressed her forehead against his chest and felt very small, very fragile. He thought of what Koni had said, that someone had foreseen her murder, and the fear that filled him was crushing. He pushed it aside, though. No time. And it was not going to happen.

He kissed her palm. When he let go, she placed it above his heart, and the warmth that spread between them was so overwhelming that he wanted to kiss her until she begged him to stop.

"I'd like that," she whispered.

Lannes fought to control himself. "You know I'm not human."

"Yes," she said dryly. "You're worried what I'll think of you."

"It's a concern."

"Were you burned once?"

"I never let myself get close enough to be burned."

"What about your own kind? Women, females."

"I've . . . known some of them," he said awkwardly. "But they mature faster than us, and I was always a bit . . . bookish."

Lethe laughed quietly. "You're a nerd."

He bit back a grin. "You could say that."

She continued to laugh, but it was filled with delight. "And what? What made the others more attractive?"

"You'd have to ask *them*," he said, and held her hand against his chest like it was all that was keeping his heart beating.

Lethe stood on her toes. "Kiss me."

He could not help but tease, mostly to cover his

overwhelming emotion at hearing her say those two words. "I suppose that means you liked it before?"

"Kiss me," she repeated, her smile fading. "Lannes."

He wrapped his arms around her waist and pulled her up tight against his body, her feet dangling below his knees. Her scent filled him, clean and warm as a summer day, and he savored, with a great deal of heartache and wonder, the desire she felt for him.

For *him*.

He kissed her, which felt no different than plunging one thousand feet off a cliff in the Himalayas. She stole his breath in exactly the same way—in a rush— his blood tingling and his body aching in all the right ways. She wrapped her legs around his hips and gasped as he jerked against her, just once, and the sound of her pleasure, the sensation of it rolling through his mind, was so overwhelming it was all he could do not to drag her into the bushes and bury himself in her body. He had never felt such arousal—never allowed himself to indulge this far, this long—and it made him blind and deaf to everything but her.

Which was probably why he did not hear the rumble of an approaching engine. Or Koni's hiss of warning. He heard nothing until it was too late.

A police cruiser rolled into the parking lot.

CHAPTER SEVENTEEN

My luck, Lethe thought, *well and truly sucks.*

Lannes set her down slowly as a pair of headlights burned into her retinas. She resisted the urge to shield her eyes, though Lannes did it for her when he stepped in front of her body, his hands loose at his sides.

A police officer got out of the brown sedan. He did so carefully, with one hand on his weapon and another holding a Mag-Lite, which he shone from Koni— who stood by the Humvee—over to Lannes and Lethe. Rictor was nowhere in sight.

"All right, everyone," said the officer, his voice sounding young and nervous. "Over to one side, please, and keep your hands in front of you."

They did as he asked. No bullets had been fired yet, which was some consolation. The officer looked as young as his voice, had clean-cut good looks and short brown hair. His uniform looked immaculate, and his eyes were intelligent. And wary.

"What," he asked slowly, "are the three of you doing here at this time of night?"

"Actually," said Lethe, trying to sound very feminine and very reasonable, "we were just out for a drive. It's a nice night."

"Your plates are out-of-state," he said. "Maine. Illinois."

"We're staying at the West Baden dome," Lannes said, his tension rolling keen and fine through her mind. "Tourists."

"Old friends," Koni said.

The officer did not look entirely reassured. "Licenses and registration. I'll want to check your cars, too."

The blood in the Impala. Shit.

But something happened. The officer shone his light over her face a second time, and the beam stayed there, flicking down an inch so it would not blind her. He stared, as though wheels were turning in his head, and his focus was suddenly so overwhelming that she thought her heart would pound a hole through her chest.

"Alice Hardon," said the officer. "My God."

The name sent something cold and serpentine slithering down her spine, a sensation not improved upon by the rolling wave of alarm that pushed from Lannes into her mind like a tsunami crushing the shore.

"Alice," the cop said again, some of his excitement fading at her silence. "Ms. Hardon. Is that your name?"

"Yes," Koni said smoothly. "I think she's just surprised you knew it, too."

Lethe's knees almost buckled. Her name was Alice
Hardon. But hearing it gave her no pleasure. In fact, it
made her want to run far, hands clapped over her ears.
She wished she had never heard the damn thing.

Maybe her distress showed; the officer tensed, shining his light again on the two men.

"Ms. Hardon," he said carefully. "Do you know
these guys? Are they friends?"

"Yes," she said, forcing herself to focus. "What's
wrong? Why *do* you know who I am?"

The officer did not relax. "You've been missing for
three days, but the search only began this morning.
Your family alerted our local station and said you had
been down in this area, so we started asking around. I
was at the hotel an hour ago. They said someone fit-
ting your description had been around."

"I was on a road trip," she said, fighting for words.
"I lost my cell phone. I didn't think anyone would de-
clare me missing."

The policeman still looked at Lannes and Koni.
"You sure you're okay?"

This time she found it easier to put a smile on her
face. "Positive."

"Okay, then." The officer took a step back toward
his car, which was crackling with radio chatter. "If
you don't mind, ma'am, I'd like all of you to come
to the station with me. I need to let people know they
can call off the search. And you should call your
parents."

Parents. Family. She felt dizzy. Terror clawed up her throat.

No, she thought. *No.*

Lannes swayed toward her, the edge of his wing brushing her arm. "I don't suppose she could make her calls from the hotel, could she? You can call off the search, but as far as letting her family know . . . the hotel would be more private."

"I'm sorry," the officer said, still moving backward toward his car. "I need to call this in."

At the back of her mind, the anchor stirred. That voice. *Runa.*

The dead woman's presence poured up from the abyss of Lethe's lost memories like a flower blooming in fast motion, filling her, but this time not in complete control.

Do it, Runa said. *Stop him.*

No, Lethe replied. *I won't hurt him.*

No, the voice explained. *Like this.*

And then Runa did take control, but only just, and before Lethe could resist she felt herself plunge into the police officer's mind and rip out his memories.

She didn't take all of them, just the past ten minutes. It felt like scraping a spoon along the inside of an avocado to dig out the flesh, and it was the most horrifying, damning thing she could have imagined doing to anyone. But in less than three seconds the deed was done. And the officer was down on the ground, alive but unconscious.

Lethe collapsed to her knees, digging her fists into the concrete. She scraped them so hard her knuckles bled, but she did not mind the pain. She wanted the pain.

There, said Runa. *You see how it's done. Again.*

Go to hell, snarled Lethe. *Fuck you.*

I know what you are planning. That you wish to kill me, or break us apart. Do as you wish, but you will not harm me. You cannot. Not until we are done.

Lethe screamed at her, except she was suddenly not screaming in her mind, but with her voice, and Lannes was there, holding her tight. Koni—and Rictor, who had reappeared—were placing the police officer into his sedan.

She could not breathe. Her heart was going to explode. She lay down on the parking lot, pressing her cheek into the cold concrete, sobbing. The sensation of tearing out those memories felt like poison in her brain. Like she was going to choke to death on them.

And for a moment—just one—she realized she could take out those memories. Her own memories.

Again, Runa had said.

Lannes dragged her into his arms. He stood, curling her tight against his chest, his wings draping over her body, and she clung like it was him or death.

"He has a camera in his car," Lannes rumbled.

"Taking care of it," Koni said.

Lethe felt herself carried some distance away, and then Lannes set her down just for a moment against the Impala. He opened the door. Helped her in. But she did not loosen her grip around his neck. She could not.

"I took his memories," she whispered, hardly able to speak past the tears. "I took them. Of us."

"I know," he said heavily, kneeling outside the car. He brushed his lips against her brow, and then her lips. "She was inside your mind. I felt her take control."

"Lannes," she breathed, drowning in horror. "I think I did this to myself."

His gaze was impossibly grim. Rictor appeared behind him. "We're ready to go."

Lannes did not look at him. "We'll be right on your tail."

LETHE KEPT HER EYES CLOSED WHILE THEY DROVE. LANNES was a constant presence in her mind, but his warmth did nothing to assuage her guilt. She had killed an old man with her bare hands, but somehow, as horrible as that act had been, it did not feel nearly as obscene as what she had just done to that police officer.

Even if Runa had made her do it. Even so.

"Talk to me," Lannes said roughly. "Lethe."

The leather seat smelled like blood. "You knew that other name, didn't you? The one the officer called me?"

"Ali—"

"Don't say it ," she interrupted fiercely.

Lannes hesitated. "Koni and Rictor told me."

"Who was she?"

He took a moment to respond, and she realized it was her wording that had stopped him cold. *Who was she?*

And not, *Who am I?*

His voice was hoarse when he spoke, almost broken. "I don't really know who she was. She was hurt by

some members of her family. Kidnapped. I guess. . . .
Koni met her, after she had been . . . rescued from
them."

Lethe rolled those words around, finding herself
too numb to appreciate them. "That wouldn't be
enough to commit the suicide of your memory. Unless
there's something else you're not telling me."

There was. She felt it in that instant. There was a secret. It was burning him up. She remembered the hotel,
and his eyes when she had walked into that room. His
grief, his desperation.

Because of her. Something they had told him about
her.

"Say it," she whispered.

"I don't want to."

"I hurt you, is that it? Something I did—"

"No," he rasped, as the Impala swerved. "It was your
family. Your great-aunt. It was her. She captured us.
My brothers. Me. She was the one who tortured us."

Of all the things he could have said, that was the
least expected. And the most horrific. It was so awful
that all she could do was stare at him, numb, blood
roaring in her ears.

"No," she said. "That's impossible. They're wrong.
They must be wrong."

"I don't think they are."

"Did they give you proof?" Her voice broke. "Pic-
tures?"

"They *recognized* you. They knew your face."

Lethe closed her eyes, shuddering. Lannes swore, and
pulled off the road. The Impala bounced, something

crunched. Ahead of them, the Humvee also pulled over. She saw a faint light out the window. Eastern sky. A hint of dawn.

Lannes undid her seat belt and dragged her into his lap. It was uncomfortable—the wheel dug into her back—but his arms were strong and his voice rumbled like thunder in her ears, in her mind.

"It wasn't you," he whispered again and again. "It wasn't you."

"Close enough," she replied, ragged and soggy, unable to breathe through her nose. "I don't . . . I don't know the details of what you went through, but I know it was bad. How can you be near me and not think about what happened?"

"Easily," he said. "You make it better."

A sob rose up her throat. She could not choke it down. Lannes cradled her against him.

"You asked me if you were a good person," he said quietly. "The answer is yes. You were a good person, Lethe. Memories might shape you, but they don't make you. Not where it matters. Not here." He placed his hand over her heart.

He was not lying. He meant every word—she could feel it in him. If the link had not been there, she might still have believed him. He could hide nothing in his eyes. Despite his mask, he was guileless.

So are you, he whispered inside her mind.

I'm not safe, she told him. *There must be more to why I destroyed my memories.*

"You're assuming too much," he said out loud. "What makes you think you had a choice?"

"Because I did," she said, certain of it. Ahead, a car door slammed. Rictor appeared. Lannes rolled down the window. Lethe buried her face in his chest.

"Everything okay?" asked Rictor.

"Just need another minute or two. Where are we going?"

"Charlie called Koni. He came through with the address and number for Ed. He lives nearby."

Lannes frowned, and Lethe could feel in his mind a hint of confusion that his brother had not called him directly. "Okay. Like I said, another couple minutes."

Rictor seemed to hesitate before walking back to the Humvee, or maybe that was Lethe's imagination. She felt him look at her though—a glance that broke through her like she was made of air and glass. It made her uneasy. She wondered what he knew about her.

Lannes rolled his window back up. "Will you feel like talking to Ed?"

"I have to," she said. "I don't think he trusts you guys as much."

"Then let's get you cleaned up," he murmured, and helped her sit back. He dragged a box of tissues from the backseat, and she blew her nose while he got out of the car to dig around the trunk. He came back with a clean rag, a bottle of water and a teddy bear.

Lethe stared at the bear. Lannes said, "My niece. I bought it for her."

A smile bubbled out of her, a weak one, and he said, "There. Good. Hold the bear."

"Don't be ridiculous," she muttered, but she took

the stuffed animal and hugged it to her chest, watching him as he dampened half of the rag and began washing her face. She let him do the first few strokes, just because it was the first time she could remember being babied, but then it started to feel like he was going to scrape off her cheeks. She took the rag from him, and he sat back, watching. His eyes glittered in the shadows.

"Feel better?" he finally asked.

"Better," she said. "Thank you."

Lannes nodded roughly. Ahead of them, taillights winked. He leaned over, planted a hard quick kiss against her brow and then started the engine.

Ten minutes later, they drove up to Ed's house.

The old man lived on a back country road that was more gravel than concrete. It was still dark, but the sky had lightened enough to illuminate the individual silhouettes of trees and fence posts that bordered large meadows filled with vague dark blobs that were probably cows and horses.

Ed had a long driveway, and they parked at the end of it. He lived in a manufactured home that had been neatly maintained. He was up—or at least his light was on. Through the window Lethe saw the old man puttering around, dressed in pajamas.

The predawn air felt cold and good on her face. Koni approached and gave her a long look that was surprisingly kind. "Are you okay?"

"Fine," she said, trying not to think about the fact that he knew her—the other her—and had not said a word. Although, in hindsight, the way he looked at her had been revealing enough.

"I called ahead," Koni said, as Lannes tucked Etta's shoe box under his arm. "Told him we were checking out early but wanted to say good-bye."

"I like him," she found herself saying, as if it would bring her comfort. And it did, in a way. She liked Ed. She. Now. She was still a person, her own person, and no matter what had happened in the past, no matter whom she was associated with, her future was her own.

More or less. If she kept telling herself that, maybe she would finally believe it.

Ed disappeared from the kitchen window as they walked up to the house. An orange cat appeared from inside a small doghouse and started purring like a freight train. The cat was especially taken with Rictor and kept jumping in front of him, wildly leaping to rub against his legs.

Koni grinned. Rictor glanced at him. "Not one word."

"Wouldn't dream of it," the tattooed man replied.

Lethe raised her hand to knock on the door. It opened before she could, and Ed greeted her with a gentle hug that left her breathless.

"You've been crying," he said, holding her at arm's length. The porch light felt hot on her face.

"It's why we're leaving early," she said.

Concern flickered in his eyes. "I'm sorry. Come on in. I'll make you all some coffee. Or do you prefer tea?"

"Anything," she said, while the others made polite little grunts of vague approval. The cat followed them in, meowing plaintively at Rictor. It was rather big, with white socks, a round tummy and a stubby tail.

"Roxanne," Ed said. "Hush."

The cat only got louder, standing on its hind legs and digging her claws into Rictor's leg. Koni covered his mouth, facing the wall and a long line of photographs that seemed to consist of young children under Christmas trees or standing in the grass surrounded by dogs and the legs of adults.

Ed's home was simple but cozy. It had tan carpet, a small dark green couch and a coffee table covered in magazines and books about World War II. The American flag, hanging from a pole, had been propped up in the corner, and beside it was a box filled with wrapped presents, lovingly covered in glittery ribbons.

"Christmas shopping done early?" she asked Ed as he handed her a cup of coffee.

He looked sheepish. "I can't help myself. I see little things here and there, down in Jasper or Paoli. I don't have anyone else to spend on but my grandkids."

"I bet they love you," she said, and he blushed happily, shaking his head as though having their love was something to which he was far too modest to admit.

She looked up and found Lannes watching her. Her heart twisted in her chest, pounding fast with grief . . . but also hope. His eyes were filled with concern, but there was nothing but warmth on the edge of his mind; his heart was sweet against her own. "Ed," Lannes rumbled, tearing his gaze from her. "We have a picture we wanted to show you. We were hoping you might recognize some of the faces."

The old man clapped his hands together and rubbed them. "I would be delighted."

Behind him, the cat was still having a vigorous conversation with Rictor, who, in a sudden burst of motion, swept down and scooped her into his arms. Four white paws curled in the air. The cat chirped once, then fell silent.

"Huh," Ed said, frowning at the orange tabby. Rictor remained utterly impassive.

Lannes opened the shoe box and removed the black-and-white group photo. Ed carefully took it from him and sat on the couch. He stared for a long time. Long enough for Lethe to take a sip of coffee and realize that she hated the stuff.

"I know these people," he said, finally. "All but one."

He pushed aside some magazines and laid the photo down. "Here, this little girl is Milly. That's Etta Bredow beside her. The two boys are Marcellus and, well, Simon. This here is William." Ed tapped the young man's face. "He had a good heart. Always a kind word. His parents owned the spread where this picture was taken."

"His family owned a cemetery?" Lethe asked, finding that rather odd.

"Not *just* a cemetery," said Ed, tapping his chin. "And by the thirties they had stopped burying local people. Maybe any people at all."

"Um," she said, and pointed at the child in William's arms. "How about this little guy?"

"He's the one I don't know. Probably because he was too young to come out and play."

She glanced around to see if the others had questions, and found Koni staring at the photo with unnerving intensity.

"Where," he said slowly, "did you say this was taken?"

"The farm is in Cuzco," Ed replied, looking at him curiously. "Fifteen, twenty minutes from here."

Lannes also glanced at Koni. "Is it still owned by the same family?"

"I assume so. Every now and then I hear rumors that William still visits the place."

"He would have to be near a hundred years old," Lethe replied.

"Young lady," Ed said, "a man is quite capable of living that long and doing things, even if he's got one foot in the grave."

Lannes smiled and started to put the photo back into the box. Ed stopped him and reached inside. He pulled out a pink piece of paper, his hand shaking slightly.

"Runa's stationery," he said reverently, though hearing that name made Lethe's stomach twist. "She used to write grocery lists on this stuff. I would do her shopping when she was busy."

He glanced at Lethe. "May I?"

She hesitated, afraid of what he might read, but Ed did not wait. He unfolded the paper, his eyes scanning words.

" 'Dear Abigail,' " he read out loud. " 'Aware as I am that you no longer welcome my letters, I nevertheless feel compelled to try one last time to make you understand the very real danger that threatens your children. I confess to having serious concerns about Simon. He is a bad influence, and the ill-advised present of that blasted grimoire does little to assuage my fear that he will commit to a grievous action beyond our ability to repair. I warn you, Abigail, Lucy and Barnabus feel the same and have ordered William to take special care when around that child. He is not to be trusted. Nor will your children be, should they continue to keep his company.'"

Ed stopped reading and set down the letter. He stared at it, his hands pressed flat against the table. Lethe forced herself to breathe, those words ringing through her as though she could hear them in her head. Which, given the nature of things, would not have been an incredible surprise.

Koni and Lannes appeared equally troubled, while Rictor displayed a cold glimmer in his eyes. The orange tabby hung over his shoulder. The entire front of his body was covered in cat hair.

"Some letter," Ed whispered. "Bitch."

She stared, startled, but Lannes was on his feet in a moment, slamming a hand against the old man's shoulder. He bore him down against the couch, and Koni leapt over the coffee table to take his other arm. The old man did not struggle. He looked at Lethe, and smiled.

"Amazing, the things you learn when you eavesdrop," said Ed, though his voice was suddenly low, hoarse.

Even his face looked different, and the muscles in his jaw were trying to rearrange themselves.

"Simon," Lethe said. "Get the hell out of that man."

"You have no patience whatsoever. Please. Sit. Relax. Let us chat a spell. And while you're at it, get your monsters to stop touching me. They'll leave a bruise on this nice old man."

Lannes leaned forward. "You hurt her, you hurt him, and there will be no talking. I'll find you myself, and rip off your head."

"You leave me shaking in my skivvies, beast. Now, please, if you would." The old man—Simon, really—gave them a rather ghastly grin. Lannes and Koni, sharing a long look, eased off. But not far. Behind Lethe, Rictor moved close. Still holding the cat.

"Talk," Lethe said.

"We have options," the man remarked. "As I said while dangling from the seat belt of that awful truck, I am prepared to offer you a deal. You kill the thing inhabiting you, and I will let you live."

"Gee," Lethe said, "what a bargain."

"It is," he replied. "I can be anywhere, in anyone. All I have to do is think it. And you're dead."

"Really," Lannes said. "If that's the case, then think your way into me."

"Or me," Koni said.

"Or please," Rictor added coldly, "try *me*."

Simon hesitated. Lethe smiled. "You are so desperate. And you are such a loser. Runa saw it. She hated your guts, and you knew it. So you thought you'd get even by hurting her little girl. You thought that would prove yourself to everyone. You little shit."

Ed's face froze in an ugly grimace. "Don't you say that."

"Murderer," she snarled. "Spoiled fucking brat."

"I'm gonna kill you," he whispered. "Oh, God, I'm gonna kill you."

Lethe felt a pulse at the back of her brain. It was Runa, waking. Lannes gave her a sharp look and took a step. Too late. The dead woman entered her mind like a ghost, intangible but full and rich.

Lethe could not fight Runa, and her mouth moved, speaking words not her own. "For my daughter," she whispered. "You will never have peace."

And then she used Lethe to slam into Ed's mind. Simon had a barrier up, but it buckled under the onslaught, and quite suddenly Lannes was there with her, too, skimming the outside of her thoughts. His strength poured in deep and true.

They did not break the wall, but Ed cried out, the tendons of his neck straining, and just like that, Simon fled. Back to the foxhole, wherever he lived.

Runa retreated as well. Lethe's knees buckled, and Rictor caught her arm, the cat on his shoulder jumping off with a disgruntled yowl. Lannes reached her in the next heartbeat, his jaw set, his eyes so dark with concern that all the blue seemed to have been traded for black. His passage sent magazines flying off the coffee table, victims of his wings.

"I'm fine," she muttered. "Ed?"

"Okay," Koni said. "Just unconscious."

Lethe sat down on the floor, resting her forehead against her knees. "That went well," she said, and promptly leaned over to vomit.

CHAPTER EIGHTEEN

I T took several hours to take care of Ed. His pulse was fine, his breathing regular, but he was unconscious for such a long time that Lannes grew concerned about brain damage. Unfortunately, that was nothing a doctor could fix. Psychic trauma had to heal itself, or not heal at all.

But the old man woke. And after a lengthy conversation in which Ed confessed remembering nothing after seeing the photograph—and Lannes determined that no permanent damage had been done—they bundled themselves up, said good-bye to the cat, and drove away, waving to the old man who stood on his stoop and watched them with a smile, sadness in his eyes.

They stopped briefly at a little café near the lake. Lethe had used the bathroom at Ed's house, so she stayed in the car—just in case someone recognized her—while the men went in and bought some food. It took only a few minutes to do that, and less than that to decide where to go next.

"I've been thinking about crows," Lannes said, as

they stood outside eating. "Crows with odd behavior, protecting large tracts of land."

"I haven't heard this story," Lethe said, talking around a roasted chicken sandwich. Odd breakfast, but the café served fishermen who wanted to buy lunches for the entire day. Sandwiches fit the bill.

"You think the farm in the picture is there," Koni said, looking rather ill.

Lannes shoved some roast beef into his mouth. "You must be a mind reader."

"Do you think William will be there?" Lethe asked them. "If he is, it could go badly for him."

Koni tensed, his reaction seeming rather more personal than simple concern over a stranger's welfare. Lannes frowned at him, and to Lethe said, "I'm not throwing you in the trunk of the car. Forget it."

"Duct tape, then. Rope. If he was part of that group, he could be in danger from me."

Lannes finished off the rest of his sandwich. "Based on Runa's letter, I doubt he did anything to harm her daughter."

"I'm not willing to take the risk."

"You'll have to," Rictor said, leaning against the car, deceptively casual. "You're too powerful. Even if we tied you up, you'd still break free. I don't even know how well a sedative would work. The only way to really stop you is to put a bullet in your brain."

"Stop," Lannes said. "Don't go there."

Rictor shrugged. "It's the truth. Deal with it, or not. She's dangerous. And once this is over, *if* it's over, she—"

"I'm right here," Lethe interrupted.

"Is going to need training," he finished.

" 'Training,' " she repeated. "Or is that another way of saying that I'll need to be watched, to make sure I don't cause trouble?"

"You *are* trouble," Rictor said. "It's in your blood."

Lannes stepped toward the man, who was a full head shorter but looked perfectly capable of handling himself against the gargoyle. They stared at each other, and there was no remorse in Rictor's eyes. No calculation, no emotion. Just flat, hard calm.

Everyone fell silent. Then, carefully, Koni said, "We're too exposed. Let's go."

Lannes and Lethe pulled out first in the Impala, leaving the Humvee a fair distance behind. For good reason. Five minutes later, he saw a crow fly free of the large black car. Koni, going scouting. Still attempting to keep his secrets from Lethe, which at this point, seemed rather ridiculous. Soon after, Lannes let Rictor pass him.

It was still morning. Lannes saw very few homes and hardly any people—just two boys playing basketball in the parking lot of a church—but the sun was shining, and the air flowing through the open window tasted rich and sweet and wild as they traveled down narrow country roads winding through land still heavy with mist. The gold of autumn was in full riot, brilliant against green meadows nestled along swollen silver creeks that captured the dawn light as though the waters were full of magic.

"There's a crow following us," Lethe said, peering out the window.

"Um," Lannes replied. "Really."

She gave him an odd look. "You do realize, don't you, that this link goes both ways? I might not be able to read your mind all the time, but I know what you're feeling."

"Might as well be the same thing," he muttered.

Lethe looked out the window again, staring into the sun, her hair shining golden and fine. Her face finally had some color, a touch of rose in her cheeks, and her eyes carried a deeper, richer green than he remembered. "I have instincts about things. Not memories, and not those random facts I spout. Just . . . feelings that seem to rest in between." She pointed out the window at the crow winging high above the Humvee. "Like instincts. And that bird, if I can allow myself to say it, is not normal."

Lannes sighed. "Don't ask me to explain."

"But I'm right."

He smiled. "You're sitting in a car being driven by a gargoyle disguised as a human man, while *you* are capable of moving objects with your mind, as well as reading minds. So yes, probably most anything your instincts tell you about this world, no matter how strange, is going to be possible."

The Humvee began to slow. Lannes looked around. He had not paid attention to where they were driving. Harvested cornfields were on his left, and on his right, a thick forest. Ahead, the crow wheeling in the sky suddenly twisted to the left, diving toward the ground, and Rictor braked so suddenly that Lannes almost crashed into his bumper.

Just as he slowed, Lannes felt a hum in his blood, a flutter of energy . . . and then a black wave of feathers erupted over the golden forest, careening en masse towards the one black bird struggling to get away.

"Shit," Lethe said.

Rictor jumped out of the Humvee and ran toward the edge of the road. Lannes and Lethe got out as well, joining him. The one small crow began flying toward them, but the sheer number pursuing him was terrifying, even to Lannes. At least a hundred crows, maybe more, their shadow passing over the cornfield like a giant fist. Rasping voices screeched, so deafening he could feel the vibration in his chest.

Rictor glanced down at Lethe. "You can save him."

She blinked, clearly startled, and the man grabbed her wrist. A cold smile tugged at his mouth. "Make something of yourself."

Lannes grabbed her other hand. "Put up a wall," he said urgently, traveling along their link. "Just see it in your head."

He felt her bewilderment, but it was followed by the roar of her quick mind. She stared at the birds, her focus sharpening to a razor point, and narrowed her eyes.

Power roared across her skin into Lannes' own body, like a lightning bolt shooting up his arm and into his brain. Her eyes flashed with actual light, her mouth tightening into a hard line, and a moment later all of the crows crashed against an unseen barrier. None of them dropped all the way to the ground, but they hovered, flapping furiously, blocking out the morning sun.

Koni fluttered past, directly into the Humvee. Rictor slammed the door behind him.

"Move," he snarled at the others, and then froze, staring into the woods. Lannes turned and saw nothing. Lethe grabbed his arm.

"I lost control of them," she snapped, and raced for the car. Lannes looked over his shoulder in time to see a black wave rushing forward. He leapt into the Impala, fighting to roll up the window, and gunned the engine.

The crows flew past both vehicles into the woods. Not one of them hesitated. They were a dark massive blur that rocked the Imapla on its wheels until . . . . nothing; they were swallowed by trees. It was as if the crows had never existed.

Lannes sat staring, his heart racing faster than the thoughts flitting through his memory, as he watched again and again that remarkable disappearance.

"Forget normal," Lethe said. "*That* was crazy."

Lannes agreed. But it also meant they were on the right track.

THEY DROVE FOR ANOTHER FIFTEEN MINUTES BEFORE finding a road through the woods. It was just as wide as a car and packed with dirt—a lane, Lannes might have called it, except that a rusty chain ran across the entrance, and there was a sign that quite clearly said, NO TRESSPASSING.

The Humvee door kicked open, and a barefoot,

half-dressed Koni tumbled out. His hair was wild, his shirt off, displaying his impressive array of tattoos, and his jeans were hardly zipped, revealing the fact that he did not wear underwear.

Koni's eyes flashed with golden light. He walked up to Lethe, ignoring everything and everyone else.

"Thank you," he said, with a great deal of sincerity.

"My pleasure," she replied, with just as much dignity.

Lannes bent down and rattled the lock on the chain across the road. He made a sharp twisting motion, and it fell broken into the dust. The chain slid apart, pooling into the narrow lane.

"Oops," he said. "Look at what I did."

Lethe smiled. "Guess this means you need to find the owner. Offer to buy a new lock."

"Assuming you *reach* the owner," Rictor said, staring at the woods.

Koni followed his gaze. "Just so everyone knows, I'm not biting it, *Blair Witch*–style."

"I'll put you out of your misery before it comes to that," replied Rictor, and it was difficult to tell if he was serious. He marched back to the Humvee, glancing over his shoulder at the rest of them. "Stay in the car, no matter what you see, no matter what happens. And keep your windows rolled up."

Koni grimaced. Lannes and Lethe shared a long look.

"Does he know something we don't?" she asked them.

"He's Rictor," Koni said, as if that was all the explanation necessary.

They started driving. Humvee first, Impala close behind. Lethe rolled down the window just a crack to air out the scent of blood—which was either fading or becoming something she was accustomed to.

"I've had this car for forty years," Lannes told her. "It was a birthday present. I would cruise around on short road trips whenever I needed to clear my head."

"It's not completely ruined," she told him, then stopped. "Wait, forty years? Just how old are you?"

"Um," he said, his hands tightening around the wheel. "We age a little differently than humans. I suppose in your years, I would be in my thirties. But chronologically I'm in my late seventies. I was born in 1930."

"Wow," she said. "So, the normal lifespan of a gargoyle . . ."

"We can live up to three hundred years," Lannes replied, "and we usually do. Especially now that we're no longer hunted."

You'll outlive me, he heard her think. Which was not something he wished to contemplate. At all.

The forest was beautiful. Lannes had thought it was lovely on the outskirts, brushed in the gold of autumn and the lingering green of summer. But here, deeper inside the forest, was another kind of wilderness. He could not see past the border of trees, which seemed to form a wall on either side of the road, filled as it was with brambles and wild stinging plants. To others it might have been inhospitable, but to Lannes it seemed nothing more than the first barrier to a mystery.

He looked for mysteries. His heart felt open to

them. If nothing else, he half-expected to find his car attacked by a cloud of angry crows. But nothing happened, and after ten minutes spent pushing down the incredibly long drive, the trees opened up, splitting apart to reveal another world.

A vast lush meadow spread before them, the grass soft and green and scattered with wildflowers. Fruit and nut trees dotted the surroundings, as did several grazing horses, brown coats shining. The drive snaked through the meadow, and at the end of it, surrounded by fat ancient oaks, was a large house, clearly old but lovingly cared for. A fresh coat of blue-gray paint had been applied, and the roof, old and made of metal, resembled the scalloped back of a dragon.

To the right of the house, at the end of the drive, was a cemetery.

"Well," Lethe said, glancing at him, "I guess we know where Etta's picture was taken."

They parked near the house. Everyone tumbled out. The air smelled fresh and clean, and not one sound of the modern world broke through the birdsong. Neither car nor plane. It was like being wrapped in another century.

Rictor still stared at the woods. Lannes moved close, following the direction of his gaze, trying to see what held him so captive—unhappily captive, he thought. He found nothing, though he sensed an odd tingle on the edge of his mind and remembered the crows blotting out the sun.

"There's something in there," he said.

"There's something everywhere," Rictor replied.

Roses surrounded the old house. Koni knocked on

the front door, while the rest of them hung back on the porch. Hummingbird feeders had been set out, and the cushions on the scattered chairs were covered in cat hair. Lannes saw a small wooden box filled with gardening gloves, a sagging bag of sunflower seeds, and a tattered bird-watching guide that was missing half its cover.

It was very warm and charming. He felt bad for interrupting.

No one, however, came to the door, and Lannes strolled to the end of the porch and peered over the rail.

There was a large garden behind the house surrounded by a pale blue picket fence. Despite the late growing season, he glimpsed red tomatoes, staked and tall, and rows of cauliflower and other leafy greens. A man stood among the vegetables. His back was turned to them, and he held a hoe in one hand. A crow perched on the other. He wore a straw hat.

Koni joined the others at the end of the porch. Rictor hung back, leaning against the rail, arms folded over his chest. Staring out at the woods. He did not appear particularly surprised or interested that there was a man on the other side of the house, and Lannes, recalling what little he knew of him, wondered if Rictor had been aware of this place's existence all along.

"You should go introduce yourself," Lethe said, holding back. "I'll just, uh, wait here."

Lannes hesitated, but it was quite clear she was not going to budge. Perhaps she felt Runa would return for more mayhem. He stooped down, kissed her cheek, and stepped off the porch onto a little beaten path lined in moss and stone. The crow watched his approach, its eyes profoundly intelligent.

"Hello," Lannes said, when he reached the fence. Koni was close behind. No sign of Rictor or Lethe.

The crow tilted its head, and after a curiously long moment, the man turned slightly, revealing a weathered and chiseled profile. He was old, but his body was so big and strong, Lannes had thought the man would be much younger.

"Well," said the stranger, with a small smile, "it's about time."

Lannes hesitated. "You know us?"

"I know enough," he said, and flicked his wrist. The crow flew into the branches of an oak, and the old man tapped his forehead.

"I'm the one who walked away," he said.

THE OLD MAN CALLED HIMSELF WILL, CLAIMING THAT William was a name used only by strangers and angry mothers. Also, according to him, it was too nice a day to be inside. There were chairs in the garden and a cooler filled with water, juice and ice. Rictor stood apart, waiting beside a tangle of tomato vines, his gaze sharp, intense.

"I believe we can talk candidly," said Will. "Seeing as how we're all a bit . . . different."

That's an understatement, thought Lannes, his hand brushing up against Lethe's knee. It had taken some persuasion to make her come this close to the old man—who finally had told her that he had *never* been involved in any of Simon's antics. Least of all those that harmed a child.

Lannes himself was perched on the edge of a stump, but he was so big in comparison, he felt rather like an elephant trying to make itself comfortable on a thimble.

"I know your face," he said to Will. "We have a picture of you when you were younger."

"Ages and ages ago, no doubt," he replied easily. "But I still have a young mind and a young heart."

Rictor shook his head and looked away at the woods. Will smiled at him.

"I was surprised to learn you were part of this. Given your current state."

"Were you?" replied the green-eyed man. "How remarkable that you would be surprised by anything."

"And yet, you. Always. Are a revelation." Will's voice was kind, but it carried a clipped sense of humor that made Lannes stare.

"You know each other," said the gargoyle.

"We met briefly, long ago," replied Rictor, still staring at the woods.

Will followed his gaze. "She won't bite, you know."

"I believe I know her a little better than you," the man replied tersely. "She dislikes me. Most of them do."

"What are you talking about?" Koni asked, staring at them both, seemingly just as surprised that Rictor and Will seemed to have a prior relationship.

Will smiled. "Our Lady of the Wood. I believe you had a taste of her temper."

Lethe made a small sound of protest. Lannes raised his hands. "How is it possible you know each other?"

Will glanced away at the woods and the house, the garden. Up at the trees and the crow watching them, then down at his hands. Anywhere but at him.

"My last name is Steele," said the old man. "I'm sure you're familiar with it."

Lannes was not, at first. He was tired, dense. He had to roll the word in his mind like a stone.

Steele.

And then it hit him, and Lannes could not look away from the old man. Indeed, he was gawking, but he could not make himself stop. Of all the things he might have expected, this was not it.

"You founded Dirk & Steele," he said. "You created the agency."

"Don't give me too much credit," Will replied easily, with a twinkle in his eyes. "The framework was in place long before I was born. My wife and I merely . . . expanded on things." He smiled, gesturing. "This place, what you see here, was—and still is—a sanctuary. For those who are . . . different."

"Like Simon was different," Lethe said in a heavy voice. "Or Etta . . . or Marcellus."

Lannes' curiosity flared, but he held himself reserved, thinking of his vision at the hotel—the stink of evil that had crowded his senses like raw sewage served as soup—and he looked at Will and found the old man staring back, his smile thoughtful and tainted with regret.

"You want to know about Simon Sayers," said the old man. "Little Simon Says."

"I'm beginning to hate that nickname," Lethe told him. "Who gave it to him?"

"His father. He thought it was . . . cute . . . that his son could make people do things against their will. And Simon liked to please his father." Will faltered. "I suppose we're all victims of such feelings."

Lannes thought of Frederick for some reason, recalling the difficulties his friend had faced in breaking away from his father—to live his own life, to write instead of carrying on the tradition of bookbinding. The split was older, and ran deeper than a mere career choice, but that had been the final cut between them. Alex Brimley and his only child had spoken little afterwards, and resolved nothing before the older man's death.

Lannes found Will watching him with uncanny, far-seeing eyes, and wondered if he could see beneath the illusion. The possibility made him feel vulnerable, despite the circumstances. Or, perhaps, because of them. William Steele was not just a stranger—he was a *powerful* stranger—and Lannes did not like having his secrets thrown about, or his armor weakened, in front of men who were undeniably mysterious.

"Koni," Lannes rumbled. "Did you know about this place?"

"No," replied the shape-shifter. "But I recognized the face in the picture when I saw it."

"We've never met," William said to him, though

there was a glint in his eye that made Lannes wonder
if that was half a lie.

Koni shifted uncomfortably. "I like to know who I
work for."

"Little spy," said Rictor.

"Whatever," Lethe interrupted. "I don't mean to be
rude, but I have a problem."

"We all do," William replied. "This is something
that should have been resolved seventy years ago."

"You'd think," she said coldly. "A little girl was
murdered."

The old man stared down at his hands, which were
strong and tanned, and surprisingly youthful. "Milly
was very sweet, not a mean bone in her body. She had a
way with animals, too. I found a fox and rabbit sleeping
in her bed once, together, because she . . . convinced
them it would be all right." He smiled sadly. "Remarkable girl. So was her mother."

"And afterwards? Obviously no one was punished."

"Never had a chance," William said. "You have to
understand something, young lady. My mother and father, those who came before them, were guardians of
this land, this old trust. People would come here because it was safe. But they didn't always get along. My
parents didn't expect that divisiveness to happen. They
assumed everyone would be as grateful as they were
for a chance to . . . be themselves. Human or otherwise.
A home of the heart for people without one." Bitterness
entered his voice. "The Sayers and Bredows were
trouble from the start. They came because they couldn't
help themselves, but they looked down on the area and

the people. They thought they were better. By the time we found out just how spoiled the children were, it was too late."

"They tried to summon something," Lannes said, as Lethe edged closer to him. "Do you know if they succeeded?"

Rictor shifted slightly, and met William's gaze. Which surprised not only Lannes, but Lethe and Koni as well. Lethe's confusion was a soft twisting cloud inside his mind, but Koni leaned forward, golden eyes simmering with a hot light.

"It was taken care of," William said finally.

"Permanently," Rictor added, and turned his back, facing the forest.

Koni let out his breath, slowly. "Shit. You've been holding out."

William gave him a hard look. "He does what he must."

"And the others?" Lethe snapped. "Why wasn't Simon . . . taken care of?"

"Because he was gone. All of them left immediately. They had no choice." Will plucked a small tomato from the vine and popped it into his mouth. "Runa was my mother's best friend. What happened to them changed everything."

Lethe leaned forward. "Runa's not entirely gone."

"Oh, I know," Will said, and offered her a tomato. "She's out sleeping in the woods."

CHAPTER NINETEEN

IT seemed like a fairly complicated problem to Lethe—how to reconcile the idea of an allegedly dead woman, more than seventy years gone from the world, with that of her still breathing and camped out in the forest. Will, however, assured her that it was really quite simple.

"Magic," he said. "Belonging to a creature so old, she cannot remember whether she was born or made."

They stood on the edge of the woods facing a wall of leaf and bark that was endlessly dense and impossibly green. Autumn, it seemed to Lethe, had not affected the woods in this place quite as much as the rest of Indiana, and though she could see almost nothing of the interior, she caught glimpses of shadows just beyond the foliage that heaved with more size and strength than any mere squirrel could account for.

"We will not enter the wood," Will said. "Our Lady claims to dislike guests but manages to keep more than her fair share of them—far beyond what a polite host should."

"In other words," Rictor said, "she's fucking dangerous."

"And how do you know?" Lannes asked him. "Personal experience?"

His green eyes glinted. But he did not say a word.

"You keep your distance, too," Will said to Koni. "She's prickly about shape-shifters."

Shape-shifters, thought Lethe, wondering when the madness would end. Gargoyles, men who flew as crows, dead women filling her brain . . .

She could not say she was surprised or puzzled by anything, anymore, but it was still surreal. And unaccountably familiar—on a gut level—same as she knew music and history. As though all of everything that had happened—all these people—were part of some inescapable truth.

Koni said, "I'll be fine."

"Try not to look like you're pissing yourself when you say that, and maybe I'll believe you," Rictor replied.

Will frowned. "Are all of you usually this contentious?"

"It keeps the love alive," Koni said.

Lethe's stomach churned. "You're certain Runa is in there?"

Will sighed, stooping to pick up some rocks in the grass. Despite his appearance, he had to be almost one hundred years old, yet he still moved with complete grace. "The Jesuits who found her body thought she was dead. Her heart had stopped beating, so technically she was, but technical is not the same as actual— and she was *not* really, *really* dead."

"What's the difference?"

"The difference," Will said, juggling the stones, "is in the soul. If the soul resides, then something—however drastic—can be done. If the soul has fled . . . well, as they say, you're dead."

Lannes was rubbing his eyes. "So Runa's soul remained, and you—what? Shoved her into the forest?"

Will stopped juggling, catching the stones in one hand. "Our Lady of the Wood had a special affection for my mother. I suppose one could say they were friends. Helping Runa was born of that friendship."

And then he turned and threw the stones into the forest. Lethe did not hear them fall but instead heard the chime of bells, small and delicate. The sound cut through her. But no more so than the sight that parted the brambles like silk.

A white stag appeared in the shadows. Its body glittered as though covered in starlight, its hooves gleamed like pearls, and in its eyes she saw a wild light that flickered as though lightning ran through its blood.

Behind the stag, a woman appeared. Pale and slender, she had hair so long it touched the ground. White furs caressed her body, surrounding and lifting round naked breasts painted in pale lines that could have been words or an illustration of wings. When she moved, she seemed to float, and everything about her shimmered like moonlight on ice. Her eyes were cold, flat and hard and assessing.

Inhuman. So far beyond human that Lethe hardly knew whether to be terrified senseless or utterly in awe. She was afraid to look away, though she wanted, des-

perately, to see Lannes' reaction. Instead she fumbled
with her mind, reaching for his thoughts, and found
herself met halfway in a tumble of emotion and one
brief word:

Faery.

Both the woman and the stag stopped just at the forest's edge, and to Lethe it was like being caught on the
other side of a wall—a wall through which she gazed
upon another world, whose wonders the mind could
not dream.

But Lethe might very well have been a smashed
flower for all that the woman seemed to notice her
presence in return. She had eyes only for Lannes, and
her breasts flushed a rosy pink, their pale nipples hard-
ening.

"Now this," she whispered, "is a first in a great long
time. I have not seen your kind in years, gargoyle.
Come a little closer, so that a Sidhe queen might look at
you beneath your mask."

Lannes straightened. "I am not here for games. Or
for you."

"You would deny me?" she asked softly. "Even just
a word?"

"I have no time for words," Lannes said. "I think
you know that. I'm certain you know why we're here."

For one moment, Lethe was sure something terrible was about to happen. She felt the weight of a great
force, much like the one in her vision of the dome,
only colder and wilder, as though one word from this
queen could unleash a thousand needles made of ice.
Fury flashed through her eyes, which were a startling

shade of green and filled with a hunger that chilled Lethe to the bone.

But the moment passed. The queen's emotion subsided, though her gaze was sharp.

"I saw, and I heard," she said, "And if it were not for the memory of one mortal woman, you would be mine, gargoyle. I would take you. And I would never let you go."

Her gaze left him, traveling to Rictor, who tensed slightly. A cold smile touched her mouth.

"Half-breed," she whispered. "They still let you live?"

"My lady," he said quietly. "Still singing in your cage?"

Her mouth twisted in displeasure. Will stepped in front of Rictor, facing down the inhuman woman with calm and quiet dignity.

"Please," he said. "For my mother."

The queen's gaze darkened, but she glided back into the shadows, the stag moving with her. Where she'd stood, the brambles began flowing like silk, tree branches heaving aside, and it was as though distances flowed like water—here, there, everywhere. A small clearing appeared, filled with a silver brook and a shaft of sunlight that pierced the canopy just so, striking the base of an enormous oak. And at the base of the oak, tangled in its roots, lay a woman.

A woman wearing Lethe's own face.

She hardly knew her own face, but the resemblance was unmistakable. Runa could have been her twin. Her eyes were closed and her chest was slowly moving, as though she were deep in sleep. Her skin looked as if it had been dusted with gold powder, and her hair resembled roots, twisted and draping past her hollow face. She was naked, but moss had crept over parts of her body, and a delicate fern grew between her breasts. Violets blossomed around her toes.

"Runa had several sisters," Will said quietly, glancing at Lannes. "Only one of them had a heart. The rest hardly had souls."

Lethe forced herself to breathe. "Did any of them have children?"

"Just one. I suppose you look like her, too."

"Blood," Lannes said heavily. "That was how Runa did it. You had a blood connection."

Blood. Lethe stared at the golden-skinned woman, and felt no joy, no sorrow—nothing but dread. Here was a connection, a root to her past, and she wanted nothing more than to run from it with all her strength. Or destroy it.

"I gave her a choice," said the queen, drifting into view inside the clearing. "A fair one. She agreed to stay here and feed my tree, and in return I gave her immortality. Until she avenges her daughter's death. And then she is free." The queen smiled. "It is a lovely tree, is it not? So full of human dreams."

Lannes' hand brushed against Lethe's arm. "Why has it taken Runa so long to seek out her daughter's murderers?"

"She had her obligations to fulfill. And I lost track of time." Her smile grew colder. "Better late than never."

"Is she awake?" Lethe asked, afraid it would show

too much weakness in front of the queen to take Lannes' hand, even though she needed his comfort, ferociously.

I am here, he whispered, his arm still touching hers. *You're not alone.*

The queen nudged the woman's foot. "My sweet fertilizer has ears. She can hear you, if you desire to speak."

Lethe gathered up her courage and crept forward, trying not to allow the ferociously bizarre quality of the moment to incapacitate her with fear. Lannes held her arm, and when she was within a foot of the tree line, he refused to let her go further.

"Runa," she called, straining against his arm. "Runa, I'm here."

"Speak louder," said the queen, smiling. "Reach into her dreams."

Lethe shivered. "*Runa.*"

A hum filled the air, as though the bark and leaves and roots of the forest had a voice soft and strong as spider silk, clinging to her mind, coating her heart with a heaviness that felt like death or sleep. She felt Lannes join her side, his thoughts trying to push against her, but it was impossible to respond.

The queen said, "How short-sighted. You left nothing of your mind."

And just like that, the world disappeared.

YOU'RE GOING TO DIE, YOU'RE GOING TO DIE, YOU'RE GO-*ing to die*.

Right now.

Hold on.

Alice. Alice, you dirty girl. Look what you made me do. Now be still. This will be over soon and never mind that man oozing shit beside you because he's dead gone anyway, soon enough, and it's your blood that matters, and your pretty little face. Little girl. Sweet little girl. My favorite grandniece.

Lethe could not open her eyes, but she did not want to. All she could hear, all she could feel, was that voice—sly and sibilant—filling her up as though there was a hole in her brain attached to a running hose. It was drowning her mind.

And then the voice shifted into something softer, kinder.

You're going to die. Don't know when or where, but just the how. A knife in your eye. Oh, God, I'm sorry.

Light bloomed on the other side of Lethe's eyelids. More voices.

The gallery is going under, darling, but don't worry, I'll take care of it. I just want you to smile again—and please, please, tell me where you were all that time. I don't know why you won't talk about it, and now with so many of us dead—

Dead, not all of us are dead—

We're monsters—

Not all of us—

I don't want to die, I wish I never knew, I can't live like this, I can't live—

So don't, whispered another voice; Runa, familiar

and old. *Give yourself to me. Help me. You must. I will not let you go.*

I will cleanse you of your pain.

LETHE FELT GRASS AGAINST HER CHEEK. SHE OPENED HER eyes, or tried to do, but her eyelids felt sticky and there was a bad taste in her mouth.

I'm here, Lannes spoke inside her mind, words followed by a torrent of desperate concern. *Stay with me.*

She managed to peel open her eyes, just a crack, and was nearly blinded by the color of the grass and the sky. Every line, every detail, was crystalline in its perfection, as though she was seeing the world for the first time.

Lannes crouched beside her, and his irises glinted with veins of blue light. For a moment she saw past the illusion, her vision filled with lavender skin and sharp bone, but the mask faded back into place, though his eyes remained the same. He folded her into his arms, pulling her up so that she leaned hard against his chest.

I was with you, said Lannes grimly, his voice soft inside her mind. *I heard everything.*

The Sidhe queen stood at the edge of the woods, the vision of the oak, and Runa, fading into darkness behind her.

"Green eyes," the queen murmured, meeting Lethe's gaze. "That blood always runs true."

She glided back a step and looked at Will. "You continue to keep strange bedfellows."

"I like to keep you amused," he said, smiling faintly.

"And you are, as always, exquisite to behold. My Sidhe queen."

She inclined her head, then passed her gaze over the rest of them, lingering last on Rictor.

"Do not come here again," she said quietly. "I do not wish the association. Not if someday I am to be free."

Rictor said nothing. The queen waited, as if she expected him to speak, and when he did not, her frown became dangerous. But she remained silent and drifted back into the forest, fading like a ghost, disappearing into the gloom.

"I don't know about all of you," Koni said, after a long moment of silence, "but I don't feel any better."

IT WAS LATE IN THE AFTERNOON. LETHE WAS QUITE CERTAIN that the amount of weirdness her brain could handle had reached its limit, and so she found herself seated at a battered kitchen table feeling numb, suffering an odd disconnect between the mundane and surreal, as she watched William Steele don an apron covered in faded cherries and start whistling "Lavender Blue."

The kitchen was small, with hardwood floors, large airy windows and a giant fireplace at one end, currently unlit. Lannes stood behind her shoulder. No chairs were large enough to support him. Koni lounged at the table, running his fingernail through some old grooves. Rictor was nowhere in sight, though Lethe had a sense that he might be as close as the hall. He seemed like the kind of man that needed isolation but not distance.

"So you see," Will said suddenly, pushing sand-wiches in front of them, "things are complicated here."

"Why haven't you told the others in the agency about this place?" Koni replied.

William picked something invisible off his apron. "Because there are some things that must not be told. Not yet. Perhaps, not ever. This place, what it holds, is one of them. Not even my own grandchildren know of it, though that will have to change soon enough."

"Are you referring only to the Sidhe queen?" Lannes asked. "Or are there other secrets?"

"There are always secrets," replied the old man. "Now eat. Then rest. Not much else can be done at the moment."

Lethe disagreed, but only out of principle. It was her mind on the line, not his. Her life that had been rocked to murder and magic, with no end in sight.

Her stolen life. A life she had stolen from herself, with help.

And what she had left behind, those voices in her head . . . glimpses of memories . . .

Her sandwich tasted like sawdust. She remembered Runa sleeping in the forest, and rocked slightly in her chair, overcome with a feeling of pure futility. There was no way she could go up against that. None.

Lannes laid his hand on her shoulder, and she reached back without thinking, sliding her fingers against his warm skin. She felt sinew and bone and recalled again her brief vision of him in the dome.

This is *a fairy tale*, she thought. *But what am I? One of the monsters?*

A princess, Lannes spoke inside her mind. *A lost maiden.*

She closed her eyes. *Are you my knight?*

His hand closed around her own. *I'm the thing the knight would kill.*

Lethe squeezed his hand, turning in her chair to look up into his eyes. He avoided her gaze at first, then met it square and true.

"No," she said, and felt eyes staring at the back of her head. Koni and Will. She did not look at them but stood slowly and walked out of the kitchen, pulling Lannes behind her. Rictor was in the hall, just where she had imagined him, sitting on the bottom of the stairs. He said nothing when Lannes and Lethe left the house, though his green eyes tracked them with cutting intensity.

The sun still shone. Looking at the woods made Lethe's skin crawl, but there were plenty of places that the forest did not touch, and she and Lannes ambled in comfortable silence, finally stopping when they reached a lush meadow overlooking a pond.

They sat in the grass. The air was warm.

Lethe said, "Did you know anything like that could exist? Anyone like *her*?"

"I knew of her possibility," Lannes replied, picking at grass. "But it's not something you think about. Or *want* to think about."

A chill stole through her. Those images, the Sidhe queen's voice, all were burned into her mind. "I can't fight Runa, you know. I can't kill her or hurt her. And not because she's protected in that wood. I just . . . it wouldn't be right."

"She's using you. That's not right."

Lethe leaned against him and ran her fingers over his chest through the illusion of his shirt. He began to hold her hand, but she pulled away.

"I'm sick of the mask," she said bluntly. "I know why you use it, obviously, but it's not you, I can see it's not you, and not being able to look at your real face is driving me nuts. So take it off. Please."

He leaned back, staring, and the trepidation that rolled through their bond made her teeth hurt. Up until that moment, she had thought that he might have seen inside her head the images she had gleaned from their shared vision in the dome, but it was obvious he had not. He did not know that she was already aware of what he looked like. Unless that had been a hoax, as well.

"Don't ask me if I'm sure," she said, when he opened his mouth to speak. "Just do it."

Lannes said nothing. He turned away from her, shoulders hunched, still playing with the grass between his fingers. At first she thought he was ignoring her, but then she noticed a shift in his appearance, a subtle one.

The easing off of his mask happened slowly, in bits and pieces. His skin became splotchy, as did his shirt, until finally he wore no shirt, and she could appreciate a broad chest thick with muscle and skin the color of dusk. Bits and pieces of the illusion frayed from his wings as well.

Watching it was another kind of enchantment. He

had no idea, she realized. Not one clue. To see him like that, so natural, so *real*, made her heart leap into her throat with a painful stutter. Maybe it was affection, maybe her own eccentricity, but much to her relief she found him almost painfully attractive, and unconditionally masculine. His profile was hawkish and sharp, his long black hair flowing wild around his shoulders between his flowing cape-like wings. Every hard muscle was chiseled as though from stone. He was physically perfect, if rough around the edges. Or perhaps because of it.

And he was kind. Effortlessly kind.

Lannes glanced sideways at her, and Lethe slid her hand under his jaw, making him fully face her.

Nothing had changed from her dream of him in the dome—except, this was no vision, and she was under blue sky with the sun shining. No monsters were breathing down their necks. Not yet.

"I like your face," she said. "I love your face."

Lannes went very still. Lethe slid her arms around his waist and held on. Between their minds, she tasted a thrill of wonder and fear.

Lethe kissed him. It was no different now, without the mask—no, that wasn't true; it was even better, she thought, taking a visceral pleasure in being able to open her eyes and glimpse something real and true. His face. Craggy as a mountainside, almost as rough, but his mouth was hard and his tongue slipped against hers, and a thrill raced from her heart to her stomach, making everything tighten, and ache.

You're not alone, she told him, so filled with emotion she could not have spoken out loud had she tried. *Lannes, you're not alone.*

He made a small desperate sound, his hands creeping around her waist, and she slid even closer, her mouth moving over his warm skin as her fingers danced across his back, stroking the edge of his wings. Lannes arched his back, breath rattling in his throat. Her fingers slipped across his stomach, sliding beneath the waistband of his jeans. Picking up where she had left off.

Lethe unbuttoned his pants slowly, leaning back to watch his eyes. And to let him watch her. She could feel him searching her mind, her face—every part of her—for some sign of rejection. Anything.

But all she felt was reckless tenderness, a need for him that went beyond mere desire, that was rooted deep in her soul, in every breath, in her desire to keep living. She wanted to live. With him.

Lannes's eyes darkened, and he grabbed her hand. Lethe tried to pull away, protesting. "You're not going to stop me this time."

"I didn't plan on it," he muttered hoarsely, dragging her close. "But you need to know something before we do this."

"Sounds ominous."

"Maybe." Lannes slid his hands into her hair, holding her face. His palms and fingers were huge and gnarled, his nails dull as silver, and sharp. But he touched her so carefully she hardly felt his strength, and his blue eyes held veins of light.

"If we do this," he whispered. "You're mine. And I mean that, Lethe."

"Promise?" she breathed, beginning to tremble.

Lannes inhaled sharply. "Just like I'll be yours."

Lethe leaned in, pressing her lips to his ear. "Is this a gargoyle thing?"

"No," he murmured. "I just love you, that's all."

She bowed her head, sagging against him. Opening her mind. There was so little of it left, her mind, but she bared it all and the link between them burned white-hot, as though she had the sun in her soul.

I cannot imagine my life without you, she whispered in his mind.

Then don't, he told her. *Don't, when you know how I feel about you.*

She wrapped herself around his body. Heart to heart. Massive muscles gliding beneath her hands. Being held by him felt the same as nesting in some soft warm home, and she was hungry for a home, aching to feel safe. She tried to see him, all of him, but he was so big and so close that all she could savor were snatches of his face, and hard muscle, the curve of a wing arched over his shoulder. He smelled sweet, like vanilla and cinnamon. Same man, she told herself. Real man. Not a mask of light and air, but something else.

He was awkward with her clothes. She ripped them off while he shoved down his jeans. She did not give him time to push them past his knees before she pounced, dragging her tongue over his shaft. His fingers dug into his scalp, and he let out a stifled groan. Lethe laughed.

"I hope you're not laughing at me," he rasped, though his voice also shook, and he ended up collapsing on his knees beside her. "I have a delicate ego."

"Nothing about you is delicate," she said, then straddled him, burying her hands in his hair, kissing the tip of his ear. "Except this."

She kissed his eyelid. "And this."

Her lips brushed his lips. "And this."

"How about my heart?" he whispered against her mouth.

"How about mine?" she replied.

She gasped as he laid her down in the grass, his lips and hands caressing her breasts—gently at first, then harder. She arched her back, trying to wind her leg around his hip, but he slid away, moving lower, with an awkwardness that was so tender she could hardly stand it. When he hooked her legs over his shoulder, she said, "Have you done this before?"

Lannes mumbled something. Lethe said, "What?"

"I read a lot," he said, and before she could say another word, he did something with his tongue that made her cry out, bucking against his mouth. He did it again, harder and faster, and she brushed her heels against his wings.

He stiffened slightly, gasping against her, and when she did it a second time, he stopped and gave her a look that was so hot and hungry, and so harassed, that she didn't know whether to laugh or beg for more.

"I don't have much practice at this," he said, and his mouth twitched into a smile. "Don't distract me."

"I'll just lie here, then," she said tartly, brushing his wing again with her heel. He closed his eyes, exhaling sharply—something she did as well, when he twisted his hips and she got another good look at his shaft. Desire pummeled her, and every part of her— *everything*—ached to have him inside her.

She reached down and grabbed his hair, tugging. "Come on."

"What if I want to slow down?" he asked, his fingers lingering between her legs as he moved up her body. She swallowed a gasp as he started a fast rhythm of caresses and penetration, and clamped her thighs around his large hand.

"In me," she gasped. "Now."

Lannes did not laugh or argue. He slid on top of her, and his weight felt so good she almost came just from having him rest heavy between her legs. She wrapped her thighs around his hips, arching her back with a low cry as he pushed slowly into her, filling her body so completely she lost all coherent thought. And when he began to move—slowly at first—she rocked hard against him, forcing him deeper, sharper. He groaned, and she reached around to stroke his wings.

Pleasure rocked down their link, so powerful she came right then, her orgasm spiking through her with a violence that cut the breath right out of her lungs. And then Lannes started moving faster, harder, grinding her into the grass—and she came again, lost in the mirror of his own pleasure and hers. He did not stop. She felt the building wave of his orgasm, and it was making him wild. She wanted him wild. Lethe did not remember having sex, but seeing him crazed made her so hot she could hardly stand it, and she tugged at his wings and hair, surging upward to bite his shoulder.

He came when she did that, and the pleasure that surged though their bond sent her over the edge again and again, until it was all she could do to breathe, gasping at aftershocks.

"Oh," she rasped, practically blind. "Holy shit."

Lannes, still buried inside her, started laughing weakly. The movement made her writhe, gasping, and his hand curved around the back of her head.

"Don't hurt yourself," he said, still grinning, and she punched his shoulder with a sharp laugh. He collapsed on top of her again, stretching out against her body, and she hugged him as tightly as she could, afraid he would roll away.

"I'm not leaving you," he said, his smile fading. "I couldn't, even if I wanted to."

"Let's not get to the point where you want to," she rasped. "Oh, man."

He almost started laughing again, and then stopped quite suddenly and said, "Was it strange for you?"

"Strange?"

"You know." He gestured at his face, and then his back, where his wings had finally collapsed around them.

Lethe stared. "Was it strange for *you*?"

"Of course not."

She kissed his throat, sliding her hand into his hair.

"Does this happen often? Between your kind and humans?"

"No," he said, holding her tight. "But it's not unheard of. It's frowned upon, maybe. But my brother has a human wife."

Lethe searched her heart. "It feels . . . natural."

"Oh. Well," he rumbled, "I'm all about being natural."

She bit back another laugh. In their clothes, a cell phone began to ring. Both of them flinched, and Lannes reached out with one long arm to snag his jeans. He dragged them over and fished out his phone.

"Hey," he said. A heartbeat later, a wave of confusion poured through their bond. It was serious enough that she started scrambling out from under him, reaching for her clothes. She was almost dressed when he hung up.

"I'm ready," she said, her knees still weak. "What happened?"

"It's Frederick," Lannes said, dazed. "He's here."

CHAPTER TWENTY

HE took a risk and decided to fly back to the old farmhouse—for speed, he told himself. Carrying Lethe over his shoulder, he climbed an oak—and once he was high enough, swung the woman into his arms and jumped, wings opening with a snap. He glided just below tree level, and it felt good to be free. Nor did he reassume his illusion. A deliberate oversight. Lethe was in his arms with a look of wonder on her face, and he reminded himself that the people he was heading towards knew him, and what he was.

He did not have to hide. He was not going to hide, even though something was wrong.

Something very wrong. There was no other reason Frederick should be here. No way, no how, he should have known where to find Lannes.

My brother must have told him, he thought, but that didn't feel right, either.

Lannes landed behind William's garden, momentum forcing him to run several steps, narrowly missing the fence post. Lethe laughed quietly, and he hefted her higher, closer, against his body. Everything still tingled. She weighed next to nothing, and it was a miracle to him—a true marvel—that she was looking at his face— *his* face—with no fear, no question.

They walked from the garden to the front porch. Lethe no longer limped—all those stolen moments healing her had paid off—though there was something just a bit stiff in the way she walked. Him, too. He was sore in unexpected ways. Deliciously so. He wanted to tell her that, but suddenly felt shy. And then concerned—again—as he saw that the front of the house stood open.

Koni stood just inside. His denim shirt hung open, tattoos dark and tangled against his chest. Faint amusement filled his eyes.

"Nice to finally see what you look like," he said.

"Thanks for the call," Lannes replied.

Koni's smile widened. "Better not thank me. I went looking for you first."

"Ah," Lannes replied, sharing a quick glance with Lethe, thinking very hard about what a flying crow might have seen. Ah well. It was what it was.

At the end of the hall, a door opened. Footsteps echoed in the hall, and Will appeared. Frederick followed him.

It was difficult for Lannes to reconcile the sight. Despite what Koni had told him over the phone—which was very little—seeing Frederick in the flesh was incredibly difficult. Much like having the flat of a red-hot knife sear his eyeballs. His old friend was wearing corduroy and tweed, and there was a smile on his face. A smile that faded when he saw Lannes. His hands started shaking so badly that he had to shove them into his pockets.

"This isn't what it looks like," Frederick whispered.

"Good," Lannes replied. "Because this looks like a lot of things."

"We should sit down," Will said.

Lannes' feet felt buckled to the floor. "You know each other."

Frederick looked miserable. "Almost all my life."

Breathe, Lannes told himself. *Breathe.*

But it was too much. He needed air. He turned around and walked back out to the porch. He saw Rictor in the distance, at the cemetery. Koni perched on the edge of the rail, his arms folded over his chest. Lethe was out there, too, her eyes dark, thoughtful. Lannes felt like everyone was watching him, and they were.

"You must have been a kid down here," he said roughly, and remembered the little boy William was holding in the group picture—how that child had seemed oddly familiar. "You were young."

"I was three," Frederick said quietly, close behind him. "But I wasn't here because I was like the others. My father was the one who had . . . talents. It was *his* connection with Will's parents that brought him to this place. I just tagged along. I think he hoped I would discover something about myself, though I never did. I remained, as ever, painfully human."

Lannes turned on him. "Why didn't you say something?"

"Say *what*? I didn't know any of this was related. I had no idea who Orwell Price was when you showed me that name." Frederick closed his eyes, rubbing his neck with a shaky hand. "I knew him as Marcellus Bredow. It wasn't until I talked to Charlie and heard him mention Etta's name that I started making connections."

Lannes closed his eyes, and felt Lethe's hand slide down his wrist.

He means it, she said in his mind. *He's as confused and hurt by all this as you are.*

Yes. He could sense that pain from Frederick's mind. It gave him no satisfaction. He loved Frederick, just as much as his own brothers. The man was his oldest friend.

"I never lied to you," Frederick whispered. "But the subject never came up. And I *couldn't* talk about this place. It was not my secret to give."

"Did—" Lannes had to stop and take a breath. "Did your father tell these people about us? Did he share *our* secrets?"

"No," Will interjected firmly. "Until your brother joined the agency, I had never heard one breath about your kind."

"My father would have died before giving you up," said Frederick quietly. "As would I. The rest . . . was past and done. It wasn't until I talked to Charlie about his new employer and heard that name . . ."

The old man stopped, rubbing his face. "It doesn't matter now anyway. I'm here because you need me."

Lannes wanted to sit down. "How's that?"

Frederick gave him a long, tired, look. "Because I'm the only one who knows where Simon is."

LOUISVILLE. IT WAS A PRIVATE HOSPITAL. FREDERICK HAD been paying the bills for years. During the telling of it, Lannes' friend grew even paler, his cheeks sunken and shadows filling his gaze. The old man looked as though he had been wrestling with demons. He sat in a rocking chair on the porch.

"I always called him Sal," he said.

Lannes shook his head in disbelief. "Sal? Coma Sal? The Sal you've been talking to on the phone at night?"

"He needed help. He's also a distant cousin. Not something I confess easily, even though we were, at one time, close. He's had a pathetic life. I don't say that to make excuses, but it's the truth. None of them did well after they left this place. Karma, I suppose."

"Did you know what he did to Milly and Runa?"

Something awful passed through Frederick's gaze. "I was too young to understand. Only, Milly disappeared, as did her mother, and there was a great deal of shouting and crying afterwards. My father was furious. I thought he would kill the old Sayers man with his bare hands."

"And later?"

Frederick closed his eyes. "Later, nothing. Except that ten years ago, Simon called me out of the blue, desperate. He had no one and was ill with cancer. I felt bad for him. He was afraid of death, and the only friends he'd ever had were ones he eventually manipulated.

His finances were in ruin. He had no skills. Not a great personality. All I did in the beginning was pay his bills and occasionally make a call."

"So, now what?" Lethe spoke up. "How do you confront a man in a coma?"

"You pull the plug," Rictor said, stepping up on the porch. Lannes had not heard his approach; the man moved like a ghost.

Frederick stared at him, pure uncertainty flickering through his eyes. "I know your face."

"You're older," Rictor said, and moved past the old man to stand just inside the house, in the shadows.

Lethe frowned at his back. "I don't know if murder should be an option."

"It should be," Koni said, golden eyes briefly glowing. "You can try to reason with Simon when he's capable of talking to you, but in the meantime you'll still be dodging bullets. Or, I suppose, you wait for him to die. But that could be a while."

"And eventually, Runa will take over," Lannes said.

"You're for this, too?" Lethe asked him.

"I'm for keeping you safe. And let's face it, Simon's not exactly helpless."

"He's an old man," Frederick growled. "As so many of us are. I didn't come here for you to murder him."

"Then, what?" Lannes asked, knowing his anger showed, but unable to help himself. "He himself is a murderer. And even if you could chalk up what he did in his childhood to accident, he's been trying to kill Lethe. And he's done so with such ease and so little apparent conscience that I can only assume he's had considerable practice at this sort of thing in the past."

Exhaustion filled Frederick's face. Lethe grabbed Lannes' arm. "The issue isn't what he's done wrong. The issue is whether you're going to stoop to his level."

"Of course I will," Lannes replied. "I won't enjoy it. I won't want to do it. But if it keeps you safe, I *will* end that man's life."

"Enough," Will said quietly. He had to be older than Fredrick by almost fifteen years, but he looked as though he could run a marathon, chop down a tree, and juggle rocks one-handed—all in the same day. He was youth, bottled up, and it hurt Lannes to see Frederick look so frail in comparison.

"We'll go to him," Will continued, with a sudden formality that reminded Lannes of why he was the boss—even if it seemed that most of the people in his employ had never seen him. "We'll see what can be done. Ms. Lethe, I recommend that you remain here. I'm certain that Rictor won't mind keeping you company."

Rictor raised an eyebrow. Lannes said, "Not to step on any toes, but I prefer to stay with her as well."

Will smiled faintly. "I know you would. But you have some mental abilities, and besides me and perhaps Ms. Lethe, there's no one else here with that skill." He glanced at Rictor, whose jaw tightened, his gaze flicking away to the forest. "I would say that two of us, in dealing with Simon, are better than one."

Lethe nudged Lannes with her elbow. "I'll be fine."

Maybe, he whispered in her mind. *But I don't like it.*

CONVERSATION WAS LIMITED AFTER THAT. EVERYONE started heading toward the cars. Lannes held back, catching Lethe's hand. He pulled her near, watching the concern in her eyes, sensing the unease in her heart. The bond between them felt as strong as a vein of marble cut from a mountain: old and weathered, timeless.

"Don't," she whispered. "Don't do anything you'll regret, just for me."

"It wouldn't just be for you." Lannes cupped her face in his palm, riding a sense of wonder that his hand—his real hand, dark and craggy—was touching her cheek. And that her eyes were gazing into his real face with a warmth that he could not fathom.

"It would kill me to lose you," he said.

"Lannes," she whispered, and he swooped close, pressing his mouth to her ear.

"I am almost eighty years old," he told her softly, "and I have never been in love. But I love you. I love you, Lethe. And no matter what you say, I will protect you."

He pulled back just enough to kiss her, his sun-warmed wings arched and aching. Lethe clung to him. And when he moved yet again to look into her eyes, he found them glistening with unshed years.

"I want you to be safe, too," she said hoarsely, rubbing her eyes.

He tried to smile for her, and pointed at his face. "Take a good look," he told her, then reached deep, searching for the magical mask, triggering the spell, embracing the energy flowing through his heart. His hand, still touching her cheek, began to shimmer. Within moments, the illusion was remade. He looked human again.

Lethe smiled, shaking her head. "I hope you believe me one day when I tell you that I prefer you the other way."

"Just don't ever stop saying it," he said, and kissed her cheek.

He left her standing on the porch. Rictor was in front of him, near the cars. Lannes paused by the green-eyed man. "Koni says you're immortal."

Rictor shrugged. "I suppose." It was said as if it was nothing, a bore, even a burden.

Lannes looked him dead in the eyes. "If she gets hurt, I'll put you in a place no one will ever find you. And you'll just sit there. Forever."

Rictor smiled coldly. "Doesn't sound much different from what I'm doing now."

Lannes shook his head. "Just take care of her."

Then he got into the Humvee with the others, and they drove out.

IT TOOK THEM AN HOUR TO GET TO LOUISVILLE. NO ONE talked much until the end.

"You've changed," Frederick suddenly said to Will. "You used to be nothing but an innocent farm boy in love with the land."

"And you were in love with words." Will's gaze grew thoughtful. "Being able to see into the minds of others can change a person. There are no masks, no walls, no prisons. You find yourself wishing that there were."

Simon was being treated in a private establishment on the east side, near the old neighborhoods where the city's rich kept their homes. The streets were filled with golden fallen leaves. Lannes thought of the Yellow Brick Road. Memories flashed in his head. Everything made him think of Lethe. He was wearing the illusion, but it felt different now. He had changed on the inside. No matter how many different ways he looked at his situation, he no longer felt as though he was hiding.

Instead, he was simply traveling. It was as though the illusion were nothing more than the key to a door. Not a mask, not a burden. He was not afraid. He was not cowering behind a psychic trick of light. And though it might seem weak and silly, the memories of Lethe's eyes when she had looked into his true face were pillars inside his heart, holding up everything. There had been no fear in her gaze. No disgust. Just acceptance. And desire.

She did not care that he was different from her. Not one iota. She had made love to him.

They had made love.

"Are you certain that Simon never managed to manipulate you?" he asked Frederick, wondering briefly if he could trust his friend. He had no mental bond with the old man—certainly nothing that could provide him with the certainty he needed—but the emotions that rolled off Frederick when he asked that question were genuine enough, and made him hurt a little for his friend.

"I'm certain," Frederick said quietly. "You don't live among individuals of certain talents without acquiring a particular awareness of things."

"Does my father know?"

"Undoubtedly," replied the old man. "You remember how they were. Like brothers."

Like us, Lannes thought. "And here, now? How do we handle Simon?"

"You don't," Will interjected grimly.

"He's near death," Frederick said.

"He's a murderer," Lannes replied.

Koni said, "There are cops outside the hospital," speaking for the first time in an hour. He pulled over to the side of the road, and all the men peered out the window. No police sedans were in sight, but there were several men and women in uniform standing in front of the double glass doors of the modern structure, walkie-talkies in hand.

"Would he know that we're coming?" asked Lannes.

"Come on," Will said, opening his door. "Best to just ask."

Lannes thought that asking the police anything at all was inviting trouble, but he followed the two old men. Koni stayed with the car. Ready for a fast getaway, he supposed, which was little comfort.

The three of them, Lannes, Will and Frederick, strolled up to the hospital as though they owned the place, and when they got to the doors and began to go in—without being stopped or questioned—Will paused and looked one of the three loitering officers in the eye.

"My goodness," he said, every inch the distinguished gentleman. "Has anything happened?"

"Eh," said the officer, shrugging. "Weirdos."

"I see," replied Will, who continued on into the hospital.

The lobby was large, decorated in natural earth tones that were pleasant but dull. Some women wearing badges around their necks sat behind a half-moon circle that seemed to be one massive front desk.

Will leaned into Frederick and Lannes. "It's nothing. Apparently, some individuals have made death threats against one of the patients. It's terribly sad."

"Heartbreaking," Lannes muttered, then felt bad for Frederick, who appeared rather ill. Will gave him a look that was particularly compassionate.

"You were trying to be a good person," he said gently. "We try to hold forgiveness in our hearts. But sometimes that's not enough."

"He's been in and out of a coma," Frederick told him. "I never dreamed he would be capable of this. Not now, after all these years."

They went upstairs to the patient rooms. The nurses at the small station recognized Frederick's name and seemed genuinely happy to meet him for the first time. The women let them into Simon's room and shut the door when they left. Lannes hardly noticed. He was too busy taking the measure of the old man who'd caused so much unhappiness.

Simon Sayers was emaciated, a skeleton in a hospital gown tucked securely within a large bed. He seemed to be breathing on his own, but an oxygen mask covered his face, and the rest of him was hooked up to a variety of humming machines. He did not look dangerous. Frederick was right. He seemed pathetic. One long life, reduced to skin and bone.

"He could have had everything," Frederick said quietly. "But he squandered it all on selfishness. And now, this is life."

"He's gone visiting," said Will, frowning. "He's empty on the inside."

Lannes placed a finger against Simon's wrist. The man's skin was cold and papery thin, and the energy in his body was weak. There was not much time left. Not much at all, and he had spent it conniving and scheming to hurt others. He was still searching for everything that had eluded him in eighty-odd years of living.

"He wanted power," Lannes said. "He had power, but he wanted more. He wanted respect. And he never got it, did he? He never had enough."

"You can't make people love you," Will said. "He had a crush on Milly, did you know that? And in the beginning, he worshipped Runa. But he couldn't handle it when she would criticize him. It made him angry. And when Milly stopped playing his games, he started to bully her."

"Simon sacrificed her to summon a demon." Lannes had not been able to name it until now, but the word rolled off his lips. *Demon*. He felt chilled, even dirty, and stopped touching the old man.

"You covered it up," he said, turning to Will. "Paid off the local cops."

"Not us. Them. We went along with it because we had little alternative. No one could afford the scrutiny. The Bredows and Sayers were no longer welcome after that, though. And I never heard about this again until some notes fell on my desk regarding Etta. I contacted her, and she was . . . willing to intervene. I didn't expect her to take poison, though. I underestimated the burden of her guilt."

A wave of nausea passed through Lannes.

And then it hit him again, followed by a pain in his head so shocking, so agonizing, he thought for certain someone had stabbed him.

And the moment he had that thought, another thought slipped into his mind. A realization.

Lethe.

He reached for her across their bond and found nothing but a thread, the tiniest of golden hums flickering in the darkness. Dread pounded through him, a fear so thick he wanted to scream.

"Lannes," Will said, frowning.

"Something's happened," Lannes whispered, staring at Simon. "He's hurting her."

He did not think. He grabbed a pillow and ripped off the old man's oxygen mask. Will grabbed his arm, his gaze burning with a power that reached even through Lannes' desperation and rage.

"I'll handle this," said Will. "Go to her."

Lannes froze a moment, then dropped the pillow and staggered backward. Inside his heart he reached for Lethe but could only find a glimmer, the echo of a flame.

She was dying.

CHAPTER TWENTY-ONE

THE trees were full of crows. Lethe noticed that almost an hour after Lannes and the others had driven away. She felt uncomfortable in the house and had started wandering. Just to the garden, the edge of the meadow where the horses grazed.

The crows were silent and watchful. It made her uneasy. She saw Rictor over by the cemetery and went to join him.

He stood by the wrought-iron fence surrounding what must have been several acres' worth of gravestones, arms folded over his chest, green eyes thoughtful. He did not look at her.

"You've adjusted well to all this," he said.

She studied his profile, then turned away to stare at the sea of buried dead. Monuments to mystery, lives long gone. "My memories might be lost, but not my instincts. And given what little Lannes has told me about my family, I would guess I've had some experience with strange things. The initial shock was the hardest part. Now it's just beginning to feel . . . natural."

And then she asked something that had been bugging her for some time: "What did the Sidhe queen mean about my eyes?"

Rictor walked through the gate into the cemetery. Lethe followed. "Your eyes are green," he said.

"Lots of people have green eyes," she replied. "Like you."

"Like her."

"I'm talking about normal people."

"And there are many. But not you." He finally looked at her, and being the focus of his gaze felt like standing naked on a freeway, playing chicken with a semi. "Something in your blood isn't entirely human. Just like the rest of your family."

The hairs rose on the back of her neck. "What do you know about my family?"

Rictor turned away from her and began staring at the graves again. "Some of them were dangerous. The older women especially, though they're all dead now. You're not as powerful as they were, but you have the potential. If you ever set your mind to it. Then again," he added slowly, "maybe you decided not to."

Lethe's pulse quickened. "I tore out my own memories. I believe that now. You're saying that's why?"

"I'm not saying anything," Rictor replied. "I don't know anything, anymore."

And he walked away, following a path amongst the graves. Lethe did not follow. Talking to Rictor was almost as bad as being stared at by a tree full of crows. She ambled back to the house. This time she was going to stay there. Maybe she'd read a book. Or, at least, maybe she'd discover the kinds of books she liked. Which made her wonder about Lannes. She knew almost as little about his life as she did about her own.

Her life. Her family. Which was searching for her.

They'll continue to search for you. Unless you go to them first.

A terrifying idea. Especially knowing what had happened to Lannes. Continuing to be with her could not possibly be safe for him. But letting go . . . letting go of him was not an option, either. Lethe had no concept of her life before, no memories to hang on to, but she knew what love was. She knew she loved him.

Lethe could not explain it, of course. She could not rationalize it. What she felt was as inexplicable as an enchanted wood, or surly immortals, or men who changed their shape with a thought. This was the modern world. Twenty-first century. People flew in planes and drove cars, surfed the Internet, watched movies with loud explosions. There was no room in the world for gargoyles, or psychics, or forests inhabited by women of temperamental powers, where the soul could reside after death. There was no room in the world for magic, in hearts or otherwise.

And yet, here she was, proposing magic. Proposing love. And she would rather be in danger with Lannes than live in safety with any other.

Near the house, an odd chill stole over her. Lethe slowed, listening, but the crows were silent. Still, a tingle hit her mind. She did not know what it meant or what to do with it, but she considered it a warning.

She stared at the house, searching the windows,

then turned and very quickly began walking back to the cemetery and Rictor. Better to be safe than sorry. She did not care if the man laughed at her.

She never made it. Halfway there, something hit her in the back. She went down hard on her knees. An arm reached around her throat.

"Told you I was gonna kill you," whispered a man. Ed. Simon.

And before she could summon her strength, something long and sharp plunged into her eye.

The pain was terrible, but it was over quickly. Everything, gone.

She passed through darkness. It was an empty place, as cold and lonely as the hole inside her memories. She searched for anything to anchor her and found two faint stars, flickering so far away that all she could do was stare and wish and desire. Two stars, one brighter than the other. Her only light.

And then, in the darkness, she sensed a presence. Not alone. She was not alone.

Little pet, whispered a smooth feminine voice. *How sweet to have you here.*

THE SPEED LIMIT ON 1-64 WAS SEVENTY MILES PER HOUR. Lannes pushed the Humvee to one hundred twenty, with Koni at his side, buckled in, feet braced on the dashboard. It took him less than forty minutes to return to the farm in Cuzco, but that was forty minutes too long.

There was a body sprawled in the driveway when they reached the farm. A man. Lannes almost did not brake in time. He and Koni scrambled out of the car, but only the shape-shifter ran to the man.

"It's Ed!" he shouted, but Lannes had already glimpsed another distant figure, and he took off running, crossing the meadow in tremendous strides that took him into the air in leaps and gliding bounds.

Rictor knelt on the edge of the forest. He was covered in blood. Lannes slammed into the earth beside him, grabbed his armpit and shoulder, and hauled his entire body into the air.

"Where?" he snarled.

"There was still a chance," Rictor said hoarsely. Lannes dropped him, and spun around to face the forest. He did not stop to think. All that was left of Lethe was a spark in his heart, their bond shriveled to a thread. Around that small light his soul felt like the yawning abyss: gone, dead, never born.

He plunged into the forest. It was like diving through a curtain of green shimmering light. Nothing touched him, not leaf or thorn. He fell through the forest border and found himself on a path made of roots and stone.

The Sidhe queen was there with him, seated atop the white stag on a saddle in the shape of a frog. Silver bells hung from her wrists, and diamonds were braided into her long pale hair. She was naked, and her eyes glinted green.

"My lord," she said with a smile. "Come for a visit to my realm?"

Lannes strode to her in two steps, feeling his illusion strip away into his real skin. The blood burned in his veins, and he could hardly breathe past his rage and grief. "Where is she?"

The queen's smile grew colder. "You are a curious beast, to be so fascinated with a mortal lover. They are so easily broken."

Lanne grabbed her fine white ankle. "Take me to her."

"A kiss first."

He snarled, and she slipped out of his grip, the stag leaping backward. The queen sat upon its back light as air, but her smile was gone, her gaze sharp as knives, and she looked sideways, in the direction Lannes had come.

"The half-breed knocks," she whispered. "He wants in."

"The woman!" Lannes screamed at her.

The queen went still, settling her gaze on him, bleeding disdain. "You mortals and your love. It never lasts, in any shape or form. And yet you pretend so dangerously."

"We do not pretend," Lannes said, grief breaking his voice. "And if you will not give her to me now, then kill me. Or take *me* instead of her. I don't care. But do *something*. *Be* something."

The queen stared at him, her eyes so ageless, so implacable, it was impossible to tell what she was thinking. But her mouth tightened and she looked away. Golden light touched the side of Lannes' face. He turned and watched as the forest shifted upon itself, trees melting and stone groaning. Until in front of him was the mighty oak. In its roots, Runa slept.

And beside her lay Lethe.

Her face was a ruin of blood. Something had been plunged into her eye, and the wound was another murder, this one in his heart. He scooped her into his arms, hugging her limp body against his chest, and his pain was so terrible, so horrifying, he could not make a sound. He could not see or hear past the roar of his blood and the pounding of his pulse.

"Her soul resides," said the queen, still seated atop her stag. "She can be saved."

"Then save her," Lannes whispered, rocking them both. "I will be yours if you save her."

"Ah," sighed the queen. "You, gargoyle—I see stories inside your heart. You, who fought the stone of the witch to save your soul. You would give yourself to me, for her?"

"Yes," he said, closing his eyes. "For her."

A great shudder filled the trees, a soft roar that echoed from the leaves. All around him, a sigh arose, and a soft voice said, *Please.*

Runa. Lannes twisted, but the golden woman's face was still lost in sleep.

Take me, whispered the trees. *For her, take me.*

The queen lifted her chin, fierce, though her hands trembled. "Self-sacrifice makes me ill. And why you? We have a bargain."

Simon is dead, breathed Runa's soft voice. *All of them are dead.*

"For summoning an abomination, even as a game," said the queen, "death was too kind."

But I am free, continued Runa. *And this girl is dead*

at Simon's hand because of me. There is blood on her hands that would not have belonged there. Memories, which I compelled her to steal. She was of my blood, my tool, my last chance to kill.

Images flashed through Lannes' mind, blinding him; the glow of the dome, Lethe standing in light with her hair like golden fire and her eyes old, dead as ash, without the vitality he knew in her. All he saw when he looked at the woman was despair, relentless and overpowering.

Not Lethe. *Alice.*

Alice, later, moving with purpose. Alice, in a hotel room. Alice, taking a meeting with three men. Men with guns.

Alice, also armed, shooting them.

The images made no sense, not without knowing what was in her heart, but he saw the horror on her face afterwards, and saw her hand scrabble for paper and a pen. Of her own free will or not, he wished he knew. But he saw her write. He saw the word, *RUN.*

Then, nothing. Darkness swelled in his vision, slowly eaten back by green and gold, and the cold body in his arms.

So take me, Runa was whispering. *Take me as I took her. It is only right. I will feed your tree with human dreams. But take me.*

"Gah," said the Sidhe queen, disgust flickering across her face. "Damn you both."

She began to turn the stag then stopped, staring into the rich shadows of the forest gloom. Her hair shimmered like moonlight caught behind a veil of mist. A shudder tore through her body, though it was as delicate as the tremble of a ripple on water.

"You would do anything for her?" she finally whispered, glancing at Lannes.

He could hardly speak. "Anything."

"Even return to your cage?"

Terror filled him, but he hugged Lethe's limp body even closer to his chest. "Yes."

"Ah," sighed the queen, and in his arms, Lethe stirred. He gazed down at her, stunned, and found the hole in her eye gone, though her face was still covered in blood. Her presence in his mind and heart, small as a spark, suddenly expanded like a rose in bloom.

And his body turned to stone.

His legs hardened first, and then his torso. He released Lethe before his arms could be stolen, and it was like drowning in slow motion, dying in quicksand. He did not shout, though, and he did not fight. He was terrified, but all he could do was look at Lethe—breathing, eyelids fluttering—and the miracle of that allowed no regret.

She opened her eyes at the last moment. Looked straight at him. Confused at first. He tried to smile for her, but his chest stiffened and he could not breathe. Her gaze dipped, and he watched as dull incomprehension was replaced by horror.

"No," she rasped, and grabbed his hand. It was already stone, cold and unfeeling. She flung herself up on her knees, reeling, and slid her arms around his neck. He still had skin there, and her touch on the last remains of his body made him shudder with grief and pleasure.

"Come away from there, young mortal," said the queen, hovering behind Lethe. "He is mine now. Such a gallant creature, giving his life for yours."

Lethe did not look at her, but pressed close instead, bloody and pale. "Lannes, fight."

"No," he whispered, trying to memorize her face. "You run."

She snarled at him, and tangled her hands in his hair, yanking hard. *"Fight."*

"Lethe," he said, but suddenly she was inside his head, filling him up so full it was as though she was trying to become him, live wholly inside him. Control him.

I won't leave you, she said inside his mind. *I won't. My body will rot and die, and I'll just live with you, here. Forever. That's what's going to happen if you don't fight.*

I gave my word, he told her, as the stone crept over his jaw. *Damn it, Lethe. Go.*

Go, and do not tempt me, he wanted to add. Terrified that if he did, the Sidhe queen would kill her. He would rather die himself. He would rather spend the rest of his life in a cage.

You gave your word, Lethe shot back. *I didn't.*

Lannes felt her hammer on the inside of his mind, and her desperation was as raw as his, wild and crazed. *What are you doing?*

Give yourself to me, she said, her mental voice

breaking on the words. *Let me have control over your body. It'll be my fight then, not yours. No broken promises.*

No.

Then I'm staying.

The stone was almost to his eyes. He looked at the queen over Lethe's body and found her staring at him with cold pleasure. The Sidhe knew, he realized. She knew exactly what Lethe was doing. The queen wanted it that way. To imprison them both.

Trust me, Lethe whispered in his mind. *I know you have no reason to, I know what this means, Lannes. But trust me.*

Trust her. Trust a member of the same family that had tortured him, tried to force him into giving what she was asking for now, freely. His soul.

I'd rather be in hell, she whispered. *Rather in hell with you than anywhere else.*

Lannes felt the same.

Take it, he told her, free-falling inside his heart, opening the last, most precious part of him to her mind. *Take it all, Lethe.*

And she did, but it felt like being buoyed by a sea of pure light, and her love washing over him was so brilliant, so desperate and powerful, he felt more alive in that moment than in any other. As though his skin were made of the sun.

Until he lost himself in that light, and Lethe took over his body.

It was not painful. It was not frightening. She slipped around him like a glove, and it was as though every lonely moment of his life, every hurt and slight and fear, was eased away by the gentleness of her spirit.

If we stay like this forever, she whispered, *we'll be all right.*

But even as Lethe spoke those words, Lannes felt another blossom of light, a force anchored to her spirit.

Runa.

He heard no words, but he felt something pass between Runa and the Sidhe queen, a heave of light and energy that was as heavy and sharp as the edge of a knife. Turmoil, a ripple beyond him, in the forest. He was stone now, as he had been years ago with the witch, but he felt no fear, no pain. Just Lethe. He clung to her soul—she clung to him—and they were so close in that moment, he was convinced that no force, nothing in this world or the next, would ever separate them.

Until, quite abruptly, the stone disappeared from his body and he could move again.

Lannes fell forward, gasping. Lethe was inside him, and her body was on the ground, breathing but still as death. He did not hesitate. He hauled her into his arms and staggered to his feet. On his left, Runa was gone from the roots of the oak.

Her flesh had been golden and shining, and now there was nothing left but bone and rock and moss. The Sidhe queen knelt in the shadows of the great tree, her pale face hidden.

"Go," she whispered. "Both of you, go. You fools. Runa gave her life for you both."

Lethe curled away from his mind, leaving a cold empty spot in his soul. Her chest rose and fell with a deep breath. Her heart pounded. Lannes swayed, weak in the knees, the separation of their minds making him feel as though he were dying all over again.

"Why are you allowing this?" he asked.

The queen closed her eyes. "Because I take, and I take. And though I take because I love, nothing remains, nothing keeps. What I take, I kill. Except for one woman. One woman I freed. Lucy Steele. And she returned to me again and again to sit outside my cage and read." Her mouth twisted into a snarl, tears glimmering in her eyes. "And it made me *weak*. Weak enough to give once more."

She flung out her arm, silver bells chiming. *"Go."*

Lannes did not argue. He ran, and the forest melted around him like some bizarre dream, though it was not his imagination that trees bent and the ferns danced, and that the brambles twisted like skeletal hands.

He saw sunlight. He burst free.

And he was back in the meadow, Lethe in his arms. She was alive. Burning a hole through his heart.

Lannes fell on his knees. He heard shouts, feet pounding. Shadows fell over him. Lethe's eyes fluttered open, and her face crumpled when she saw him. Lannes kissed her mouth, shaking.

And he felt, on the edge of his mind, a presence—cold and worn and bitter. Lethe stiffened, as well, her mind melting into his.

I am not sorry, whispered a dry masculine voice, skimming the edge of their thoughts. *My body may have at last given out, but my mind never will. I will never be sorry.*

"Liar," Lethe breathed out loud. "Simon Says, you big fat liar."

Lannes closed his eyes and sent his mind lunging toward that presence, swinging power like a hammer. He made contact. He felt a crack.

And the presence fractured. Simon disappeared.

But whether it was for good, Lannes had no idea.

EPILOGUE

NEW York. Upper East Side. It was snowing early for the season, but Lannes did not mind the cold. He wore the illusion of a coat and had a woman tucked close to his side, under his arm. It was night and the city was bright in his eyes. Central Park was on their left.

Lethe was quiet and had been for most of the drive from Indiana to New York. They had only arrived this morning. Something needed to be done, and it could not wait.

"Frederick called," he said, heart aching, knowing she was trembling from something other than the cold. "Ed finally woke up."

"Two weeks was a long time. Any permanent damage?"

"No," Lannes said. "He was worried about his cat."

She smiled, but only briefly. Her face was small and pale beneath her chunky blue hat.

"I'm scared," she said.

"I know," he replied.

"I think I miss Runa." Lethe smiled weakly. "She knew what she was doing, even if it wasn't nice."

"I behaved like her," Lannes rumbled. "Years ago, after I was free from the witch. I had lost nothing but my pride and my freedom, but once I had those back, I still behaved as though I was in a cage. I can't imagine all that time I wasted."

They stopped in front of a glistening building, shining with glass and stone. It was old, expensive. Lannes had memorized the address from a piece of paper crumpled in his fist. Both of them stopped, staring at the doors. A man in uniform huddled just inside, staring back at them.

Her family lived there. Alice's family. Lethe's family. Good, normal, fabulously wealthy people. Not a psychotic amongst them, or so Charlie and Will and all the resources of Dirk & Steele had confirmed. The witches, the sisters who had hurt him, and others, were dead. As far as anyone knew.

I was terrified of becoming like them. And of knowing I would be murdered, Lethe whispered inside his head. *That's the only reason I can think of for destroying my memories. To give myself a new beginning. A chance to start over.*

"And here you are," he said, hating himself. "I can't go with you. I can't take the risk that some of them will be able to see through the illusion."

"You know I understand," she told him. "And I don't have to go, either. In fact—"

Lannes shook his head, close to tears, and kissed her palms. "If you don't go to them, they will always hunt you. If you go to them, you may find freedom. They're not . . . all bad. Not that we've found."

Her face crumpled. "How will I know? I don't remember them, Lannes. What if they try to keep me?"

"Then call for me," he whispered, pressing her hands over his heart. "And I'll come for you. No matter where you are or how long it takes. I'll find you."

Lethe closed her eyes, leaning into his body. "I've never been away from you."

"You may like it," he said. "Enjoy yourself here. See if you enjoy being Alice. You have family. Don't take it for granted." Then he pulled away from her, dying a little on the inside. She pressed her lips together, mouth firming into a stubborn smile, and nodded.

She turned and walked into the apartment building. Lannes waited, hoping she would come back out again. But she did not.

He crossed the street to Central Park.

A forest in the city. He thought of the Sidhe queen and smiled to himself as he found a tall tree and climbed it. He whispered words, and his body shimmered. Less than invisibility, more than a shadow. It was a dangerous risk, but he had no choice.

He leapt into the sky, catching a draft, and flew upward, circling until he felt Lethe's heart. He focused on it, following her inside the building until he felt her slow in front of one apartment in particular.

There was a balcony. He landed softly on it, peering

through large windows. It was a cold home, he thought: all modern sophistication, sleek and gray, with touches of red like splashes of blood. No clutter, few photographs.

But he saw a wall full of books and a grand piano that a child was playing, and when Lethe entered the apartment, the smiles and tears that greeted her were genuine. A tall blond woman dressed in sleek black collapsed on the couch, sobbing. Lethe stared at her, helpless. She looked so alone, Lannes almost rapped on the glass. He wanted to go to her, he wanted to touch her and stand with her in that lonely crowd.

Lethe looked past those faces, directly at him. He was deep in shadow, and invisible. He knew she could not see him through the glass, but their link flared white-hot, and he felt warmth shimmer through him like the sun and the stars. The loneliness in her eyes almost killed him.

And then he stopped seeing her eyes as a tall handsome man swept between them and wrapped Lethe in his arms.

The man kissed her. He kissed her so hard he swept her backwards, and everyone in the room cheered. Lannes wanted to rip out his own heart—and throw that human man off the building.

Lannes did not wait to see what happened next. He turned away, gripping the balcony behind him so hard chunks of stone cracked beneath his claws. Memories danced—what felt like a lifetime of memories—from the first moment he had met her, bloody and defiant, until now, and everything, every joy and sorrow in between. He loved her. He wanted her to be happy. He wanted her to have a chance at every happiness.

It feels as though all I've ever known is you, she had said to him during the long drive here, and though she had said those words with love—love, that he had felt in her mind, in her heart, burning up their bond—he wondered if that was fair to her. He was not human. And though he could wear a human mask, he would never *be* human. He could not give her children. He could not age with her. He was not . . . normal.

She doesn't care, you fool, whispered a small voice in his heart. *And it's not as though* she's *normal, either.*

But it was different. She needed to have the choice, the opportunity to see what she had left behind. Lannes would not be responsible for putting her in a cage, no matter how much he wanted her at his side. He'd realized as she'd joined him in the Sidhe queen's condemnation of stone: No one should be caged. Not even in a cage of love. He wanted her to be free.

He threw himself off the balcony, plunging six stories before his wings snapped open.

The next morning, he was back in Maine.

Two days later, Lannes found himself sitting at the end of a long pier, whittling away at a pine block, searching for a face in the wood while his toes dipped into the cold Atlantic. There was a storm on the horizon, the wind brisk. Lights on the distant shore were winking on one by one as evening pulled near. The coast of Maine was always nice to look at. Mainbow Island, home of the Hannelore brothers, had a good view of most everything.

Charlie was nearby. Aggie and Emma were up at the house. Lannes had been promised stories about the "damn gnomes."

His brother pulled up the crab nets, the muscles of his long arms straining. "Just so you know, you're a wreck."

"Thanks," Lannes replied, "for nothing."

"Whatever," said Charlie. "The others are worried."

That, Lannes thought, was precisely the problem. Too many family members who did not know how to mind their own business.

"I think," he said carefully, "that I am doing quite well, considering."

Charlie dragged two massive nets out of the water and dropped them heavily on the dock. Crabs shuffled inside, waving their pincers. Lannes could tell from looking that a good handful would have to be thrown back for size, but the rest were destined for the big pot in the kitchen.

Charlie's wings swayed in the wind. "You should call her."

Lannes replied, "I know."

"We can handle her family."

He thought about the man who had kissed Lethe, something he had not yet shared with his brother. His heart ached. "Maybe you won't have to."

"Stop feeling sorry for yourself."

Lannes glared, but his brother had knelt and was

sorting through the doomed crustaceans, tossing some in a battered bucket—the sides of which had been crudely painted with rainbows and daisies. A little girl's touch. A human's touch. Odd, in this place of gargoyles.

Lannes pulled his feet out of the icy ocean. "You're trying to goad me."

Charlie grinned, ready to respond, but someone whistled at the end of the dock. Both brothers looked up.

Two human women stood by the rocky shore. One of them—Agatha—was tall and dark, with curvy hips and long wavy hair. The other woman was also tall, but pale and blond. Lannes stared, stunned that he had not felt her coming.

"Dude," Charlie said, "I'm out of here."

Lannes hardly noticed his brother's departure. He had eyes only for Lethe. She smiled briefly at Charlie, shook his hands, even—but then she was there, in front of him, and he could not breathe.

"You left," she said, quietly. "You really left. I went back to the hotel, and you had checked out."

He had been a coward in some ways. "I stayed long enough to make certain you would be all right, but I didn't want you to feel obligated to see me again."

Lethe folded her arms over her chest. "You ran. You saw that man hugging me and you dodged so fast I saw tracks in the sky."

"I saw him *kissing* you," he muttered, skin growing hot.

She stood very still, holding his gaze. "I wasn't kissing back. He caught me by surprise."

Lannes nodded, digging a claw into the wood block. "And?"

"And he was a boyfriend, I guess. Tennis player. Doctor. Voted most likely to succeed in his college yearbook." She smiled wryly. "Those were the first three things he told me when he found out I had amnesia."

"Ah." Lannes felt rather ill. "Accomplished. I suppose handsome should be added to the list."

"I suppose." She walked toward him, slowly. Lannes held steady, his heart hammering. She was so very beautiful, and he was so very relieved to see her that he could have sunk down on his knees and stayed there.

"I called Will," she said. "He told me how to get here."

"I wanted you to have freedom," he replied. "To make your new life without . . . me hanging around your neck."

"After all we went through?" Lethe asked him, smiling gently. She stopped in front of him, very close. "I have to ask you something. I have to ask if you still want me."

It was hard to breathe. "You shouldn't have to ask. You know what I feel."

Her gaze searched his face, and there was a pain in her eyes that mirrored his own enough that he reached up and slid his knuckle along the soft skin of her jaw. She closed her eyes, leaning in to his touch, and he bent down and kissed her mouth.

Lethe leaned into him, shuddering. "I wished you could have been there. I couldn't stop thinking of you.

It was awful. Not in any magical weird way. That subject didn't even come up. It's just . . . I don't know them. My own parents, my friends. I think . . . I think I must have been some kind of socialite before. They expected me to be a certain way, and I wasn't like that. Not anymore. It disappointed them a little."

"They'll learn to accept you."

"Maybe." Lethe kissed his throat. "They want me to live with them. They want to take care of me until my memory returns."

His gut tightened. "That's kind of them."

Lethe laughed quietly. "Tell me how you *really* feel."

How he really felt? He hardly believed there were words for that.

Lannes held her waist and picked her up. She wrapped her legs around his hips with an ease that stole his breath.

His wings arched, spreading around them. Lannes, his body growing hot and hard, pushed closer to her.

"Tell me," Lethe said.

"I want you here," he rasped. "I want you with me. I want to care for you and love you and have you with me every moment, every day, for as long as we live. I want to be the one to protect you. Not them, not anyone else, ever. And all those . . . handsome doctors and tennis players and men who know their wine can just . . . go away. Because I might not be as handsome as them, and I may not even be as *human* as them, but they will never believe in you the way I do, and they will never know you as I do, and they will never, *never*, come within a breath of loving you as much as

I do. Never, Lethe. And if ever there should be a man who loves you more, then I bow to him. Because you deserve nothing less."

She stared at him, eyes red rimmed, glistening with unshed tears. He felt rather weepy himself.

"I would have settled for some help unloading my bags from the car," she whispered. "Because, you know, I was going to move in whether you wanted me or not. But what you just said was . . ."

"Better than luggage?" Lannes asked.

"Yes," she said simply, tears finally spilling free. "Yes, Lannes. I think maybe you're better than anything I could have imagined. And I'm *glad* I don't have my memories. I hope I never do. Because when I look back, fifty years from now, I want all my memories to begin with you."

"It won't be easy," he rumbled. "There's so much against us."

Lethe stood back from him, and pulled a pocketknife from her pocket. He stared, startled, as she unfolded the blade.

"I learned something by accident," she said. "Yesterday."

"Um," he said, and then bit back a shout as she dug the blade into her hand. Blood welled. She paled, hissing. He grabbed her wrist, but she said, "Wait," and though he wanted to shake her, and though it terrified him, he did as she said.

And the cut, right before his eyes, healed.

"We did something in those woods. I don't know

what," she whispered. "Or . . . maybe the Sidhe queen did it? Either way . . . maybe there are some things we won't have to worry about."

An image flashed from her mind; Lethe, gray and wrinkled, in a wheelchair, ancient-looking, and him, still as he was. Fear tightened his stomach. He had thought of this, too, and it was his nightmare.

"I would never leave you," he whispered. "You know that."

Lethe held up her healed hand, cheeks flushed. "Maybe it won't be a concern."

He closed his eyes, dragging her near. "We'll figure it out, one way or the other. We've handled worse."

"To hell and back," she told him. "I'll fight for you with my last breath."

"And I'll love you with mine," he said, and wrapped her in his wings.

THE NIGHT HUNTRESS NOVELS FROM

JEANIENE FROST

✠ HALFWAY TO THE GRAVE ✠

978-0-06-124508-4

Kick-ass demon hunter and half-vampire Cat Crawfield and
her sexy mentor, Bones, are being pursued by a group of kill-
ers. Now Cat will have to choose a side…and Bones is turning
out to be as tempting as any man with a heartbeat.

✠ ONE FOOT IN THE GRAVE ✠

978-0-06-124509-1

Cat Crawfield works to rid the world of the rogue undead.
But when she's targeted for assassination she turns to her ex,
the sexy and dangerous vampire Bones, to help her.

✠ AT GRAVE'S END ✠

978-0-06-158307-0

Caught in the crosshairs of a vengeful vamp, Cat's about to
learn the true meaning of bad blood—just as she and Bones
need to stop a lethal magic from being unleashed.

✠ DESTINED FOR AN EARLY GRAVE ✠

978-0-06-158321-6

Cat is having terrifying visions in her dreams of a vampire
named Gregor who's more powerful than Bones.

✠ THIS SIDE OF THE GRAVE ✠

978-0-06-178318-0

Cat and her vampire husband Bones have fought for their lives,
as well as their relationship. But Cat's new and unexpected
abilities threaten the both of them.